THE SHEPHERD'S CALL

BY

PENNY HARRIS SMITH

Published by Penny Harris Smith
ISBN: 978-0-9677490-0-6

Visit Penny Harris Smith's official website at
www.PennyHarrisSmith.com for the latest news, book details, and
other information.

Cover Design by Sarah Whelan, Life In Stills, LLC
Layout formatting by Guido Henkel, www.guidohenkel.com

DEDICATION

This novel is dedicated to God, the Father Almighty, who in His eternal love and mercy, led me to my Lord, Jesus Christ, and through His Spirit, enabled me to write this book. May all glory and honor be yours forever and ever!

"…yet for us there is but one God, the Father, from whom all things came and for whom we live; and there is but one Lord, Jesus Christ, through whom all things came and through whom we live."

1 Corinthians 8:6 (NIV)

CHAPTER 1

KENDRA MATTHEWS INTENDED TO ASK HER STUDENTS "WHAT is the truth?" relating to the strength of an egg's shell. The unconscious omission of '*the*' energized a discussion which lasted the entire class period. She uncharacteristically closed the classroom door after ushering out the students who were reluctant to leave. For three years, she used the egg demonstration to reinforce the importance of verifying facts. The principle behind the demonstration was simple. A crack-free egg will not break when squeezed in the palm of a jewelry-free hand. Every student in her class tried and all failed. They accused her of using boiled eggs until she allowed them to crack the shells using techniques ranging from gently tapping with a hammer to dropping the egg on the table. Placing each egg in a plastic sandwich bag increased the dramatic effect and reduced cleanup. While monitoring the contained messes being dropped into the trash, a mandate from the principal to prevent a reoccurrence of last year's senior prank, Kendra felt like she had been hit by a hammer.

Alone in the classroom, Kendra reflected on her childhood Sunday school teacher's egg analogy. Her voice was distinctively clear in the recesses of Kendra's mind. "The relationship between God the Father, Jesus and the Holy Spirit is like the parts of an egg. The Holy Spirit is the shell which is the visible power of God. The egg white represents Jesus, who's recorded as saying that no one can come to the Father except through him. The Father is the yolk; the center and source of all life." Kendra stood over the trash can trying to reconcile the concept of an indestructible God with the broken eggs. Her most vocal student's declaration was hard to ignore. "Religion's a tool for the powerful and a crutch for the weak." Kendra's thoughts raced faster than her heart. "When my life was falling apart, I clung to Dale's faith. Did I ...Stay busy!"

Kendra struggled to dismiss the escalating anxiety while eating her turkey sandwich. After preparing the lab stations for the advanced class' tornado experiment, she had ten minutes before the bell. Although she wanted to call Dale who could certainly erase her doubts, she remembered her vow and called his wife, Sharon, instead.

Sharon McKinney stared out the window in her family room. The ringing telephone interrupted her train of thoughts. She looked at the display before picking it up. "To what do I owe this honor?"

Kendra sat on a lab table. Despite being thirty-one, she looked more like a student in her khaki slacks and long-sleeved polo shirt. "Can't I call in the middle of the day just to say hello?"

Sharon looked at the clock on the fireplace mantel. It was almost one. "Shouldn't you be a little busy?"

"It's my lunch break." Kendra paused. "I just wanted to check on things in St. Louis. Is this a bad time for you?"

"Actually, your timing's perfect. I was just thinking about you. Have you talked to Dale?"

"Not since I talked with you both at Christmas. How's his new job working out?"

Sharon sat on the sofa, put the phone on speaker and resumed folding the warm load of clothes. "Leon, the senior pastor, died a few weeks ago. He had a massive heart attack while shoveling snow from his driveway."

"Wow...Dale said he really liked working with him. Hopefully, his death won't affect Dale's Bible studies."

"That's an understatement of epic proportion. Dale's the interim Senior Pastor while they organize a search committee. Everything's so unsettled right now."

Kendra massaged a shoulder, an automatic response to increasing tension. "Don't sound so concerned. Dale's a natural-born leader. Maybe, this is God's way of putting him where he belongs. He certainly was instrumental in redirecting my life. You both were."

"Well, the feeling's certainly mutual. If it wasn't for the trust fund you set up, Dale would have never changed careers so abruptly…or so frequently."

Kendra stood and paced the room, wondering if she ruined Dale's career by her zealous actions. He was a successful marketing executive when they met.

Sharon continued, "I just don't think he knows what he's committing to. This church might jump at the chance to get a 'free' pastor." Sharon tossed a shirt into the basket of clothes which needed ironing. "But enough about us…are you still enjoying all the changes in your life?"

"Teaching's going well. The principal held a special assembly this morning to announce that I'm a Texas finalist for Science Teacher of the Year. Needless to say, the entire school's excited because we could get a new science lab."

"What do you get?"

Kendra paused at the trash. "All the finalists are invited to the White House for a special reception with the President, but I'm not teaching for recognition. The fact that a record number of students are choosing to take physics is reward enough." Kendra resumed pacing. "Motherhood's a different story. Even with Eric's help, trying to get everything done is literally wearing me out. Mom made it look so easy." Kendra felt the muscles in her throat tightening and redirected her thoughts. "Have you joined Facebook yet? I posted some great pictures of the boys."

"Facebook will have to wait a lot longer for me to join the ranks. I'd much rather keep up with my true friends the old-fashioned ways, but monitoring Shawn's internet activity is keeping me from becoming too technically obsolete."

Kendra walked to her desk and sat down, remembering the week she stayed with Sharon's children while their parents went on a cruise. It was the first time she seriously considered having children. "You're a smart mother! It's hard to believe Shawn's thirteen already."

The buzzer on the dryer sounded. Sharon carried the phone to the breakfast table and continued the conversation and the laundry. "Five years can make quite a difference, especially in the amount of dirty clothes and groceries. Just wait! You'll see exactly what I mean, especially with two boys so close in age."

Kendra sighed. "I wish these years had made a difference in Jessica. I love her like a sister, but there's only so much I can accept. A five-year affair with Jonathan is bad enough. Now, she's allowing her daughter to become attached to that monster. Simone would have been better off not knowing her father. And if Jessica tells me one more time that I just need to get to know him, I'm going to scream." Kendra felt her hastily eaten lunch churning in her stomach. "Just thinking about him makes me nauseated. I can't imagine getting to know him."

Sharon deposited the load of clothes from the dryer on the loveseat, resisting the urge to tell Kendra that her friendship with Jessica was borderline toxic. Returning to get the phone, she noticed the sink filled with dirty dishes. "Did the book I recommended help any?" She moved the phone to the kitchen counter then opened the dishwasher to unload it.

"I read it before sending it to Jessica, but she won't read it! Dale's divinity degree is in counseling. Should I talk to him about what to do next?"

"Need I remind you that he left counseling for a reason? He's better equipped just to teach the Bible. Hopefully, they'll find a permanent replacement for Leon soon. I'm definitely not qualified to be a minister's wife."

"God might have different plans," Kendra said.

Sharon continued unloading the dishwasher with military precision. "How's your dad adjusting to retirement?"

Kendra wondered why Sharon changed the subject so abruptly. The sound of the school bell prevented her from asking why. "It's working perfectly for the both of us. He's a great sitter.

My lunch period's over, so I'll let you get back to what you were doing." Kendra stood and stretched. "My Spring break's next week. Eric and I are taking the boys to South Padre Island for their first beach vacation. Pray we'll survive and won't bring home too much sand." She walked across the classroom and opened the door.

"Have fun and send some pictures, the old-fashioned way," Sharon teased.

"I'll try. Give Dale and the kids my love. We'll talk soon." Kendra pushed the end call button and returned the phone to her purse. Despite her students' eager anticipation for the day to end, she dreaded the week long exile from the one controllable aspect of her life. A strong sense of foreboding permeated her entire body. The excited students walking into her class assured that she could delay dwelling on the last time she experienced a similar feeling.

***

The following Monday afternoon, Kendra merged her car onto the Dallas highway. The realization that the test results were neither a poor attempt at humor nor a lab error had paralyzed her mind, rendering it incapable of sensing the dangerous temperature when she entered her car. Sweat dripping from her eyebrows finally snapped her mind back to a functioning state; too late to prevent the all cotton sweater set, selected because of the frigid conditions in her doctor's office, from being saturated by her body's survival instinct. The air conditioner stayed in the automatic mode, so there was no need to adjust the controls. She held her hand in front of an air vent which confirmed the obvious. The car would cool faster than her clothes would dry. The high probability of causing a multiple car collision made removing the top layer of clothing a risk not worth taking.

Kendra's left hand wiped her brow before fingering her short, curly brown hair. After giving birth to her second son, she walked into the hair salon with shoulder length, chemically straightened hair and came out with a military cut; the first of many time saving changes in her life. She glanced in the rearview mirror to reassess her decision. The murky brown eyes in the reflection eerily resembled those of the deer that crossed Kendra's path years earlier when she was living in St. Louis. The animal darted onto the road and then stopped. After Kendra's car came to a screeching halt, she looked at the still motionless deer and cursed both their stupidity. She had been warned of deer activity in the fall. Her eyes returned to the current traffic. For a brief second, she wondered about the fate of that deer. "Why this?…Why now?"

Refusing to be a victim of her emotions, she recited the words relentlessly drilled into her students, "The first step to solve any problem is careful analysis of all the facts." Her mind raced through the facts before returning to the unanswerable 'why'. A scream crept from the depths of her soul but it would never leave her mouth. The merging tractor trailer that missed her car by inches convinced her that trying to navigate both the traffic and her thoughts was too dangerous. With the skill of a master, she quarantined the disturbing thoughts. A shiver caused her to adjust both the air vents and her plans for the remainder of the afternoon.

While waiting for the garage door to open, she scanned the yard for anything out of order. A robin gathering nesting materials drew her attention to the recently mulched flower beds. The first wave of perennials, carefully selected and strategically planted to ensure blooming flowers throughout the growing season, was emerging. Sitting in her idling sports utility vehicle, she would have traded all the flowers surrounding her home for more time with the original gardener. She eased the car into the garage. The wheeled recycling bin was kept beside the door leading to the laundry room to ensure that junk mail never crossed the threshold. Supplies for their automobiles were on the metal shelving at the front, adjacent to the cabinet for lawn supplies. The lawn equipment and tools were on the left side. Their trail bikes and strollers were on the right. Hoping her father had not heard the garage door open, she tuned off the engine but her hand paused before removing the key. Not enough time passed before the door to the house opened. She pulled the key from the ignition and exited the car.

Caleb Jones hovered in the doorway of the house that he meticulously designed decades earlier, ready to offer assistance. Since the day he gave Kendra and Eric the house for a wedding present, Caleb knew he received the greatest benefit. Even though he lived in a condominium nearby, the house would always be home. When his daughter mentioned she was using the first day of her Spring break to take care of a few things, he jumped at the opportunity to spend more time in the house with his grandsons. He waited for his daughter to reach the door before speaking. "I didn't expect you back so soon. Do you need help carrying anything in?"

At sixty-two, Caleb's short, cotton soft hair was solidly gray and his hairline was like a receding ocean wave. He once towered over his daughter, but with each passing year the gap between their heights narrowed. His posture and disposition still reminded Kendra of the father in the Broadway show, 'The Lion King'. People often commented that father and daughter were cut from the same rock, although Kendra never believed it.

She pressed the button to close the garage door. "No." Brushing past him, she hoped that he would leave without needing an explanation. She set her purse on the center island and listened to the baby monitor. The familiar sound of their breathing was a welcomed relief.

Caleb waited to verify that the garage door closed completely before joining his daughter in the kitchen. "How was your appointment?"

"Fine," she said, looking around the kitchen for any task that could provide an excuse to avoid her father's inquisitive gaze. Since the front of her sweater appeared to be dry, she leaned against the counter to keep the watermarks on the back of the sweater hidden.

He leaned against the door frame. "You don't look fine. Is everything okay?"

Too exhausted to continue standing, Kendra plopped on a chair at the round oak table bearing permanent scars from her childhood despite several refinishes. "Did you have trouble getting the boys down for their nap?"

"Not at all. Since it was such a nice day, we played outside after lunch. They might be sleep for a while. Danny's going to be an early walker, just like you were!"

Kendra stared in the direction of her father, still avoiding direct eye contact. She was not ready for the words to come out of her mouth. "Thanks for staying with them."

"Did your doctor give you a clean bill of health?"

Kendra hesitated, increasing both their levels of anxiety. "Yes."

"Then what's wrong? ... And don't you dare say nothing either; I know you too well."

"I'd rather not talk about it," she said rubbing her forehead. "Besides, I've imposed on your time long enough and I need to change clothes before the boys wake up."

Her father sat in the chair next to her. "If you think that I'm leaving before you tell me what we're facing, then you don't know *me* very well!"

Caleb's concerned expression finally penetrated her mental barrier. "Dad...it's not cancer!" His visible relief prevented her from stating that it was almost as bad.

"Thank you, God." Caleb waited for his daughter to speak. When she didn't, he did. "What else could have you so upset? You were fine when you left."

She remembered the last time she tried to keep information from him. "I'm pregnant...again." The words sounded more like an indictment than an announcement. Kendra watched her father carefully for signs of shock or disappointment.

He exhaled. "Why so glum? You screamed with excitement the first two times."

"Those were both carefully planned pregnancies, so I wouldn't miss any of the school year." Kendra winched thinking again about the December due date. She had finally convinced Eric that they needed to wait at least two years before even discussing more children.

"Do you think this one will be a girl?"

"I don't know…" Kendra gently slid her finger across a deep groove in the table, remembering the day it was etched.

"Yes, you do. Your mother said that a woman's intuition is always right. Are you awaiting another son or a daughter?"

She looked around the kitchen that her mother had redecorated during her fatal battle with cancer. When she moved back into the house, she decided not to change anything. Every detail in the kitchen served as a visible reminder of her mother's essence. "Probably both, I'm having twins."

"How can they tell so soon? Did you know you were pregnant?"

"No, I didn't *know* I was pregnant! I've been so irregular since the boys were born. They did a pregnancy test as a precaution since I wanted to get back on birth control pills. When the test was positive, they did an ultrasound to confirm the results." Kendra had a grainy picture of two dots that the doctor assured her were developing fetuses in her purse.

Caleb beamed. "Baby, this is wonderful news. I don't think we've had twins in the family!"

Her fists hit the table. "*No*, it's not wonderful… I wish *men* would stop saying that it is! First my doctor, and now *you*. It's bad enough that I'm pregnant again so soon. Now, we're going to have four children in three years!" She knew exactly when she conceived. Since she was still nursing Daniel, she thought their Valentine Day celebration would be harmless.

Her father abandoned the attempt to contain his joy. A broad smile spread across his face. "And you thought you'd never have children."

Kendra leered at her father. "This is your fault!"

Her father chuckled. "Okay. Maybe I'm partly responsible since I did help produce you."

"That's not what I'm talking about. You said that I was going to have a house full of children. Apparently, those words traveled directly from your mouth to God's ears."

Caleb had made the statement in jest when she expressed concerns about being able to conceive. He raised his hands in the air. "To God be the glory!"

"There's no glory in this Daddy." Kendra propped her elbows on the table, closed her eyes and massaged her temples. Prior to having children running was her escape. Last week, she was barely able to run a mile, now she knew why. A thought flashed in her mind about running until the contents of her womb broke free. Then she remembered her own words to Jessica after she announced her plan to get another abortion – "You will be killing a gift from God." Her heart burned from the searing irony. "I didn't mean that…" She longed for the days when her father could tickle away her concerns.

"What did you mean?"

Kendra sighed in frustration. "I don't want to be ungrateful, but I can't keep doing this. Joshua and Daniel are already a handful. How in the world am I going to handle two more?"

"Baby, God never gives us more than we can handle."

Kendra thought about the broken eggs. "I'm already under so much stress. Between teaching, the boys, and the house, I'm constantly juggling my time."

"Maybe you should stop teaching for a while; at least, until your children are older."

"That's what Eric said this morning, without knowing that his brood's about to double." She slipped off her shoes.

"Consider yourself blessed. You don't have to work for a paycheck. Eric makes more than enough to support the family and I suspect that you haven't even touched the money from the lawsuit."

"It's not about money. I love teaching and it seemed like I'd finally found my purpose."

"Not working at a school doesn't mean you aren't teaching. Besides, at the rate you're going, your own children could fill a classroom."

The news interview with the woman who had nineteen children suddenly seemed relevant. "That's not even remotely funny. If you're trying to cheer me up, please stop."

"It wasn't supposed to be funny. Home schooling is becoming very relevant in today's culture." Kendra's father reached for his daughter's hand. "I know the news about twins is a bit overwhelming right now, but Eric's going to be thrilled. It's no secret that he wants a lot of children."

"That's because he has the easy job. Well, he'd better be content with four. If he doesn't do something, I will."

"Sweetheart, you don't mean that. You're not thinking clearly right now."

"Then why did you and Mom only have two?"

Sadness filled her father's eyes. "Because that's all God gave us."

Sensing her father's remorse, Kendra regretted asking him the question. "Daddy, families don't need a lot of children anymore. Parents don't know how to handle them. Besides, we don't have any fields to plant or cows to milk or whatever children did back then to make them an asset."

"I disagree. Children are our contribution to the future. If more people realized that, they might do a better job raising them."

Kendra glanced at her father, hoping she could make him understand her turmoil. "Some women are better suited for motherhood. It seems that I'm not one of them."

"If that were true, you wouldn't be so fertile."

"Giving birth to children has no correlation with ability to produce the next generation of human beings. The nightly news is proof of that. If you want more proof, spend one day with me at the school. The effects of bad mothering are all around us. " Kendra appreciated her father's good intentions, but she doubted he would ever understand. She wanted her mother to be the one sitting next to her.

"I think that society at large is more to blame. You're exactly the kind of woman who should be mothering the next generation. You're intelligent, caring, hard-working and, most importantly, committed to doing things right. Even though your mother's time with you was cut short, she died convinced that you were prepared for whatever life had in store for you."

"Everything was so easy for Mom. What am I doing wrong?"

"Appearing easy and being easy are not always the same. You're just encountering a little friction as you change gears and it may take several adjustments before you find the gear that works best for you." Her father chuckled. "If memory serves me right, your mother had a rough start with you and your brother. Be patient. On average, it takes almost ten years of hard work to master any new skill."

The thought of ten years of mistakes frightened her more. She'd read that the battle was won or lost in the first seven years of a child's life. "Why did Mom have to die? We still need her...I still need her."

"Remember not to lean on your own understanding..."

Kendra held up her hand to stop her father. "You don't need to finish it."

"Are you sure?"

"Oh yes, I'm sure," Kendra said with a reluctant smile.

"So, when are you going to tell Eric about the twins? I'd love to see his reaction."

"I might wait until they're born to surprise him." Kendra looked at her stomach trying to imagine the expansion required for two. Instinctively, she wanted to call Jessica, her best friend and confidant. Knowing her response, Kendra decided the news could wait until Jessica returned from the conference in Hawaii.

***

Sharon McKinney sat on her expansive deck savoring her solitude and looking for buds on the trees. Although the temperature barely reached seventy degrees, the sunshine made it feel warmer. The trees were still bare but anticipation was in the air. Spring popped quickly in the Midwest. The deep furrows between her brows matched the intensity of her thoughts. The garage door opening could be heard from the deck. Hoping that her day was not about to get worse, she mentally followed her husband's routine. Right on cue, Dale walked onto the deck. She decided to let him unload first. "How was your first Deacon Board meeting as the senior pastor?" When he stood between her and the sun, she motioned with her hand for him to move before he could answer.

Dale pulled a chair into the sunshine and sat down. "Apparently I'm ruffling a few feathers. Half of the group was guardedly polite, but several were quite vocal about every change that I suggested. Someone was actually upset because I expect people to bring a Bible to church services."

Sharon looked at her husband whose clothing style was unaffected by his mid-life career change. In his dark slacks and starched white, long-sleeved shirt, he looked more like the corporate executive than a fledgling minister. At six feet-three inches, his height was equally intimidating. She wondered if Dale's strictly business attitude was the root of his difficulties. "I can imagine your response."

"I simply said that if people don't want to bring a Bible to church, we could provide some for them; they then instructed me how to submit a *request for procurement*. I never imagined that running a church could be so frustrating...or inefficient...or political."

Sharon observed her husband of eighteen years carefully. At forty-four, he was relatively young; yet it was difficult for her to ignore the light gray strands which seemed to appear overnight. "Do you think the stress caused Leon's heart attack?"

"No, I believe it was just Leon's time to rest. This afternoon, I found myself envying Moses' ability to speak with God face to face."

Despite having a million dollar trust fund, Sharon wondered if they had made a mistake. "I never imagined when you accepted the job working for Leon that you'd be in his position a few months later."

"Well, a certain member of the board, who shall remain nameless, pointedly reminded me that I was only the *interim* senior pastor, so I shouldn't get too full of myself. Those were his exact words."

"The fact that they don't have to pay you might be incentive to give you the job, if this is what you want to do long term." Sharon debated asking, but she had to know. "Is it?"

"Honestly, I don't know. Someone actually asked me 'why on earth would I work for free?'"

"What did you say?"

Dale clasped his hands together. "Leon and I agreed that drudging up the details might not be a good idea, so I just said that God provided for my family's needs so the church's funds could be used for more pressing work."

"Hopefully, no one will go digging into your past."

"Sharon, I'm not ashamed of my actions."

"You don't have to be a minister to serve God, or to honor the terms of the trust. If you got a PhD, you could teach at the seminary."

"I have no desire, whatsoever, to be theologian. I just want to help others make the connection between the God of the Bible and their personal experiences. Leon hired me, so to speak, because he wanted the church to start a serious Bible study program. Unfortunately, he died before we could implement our plans." Dale paused. "I didn't know that the only reason the board approved my addition to the staff was because they didn't have to pay me."

"They told you that."

"Oh, yes. It also slipped out that the associate pastor whose position I filled turned down the offer to return as senior pastor. Leon isolated me from so much." Dale looked skyward resolutely. "Thankfully, God equips us for the work." He looked at Sharon again. "If people could just stop bickering and get with the program!"

"You know that I'll support whatever you decide to do, within limits."

Dale leaned back in the chair. "How was your day?"

"Things were so much easier before our son became convinced that he knows everything. I'm struggling not to reach out and show him the kind of love we grew up with."

"What did he do?"

"What he did initially wasn't that bad. He got a *D* on a test, so his teacher called because she knows he can do better. When I asked him why he didn't study for the test – which I know he didn't because if he had, he would have aced it—he had the audacity to ask me – let me put this in his words – 'Why was I making such a big deal over *his* grades?' Dale, I don't know what's gotten into him—nothing but divine intervention, and the law, kept me from flying across the room to knock some sense into his head."

"Where is he?"

"I told him it was safer for him to stay in his room until you got home. Dale, I'm not going to have disrespect in this house. What did our parents tell us? – 'I brought you into this world and I can take you out!' That's how I feel right now. Has he lost his mind?"

"From what I've read, it's just not finished developing." Dale smoothed his mustache to conceal the smile. "He's testing us to see what he can get away with."

The sun was retreating too quickly, causing a noticeable chill in the air. "I do not have the patience to be tested by a thirteen year old!"

"You're going to get a lot of opportunity to develop some. Did you actually think we would waltz through the teen years, especially with what they're exposed to today? If Shawn's anything like I was, we have an interesting road ahead."

"I'm just thankful that Paige is so easy going."

Dale raised an eyebrow. "What were you like as a teenager?"

"Oh no, you didn't just go there! Remind me again why we wanted children so badly."

Dale stood up. "I'll go have a heart to heart talk with our son. If that doesn't work, we'll have to try something else. Is Paige in her room, too?"

"No, she's next door playing. I talked to Kendra this afternoon. Guess what?"

"She's pregnant?"

"How'd you know that?"

"She's an over achiever. When is this one due?"

"The *twins* are due in December. She sounded really upset."

"I can only imagine. She likes to be in control."

"Those days are definitely over," Sharon said with a noticeable tinge of bitterness.

"I hope you didn't tell her that."

"No I didn't, but I did suggest meeting somewhere. She needs some time away from the boys, even if it's just for a weekend. Can you and the kids survive without me for two days?"

"Probably, seeing how it's for a good cause. I'm glad you and Kendra keep in contact."

"It looks like I'm becoming a surrogate mother."

"You're too young to be her mother, but she did tell me once that she regretted not having a sister. Maybe she sees you as the older sister she always wanted and apparently needs."

"I'll do whatever I can to help her. Maybe when I come back, my family will appreciate me a little more."

"We appreciate you. Certain members of this family just need to learn about respect and responsibilities." Dale hesitated. "All signs point to a light dinner."

Sharon checked her watch. "I read that the cook's attitude affects the quality of the food. My cooking's bad enough."

"You've never heard me complain. Do you want me to order a pizza?"

"No. You deal with our son and I'll manage dinner."

As Sharon sat on the deck thinking about a weekend away from home, a larger plan took shape. She picked up her phone and scrolled quickly through her contacts list. Excitement built with each second of waiting to hear Karly's voice. Since she moved to Minneapolis, they often discussed taking a trip together. Finally, they might get the chance.

***

In Atlanta, Jonathan Grey inspected the contents of his shaving kit before snapping it closed. At thirty-five, his wavy brown hair was freshly trimmed, his body rock solid and his coffee-colored skin flawless but his deep baritone voice was what everyone noticed most. The joy of traveling to Hawaii for the first time was dampened by the possibility that something might go wrong. He allowed himself to be convinced that the well-timed trade conference provided the perfect opportunity for a romantic anniversary getaway and the rewards would greatly outweigh any perceived risk. Jessica, the mother of his illegitimate daughter, was extremely convincing. It had been four years since the birth that solidified a permanent relationship; exactly five years since he walked into her office. Although he knew that she wanted the impossible, their addictive relationship continued. Leaving his wife for Jessica, a mistake her first husband made, was not even a consideration; still he could not resist what she offered, despite several earnest attempts. Working for the same corporation, but in

23

different cities, facilitated his unfaithfulness. Spending the night at her house when he was in Chicago for business was one thing; risking being seen romantically with her in Hawaii was a totally different story. Jessica reassured him that they would be extremely discrete.

Jonathan heard Lori, his wife, coming up the stairs. When she entered their bedroom, he analyzed the contrast between the two women. Everything about Lori was average: her height, weight, coloring, hair, and even her gestures. Yet, the combination of her features and personality produced a disarming charm. Complete strangers seemed like old friends after a few minutes in her presence. Nothing about Jessica was average. Jessica was most men's desire with a sensuality that was impossible to resist. Lori's smile compelled him to smile with her; Jessica's smile compelled him to want her.

Lori watched him put the shaving kit in the suitcase and zip it shut. "I was coming to help you pack."

Hoping to mask his guilt, Jonathan forced a smile. "You have enough to do already. By the way, dinner was delicious."

"Thanks." Lori twisted her wedding ring on her finger. "I've been dreading this trip ever since you told me about it. Managing without you during the week's hard enough, but we really miss you on the weekends."

"Our livelihood depends on the contacts I make at these conferences. Don't look so glum. The days will fly by for us both. But if it makes you feel any better, I'll hate being away from you and the kids." Jonathan went into their bathroom before continuing. "The time difference will prevent me from calling very often."

"That's fine...I just wish you didn't have to travel so much. Maybe it's time I went back to work. Jason will be starting kindergarten in the fall."

"Lori, we've talked about this before. Let me worry about the money; besides, taking care of four children is a very demanding job."

Lori reached to open his suitcase. "Do you have everything you need?"

He eased the suitcase from her grip and set it by the door. "I think so."

"I wish we could spend five days in Hawaii together."

"You know we can't afford it, besides the kids would never let you leave them for that long." He checked his briefcase hoping to mask his nervousness. "With the trip to Disneyworld this summer, we need to save every penny." This fact was his last line of defense with Jessica. He finally relented when she agreed to pay for everything that the company would not. "Besides, you'd be bored with me in meetings all day and entertaining clients at night."

"I wouldn't mind giving 'bored' in Hawaii a try."

"Maybe in a few years, we'll be able to take the entire family."

"I miss the way we used to be. We never get time alone anymore," she said.

The sadness in her eyes caused him to momentarily reconsider his plans, again, but it was too late to do the right thing. "Unfortunately, life requires sacrifice and compromise." He knew that he needed to do something to ease his conscience. Lori deserved better. "If your mother can stay with our children, maybe we can drive down to Savannah for a weekend. That way, we can spend some quality time together without crippling the family budget."

"It's not Hawaii, but I guess beggars can't be choosey...I love you, so much!"

He pulled his wife from the bed and embraced her tightly. "I love you, too."

"What time do you want to leave for the airport?"

He stopped their embrace. "We can leave now, so you won't be out so late with the kids."

"I still can't believe they're making you connect through Chicago. There are direct flights to Hawaii from here."

He preferred a direct flight but was unwilling to risk Jessica meeting him in Atlanta. With his luck, someone he knew would be on the flight. "Lately, the company's always counting pennies. They probably saved a few bucks on the ticket."

Lori walked towards the door. "I'll get the kids ready. Give us ten minutes."

***

The Sunday morning after Dale's insightful deacon board meeting, the music director ramped up the volume and tempo causing the song's lyrics to resonate throughout the main church building. "It makes me want to shout Hallelujah! Thank you, Jesus…." Dale stood and enthusiastically joined the choir. When the song ended and the choir members, many fanning themselves with their bulletins, had taken their seats, Dale walked purposefully to the pulpit with his Bible and sermon notes in hand.

"I want to thank the choir for singing the song which so clearly expresses the joy of knowing God. He truly picks us up, turns us around and places our feet on solid ground. Remember Jonah." Laughter filled the air. "As many of you know, I'm a novice at leading a congregation. When I joined the staff, I anticipated having years of training with Pastor Lowe. Apparently, the Lord had different plans, at least for the interim." Dale glanced at the scowling Deacon Jones, sitting on the first pew with one of the new Bibles in his hand. "While working on this morning's message, I was overcome by a feeling of immense inadequacy. Teaching the Word of God is an awesome privilege and huge responsibility. I didn't realize that when I harshly criticized most of the sermons I heard. Standing before you now, completely humbled, I should have heeded Jesus' warning 'For in the same way you judge others, you will be judged, and with the measure you use, it will be measured to you.' Learn a lesson from my mistake and temper your critiques. You never know what God has planned for you."

As Dale looked around the sanctuary, Jeremiah's words regarding God's people being lost sheep forced to roam the mountains because their shepherds led them astray resonated with him. "This feeling of inadequacy brought to mind an email that I received a long time ago. Then, it was amusing. Now, it seems prophetic. The email told the story of a man who lived at the top of a high hill in a remote country. Every morning, the man tied two large stone water jars to a pole and carried them down the hill to the river. After filling them to the brim, he hauled them back up the hill to his house." Dale walked down the aisle as if he were carrying the pole with the heavy jugs on his shoulder before lowering the imaginary jars to the ground.

"After many years of use, one of the jars developed a crack. Over time, the crack got larger and larger until it reached the point that the jar was almost empty by the time the man reached his house. The jar knew it was only a matter of time before the old man realized how useless it was and replaced it. Every day, as the jar was carried up the hill leaking its content, it compared itself to the other jar which only made the situation worse." Dale perched at the center of the aisle.

"Eventually, the jar couldn't take the waiting any longer. As the old man sat the jars beside the door, the cracked one cried out to the old man. 'Why do you continue to use me? You work so hard to fill me but before you can get back home, I've spilled most of the water.' The old man smiled as he responded. 'It's your crack that makes you more useful to me. I saw how you spilled your water along the path. So I planted seeds on the side that you watered. Now look at the beauty that you helped me create.' Along the path was a beautiful trail of flowers of every size and color. You see, the jar's focus was too narrow."

Dale returned to the pulpit. "Ladies and gentleman, I'm a cracked vessel and some of you are too. We can sit around and bemoan our faults and compare ourselves to others. But what we must realize is that God's fully aware of our cracks. God doesn't call the qualified, God qualifies the called. Please turn with me in your Bibles to the gospel of John, chapter 3. If you didn't remember to bring your Bible, God graciously provided extras for the pews. But next week, please remember to bring your own."

Deacon Jones cleared his throat in a vain attempt to command the attention of Dale, who opened his Bible without missing a beat. "For the last few weeks, I've stressed the importance of bringing a Bible to church with you and signing up for the new Bible studies. What I failed to remember is that the only person who likes change is a baby with a dirty diaper. People willingly change only when they see how it benefits them. Our subject this morning is 'Why we need the Bible'."

An hour later, Dale closed his Bible surprised at how quickly the time passed. "Using just a few verses throughout the Bible, I tried to show that knowledge of God, an understanding of the work of Jesus Christ and unwavering faith are all required. It's like a three-legged stool. We need God's Word as much as we need His Spirit. How could I expect Shawn to drive a car, if he's never received the right instruction?"

Dale scanned the crowd, most of whom were shaking their heads in agreement. "We'll continue with this next week. If you are here without a church home…"

When the main sanctuary was finally empty, Dale returned to his office to record a few notes and reflect on the feedback he received. Sharon and his children went home after the benediction, eliminating his need to rush. A knock on the door interrupted his solitude. Dale looked up, expecting to see Deacon Jones. Instead, Leon's son lingered in the doorway. The physical resemblance to his father was strong and Dale suspected that the similarities went much deeper.

"Pastor McKinney, do you have a few minutes?"

Dale stood and gestured for the young man to enter. "Sure Henry, what can I do for you?"

He walked into Dale's office and closed the door. "I really enjoy your sermons. My father was right about God using you in a powerful way."

"Remember, we're just the cracked vessel." Dale motioned for Henry to sit.

Henry perched on the edge of the chair facing Dale's desk. "I want to thank you for allowing my mother to stay in the parsonage until my father's estate is settled. I heard that the board of deacons was split on the matter."

"Don't worry about it. My family had no plans to move into the parsonage anyway. Make sure your mother knows that there's no rush. She can live there as long as needed."

"Momma's planning to be settled before summer. She wants me back in school as soon as possible. But that's not what I wanted to talk to you about."

"What is it?"

"Pastor, I know that you're an honest man, which is the only reason that I'm coming to you. I think something shady is going on with the offerings. I don't have any hard proof, just something in my gut. Dad taught me that I should never ignore these feelings because it's often from the Holy Spirit."

"What do you think is happening?"

"Well, I noticed in the bulletin that the offering last week was about the same as usual."

"What's so strange about that?"

"Since I've been back home, I usher whenever I can. The ushers notice what goes into the offering plate. I expected that the offerings would be at least double. But when I looked at the bulletin, I couldn't believe my eyes. You might want to check into this. Finances have brought down a lot of churches. I'd hate for this church to be one of them."

"Me too." Dale rubbed his temples.

"I don't need to tell you that some of our deacons are wolves in sheep's clothing. They gave Dad one problem after another. Someone may be taking advantage of the situation."

Dale stood up. "Henry, I appreciate you bringing this to my attention. Have you told anyone else about this?"

"No sir, not even my mother. I wanted to see what you thought first. What do you think we should do?"

"I'm not sure. Let me give this some thought. Will you do me a favor?"

"Whatever you need, I'm your man."

"Don't mention this to anyone. If someone's doing something wrong, we need to be careful how we handle it and the only one I trust completely is God."

Henry stood up. "I won't say a word, but next Sunday I will definitely have my eyes and ears open. If I hear or see anything, you'll be the first to know."

CHAPTER 2

AFTER THREE WEEKS OF WAITING, KENDRA WAS THOROUGHLY enjoying her time away from home. A quaint bed-and-breakfast in central Arkansas met all of the criteria: centrally located, warm climate, easy access, and relatively private. Jessica was a late addition to the group. Sharon and Karly shared one suite in the old converted farmhouse; Kendra and Jessica shared the other. The group coordinated their flights into Little Rock, Arkansas for Friday evening and rented a car for the late night drive.

Saturday morning after eating a southern comfort breakfast, Jessica dragged Kendra back to their suite and sat her at the Queen Anne writing desk. She eyed the bed ready for a mid-morning nap. Jessica removed the book from her suitcase and presented it to Kendra with the pride of a child sharing their first great work of art. Expecting to see pictures of her beloved god-daughter and namesake, Kendra opened it excitedly. Her expectations were dashed with the first page. The scrapbook was a magnified view of the issue that strained their friendship. After the last argument about Jonathan, they agreed not to discuss him or the relationship again.

The ticking of the mantle clock became more pronounced with each passing second. Every detail of the room was intended to create a sense of tranquility and romance. Kendra felt neither. One hand propped up her head while the other methodically turned the pages. As much as Kendra wanted to find something positive to say, every thought was negative. Her emotions vacillated between adamant disgust and genuine sympathy for his wife. "I didn't know that he went to Hawaii with you."

"I didn't tell you because we agreed not to talk about him." Jessica reclined on the bed. "Aren't the pictures great? Everyone kept commenting on what a great couple we made." Tick... Tick...Tick. "I never thought I was the scrap booking type but once I got started, it was fun. I probably should do one for some of Simone's pictures."

"I can't believe he agreed to be photographed with you like this."

"Jonathan didn't know some of them were being taken. Those really captured the intensity of our relationship. Technology has definitely improved."

"Intensity is putting it mildly...Look Jessica, I know we've been through this before and we agreed to avoid the subject. But since you opened the door by flaunting these pictures, I deserve the chance for rebuttal."

"Okay...shoot."

"What you're doing is wrong and you've got to stop it. Nothing good will ever come of this."

"Something good already has—our daughter, who just so happens to be your godchild." Jessica sat up on the bed and adjusted the elastic band on her copper colored hair. "This may actually surprise you but I reconsidered everything that you've said over the years about my relationship with Jonathan. Working on this scrapbook was therapeutic. It gave me lots of time to think. After a lot of deep reflection, I can honestly say that our relationship's not wrong."

Unable to process the remaining images, Kendra closed the scrapbook and tried to comprehend the words which defied logic. Despite Jessica's well documented intelligence, Kendra was still amazed by her lack of common sense. "By who's standard?"

"By yours, of course..."

"Excuse me. My standard for right and wrong is God's Word, the Good Book...the B.I.B.L.E."

"I know and according to the B.I.B.L.E., Jonathan and I are not doing anything wrong."

Kendra shook her head in disbelief. "What are you talking about? Adultery's one of the Ten Commandments. Even you have to know that!"

"I'll overlook that statement. But since you're such an expert, consider this. My mother dated a minister who said, according to the Bible, a man is allowed to have relations with other women as long as he doesn't leave his wife or treat her badly. Well, Jonathan has made it clear that he's not leaving his wife and he treats her like a queen, if you ask me." Jessica crossed her legs. "And I've checked out what else the Bible says about marriage. Jacob had between two and four wives, depending on how you want to count them. The great King David had several wives and the wisest man to ever live had three hundred wives, not to mention all his concubines. And wasn't it Bathsheba who gave birth to the wisest man. David and Bathsheba's relationship started just like mine, except Jonathan didn't have to kill anyone to get me. So now will you please stop judging us? Jonathan just has two wives, like most of the men in the Bible. Case closed…"

Kendra wondered if Jessica was purposefully ignoring the fact that David and Bathsheba's child conceived in adultery died. "Jessica, I know you don't believe that. You're *not* his wife. And for your information, God created one woman for Adam, not two."

"I may not be Jonathan's wife legally, but in every other way I am. And if it were legal in this country, I know that he would marry me."

"Jessica, you're really starting to scare me. There's no way you can justify what you're doing. Your relationship's adultery, plain and simple and you've got to stop it before it's too late. Read the Bible a little closer. In every case, those extra wives caused great hardship for the men."

"I know you mean well, but Jonathan, Simone and I are a family. We can't be together as much as I want, but when we are together, it's perfect."

"Jessica, what's it going to take to get through to you?"

"I don't know why you still don't understand. These pictures should convince you how much we care for each other. You should be happy for me."

"And what are you going to tell Simone when she's old enough to start asking questions?"

"The truth…Her father and I love her very much and stayed together for her sake."

Kendra remembered her students' discussion of truth. "Oh please… Simone has nothing to do with this. You and Jonathan are together for your own selfish reasons. Can't you see that he's using you?"

"If anybody's being used, it's him. Now, let's change the subject. Apparently, we'll never agree on this one. So when are you and Eric going to stop having babies? Your body will never get back in shape and that hair cut has got to go. Short hair is definitely not the style for you."

A soft knock on the door was a welcomed relief for Kendra.

Sharon stood in the doorway in riding clothes. "Jessica, are you ready to go?"

Jessica jumped off the bed. "I wondered what was taking you so long!"

Kendra gave Sharon an apologetic look while Jessica grabbed the scrapbook and put it back in her suitcase. She bolted from the room without saying another word.

***

Unfiltered sunshine rapidly caused perspiration to trickle down the ridge of Sharon's nose. Resenting being pressured by Jessica's pace, she wondered if Jessica was intentionally increasing the distance between them. Sharon took a riding class in college as an elective, but it had been years since she rode. Once in the saddle, she remembered enough to appear proficient.

After a quick glance back to confirm that Sharon was keeping pace, Jessica spotted a tree-covered knoll. She raced towards the trees and away from her thoughts of Jonathan. Both the rider and the horse were winded when they reached their destination. By the time Sharon joined them, Jessica was sitting on the ground in the shade of a sprawling tree. Jessica learned to ride horses at the summer camp her mother sent her to once Jessica was old enough to attract the attention of her mother's male companions. After the first summer, Jessica looked forward to school ending and going to camp. When she turned sixteen, Jessica got summer jobs but her minimum wage was not sufficient to support her love of horseback riding. Her desire to ride horses was what helped Jessica discover her power with men.

Sharon dismounted and walked her horse to the tree. "What's the hurry? You're going so fast, you're missing all this beauty."

Jessica looked at a patch of wildflowers blooming near by. "I get on a horse to ride, not look at the scenery."

"I like to do both." Sharon took a deep breath.

"Someone like you would."

Sharon let the words sail past realizing that life with a thirteen year old had its benefits. Words intended to inflict pain lost their sting.

Jessica tilted her head back to get the full benefit of the breeze. "It's been too long since I've been on a horse. I almost forgot riding's power to purge the mind."

Sharon sat a few feet from Jessica, whose flawless beauty and youthful energy was hard not to envy. Her dark brown riding pants clung to every inch of her legs highlighting her perfectly toned body. "What are you trying to purge?"

"My inability to get the one thing I want most in this world and Kendra's inability to understand."

Given Kendra's expression before they left, Sharon feared Jessica was about to ruin the weekend. "Sometimes, what we want is not what we need."

"In this case, what I want and need is the same thing. It's just taking too long to get."

Sharon paused trying to determine the best way to deal with Jessica. "Get it or get him?"

"Same thing…" Jessica plucked a long blade of grass. "So, how much do you know?"

"About what?"

"Don't play innocent with me. How many of my dirty little secrets have you been privy to? I know Kendra has told you something about my current situation. She mistakenly believes that my soul needs saving from the fires of hell. If you ask me, there's enough hell here on earth. Why worry about some eternal hell that probably doesn't even exist?"

Sharon sighed. "I know that you're having an affair with a married man who's the father of your child. Given the age of your daughter, this affair has been going on for some time."

Jessica tossed the grass blade on the ground and rubbed her hands on her pants. "I guess you know enough."

"Jessica, can I ask you a question?"

Jessica glared at Sharon. "Why did I get involved with a married man?"

"Especially if you knew he was married from the beginning."

"Genetics, I guess. Like mother, like daughter."

Sharon looked at the ground. "It appears that this man has the morals of a snake."

"You know what they say—birds of a feather flock together."

Sharon did not know whether to pity her or slap her. "Jessica, you're an intelligent, beautiful woman. You deserve a man who'll be committed to you and only you."

"I've learned that commitment's highly overrated and very rare these days. You should probably keep very tight reins on your husband and worry less about my affairs."

Sharon restrained her hand from making the decision for her. "I don't have to worry about my husband."

Jessica smirked. "I could probably prove you wrong. But if you say so…"

The smugness intended to offend only confirmed Sharon's suspicions. Behind the tough exterior was a soul in desperate need of help and she had to try, despite her personal feelings. "Jessica, it may surprise you that not all men are controlled by lust. Take my advice, you need to stop letting lust control you too."

"If I wanted your advice, I'd ask for it. But since you've started this, let me give you some advice. Stop assuming that Jonathan doesn't love me because he does. Our relationship may have started with a strong physical attraction but it has developed into something much more. And I'm not about to let him go, regardless of what anyone else might think."

"Jessica, listen to what you're saying. You're trying to fill a void that can only be filled by one person and it's not Jonathan. It's God."

"Not you, too," Jessica snorted. "I should've checked into a convent. Well, so much for a fun girl's weekend. I should have known better. This is just another attempt by Kendra to brainwash me. Well, I've got news for her. It's not going to work."

Sharon struggled to her feet. "I think it's time we get back."

Jessica stood and dusted off the back of her pants. "What's your problem?"

"The saying 'you can lead a horse to water but you can't make them drink' is very applicable. You need water, but apparently you're not thirsty enough. So let's finish our ride before it gets too hot." Sharon grabbed her horse's reign. "Jessica, your best friend's going through a very difficult time. I can't imagine why she would want you here, but she does."

"Kendra doesn't need me. She has her God!"

"That's true. But right now she needs others to remind her that God is enough. Maybe she's hoping that you'll both learn that this weekend." Sharon mounted her horse and rode off without waiting for Jessica.

***

After showering from her ride, Sharon walked to the kitchen to sample the fresh squeezed lemonade announced at breakfast. She looked out the window and saw Kendra sitting sideways on the wooden swing, unconsciously rubbing her abdomen. Since she stepped off the plane, Sharon wondered whether the noticeable bulge was due to this pregnancy or leftover from the last. Deciding that the lemonade might do them both good, Sharon postponed her plans to read in her suite.

The screen door leading to the covered porch squeaked as Sharon walked outside carrying two glasses dripping with condensation. "Feeling anything yet?"

Kendra's hand stopped abruptly, as she moved her feet so Sharon could sit. "Not really…"

Sharon handed Kendra a glass before sitting. Her legs propelled the swing back and forth in the same slow rhythm that had calmed both of her children through colic and teething, hoping the motion would bring temporary peace to Kendra. "How was your walk?"

Kendra smiled sheepishly. "This is as far as I made it."

Sharon was happy to see a genuine smile. "You'll get your energy back soon. Enjoy your pregnancy. I wish I had."

"You and Dale should have more children."

"Oh, no… It's too late for us!"

"Not these days. Women much older than you are having their first child."

"That's great for them, but my doctor obliged my request for permanent birth control before I left the hospital with Paige."

"I want to do the same thing, but Eric doesn't think I should."

"In my case, it wasn't Dale's decision to make." Sharon looked into the garden. "But don't let hormones motivate your actions."

Kendra fished the slice of lemon from the glass. "Do you regret your decision?"

Sharon paused as she contemplated whether it was regret or guilt that she felt over the years. "At the time, I was so certain it was the right thing to do. Both my pregnancies were so difficult. But now, when I look at Shawn and Paige, I can't help wondering what might have been."

"You could always have the surgery reversed." Kendra grimaced as she sucked the juice from the lemon slice.

"Nope. I think it's better for me to accept the consequences for my actions and move on. Otherwise, I could spend valuable time, money and emotions chasing a missed opportunity."

"Well, at the rate I'm going, I'll have enough children to share."

"And whenever you're ready to leave them with someone, their Aunt Sharon and Uncle Dale will be ready and willing."

"Be careful what you volunteer for. Eric and I may take you up on the offer. Dad's great with two, but I think four may be a bit much for him to handle." Kendra returned the lemon to the glass and took a sip. "This is delicious, just like my mom used to make." Tears threatened to fall, instinctively triggering a change in thoughts. "Truthfully, how was the ride with Jessica?"

Afraid their conversation might be overheard, Sharon filtered her words. "Jessica rode faster than I would have preferred. The hot bath helped. I probably should have stayed here with you and Karly."

"I love Jessica but she can be trying, especially for people who don't know her well."

The impulse to ask why Kendra maintained any contract with Jessica was blocked. Instead, Sharon continued powering the swing and waited patiently for Kendra to speak again.

Kendra sighed. "It feels like I'm in a vortex, getting sucked to the bottom of some horrible pit. I'm trying to be thankful for this pregnancy but..."

"Give yourself a break. Two small children can be physically overwhelming, even if you weren't pregnant again. I was exhausted all the time when my children were still in diapers. You might even have postpartum depression which can last for years after giving birth based on an article I just read."

Kendra leaned her head back and closed her eyes. "It's more frustration than depression. Finally, I thought I knew God's will for my life. Teaching's clearly my gift, and I love making a difference in the lives of my students. You should see their eyes light up with excitement for learning. Just when I get to the point that I know what I'm doing, I have to stop."

"Life's a marathon, not a sprint. You can return to teaching when your kids get older."

Kendra chuckled. "That's assuming we ever stop having them!"

"God will not give you more than you can handle."

"That's what Dad keeps saying, but he's a man." Kendra opened her eyes and looked at Sharon. "I want to ask you something and I need you to be totally honest with me."

"I'll try."

"Do you enjoy being just a wife and mother?"

The swing stopped. Sharon wondered if she had unconsciously said something that revealed her own state of mind. "What do you mean by enjoy?"

"I don't know. It's just that marriage and motherhood are different from what I thought they'd be."

Sharon's legs resumed pushing the swing knowing that she needed to keep the focus on Kendra. "What did you think it would be like?"

"Not like this...and I can't see how two more children will make either any better."

Sharon's confidence in her ability to guide Kendra shriveled. Their situations were not that different. "We all go through periods of self-doubt."

"Lately, my faith in God seems so weak and everyone needs so much from me…Eric…the boys…and now the twins. My body is not even my own anymore."

"The Bible says that He who is in us is greater than He who is in the world. You have more than enough power to accomplish whatever God has in mind."

"If that's true, how do I plug into that power source?"

Sharon refused to admit that she faced the same question. "God will show you when the time's right."

The two women rocked in silence until they heard the screen door open and Jessica walked onto the porch with a glass of wine.

"Karly's waiting for you two, so we can watch the movie."

Sharon and Kendra exchanged a glance before standing up.

***

The ocean breeze created choppy waves along the Savannah coastline. Several seagulls searched the shore for their evening meal. Jonathan strolled along the shoreline, carrying his shoes. He reached for his wife's hand as they walked in silence. As the sun dipped lower on the horizon, his thoughts drifted to Jessica's comment about spending the weekend with a friend who would keep her mind off of him. Although he felt no jealousy, the thought of Jessica having multiple partners made him nervous. He hoped that she would be smart enough to protect both of them.

Lori turned to tell Jonathan something and noticed his furrowed brows. "What are you thinking about?"

Jonathan exhaled. "You know me, just some unfinished business."

"We promised that you wouldn't think about work and I wouldn't worry about the kids. This is supposed to be our time."

"Sorry." Jonathan kissed her hand. "Some habits are hard to break. It won't happen again."

Lori moved away from Jonathan to avoid a patch of seaweed. "Dinner was wonderful, but I ate too much. This walk is just what I need."

Jonathan pulled her closer. "You're just what I need." He stopped walking and looked at the sky. "Let's sit here and watch the sunset."

"We didn't bring anything to sit on."

Jonathan looked at Lori's ankle-length sundress. "That can be washed, can't it?"

"Yes…"

Jonathan sat then motioned for Lori to join him. With her wrapped in his arms, he kissed her neck.

Lori leaned her head against his chest. "This has been a wonderful day. It's been a long time since I felt so refreshed."

"Too bad it has to end. Maybe time will freeze and we can stay like this forever," Jonathan said caressing her arms.

"That would be nice, but tomorrow will be even better."

Jonathan thought about returning home to their children. His wife was right about them needing more time alone. "Is everything ready for our trip to Disney World?"

"Yep and the kids can't wait. This sunset is nice, but it probably doesn't compare to the ones you saw in Hawaii."

Jonathan's effort to steer their conversation in another direction wasn't working. Jessica's declaration resounded in his head. 'You'll never see another sunset without thinking about me.' He wished that she had been wrong.

Lori sighed. "Maybe one day, we'll get to Hawaii together."

"Let's just enjoy the present."

"Right now, I feel like the luckiest woman in the world."

"Actually, I'm the lucky one," Jonathan said, thankful that his trip with Jessica was problem free. He wondered how long his luck was going to last as he watched the sun rapidly disappear into darkness and imagined Jessica in the arms of another man.

Jonathan and Lori returned to their hotel room tired and coated with a light layer of sand. He walked into the bathroom and turned on the shower before Lori could even protest. She would take twice as long and he needed to wash away the lingering thoughts of Jessica before being with his wife. He sensed that Lori's mind was pre-occupied also. She was unusually quiet on the drive back to the hotel.

When the alarm clock blared at five o'clock the next morning, Jonathan sat up ready to start another work day. It took a few seconds to realize his location. His head had just returned to the pillow when Lori bolted from the bed and turned on the lamp.

"Come on, I don't want to miss it."

Jonathan turned his back to the light glaring in his face. "Miss what?"

Lori grabbed her clothes and walked quickly into the bathroom "Will you just get dressed?"

Jonathan clutched the pillow. "Come back to bed. We can order room service, a little later."

Lori walked out of the bathroom and tossed a pair of jeans and a t-shirt on the bed near his head. "We still can, when we get back! Now will you please hurry up? It's important."

Jonathan reluctantly opened his eyes and was surprised to see Lori dressed. He vowed to make the weekend special for his wife and this was the only thing she was insisting on. "Are you sure you wouldn't rather spend this time in bed with your husband?"

"If you will just get dressed, we'll have plenty of time for that later."

Curiosity trumped the need for sleep. Jonathan pushed the comforter away and sat up. "Oh really…"

"Yes, really. Now hurry up."

Before he could put on his shoes, Lori had her purse on her shoulder and a hand on the door handle.

"Can I at least brush my teeth?"

"I'll give you a piece of gum. Come on."

Jonathan had not seen his wife so insistent in a long time. Whatever she planned had to be important.

Lori drove and traffic was sparse. They pulled into an empty parking lot on Tybee Island just as a faint pink light appeared above the ocean. He watched Lori rush out the car and wait for him on the sidewalk. The stars above were fading with the darkness. Surrendering to her sense of urgency, he did not resist as she reached for his hand and led him towards the water. It was the most excited she had been the entire weekend.

She stopped half-way to the water's edge and turned to look into his eyes. "This is the moment I've been waiting for since planning this weekend." Lori closed her eyes and listened to the sounds around her. "Do you remember the story of creation?"

Jonathan's stomach rumbled. "God made Adam and Eve and put them in a garden. One wrong meal choice and they were kicked out of the garden. Speaking of food, maybe we should get something to eat while we're out."

Lori pulled Jonathan by the hand and walked towards the approaching light. "Will you please be serious? I've always wondered what the first sunrise looked like. I read that everything we see and experience is a mere shadow of what we'll experience after the resurrection."

As they walked, he sensed that his wife was soaking up everything her senses could process. When she paused to remove her shoes, Jonathan waited but kept his shoes on hoping to expedite getting breakfast.

"Did you know that man's the last act of God's creation?"

Jonathan wondered where the question was leading but before he could respond, Lori fired off another.

"Do you know what was created first?"

"No, but I suspect you're going to tell me."

"First, God created light and it took a whole day to do it. On the second day, God created Heaven to separate that which is above from that which is below." Lori stopped walking and smiled.

Jonathan's gentle tug redirected her thoughts and her motion. "So what came next since you've apparently dragged me out of a very comfortable bed for a Bible study?"

"This is not a Bible study, but we could start one when we go home."

"Not likely. You know how I feel about religion."

Lori looked towards the light on the horizon. "On the third day, God created the land, the sea and all vegetation."

"I think you forgot something. The sun came before the earth. It's the center of the universe."

"Not according to God's Word. The sun, moon and stars were created on the fourth day."

"That's precisely why I don't believe the Bible; too many things in it contradict science."

"Were any scientists around when God created all this?"

Jonathan knew better than to argue when it came to her beliefs, so he remained silent.

"I rest my case... On the fifth day, God created every living creature in the seas and the birds of the sky, according to their kind."

"What about all the animals?"

"God created them on the sixth day before he made man, which is probably why animals and humans share so much DNA. I like to think of it as God using the same building materials. A door and a table can be made from the same tree but the idea of one evolving from the other is ridiculous. Evolution is man's attempt to eliminate God from the equation."

Jonathan regretted leaving the hotel room. "Lori, we've had this discussion before. Believe what you want to believe but don't try to force your beliefs on me or our children."

"Our children don't need to be forced into believing in God. Even though I wish that I could, I'm not trying to force my beliefs on you."

Jonathan stopped and threw up his hands. "Then what's the point of us being here? I thought you wanted us to spend some time together."

"I want you to understand the significance of this day. God rested on the seventh day, which is Saturday, making Sunday the first day. I wanted a Sunday to be the first day of the rest of our life together." The expression on Lori's face softened. "I know things have changed between us, but change doesn't have to be bad." Lori raised a finger to Jonathan's lips to halt his mounting frustration. She looked into his eyes before her lips moved to meet his. Her lips were kissing him but her soul was praising God. Their breathing synchronized as the same air filled their lungs. When Lori finally pulled away, the sun was above the water.

It took a moment for Jonathan to speak. "Wow...we haven't kissed like that in a long time. Come to think of it, we've never kissed like that." Jonathan's desire for food was replaced by a desire for his wife. "Maybe we should go back to the hotel...now!"

Lori brought Jonathan's hands to her lips and kissed them gently. "Can we pray before we go?"

Jonathan's mind was foggy and his legs were weak. "Are you serious?"

Lori held his hands and waited for his response. Jonathan did not want to waste time arguing. When he shrugged his shoulders, Lori knelt on the sand facing him and pulled his hand gently towards her. Jonathan looked around to make sure no one was watching before relenting to the unspoken request. Lori closed her eyes and verbalized the longings of her soul to God while Jonathan waited. He tried to listen but his mind was fixed on their kiss. Although he doubted that God would comply with his request, he prayed silently that they would be able recapture the moment.

CHAPTER 3

FOUR DAYS AFTER RETURNING FROM SAVANNAH, JONATHAN wrestled through another sleepless night. Thunder shook the windows and flashes of lightening illuminated the room. Jonathan counted the seconds between the flash of lighting and the trailing thunderous boom. The storm was parked directly overhead. Crimson red numbers on the nightstand clock displayed four-fifteen. Another hour had passed but it was still too early. Even before the storm started, Jonathan struggled to quiet his thoughts so his body could get the rest it desperately needed. Since his weekend with Lori, restless nights were a recurring event, regardless of where they were spent. Sleep deprivation was taking a toll on his productivity which drove him back to Chicago and Jessica. The release he expected Jessica to provide was brief and sharpened the divide between the two women pulling him in opposing directions.

Another flash cast shadows from the hand carved bed posts which stopped a few inches below the ceiling. The elaborate king bed was too large for the room. Jonathan was amazed that neither the dimensions of the furniture nor the room were checked before Jessica purchased the set. Logistics became a factor only when the delivery crew struggled to get the headboard into the condominium. By contrast, the queen bed he shared with his wife seemed minuscule. When he suggested to Lori that they get a king bed, she resisted adamantly, stating that she preferred to sleep close to him. He knew that Jessica selected the king bed for reasons other than sleeping.

The fading rumbles carried Jonathan's thoughts to the morning on the beach with Lori. As much as he wanted to discount his feelings, he was convinced something changed. His most vivid memory hinged on the kiss. Lying in Jessica's bed, he realized that they had never kissed like that. A bolt of lightening made a connection too close for comfort. The noise caused Jessica to stir which forced his eyes to the mother and child an arm's length away. Simone joined them shortly after the storm began and was between them, snuggled safely in her mother's arms. Jonathan wondered whether one of their children had come to Lori for comfort in the middle of the night. A mental bolt of lightening more powerful than those produced by the storm sent a shock-wave through his system. The image of his childhood friend, the last time he saw him, merged with his thoughts. The man had lost everything because of a cocaine addiction. An involuntary shiver caused him to adjust the goose down covering. He knew what had to be done. He could no longer put his marriage at risk. Lori was the one that he loved and needed. The person he'd become since his involvement with Jessica was unrecognizable. Watching his daughter sleep, he knew that Simone would have to pay the highest price. Her eyes lit up every time she saw him. Walking away from their bond would be like peeling away a piece of his flesh. Despite a painful scar, he would eventually heal. The separated flesh might not be as fortunate. He was so absorbed in his thoughts that he failed to notice Jessica watching him.

"What are you thinking about?"

Her words startled him. "Nothing...It's hard to sleep through this storm." He turned towards the window to avoid looking at her. "I hope it won't delay my flight."

Jessica adjusted the pillow. "Are you in that much of a hurry to leave us?"

"Please don't go there. I promised Lori and the kids that I'd be home for dinner."

The mention of his wife's name chased away her lingering drowsiness. "I'm willing to take the scraps of your time, but please don't talk about your other family while you're with us, especially in our bed."

Jonathan detested her reference to it being their bed. Everything about the bed and the condo was hers. His money had not paid for anything. His bed was in Atlanta with his wife, where he knew he should be too. "Fine." He sat on the edge of the bed, vowing that it would be the last time.

She rose onto an elbow. "Since we're both awake, I can take Simone back to her room."

"No, don't disturb her."

"So, when can we expect you back?"

He exhaled loudly in frustration. Given his job, it would be difficult to avoid Chicago and Jessica. "I'm not sure. I have a lot of work to do before…"

"…your family vacation," she spat.

Jonathan was livid. She had listened to his conversation with Lori. He clasped his hands together tightly. "I thought you didn't want them discussed."

Jessica looked at Simone to make sure she was still asleep. "Well, since you brought the subject up. When are *we* going to take *our* daughter on a family vacation?"

"Look Jessica, I'm taking a risk staying with you when I come to town for business just so I can be a father to Simone. I'm just thankful for cell phones otherwise I'd never be able to pull this off. If you wanted a family vacation, you should have brought Simone to Hawaii."

"You know Hawaii was just for us."

"Then stop complaining. You made your choices and now you have to live with them. We both will." He went into the bathroom and closed the door behind him.

Jessica jumped out of the bed, darted to the bathroom door and flung it open, catching him off guard. "Then I guess I'll just have to take our daughter on a vacation by myself. I think she would really enjoy Disneyworld. And with a little luck, she might just get to meet her brothers and sisters." She leered at him.

His breathing increased with his heartbeat. "You wouldn't dare."

She leaned against the doorframe and smiled. "Besides, maybe it's time I met the infamous Lori!"

Jonathan rushed towards Jessica and grabbed her by the arms. The pressure of his grip was too tight, but he wanted to leave no doubt. "If you come any where near my family, I will kill you!" He whispered through clinched teeth in her ear. "Do you understand?"

She nodded. When he released her, his icy glare was convincing. She rubbed her arms anticipating bruises. "Relax...you're acting deranged. There's no need to threaten me. I just love you so much. I get a little crazy when I think about your other life."

His eyes pierced hers. "That's not a threat. It's a promise! Now, if you don't mind, I need to get dressed."

She walked out the bathroom and closed the door behind her.

When Jonathan left Jessica's place, his adrenaline was pumping. His mind wondered throughout his early morning meeting. He left the building as soon as it ended, to avoid another encounter with Jessica. By the time he reached the gate at Chicago's O'Hare Airport, his thinking had cleared but the sky had not. The severe weather had temporarily suspended flight operations at one of the world's busiest airports. Planes were lined up waiting to take off. Aware that flight cancellations were inevitable, he checked the monitors frequently. To keep his mind occupied, he made several business calls and scanned the newspaper before resorting to watching the television. After fifteen minutes, the television segments were either too depressing or repeated information he had just read in the newspaper. With nothing else to do but think, Jonathan realized that he was anxious to see Lori's smile and hold her in his arms. Their emotional bond suddenly seemed so strong that it unnerved him. The more he thought about Lori, the more he realized what had to be done. The relationship with Jessica had to end even if it meant telling Lori the truth. Given Jessica's threat, he knew it was the only way. After his weekend with Lori, he was confident that she would eventually forgive him. But before he could tell her, he had to prove how much he loved her. He opened his cell phone and waited.

Upbeat music played softly in the background as walkers trekked the mall at varying speeds. Most of the mall walkers were senior citizens or young mothers pushing strollers. The stores were not open, which was ideal for Lori since all she could afford to do was window shop anyway. When she heard her phone ring, she looked at the caller identification before answering. "Hey."

He heard the smile in her voice. "Did I catch you at a bad time?"

"Nope. Your timing's perfect. After dropping our little one at preschool, I decided to walk at the mall. For some strange reason, I want to get this body back into shape. Hum...I wonder if it might have something to do with my husband, who still takes my breath away."

Her words confirmed his decision. "You don't need to change for me. I love you just the way you are."

"Liar, but thanks anyway. Unfortunately, there won't be much change before our vacation. But with four children in tow, there won't be much time for romance anyway." Lori picked up her pace. "I saw the weather forecast on the news this morning. Please don't tell me your flight was cancelled."

"Not yet," Jonathan said, looking out the window at the line of planes which had not moved. "But you might want to say a prayer. Things aren't looking too promising on this end."

"I already did."

Jonathan shook his head, realizing that he should have known that she had. "Do you have anything special planned for tonight?"

"I was thinking about leaving the minute you pulled into the garage and not returning until Sunday night, so you could experience my world for a change."

"You wouldn't do that to me, would you? Think of our children!"

"Don't worry. I don't have anywhere to go, but don't come home expecting a great dinner."

Food was the last thing on his mind. "I'll only be expecting to hold you in my arms."

Lori's heart fluttered, leaving her speechless.

Jonathan looked at his wedding band remembering the day Lori slipped it onto his finger. They had promised to love each other for better or for worse. He wondered how he would be able to tell her the magnitude of his worst. "I'd better check the status of my flight. I'll call you before boarding." Jonathan hesitated. "Lori, I love you."

The heaviness in his voice caused Lori to stop walking. "I love you, too."

***

Kendra volunteered in her church's children ministry the last Sunday of the month. Already exhausted walking into the classroom, she distributed the handouts with the Bible lesson hoping time would pass quickly. There was a new boy in the class. Kendra had no problem remembering his name was Eric. He was so well behaved that she was looking forward to meeting his parents.

When the first parents finally came to retrieve their children, Kendra wanted to follow them out the door. However, church policy required her to stay with the teacher until all the children were signed out by the parents. As the other children left, Kendra sat with the new boy who didn't seem to mind waiting.

"There's my little man!"

Kendra's mouth dropped open as soon as she saw her. "This is your son?"

Stephanie had labored all week to select her outfit. It was a form fitting sapphire dress with a tailored jacket. "Yes, he is." Stephanie rubbed her son's head. "Baby, mommy's so sorry you had to wait. I ran into an old friend." Stephanie turned her attention back to Kendra. "What a small world?"

"Not this small," Kendra said barely audible.

"I heard you and Eric got married after our breakup." Stephanie looked at Kendra's bulging midsection. "Are you pregnant or have you just put on a lot of weight?"

"What does it look like?" Kendra snapped.

Stephanie rolled her eyes. "Everyone's been so friendly until now, but I guess I can't hold one person's rudeness against the whole church."

Kendra put her hand on her hip. "What are you doing here?"

"My son and I are looking for a new church. Didn't your husband tell you that I moved back?"

"No, he didn't!"

"Odd...he must have forgotten. Well, we've gotta run. My parents are expecting us for dinner. They're so excited to have their grandson back in town." Stephanie took her son's hand. "Maybe we'll see you next Sunday."

Eric and their sons were waiting for Kendra at the main entrance. By the time Kendra reached to the car, she was fuming but decided to give him the chance to prove his trustworthiness.

After getting their sons settled for their nap, Kendra refused to wait any longer. When she strolled into the kitchen, Eric was putting away the lunch dishes with the television playing in the background.

"Hey, I thought you were going to take a nap too."

Kendra leaned against the door frame with her arms crossed over her chest. "Is there something you need to tell me?"

Eric adjusted his eyeglasses. "I don't think so."

She stared at him.

He dried his hands on the dish towel and walked towards her. "Baby, what's wrong?"

She held up her hands, halting his approach. "What's wrong? The woman who did everything in her power to destroy our relationship waltzes into our church and you have the audacity to ask me what's wrong."

He sighed in disbelief. "Stephanie was at church this morning?"

"Oh, don't act innocent. You must have seen her. She was late picking up her son because she 'ran' into an *old* friend."

"You've got to believe me. I didn't see Stephanie at church. Her son was in your class?"

Kendra looked like a lioness ready to pounce on a defenseless prey. "Yes, *little* Eric was in my class."

His eyes closed as he shook his head. "Little Eric."

"Don't act like you didn't know that the woman who was obsessed with you, named her son after you!"

Eric picked up a glass from the table and walked to the sink. "*No!* I did not."

Kendra stood in the doorway. "She said that she saw you. If it wasn't today, when was it and, more importantly, why didn't you tell me?"

He sucked in a deep breath. "Let's see -"

"Don't lie to me. I want the truth!" she shouted, on the brink of tears.

He resumed loading the dishwasher. "Because I didn't think it was important. I ran into her at the grocery store while you were at the bed-and-breakfast with Sharon. I barely said anything to her."

Kendra's back was aching but her heart was hurting more. "Did she tell you that she had moved back here?"

"She mentioned it."

"And you didn't think that was important for me to know?"

Eric closed the dishwasher then looked at Kendra. "Stephanie's past history."

"That may be true, but history has a strange way of repeating itself."

"Well, not in this case. I've learned my lesson."

Kendra rubbed the small of her back as she walked to a chair. "But has she learned hers?"

"Stephanie can't do anything else to hurt us. We just need to forgive her and move on with our lives."

Kendra rolled her eyes.

Eric shook his head. "Look, you're the one who said that not forgiving harms us more than the perpetrator. You don't want to block our blessings do you?"

She thought about the two 'blessings' in her womb that should have been blocked. Guilt immediately followed. She slumped in the chair like a child being disciplined. "No...The sight of her set off a chain reaction. The fact that she named her child after you certainly didn't help either. I don't trust her."

Eric sat in the chair beside her. "Look sweetheart, there's nothing she can do. We're both well aware of the games that she played in the past. I was a fool once, but I won't be one twice."

"Well, she'd better not bring her trifling self back to our church."

"Kendra, listen to you. Remember, we're not to judge others. What did pastor just teach? Our job's to help catch the fish. It's God's job to clean them."

Kendra yawned. "Well, I wouldn't mind helping God gut her!"

He chuckled as he stood up and helped her out of the chair. "I think it's definitely time for you to get some rest. What time do you want me to wake you up?"

She looked at the microwave clock. "I feel like I could sleep straight through till morning." She yawned again. "How about four o'clock? Will you be okay when the boys wake up?"

"Do you honestly need to ask?" He patted her bottom as she walked out of the kitchen. "Have a good nap and please don't give you-know-who a second thought."

***

Feeling recharged from her nap, Kendra sat on the sofa in the family room watching her sons play. She dreaded making the call, but it had been two weeks since she talked to Simone.

When the telephone rang, Jessica answered without looking at the display. Jonathan had not returned any of her calls or emails. "Jessica…"

"Hey."

"I wondered when you'd finally find time to call me. How's the family?"

Kendra stretched her legs across the couch. "It's expanding by the minute. I don't know how I'm going to survive this pregnancy. I'm barely four months pregnant and already look like a blimp."

Jessica's travel confirmations and the information from the Orlando visitor's bureau were stacked on the desk. She paged through the Disneyworld website. "Just keep moving so you don't start depositing fat that you can't get rid of. No man wants to see blubber on his woman."

"Not all men want a twiggy, like you. Besides, Eric would love me whatever size I am." Kendra looked at her thighs hoping she was right.

"You and Eric are perfect for each other, still as naïve as ever."

"Coming from you, I'll take that as a compliment. So what are you guys up to?"

"Simone's in the tub and I was just trying to figure out what we're going to do at Disneyworld. There are so many choices."

Kendra was disappointed that she would not be able to talk to Simone. "You definitely have to do the Magic Kingdom. Simone will love that?"

"That's a no-brainer. Right now, I'm trying to figure out if I want to get the park hopper pass or just buy individual tickets."

"How long are you staying?"

"Three days." Jessica smiled at how perfectly her plan was falling into place. "That's as long as I'll probably be able to take my mother."

"How's she enjoying being a grandmother?"

"She loves it, as long as you don't call her one."

"So what does Simone call her?"

"The same thing I do—Liz."

Kendra frowned. "You know that's not right. Children shouldn't call adults by their first name."

"Well, then it's okay because my mother never grew up."

"I won't touch that." Despite the apparently dysfunctional relationship, Kendra envied Jessica and wished that her mother would have lived long enough to see her grandchildren. "I'm surprised that she's going with you."

"Please. My mother has friends in every major city. This way she gets to spend time with Simone and party at the same time. But enough of her, what's new with you?"

Kendra stopped the ball from rolling under the sofa and handed it to her son. "Let's see. I told the school that I wouldn't be back next year."

Jessica leaned back in the chair. "So you're really going to be one of those stay-at-home mothers?"

"Apparently, I am. Don't make it sound so bad. Guess who had the nerve to walk into our church this morning."

"You know I don't like guessing games." Jessica inspected her nails.

"Stephanie…"

Kendra had her full attention. "Not Eric's Stephanie?"

"The one and only."

Jessica chuckled. "I guess your church really does let anybody in. What does she look like?"

"She hasn't changed one bit, unfortunately. And get this! She named her son, Eric."

"Oh, she's good! Even I didn't think about doing that. She must have thought she still had a chance."

"The emphasis is on 'had' because she doesn't know who she's messing with now. I walked away once without a fight. I won't make that mistake again! If she so much as flutters an eyelash at him, she will regret it."

"Girl, what's gotten into you? Where's all that Christian love?"

"It's reserved for Christians."

"Maybe she's one of you now."

"Time will tell. Speaking of which, did you visit that Bible Study I told you about?"

Jessica grimaced. "I promised that I would."

"So, what did you think?"

"It's definitely not for me, but don't worry. I think my neighbors are trying to save Simone's soul. They take her to church every chance I let them. She went with them this morning."

"You should go with them."

"You know how I feel about churches and the people who run them."

"I keep telling you that not all churches are the same. As soon as you stop running from God, you'll be able to tell the difference."

"I'd better go check on Simone. I'll talk to you next week."

"Okay, but think about visiting their church."

"I did, I'm not, end of story. Give the boys a hug from their auntie."

***

A stale, musty smell greeted Dale as he descended the stairs to the church's basement. The deacon board meeting was the first planned activity in a day filled with interruptions. He was intent on finding out who had access to the offering money. He heard voices coming from the large meeting room and looked at his watch. It was exactly five-fifteen. His meeting was not supposed to start for another fifteen minutes. Wondering if another group had reserved the room by mistake, he paused outside the door and listened. When he heard the unmistakable voice, he opened the door, interrupting what appeared to be a heated discussion. The conversation stopped. It was definitely the right meeting. "Did I write the wrong start time?"

Deacon Jones shuffled the papers in front of him. "No."

Dale walked into the room, placed his portfolio on the table and sat down. "Then what's going on here?" The question was rhetorical. He had used the same tactics to build corporate alliances.

"Some of us needed to get together to discuss a few things before the meeting."

Dale dramatically scanned the group. "It looks like everyone was included, but me." He was somewhat disappointed that Jones had apparently rallied the support of the entire board. "Would you like for me to wait outside until you're finished, since the meeting doesn't officially start for a few more minutes?" Dale sensed that Deacon Jones was thoroughly enjoying his seat of power. An uncomfortable silence filled the room as all eyes focused on him.

"No, that won't be necessary." Deacon Jones looked at a sheepish man who was sitting by the door. "Brother Tucker, will you distribute the agenda and minutes from the last meeting."

Dale sat at the table, thankful he had spent extra time in prayer. When the handouts finally reached him, he suppressed a smile. The first item on the agenda under new business was pew Bibles. One of the new Bibles sat on the table in front of Deacon Jones.

Dale endured the formality of the parliamentarian procedures used to move through the agenda. After the minutes were read, corrected and approved, the financial report was given. Seizing an opening, he raised his hand to be recognized. "Being a novice, I'd appreciate an overview of the system for collecting and reporting the offering."

Deacon Jones reared back in his chair. "For starters, the pastor is not involved with that aspect of the church's operation. The finance committee handles it. Money's a mighty powerful tempter."

Dale met Deacon Jones' stare. "Not for me. As I've already stated, God has amply provided for all my financial needs. But for the record, who's on the finance committee and what are the procedures?"

Deacon Jones leaned forward in his chair and locked eyes with Dale. "If God has provided for your financial needs, why are you so interested in the church's money?"

"Actually, it's God's money." Dale felt every eye in the room on him. "And as pastor of this church, I'm accountable to God and all those who give, to ensure that we're good stewards of what God has entrusted to us. Not to mention, the government requirements associated with this church's tax status. I'm confident that very good procedures are in place but would still like to know what they are just in case we're audited."

Before Deacon Jones could respond, his son, Marcus, spoke up. "Pastor…"

Dale shifted his attention to the son, ignoring the elder Jones' obvious displeasure.

"The finance committee's made up of the treasurer, the head of the deacon board and four volunteer members of the church, who are appointed to one year terms."

"Thank you, Marcus. Can you summarize the procedure for me?"

"Certainly…."

When Marcus finished, Deacon Jones cleared his throat. "Now, can we move on?"

"Just one more question." Dale turned to Marcus again. "Do we keep records of individual giving?"

"If the offering envelope has sufficient information, we do. Someone from the finance committee will usually come in during the week and record the information from the envelopes. Financial giving statements are mailed at the end of January. Visitors usually give cash donations, so we can't track that."

Deacon Jones leered at Dale. "If that's all the questions about money, can we move on to *new* business?"

Dale had the information that he needed. "Of course…"

Deacon Jones picked up the pew Bible and tossed it on the table in front of Dale. It landed with a loud thud. "I speak for the entire board when I say we'd like an explanation of how *you* plan to pay for these Bibles. If you're not aware, this church does *not* pay for unapproved purchases, regardless of who makes them. And if I counted correctly, there are twice as many as the original request."

Dale was annoyed by Deacon Jones' handling of God's Word. He picked up the Bible and held it like a prized possession. "Isn't God wonderful?"

Deacon Jones huffed. "What are you talking about?"

"After the board turn down my requisition, I stopped by the Christian bookstore, planning to use my pastor's discount to personally buy them. As soon as I told the store manager what we needed, he produced two cases of Bibles that had been imprinted wrong." Dale held up the Bible. "They were able to remove the gold foil but the impression is still there, so they could not be sold." Dale passed the Bible to the person on his right. "If you hold it at an angle, you can see it."

The deacon angled the Bible and nodded in agreement before passing the Bible to the next person for inspection.

Dale continued. "These Bibles sat in the manager's office for months. He was confident that God was going to send someone in that needed them…So you see…God provided the Bibles and it didn't cost us a single penny."

***

It was the worst day of the week for the major traffic accident which clogged Kendra's usual route to pick up her sons from daycare. As the Physic club's advisor, she was required at their weekly after school meetings. The daycare's director was waiting at the door to reminded Kendra of their after hours policy. Her youngest son cried the entire drive home, pushing her stress level to the breaking point. When she walked into the house with Danny balanced on one hip and Joshua following on her heels, a trail of toys littered the floor. As she rushed to put Danny in his high chair, she kicked several toys out of her way. Following his mommy's lead, Joshua kicked a toy. The unexpected action caused her to scream "No". She secured the high chair latch and left Joshua standing shell-shocked beside his brother while she rushed to the bathroom.

She returned to the kitchen and scanned the mess. The sink overflowed with dishes because the dishwasher needed to be unloaded. She looked at her sons. Joshua had brought Danny a toy and was entertaining him, making Kendra feel worse about her harsh reprimand. "Josh, mommy's sorry for yelling. Thanks for helping with your brother." It was hard to tell how much he understood. Sometimes he seemed much older than three.

"It looks like dinner's going to be late. Would you like a snack while you watch Barney?"

Her son nodded with a smile. She went to the refrigerator to get the milk. The usual space for it was empty. The planned stop at the grocery store had slipped her mind putting both dinner and breakfast in jeopardy. The notion of loading her sons back into the car was overwhelming. She grabbed a juice pouch and bottle of formula before slamming the refrigerator closed. Struggling to keep her composure, she managed to get her sons settled in the den before succumbing to years of grief and fears. By the time

Eric walked in the door thirty minutes later, Kendra was sitting at the kitchen table crying into her arms.

He rushed to kneel by her side. "Kendra. Baby, what's wrong?"

She looked at him, searching her mind for an answer. "I don't know. That's the problem. I don't know what's wrong with me!" The tears poured out.

"Are the boys okay?"

Kendra nodded and wiped her face with her sleeve. Eric retrieved the box of tissue from the counter and handed it to her. While she blew her nose, he went to confirm his sons' well-being before returning quickly.

She heaved in breaths while he waited. "I can't do this anymore,"

Eric reached for her hand. "Do what?

"Anything…the boys, the house, the job…It's too much…" The words poured out between sniffles.

"What happened?"

"I feel like I'm losing my mind. I can't even remember simple things like stopping at the grocery store. I have no idea what we're going to have for dinner now. And look at this house? My mother never let it get like this, even when she was sick. And I'm so tired all the time?"

Eric had never seen Kendra so distraught. "Sweetheart, I can go to the store. It's not a big deal. And the house is not that bad. It's just a few toys and some dirty dishes."

Kendra gripped Eric's hand with both of hers. "What's wrong with me? Am I being punished?"

"Of course, you're not being punished. You're just trying to do too much."

Kendra stared at him. How could she tell Eric about the doubts that returned and constantly flooded her mind? His faith that God existed was rock solid. It was what she always admired in him. She didn't want him to think differently about her. "But it's never been a problem before. I've always managed to keep everything under control."

"The doctor said you'd be more drained than before. You just need to rest. Write down what we need from the store then go lie down. The boys and I will go shopping and bring home dinner. And I'll bathe the boys and put them to bed tonight." Eric walked to the refrigerator for the magnetic note pad and placed it in front of her.

"Are you sure?"

Eric patted Kendra's rapidly expanding abdomen. "You take care of these two and I'll take care of their brothers. Later, we can talk about a plan until the school year ends."

Kendra started the list; hoping exhaustion was indeed her only problem.

***

Jessica sat on Simone's bed, admiring the room that was an exact replica of a catalog display. A garden mural covered the wall with the windows. The ceiling was professionally painted to resemble the sky. During the day, clouds hovered above. At night, florescent stars sparkled like the constellations. The bedside table was a fiberglass tree stump. Both the closet and dresser were filled with clothes. Her daughter would never be an after thought or inconvenience. Jessica was determined to give Simone the childhood she never had and to be a real mother. Only one thing was lacking from her daughter's perfect world.

Simone dove onto the bed causing the springs to squeal. Her hair was in two ponytails with the ends firmly secured by satin rollers to ensure perfect curls the next day. Her complexion was flawless like her mother's, but her facial features were inherited from her father. Jessica hoped that adolescence would not ruin either as she tried to imagine Simone as a woman.

"What did I tell you about diving onto your bed?"

"Oh mommy! I'm too small to break it."

Jessica pulled the covers over her daughter. "You're growing fast. If you break this one, I'm not going to buy you another one."

Simone giggled. "Yes, you will." She reached for her over-sized teddy bear her father had given her. "When's Daddy coming home again?"

Jessica smoothed her daughter's hair. The question asked so innocently caused her to pause before responding. Jonathan was still not returning her calls or emails. "I'm not sure."

"Can we call him again tomorrow?"

Jessica hated watching her daughter's hopes get repeatedly crushed. "We'll see...he must be awfully busy not to call us back. Now, let's get some sleep." Jonathan's cruelty to their daughter confirmed it was definitely time for the ultimate gamble.

Simone threw back the cover. "Oops. I almost forget!"

"You just came from the bathroom."

"I forgot to thank God. The teacher says that praying every night's really important."

Jessica grabbed her daughter's arm halting her exit from the bed. "What are you talking about? Why is pray...talking to God suddenly so important?"

"I need to thank him for taking care of us."

Jessica released her daughter's arm and watched her kneel beside the bed.

Simone looked up at her mother. "You can talk to him too, even if you're not saved. God listens to everyone."

Jessica cleared her throat. "What does a four-year old know about being saved?"

"Mommy, I'm almost five!"

"Fine. What does an almost five-year old know about being saved, little missy?"

Simone's smile revealed a wisdom that was beyond her years. "Don't you know?"

If Simone did not look so much like her father, Jessica would have sworn that someone switched babies in the hospital. "Of course I know, but how do you know?"

"I'm learning a lot at church. Adam and Eve didn't obey God and made a mess. So God sent his son, Jesus, to clean up the mess; just like when I make a mess and you help me clean it up. Jesus even chooses some people to help him, but I'm too little." Her daughter paused. "Do you believe in Jesus?"

Jessica was appalled. Her daughter was not going to be brainwashed. "I used to believe in a lot of things, but they all turned out to be lies." Jessica was relieved that her comment went above her daughter's comprehension. Soon enough she would find out that Santa, the Easter Bunny, the Tooth Fairy, and God are all lies told for the amusement of adults. "Hurry up."

Simone closed her eyes and prayed silently.

Jessica thought about the prayer she used to repeat every night when she was little. 'Now I lay me down to sleep, I pray the Lord my soul to keep. If I should die before I wake, I pray the Lord my soul to take.' Her anger grew with the revelation that she remembered every word of the prayer. Now as a mother, she was convinced it was cruel to teach a child to think about dying every night. There was enough to be afraid of without adding death. She hoped the church had not taught her daughter that same asinine prayer. Her daughter's mind needed to be protected. She would not be attending any more church services with her friend. A minute later, Simone hopped back in bed.

Jessica readjusted the comforter. "So what did you say to God or is it a secret?"

"I thanked God for this day and for the light he placed inside me. I asked Jesus to give you one too. Sometimes you seem so sad."

"Baby, I'm not sad." Jessica resisted vocalizing her true emotion at that moment, confident that her daughter would not understand. "I just have a lot on my mind. It's not easy being an adult." Jessica kissed her daughter wondering if Kendra's incessant prayers were responsible for her namesake's sudden interest in God. "Sleep tight and don't let the bed bugs bite."

"Mommy, there's no such thing as bed bugs."

"Unfortunately, bed bugs are very real, but you'll never have to worry about them. Have sweet dreams."

"You too, mommy. I love you."

"I love you, too."

Jessica walked out of her daughter's room wondering if Kendra was praying against her and Jonathan's relationship also. It would explain why Jonathan was pulling away from her at the same time that her daughter started talking about God. Jessica pushed the thoughts out of her mind. It was too absurd even for her. She controlled their destiny.

***

Dale knew they were dealing with a bigger problem than theft, when Deacon Jones' son, Marcus, came to his office in the middle of the week and confessed to taking money from the offering. He had lost his job and wanted to prevent his father from learning the truth. With each additional meeting, they both struggled with what needed to be done. Sunday morning when Marcus cornered him and requested time to address the congregation, Dale had serious reservations, given his father's prominence. During the sermon, Dale felt compelled to yield to the request. Before the benediction, he nodded towards Marcus who seemed equally compelled. He walked purposefully to the center aisle and turned to face the congregation. He took several deep breaths. Dale suspected he was trying to muster the courage to follow through with his decision. His voice quivered as he spoke causing Dale to pray silently for him. During the public confession that revealed the depths of Marcus' transgressions, the veins bulging on the side of his father's temples and clinched jaw could be seen from the pulpit. Dale suspected that pride was the only thing keeping the elder Jones in his pew.

After the benediction, Dale waited behind a swarm of people to speak with Marcus, hoping that his father would be as merciful as the majority of the congregation. Marcus' mother cried tears of thanksgiving and praised God for interceding in her son's life. Others offered heartfelt words of encouragement, which seemed to only exasperate his father more.

Deacon Jones was waiting for Dale in his office. "What kind of pastor are you? How could you let that boy make of fool of himself like that?"

Dale paused while debating which question to answer first. Realizing that he did not have a good answer for either, he redirected the conversation. "Marcus just took a major step in his life. You should be very proud of him."

"Proud of a thief!" Deacon Jones bellowed. "The least you could have done was handled this quietly. Why didn't you come to me after he told you? I could have paid back the money."

Dale walked to his desk and sat down, hoping to defuse the situation. "Marcus is a sinner, just like the rest of us. Taking the money was just a symptom of the greater problem. I'm so glad that Marcus understands that now. He's ready to be healed and changed."

"He's not ready for nothing. He can't even keep a job. The boy's a complete failure and now the whole church knows it, thanks to you!"

Dale's compassion for Marcus increased with each destructive word from the person who should have been rejoicing the loudest. "Apart from Jesus, we're all failures. What just happened in this church should be happening more often. Marcus responded to hearing the gospel message."

Deacon Jones glared down at Dale. "He may be a failure, but I'm not."

Drained from pouring all his energy into the service, Dale knew he was in no condition to argue. "If you say so."

The response fueled Deacon Jones' anger. "Don't you get smug with me. You don't know who you're dealing with."

"Actually, I know exactly who I'm dealing with," Dale said.

"I don't know what you said to Marcus to brainwash him, but you'd better stay away from my son. You've done enough damage. And remember who runs this church. From now on, any business involving this church comes to the deacon board first."

Dale knew that he was not the one who had damaged Marcus but he was not about to get into a war of words. Marcus was safely in Jesus' care and nothing could change that. "Actually, Jesus Christ is the head of the church and I took up the matter with Him."

Deacon Jones leaned against Dale's desk. "I don't know who you think you are but if you want to continue at this church, you'd better play by my rules. One more incident like this and you'll be out of here. Some people may think God sent you here, but I'm not one of them."

"I'm sorry you feel that way." Dale picked up his satchel. "If you don't mind, I have another important appointment."

CHAPTER 4

THE MEMORIAL DAY WEEKEND OFFICIALLY ENDED THE SCHOOL year and the beginning of Kendra's new existence. The arrangement for household help until the school year ended worked better than expected. An announcement posted on the church's website produced the perfect match. Ruby Johnson was a retired school teacher dealing with the sudden death of her husband. Instead of enjoying her retirement, Ruby found herself with too much time and no plans for life without her husband. She hoped temporarily helping a young family would soothe her grief. After one week, Ruby asked if the boys could call her Nana. The next eight weeks passed quickly. Both Kendra and Ruby were hesitant for the arrangement to end, but with the school year over Kendra believed Ruby's help was no longer needed. The Friday before Memorial Day was Ruby's last working day. Kendra was startled by the tears, which she attributed to hormones, while saying goodbye.

The Tuesday following the holiday, streams of water flew in every direction. Kendra sat in a folding chair at the edge of the splashing pool and watched her sons play in their early birthday present. When her sons stepped into the pool, it was in the shadow of the house. The shade was fading quickly. Not wanting her sons or her to roast in the intense sunlight, Kendra carried the laundry basket that served as the outside toy box and sat it beside the pool. "It's time to go inside. Let's see how fast we can put your toys in this."

Kendra watched her oldest son comply with her request before bending to lift Danny out of the pool. She felt a small pinch in her lower abdomen. When she straightened up, the pinch became a sharp stabbing pain that momentarily took her breath away. She waited for the pain to ease before wrapping a towel around her son. "Joshua, the other toys can stay in the pool. Grab your towel and let's go inside." She waited nervously for her oldest son to get out of the pool and let him lead the way.

Once inside, the stark temperature difference convinced her that her boys needed to get out of their wet swimsuits. Even though their clothes were in the den, it took ten minutes to get them dressed and settled at the kitchen table with a frozen fruit bar. With the pain abating, she was ready to put her lingering fears to rest. In the bathroom, the bright crimson stain returned her to panic mode. She walked cautiously to the kitchen supporting her abdomen with both hands, afraid that every step might trigger a gush of blood, water or both. Her sons were still engrossed with their treats. Instinctively, she picked up the phone to call Eric but paused. Instead of his number, she pressed the speed dial button for her doctor and waited. Her sons were making a mess with their treat but at least they were content. She prayed they would stay that way. The automated answering system picked up. Reluctantly, she followed the instructions to speak with a human, who put her on hold before Kendra could say anything.

Kendra's patience and her sons' treats were disappearing at the same rate. The minutes continued to tick away while Kendra watched her sons and squeezed her legs together. Finally someone mumbled a scripted greeting into the phone. Kendra frantically explained her problem. The obviously overwhelmed person confirmed what Kendra feared. Her doctor was in a delivery. Kendra was abruptly transferred to the nurse practitioner. Following two rapid clicks, Kendra listened to the music desperate for reassurance that the babies in her womb were safe. When a friendly voice finally picked up the phone, she thanked God. After explaining the situation again, a barrage of questions followed. Kendra suspected that a trouble shooting chart was being used. The nurse practitioner tried to sound reassuring as she instructed Kendra to go to the hospital emergency room as soon as possible.

Since the pain had stopped, Kendra was convinced that she could drive herself to the hospital but taking her sons with her would be the last resort. It took a few minutes for her to remember her father's schedule. She looked at the clock. He would be in the middle of a golf game but he would come if she called. Although she vowed not to rely on Ruby too much, Kendra decided to call her before calling Eric.

Ruby was in her garage loading the car for an afternoon of errands when she heard the phone ringing. Since she was meeting a friend who routinely canceled at the last moment for lunch, she rushed into the house to answer it. "Hello…"

Kendra went to the laundry room to get clean shirts out of the dryer for her sons. "Ruby, it's me."

Ruby paused to catch her breath. "Well, hello. I thought about the boys this morning. Did you have a nice holiday?"

Kendra tried to control her voice which was falling victim to her escalating nerves. "Are you busy right now?"

"I'm meeting a friend for lunch. Why?

Kendra inhaled deeply and exhaled. "Never mind…" Eric would have to meet her at the hospital and keep the boys occupied until her father could get there. "I'll give you a call next week."

Ruby noticed a tremor in Kendra's voice. "Is everything okay?"

"Just say a prayer. I'm bleeding and I need to go to the emergency room to get checked out." A surge of emotions logged in her throat. "I thought maybe you could watch the boys but since you're busy, don't worry about it. I'll call my dad." Kendra tried to put some levity in her voice. "Besides, it's too hot for him to be on the golf course today anyway."

Ruby grabbed her purse off the table. "You'll do no such thing. I'll be there in fifteen minutes. Is Eric taking you to the hospital?"

"I haven't called him yet. I can drive myself, but the emergency room may be difficult on the boys."

"If there's a problem, you shouldn't be driving. Have Eric meet you at the hospital. The boys and I will take you," Ruby said.

Momentary relief washed over Kendra. "What about your plans?"

Ruby walked through the house making sure she had everything she needed. "Stella won't mind if we reschedule lunch and the boys can go with me on the other errands. Now, go call Eric and I'll be there shortly."

While she waited for Eric to answer, Kendra threw some snacks in the diaper bag for the boys. The call went to his voice mail, so she left him a short message.

The distance to the hospital seemed twice as far. Despite Kendra willing the car to go faster, she was thankful that Ruby was a cautious driver. Her boys would be safe. With Ruby in temporary control and her sons content in the rear seat, Kendra's thoughts drifted to the fate of her unborn children and her responsibility for the current situation. Had her grumbling angered God? Guilt overwhelmed her as she realized that she had responded to their unplanned pregnancy just like the nation of Israel in the desert, complaining about what God was providing and wanting things their way. She felt too remorseful to even pray.

Ruby was pulling into the hospital complex when the cell phone firmly clutched in Kendra's hand rang. She answered quickly. "Eric, you called just in time."

Eric sensed the panic in Kendra's voice but hoped it was nothing more serious than a clogged toilet. "I was in a meeting. What's up?"

"Can you meet me at the hospital?"

The word hospital caused the palms of his hands to sweat. "What happened? Are the boys okay?"

Ruby stomped on the brakes a little too sharply causing Kendra to lunge forward against the seatbelt. Kendra flinched afraid that more damage had been inflicted on the babies who were not ready for the world. After parking haphazardly in front of the Emergency Room entrance, Ruby whispered to Kendra, "Wait here. I'll get some help."

Kendra looked at her sons in the back seat who had dozed off. "There might be a problem with the twins. I'm bleeding lightly, so the doctor's office told me to go to the emergency room. Ruby offered to drive me here and keep the boys."

A tall, athletic looking man in multi-colored scrubs pushing a wheelchair rushed towards the car. Ruby struggled to stay close behind.

Kendra's pulse increased the closer they came to the car. "We just got to the hospital, so I can't talk long. Ruby's not staying, but I'll be fine until you get here. Please hurry. I'm scared."

Eric picked up Kendra's message during the lunch break. The design review was scheduled to last all day, but he would not be returning. "Don't worry. Everything's going to be okay."

***

Sharon knocked softly before opening the door to their home office. It resembled a command center. Tall stacks of papers were sprawled across the desk and a white dry erase board had replaced the framed jigsaw puzzle over the futon. The diagram covering the board resembled a large flower. One large circle was drawn in the center surrounded by five smaller circles. Every circle was titled and numbered. Color coded Bible verses covered almost every inch of the board. In the center of the desk sat a laptop computer that responded slowly because of all the open applications. The speed of the computer did not concern Dale as much as the speed of his brain to process all the information.

"You've been working for six hours. Are you ready for lunch?" She walked to the desk and picked up a thick stack of papers. "I'm surprised you got this many responses back."

Dale leaned back in his chair and stretched. "I'm sure it was because of your suggestions to make it anonymous and to include a stamped, pre-addressed envelope. It's about sixty percent of what we handed out. At the time the questionnaires went out, I wasn't sure what I'd do with the information. Now I do...What's for lunch?"

"You're in luck. The kitchen's fully stocked."

Dale attempted to organize his desk. "Have you and the kids eaten?"

"The kids have. They wanted to go to the pool with their friends. I was waiting for you." Sharon returned her attention to the questionnaire on top of the stack and scanned the responses. "Looks like you got some very interesting answers. This one defines a Christian as someone who's Christ-like." Sharon shook her head. "That's a pretty broad definition."

Dale saved the file he was working on. "There's one that says a Christian is someone who celebrates Christmas."

"That would explain why so many Americans classify themselves as Christians." Sharon flipped through the stack quickly. "Were the responses what you expected?"

Dale rubbed his eyes. "Worse... We have drifted so far from even knowing the basics, but maybe I shouldn't be surprised. Most of our members don't even believe the Bible is relevant today. Sharon, please tell me how you can call yourself a Christian without believing the Bible's relevant. That's like saying I'm a doctor because I can put a bandage on a cut. The knowledge required to become a doctor's very relevant."

Sharon failed to see the comparison. She wrapped her arm around Dale's waist as they walked down the stairs. "The fields are ripe, but the workers are few."

"Now, I'm trying to pastor this flock and there's such a wide spectrum of knowledge. How do I get everyone on the same level?"

"Don't ask me. I have my hands full with two children." Sharon opened the refrigerator. "Roasted chicken breast or smoked turkey?"

"Whatever you're having?" Dale opened the pantry to get the paper plates and a bag of multigrain chips. He placed them on the kitchen island and leaned against it. "Before you came upstairs I was thinking about how Jesus handled this issue. After Jesus fed the five thousand, a large crowd followed him. He knew many followed him only because of the free meal but the next day he still preached the gospel to them."

"If memory serves me correctly, Jesus' message wasn't received too well," Sharon said, while washing two leaves of lettuce.

Dale pulled out a barstool and sat down. "If most of those following Jesus, including some disciples, walked away from the truth, how am I supposed to teach it?"

"I'm sure you'll figure out a way."

"You want to know something really interesting that I never noticed before?"

"I'm all ears." Sharon piled the meat, lettuce and cheese on the whole wheat tortillas.

"Seriously, are you listening?"

Sharon poured salad dressing on each wrap and handed the plates to Dale. "You know I listen better when I'm doing something with my hands. Now what's so interesting?"

"The verse that records the desertion is John 6:66."

"Isn't 666 supposed to be the mark of the beast in Revelations? Kind of ironic, don't you think?"

Dale folded his tortilla to enclose the contents. "Now that I think about it, Jesus knew then and he knows now who has ears to hear His words of truth. So it looks like, I have my sermon series for the summer – the true gospel of Jesus Christ."

Sharon sighed. "This could cost the church a few members."

"Maybe, but I believe this is what God brought me to this church to do. If it separates the wheat from the chaff, so be it."

***

Lying on her back draped in a faded blue hospital gown, Kendra's bulging abdomen, tethered to twin fetal monitors, appeared more pronounced. She was visibly relieved when Eric finally appeared in the doorway. Two women on the other side of Kendra's bed watching the monitors acknowledged Eric's presence before resuming their conversation. One woman was tall and thin with short faded red hair. Given her wrinkles, Kendra guessed that she was closer to fifty than forty. The other woman had a flawless mahogany complexion, perfectly round face and naturally curly brown hair pulled into a ponytail. She looked barely out of high school. Kendra checked the badge clipped to her coat to confirm her title and resisted the urge to ask how long she'd been out of medical school.

Eric ducked under the ceiling mounted television and squeezed between the I.V. stand to reach his wife. Matching sets of wires emerging from under the dull beige blanket and the I.V. in her arm constrained her movements. He kissed Kendra on the forehead and gently held her hand. "Do they know what's going on?"

The guilt was overwhelming and the waiting only made the situation worse. Kendra looked at Eric and wondered if he would be able to forgive her. Emotions impeded the flow of her words. "Not yet."

After receiving a brief string of instructions that Kendra did not understand, the tall woman left the room. The other woman extended her hand to Eric. Her smile was warm and friendly. "You must be Eric. I'm Dr. Snyder."

Eric reached across Kendra to shake the doctor's hand. Kendra knew they were both thinking the same thing.

Dr. Snyder was used to the reaction. "Relax. Your wife's in good hands. Her doctor's in the process of delivering a baby. He asked me to make sure Kendra's being well cared for until he can safely leave his other patient. Fortunately, Kendra's not having contractions and both heartbeats are strong. However, the bleeding's cause for concern."

Eric felt Kendra's grip increase. "Does that mean Kendra might have to stay overnight?"

"That would be a best case scenario. It could be much longer. Your wife's just starting her second trimester which is a critical stage for multiple births."

With Eric at her side, Kendra could bear hearing the answer. "Could we lose the babies?"

The doctor patted Kendra's leg. "We don't have enough information to answer that question yet."

Eric's body was still recovering after sprinting from the parking lot. "What do you think's causing the bleeding?"

"Our main concern is that one of the placentas is separating from the uterus."

Tears rolled out the corner of Kendra's eyes into her hair. Dr. Snyder handed her the box of tissue kept under the monitor tray for such occasions. Kendra blotted her eyes.

"Let's hope for the best." She looked at her watch. "Radiology should be here soon to do the ultrasound. As soon as we get the results, we'll take it from there. Are there any other questions?"

Kendra adjusted her position. "Can I go to the restroom, while we wait?"

"I'm afraid not. Until we know the cause of the bleeding, you need to stay in bed; besides a full bladder will be helpful. Can you wait a while longer?"

Kendra hesitated. For the sake of her children, she would do whatever was necessary from this point on. "I think so."

"Good. But if you can't, push the call button and a nurse will assist you with a bed pan."

After the doctor left the room, Kendra rolled onto her side to blow her nose. The small movement made the fullness of her bladder more noticeable. Eric adjusted her pillow and took the used tissue. She could tell by his silence and furrowed brows that he was worried. She hoped he wasn't blaming himself. He had done everything possible to make the pregnancy easier for her.

"Eric, this is my fault. I didn't want to be pregnant again and now God's going to take them away."

Eric sat on the bed. "Kendra, if anyone's to blame, it's me. I should not have put you in this position. We should have waited or I should have used protection."

Kendra closed her eyes remembering the weeks she moped around the house, traumatized by the pregnancy. She needed Eric to understand. "This pregnancy was such a shock, but I've had time to adjust. I even have names picked out." The tears resumed. "I want the babies, Eric. Both of them!"

Eric caressed her arm. "It's going to be okay. Stop doing this to yourself. You heard the doctor. It may not be serious."

"But what if it is?"

"Then we'll cross that bridge when we get there. For now, we both need to be strong and courageous." Eric looked at the monitors again and noticed the two rapid heartbeats. "Can you try to send our children some peaceful thoughts? Stress can't be good for you or the babies."

As long as the babies were inside of her, there was still hope that God would be merciful. Kendra took several deep breaths and watched the monitors. The heartbeats slowed slightly. "You're right."

Eric smiled. "My ears must be playing a trick on me. Did you just say I was right?"

Kendra raised one eyebrow and gave Eric a faint smile. "It happens every now and then." She adjusted her position to get a better view of the monitors. One of the heart rates was slightly lower than the other. Kendra wondered if the heart rates indicated which baby was in danger. She hoped that neither baby was in pain. The first ultrasound at her doctor's office had confirmed that they were fraternal twins, so each baby had its own embryonic sack. It was still too soon to determine the sexes, but Kendra knew in her heart at least one of them was a girl. Realizing that she was hoping her daughter would survive, she quickly pushed the thought out of her mind. She wanted both of her children to survive. They had to.

Kendra needed a distraction to get her mind off her full bladder. "Will you get my cell phone out of my purse? It's in the bag. I need to call Ruby to check on the boys, and then I want to call Daddy and Jessica."

Eric walked to the chair and extracted Kendra's purse from the bag. "I'll call Ruby on my phone to check on the boys." He hesitated before handing the phone to her. "Maybe you should wait before calling Jessica."

Kendra reached for her purse wondering if Eric would ever understand the bond between women.

***

The pounding in Jonathan's head kept tempo with the steel drums in the distance. He stood in the line, trying to keep his composure. His family was two ferries away from even reaching the point where a canopy provided a narrow band of shade. It had been an exhausting five hours at Epcot. After the first two, he knew it was a mistake bringing their children. The educational experience he had hoped for turned into a battle of endurance. His children only wanted to buy souvenirs and argue about which exhibit was next. Jonathan wished they had saved the admission price and stayed at the hotel swimming pool, which was proving to be the highlight of the vacation. He watched his wife who seemed unfazed by the experience. When Lori suggested they leave and come back later, Jonathan seized the opportunity.

Twenty minutes later, they were on the ferry boat heading towards the park exit. If his youngest son, Jason, had not cried because he wanted to ride the boat again, they could have been on their way to the hotel. As the boat bobbed in the wake of a passing ferry, Jonathan looked out the window at the murky gray water. He wondered why the park did not dye the water to make it more appealing. Unable to restrain himself, he scanned the shores to estimate the volume of the lake and the feasibility of changing its appearance. While focusing on what he thought was the water source of the lake, he spotted someone who looked familiar. His pulse raced. The longer he stared the more nervous he became. Lori's nudge caused him to look away.

"Jason needs to go to the restroom. Will you take him before we head to the car?"

"Sure..." Jonathan said, returning his gaze to the window. Whatever he saw was gone.

By the time the ferry docked and was unloading, he had convinced himself that he had nothing to worry about. Taking his son to the restroom, he called Jessica just to make sure. When the call went directly to her voice mail, he hung up without leaving a message.

As they walked to the car, his wife reminded him about her spa appointment for the following day. When they checked in, she was given an envelope with her name. Inside the envelope was a complimentary certificate for a facial and manicure at the hotel spa. Lori called to confirm the appointment as soon as they walked into the room.

***

It took less than two hours for the news to reach Stephanie. Her mood improved immediately and the smile on her face was no longer forced when instructing visitors to sign in. The decision to return to the company where she met Eric was easy. Getting rehired proved more difficult. She expected a comparable administrative job, but her skills did not meet the new requirements. Stephanie felt punished for her beauty. Not only was her new job demeaning, it was also temporary. The regular receptionist was out for three months on maternity leave. Faced with eviction from her apartment, she reluctantly accepted the position which chained her to a desk and reduced her opportunities to bump into Eric since he rarely used the main entrance.

When she got the call from a co-worker about Eric's wife being in the hospital, Stephanie believed things were finally working in her favor. She spent the remainder of the afternoon daydreaming about all the possibilities. First, she thought about how to approach Eric at Kendra's funeral and how soon they could be married. With two small boys, he would definitely need a new wife quickly. If Kendra did not die, things could still work in her favor. She thought about women who went crazy after miscarriages. She dismissed that scenario because it would take too long. All she needed was one evening with Kendra out of the house. She knew Eric's one weakness and planned to use it once more in her favor.

Later that evening, Ruby had dozed off on the couch waiting for Eric to return with an update on Kendra's condition. He came home to eat dinner with his sons and returned to the hospital at Ruby's insistence. When he told Ruby that Kendra would be in the hospital for at least a week, she drove home and packed a suitcase. Eric did not even have to ask.

The knock at the door startled Ruby. She glanced at her watch before walking to the foyer. "Who is it?" she asked through the closed door.

Stephanie expected Eric to answer the door, which is why she wore a haltered midriff top and sheer skirt that hung just above her pelvic bone. "Is Eric here?"

Ruby opened the door and looked at the woman from head to toe.

Her disapproving look caused Stephanie to become more assertive. "Is Eric home?

"Why?"

The woman looked familiar but it took a few seconds for Stephanie to remember why. "Don't you go to our church?"

Ruby shifted her weight. "I thought you looked familiar."

Stephanie extended her hand which Ruby slowly accepted. "I'm Stephanie. Eric and I work together. When I heard that Kendra was in the hospital, I wanted to drop off a few things to help out. I figured he'd be busy with the boys, so I waited until they were in bed."

"That was sweet of you to go to all that trouble." Ruby reached for the basket in Stephanie's hand. "I'll let Kendra know that you stopped by."

Stephanie pulled the basket back. "I'd really like to say hello to Eric and see what else he might need."

"I'm sure you would, but he's at the hospital with his wife."

"Oh…Well, I guess I'll just check with him tomorrow at work." She gave the basket with the casserole and an assortment of cookies and chocolates to Ruby.

Ruby inspected the basket. "I'm not sure he'll be at work tomorrow."

Stephanie turned to walk away.

"Stephanie…" Ruby waited for her to return to the door. "When you go to a married man's house, you shouldn't wear that kind of outfit. It might give people the wrong impression. And there's one other thing you should know. I'll be staying here with Eric and the boys until Kendra gets home, so they'll be well taken care of." Ruby smiled and closed the door.

Stephanie walked to her car, stifling the urge to scream. She was not going to be intimidated by some old hag. Too much was at stake. As she drove back to her apartment, she had a better idea. Ruby could delay her from being with Eric, but she wouldn't be able to stop her from immediately working on Kendra.

***

Kendra listened to the hushed voices coming from the nurse's station across the hall. Based on the flurry of activity, the night staff had arrived. Frigid air blew directly on her. She pulled the thin cotton blankets up to her chin in an effort to stay warm. When Eric left after the ten o'clock news, he turned off the television and the light. Lying in the darkness, she remembered the day she learned of her pregnancy and the broken eggs in the trash can. A fresh wave of emotions burst forth. When the door opened flooding the room with light, Kendra was clutching the blankets and sobbing quietly.

A petite woman dressed in sky blue scrubs walked to her bedside. Her short curly hair was generously sprinkled with gray. The eyeglasses perched on her nose had a dangling neck chain. She looked at Kendra's medical chart. "Are you in pain?"

Kendra sniffed, slightly embarrassed. "No, I'm fine."

The nurse sat the chart on the bed table and handed her some tissue. "Then what's the crying for?" She checked her pulse.

Kendra wiped her eyes and nose, feeling like a reprimanded child. "It seems all of this is just too much for me to handle."

The nurse looked her squarely in the eyes. "Are you saved?"

Kendra was caught off guard by the bluntness of the question. "...Yes." She was too ashamed to admit she was not even sure what the word meant anymore.

"Then you don't need to be handling anything anyway." The nurse stuck a thermometer in Kendra's mouth and started to sing softly.

"What a friend we have in Jesus,

All our sins and grief to bear!

What a privilege to carry,

Everything to God in prayer.

Oh, what peace we often forfeit

Oh, what needless pains we bear

All because we do not carry,

Everything to God in prayer!"

She stopped singing and looked at the thermometer that had beeped. "I love that song. It's gotten me through many tough times. Good reminder that we're supposed to take our burdens to the Lord and leave them with Him." The nurse gently pulled back the blankets. "Let's make sure you're still doing okay."

Kendra yielded to yet another inspection by a stranger.

"No bleeding. That's what we want to see. It's late. You need to get some rest so your body can do what it needs to do."

Kendra needed reassurance to calm her fears. "I'm afraid I'll lose the babies during the night?"

"Would you mind if I pray for you?"

Kendra tried to smile. "Please do. I need all the prayers I can get." She was shocked when the nurse gently clasped her hands around Kendra's and began to pray aloud.

"Heavenly Father, God of all creation. You're our life giver and divine provider. Your grace is sufficient and by your power, all things are possible. Your daughter, Kendra's in need of your peace and healing right now. God ease her mind, protect your children that you've placed in her womb and grant her a restful night of sleep. We ask this in the name of our Lord and Savior, Jesus Christ. Amen" She released Kendra's hand, adjusted her covers and walked to the door. "Push the call button, if you need anything. Now, get some rest."

Kendra rose up on her elbows and watched the woman whose name she did not know pull the door closed. "Thank you…" As she laid her head on the pillow, Kendra thought about the words to the song, wishing she could remember them all. What she did remember was enough to divert her attention from her womb to her soul. "God, why am I feeling like this? I know you can keep these babies safe, if it's your will. Your Word is clear. With you, all things are possible. So why do I still feel this way?"

The words to the song floated through her mind. 'All our sins and grief to bear.' Her conversation with Eric replayed in her mind. 'It's my fault.' Despite Eric's reassurances, Kendra still believed God was punishing her and that she deserved the punishment. Her hand moved to her stomach and caressed the babies. She longed to see their faces and hold them tightly. With every stroke, she realized that everyone deserved to be punished but not everyone had to be. "God, forgive me…forgive me for not trusting you, for grumbling when I found out that I was pregnant and for being angry with you for taking my mother from me. It's your decision whether these children live or die. Your will be done. Thank you for sending that nurse. Bless her for helping me." Kendra drifted to sleep thinking about her many blessings.

CHAPTER 5

JESSICA RETURNED TO HER OBSERVATION POINT IN THE HOTEL lobby with an unobstructed view of the spa entrance and waited. When Lori entered the spa with the gift certificate in hand, Jessica got her first glimpse of the woman who stood between her and her happiness. She was not what Jessica expected. Lori wore an ankle length sundress with flat sandals and her thick ebony hair was pulled into a ponytail at the nap of her neck. Despite the lack of makeup, she was attractive. Jessica wondered if it was her first spa experience. When Jessica purchased the certificate, she was only concerned with getting Lori alone and ensuring everything fit the schedule. Watching her gentle disposition, Jessica wished that she had included a massage for the woman whose life was about to be shattered. Lori walked out of the spa right on schedule.

Jessica joined her a few steps later. "Hello, Lori."

Lori looked completely startled to be addressed by name. "Should I know you?"

Jessica smiled at Lori's naïve politeness, wondering how long it would last. "You should, but you don't. Can we go somewhere to talk? It's about Jonathan." Jessica watched the subtle change in Lori's eyes while the information registered.

"How do you know my husband?"

"That's what we need to discuss," Jessica said in a hushed tone.

"Look, I don't know who you are, but I don't have time for your games." Lori turned to walk away but Jessica grabbed her arm. Lori yanked it away.

Jessica held up her hands. "I don't have time for games either." Jessica knew a softer approach was needed. She took a step back to give Lori more space. "My name's Jessica Taylor. If you give me just a few minutes, I'll explain the situation."

Lori looked at Jessica then looked away. Jessica's perfume filled the air around her. Lori recognized the scent causing the blood to drain from her already blotchy face. Lori cleared her throat. "It sounds like you know my husband very well."

"Unfortunately, I do. Would you mind if we continued this conversation somewhere a little more discrete? There's a lounge on the mezzanine level." Jessica walked towards the escalator on the other side of the lobby without waiting for a response. Lori followed. When they were seated at a table towards the rear of the lounge, Jessica set her purse on the floor beside her chair and crossed her legs. "You probably have a few questions for me…"

Lori interrupted "Just one. How do you know my husband?"

"Let me preface this with how sorry I am that you have to hear this from me. But I'm tired of waiting for Jonathan to do what he should have done years ago. You deserve to know the truth." Jessica noticed Lori's reaction to the word 'years'. Jessica took a dramatic deep breath before continuing. "Jonathan and I work for the same company. We've had a very close relationship for some time now."

"I'm sorry, but I don't believe you. Jonathan would not do that to his family."

Jessica watched Lori, whose eyes reflected shock and disbelief. For a brief second, Jessica felt a tinge of remorse. Her first husband's wife was so arrogant. Jessica enjoyed flaunting their affair. Lori seemed so different, so nice. Jessica wondered if that was why Jonathan was having such a hard time leaving her. The thought validated her belief that she was helping Jonathan do what he would never be able to do on his own. Once Lori knew the truth, Jonathan would be free to do what he wanted to do. She reached into her purse and pulled out a business card and handed it to Lori.

Lori looked at the familiar logo and the title under Jessica's name. "This only proves that you work at the same company." Lori handed the business card back to Jessica.

Jessica returned the business card to her purse and took out an envelope. "Maybe you'll believe these." She opened the envelope, slowly took out two pictures and handed them to Lori.

Lori looked at the first picture of Jonathan and Jessica embracing on a dark, secluded beach. No one else was in the picture. In the second, their clothes were discarded on the sand. She put the pictures on the table face down and held her hand over her mouth.

Lori had the same expression as Simone right before she vomited. Having no desire to be in the pathway, Jessica pushed her chair away from the table slightly and waited a few seconds before continuing. "I've been pleading with Jonathan to make a choice. Finally, I decided that if he won't, it will be up to us."

After forcing air into her lungs several times, Lori recovered enough to respond. "What choice is there? Jonathan would never leave us for a whore like you and I would not ask him to. So apparently, you've wasted your time following him here." Lori stood up.

Jessica pulled another picture from the envelope but paused before handing it to her. "I know how difficult this is for you, but I have a very good reason for doing this." She handed Lori a picture of Simone that showed an unquestionable likeness to her father, more than even Lori's own children.

Unable to control the assault on her body that radiated from her core, Lori rushed to the restroom they had passed on the way to the table. Her body shook as her stomach surrendered the contents which had soured after the first pictures. Five minutes later, she was still in the stall, sweating and panting. Her mind constantly replayed the pictures. It took another ten minutes for her to return to the table. Jessica was waiting with two glasses of wine. One was half empty.

Lori sat down and pushed the glass of wine towards Jessica. "Does he know you're here?"

"He threatened to kill me, if I ever came near you. But at this point, that's a risk I'm willing to take. Our daughter has started asking questions that I can't give her answers to. It's time to end this senseless charade of his."

Lori glanced at the pictures on the table. "When were those taken?"

"In Hawaii…he didn't know they were being taken."

Lori closed her eyes to ease the pain. "Would it have mattered?"

Jessica thought about the night on the beach surrendering to the forces that used to come so naturally when they were together, before their relationship started to change. "Not really."

"How old is your daughter?"

"Simone will be five in September."

"She's the same age as my youngest…We were pregnant at the same time."

"Apparently we were." Jessica suddenly understood Jonathan's reaction to her pregnancy. Jessica worried whether Lori had enough strength remaining to confront her husband, which was critical for the final part of the plan.

Lori stared defiantly at Jessica. "So what's your next move? Clearly, you've thought this out."

Jessica handed Lori an airline ticket with Jonathan's name on it. "I thought you might need some time to sort things out, so I took the liberty of buying Jonathan an airline ticket. Our flight leaves at three today." Jessica knew that this would be her last chance to convince Jonathan. If he had no where else to go, it would make things much easier.

Lori looked at the destination and her eyes bulged. "You live in Chicago!"

"Why do you think he spends so much time there?"

"I thought he was working." Her voice was barely a whisper.

"He was working during the day, but he spent his nights with us."

Lori picked up the pictures. "Can I take these?"

Jessica savored the feeling that victory was within her grasp. "Of course. They're just copies." Jonathan had clearly underestimated her. After today, he would not make that mistake again. He would know beyond a doubt how much she loved him.

After putting the airline ticket and pictures in her purse, Lori stood up. "I never want to see you again. Is that clear?"

"Perfectly. My business with you is done." Jessica looked at her watch. She had just enough time to meet her mother and Simone for lunch before checking out of their hotel.

***

After four days in the hospital, Kendra was anxious to get home even with all the restrictions. Her doctor cautioned her that the risk of a miscarriage within the next month was high while signing her discharge papers. One of the placentas was growing too close to her cervix, requiring it to be surgically closed. With the bleeding stopped and no signs of infection, he agreed to let her go home a day earlier than planned.

Kendra knew that even if she followed every instruction, the future of her babies was ultimately out of her control. Still, she had no intention of putting God to a test. Every order would be followed. To ward off any residual doubt, Kendra constantly reflected on how God had protected her before. Her children were in good hands. All morning, she thought about the angel figurine from Eric prominently displayed on their fireplace mantle. Five years ago, she envisioned the angel's wings protecting her and Eric. Now she believed the little boy and girl represented the children in her womb. Complete peace filled her.

The steady rainfall was visible through the window but the thick walls of the hospital masked the thunder. Kendra thought of her boys, as she reclined on the bed and watched the television for any weather warnings. A cold front collided with the warm air, resulting in severe thunderstorms that she hoped would not delay Eric. When the door opened, she expected to see him. Instead Stephanie walked in carrying a large green plant.

Kendra's peace evaporated before Stephanie crossed the threshold. "What are you doing here?

Stephanie sat the plant on the bedside table. "I wanted to see how you're doing."

Kendra looked at Stephanie wondering if she owned any clothes that were not too short or tight. "No really, what are you doing here?"

"Honestly, can't a person do something nice? Don't be so suspicious?"

"Let's see…you tried to trick my husband into marrying you—then you named your son after Eric. I have reason to be suspicious."

"I was young and dumb. You can't blame me for falling in love with Eric. You did, too." Stephanie adjusted her purse on her shoulder. "Let's just put the past behind us, especially since we go to the same church."

Kendra did not need to be reminded. The church was her spiritual base until Stephanie walked through its door. "What does going to the same church have to do with anything?"

"Well for starters, we're both Christians. So I think it's time we start acting more sisterly."

"There's a difference between calling yourself a Christian and being one."

"Why would anybody call themselves a Christian if they aren't?"

"Maybe you should ask Reverend Tucker about that. Have you attended any of the new member classes?"

"Not yet. Oops, I almost forgot the card" Stephanie sat her purse on the bed, near Kendra's feet and took out an envelope. "I dropped a few things at the house for Eric and the boys the other night, but some of us at work chipped in to get you this plant and a card. Everyone thinks so highly of Eric." She handed Kendra the card.

Kendra hesitated before taking it. "What do you mean by 'at work'?"

"Didn't Eric tell you that we're working together again?"

Kendra resisted the urge to sit up. "Since when?"

"For weeks now…what are you doing dressed?"

"I'm waiting for Eric to pick me up."

"Did you lose the baby?"

"No." Having the object of Eric's betrayal in the same room was intolerable. "You've accomplished your goal. Please leave."

Stephanie picked up her purse. "If there's anything I can do to help, just let me know." She adjusted the bow on the plant before leaving the room.

Watching Stephanie walk out the door, Kendra thought about Jessica's obsession with Jonathan. Eric was blindsided by her anger, as soon as he walked through the door.

***

Jonathan lagged behind his children in the hallway. When he heard them greeting their mother, he was surprised. He had left a note on the desk for her to join them at the pool. He assumed she was still at the spa. He walked into the room, thankful housekeeping came while they were out. Lori looked at him briefly before returning her attention to their children. He knew the look. She was upset with him about something. On the way to the bed, he noticed her Bible open on the desk, next to his note.

"Mom, how was the spa?" asked her oldest son, Jon.

"It was nice." Lori kept her eyes on her children. "Go change out of your swim suits and then we'll get some lunch?"

Their younger children ran into the adjoining room, arguing over who would get the bathroom first. Jon paused and looked at his mother longer. Lori waited for the comments about her face, thankful to have an excuse for her swollen eyes and pale complexion.

"Mom, I hope you enjoyed your time at the spa."

Lori hugged her son. "Go get changed. I know you're starving."

Jonathan collapsed on the bed, ready for a break. "Didn't you get the note? We waited for you, so we could eat at the poolside café." When Lori didn't respond, Jonathan rolled onto his side to see why. Everything about his wife seemed foreign. There were lines in her face that he had never noticed before and her eyes were puffy and dark. He wondered if she was having an allergic reaction to the products they used on her face. "The kids wore me out. I guess I'm not as young as I used to be. Will you bring me a sandwich back to the room?"

"No Jonathan, I won't."

"Was the service that bad? Your face looks awful."

"The spa was wonderful, but I had quite a surprise when I came out. Apparently some unfinished business followed you to Florida."

Jonathan immediately knew that it was Jessica he saw at Epcot. Adrenaline pulsed through his body as he realized that chemicals were not to blame for his wife's appearance.

"Guess who was waiting for me, when I came out of the Spa? Now that I think about it, I'm sure she arranged our meeting."

He sat on the edge of the bed and wrung his hands together hating Jessica for forcing him to confront his infidelity at the most inopportune time. Words hurled around in his brain but none seemed adequate. What could he possible say to take away his wife's pain?

Lori stared at Jonathan. "Apparently, she got tired of waiting for you to do the right thing."

Jonathan stood up and walked towards Lori who was now standing at the desk. The depth of the pain in her eyes would haunt him forever. "I don't know what she told you, but please let me explain."

"She didn't have to say very much." Lori opened the desk drawer and handed Jonathan the pictures. "These pictures explain everything very clearly. What can you possibly add?"

The picture of Simone was on top. The next two pictures ushered him into his wife's pain. Instead of buying time to prove his love, he had given Jessica a chance to prove how despicable she was. It didn't matter he was drunk when the pictures were taken or he'd been set up. No one else was on the beach and it was the middle of the night. He stared at the picture of Simone before daring to look at Lori again. "I was going to tell you after our vacation."

"You never wanted me to go to Hawaii. Was there even a convention or was she the only business connection?" Lori continued before he could answer. "Our trip to Savannah must have been a real joke to you. How could I have been so stupid for so long?"

"Lori, I love you…you have to believe that. I never loved her."

"Do you even know what love is?" Lori spat the question at him barely above a whisper. "Did our marriage and children mean that little to you?"

As if on cue, their oldest daughter came from the other room dressed in shorts and a T-shirt. "Mom, when are we going to eat?"

"In a few minutes…" Lori escorted her daughter back into the other room and addressed all her children. "Your father and I need to finish discussing something. Get a snack out of the basket and look at television until we're ready." Lori looked at her youngest, still in his swim trunks." Jon, help your little brother change, please." Lori closed the door between the two rooms and looked defiantly at Jonathan.

"Lori, this has nothing to do with the way I feel for you or our children. Men have needs…You didn't have the time or the desire. I'll admit that I made a very big mistake, but we're both to blame."

"So, now it's my fault? Forgive me for putting our children's needs above yours." Lori sneered and lowered her voice. "I could understand a momentary lack of judgment. But somehow, I think that this is even beyond my comprehension. Five years! But you're right about one thing. Apparently you do have needs that I can no longer meet. Thankfully, Jessica's making this easy for us all." Lori walked into the bathroom and came back with his suitcase. "I took the liberty of packing for you." She tossed the airline ticket onto the bed. "She's waiting for you at the airport."

Jonathan looked at the airline ticket but did not pick it up. "Lori, you have every reason to be upset, but I'm not going anywhere."

"That's where you're wrong. If you don't get on that plane, these pictures will be emailed to your manager with a nice note explaining your lapse in judgment with a co-worker. I'm sure there's some small clause in your employment contract about morality. You'll be fired before you can sit down at your desk. Given the economy, it just might take some time to find another job but that shouldn't be a problem for you. I'm sure Jessica won't mind, as long as she gets what she wants."

Jonathan tore the pictures into small pieces and put them in his pocket.

Lori shook her head. "You really do think I'm a fool? I went to the business center and scanned the pictures. They're sitting in my email account, waiting for one click of a mouse. "

"You wouldn't do that," Jonathan said hopefully.

"All this time, I really thought you cared about what was best for the family. The years you refused to even discuss me returning to work. You just wanted to keep me dependent on you. But apparently, you can't be depended on."

"Lori, you know that's not true. Right now, we need to think about our children?"

Jonathan felt like he was betraying Simone. It hurt to tear her picture but he had no choice.

"It's a little late to think about them now. Six year's ago would have been a more appropriate time, before you gave them an illegitimate sister." Lori folded her arms on her chest and looked at the airline ticket.

"I can't leave you here with the kids."

"You left us a long time ago. And as far as this vacation is concerned, you'll be doing me a favor. It'll be one less child to worry about." Lori looked at her wrist watch. "I suggest you say goodbye to your children before I take them to eat."

Hearing the truth vocalized hurt even more. "Lori, please…"

"If you really do care anything about us, you'll be gone when we get back. I need time to think and I can't do that with you here. It's too painful to even look at you?"

Jonathan suspected she needed to switch roles from his wife to mother to cope. Her children needed her, even if she thought he no longer did. "Lori…"

She ignored him and went into the room with her children. "Kids, Daddy has an emergency at work so he has to leave. But we're going to finish our vacation. Say goodbye quickly, so we won't make him miss his flight."

Jonathan kissed his children fighting back his own tears. He would give Lori what she needed and use the time to permanently end his relationship with Jessica. If it took the rest of his life, he would make it up to Lori. They could get through this. They had too.

***

The minute the wheels of the airplane left the ground, Jonathan regretted giving in to Lori's demand. The truth was going to be painful whenever she found out. Even if he had told her first, Jessica would have still found a way to confront Lori with the pictures. Now he could start repairing his marriage. The entire flight he thought about Lori and what it would take to regain her trust. Eventually, he hoped Lori could make room in her heart and their family for Simone. Left in Jessica's care, he knew Simone would be ruined. By the time the airplane landed, he had a plan. Lori had begged him for years to go to a Christian marriage conference but he always made excuses. He would go where ever she wanted and do whatever she asked. Now that Lori knew, it would be easier. There was nothing that Jessica could hold over his head.

Jonathan rode from the Chicago airport to Jessica's condominium in silence, struggling to control his emotions for his daughter's sake. She fell asleep soon after getting buckled in. Jessica drove the familiar path, as if nothing was wrong. He suspected that she was gloating inside. Once Simone saw him at the Orlando airport, she was overjoyed. His demeanor changed as soon as she flew into his arms. He was certain that was part of the plan, making Jonathan wonder what kind of mother uses her daughter as a pawn and intentionally puts her in harm's way.

While Jessica was putting Simone to bed, Jonathan took out his phone to call Lori but he could not bring himself to make the call. After leaving her, what could he say over the phone to make the situation any better? The fact that he was at Jessica's would not help his case. He would call her from the airport to let her know that he'd be waiting for them at home. The sound of Jessica's footsteps approaching shifted his attention away from his future to the present. He did not wait for her to speak. "That was quite a stunt you pulled. I warned you what would happen, if you went anywhere near my family."

Jessica stopped to check the number of messages on her answering machine. "Last time I checked, I was still alive."

Jonathan clasped his hands together and forced himself to stay seated. He could not do anything that would keep him away from Lori any longer. He had no doubt that Jessica would call the police, just to keep him from leaving Chicago. "You can thank Simone for that. But make no mistake about it; to me, you're just as good as dead. A photographer on the beach…how long have you been planning this?"

"You left me no choice."

"Did you honestly think this little ploy of yours would work?"

Jessica sat in the arm chair and drew her knees to her chest. "What did you expect me to do? Wait around forever. Simone needs both her parents and I need you. It's obvious we belong together."

The air in the room was stifling despite the frigid temperature. "I regret the day I ever walked into your office. What kind of person does what you just did? Lori never did a thing to hurt you."

"You're just upset. I'm the best thing that ever happened to you. We're destined to be together. You'll be happier in Chicago with us. I talked with Dave and he's willing to give you a shot on his team. We can get married and…"

Jonathan laughed out loud. "Married? Have you totally lost your mind? I'll never make the mistake your first husband did. Actually, he was pretty smart. He made sure you didn't have his child. It pains me to know that my daughter has a mother like you." Looking at Jessica, he knew that he could not leave his daughter with her very long. First, he needed to salvage his marriage then he would be in a position to help Simone.

Jessica looked at Jonathan, her eyes pleading with him. "There's no one better for me than you. Can't you see that? I'll do whatever it takes to prove to you how much I love you." Jessica walked seductively to the couch. The doorbell rang startling her. "Who could that be at this hour?"

Jonathan looked at his watch before standing up. "The taxi that I called…Did you honestly think I was staying?" Jonathan walked to his suitcase sitting beside the door and picked it up. "I've already told Simone goodbye." Jonathan left without another word.

"She won't take you back." Jessica watched the door close, refusing to run after him.

***

At five in the morning, Lori led her barely awake children from their hotel room to the loaded van. She let them stay up as late as they wanted, hoping they would sleep for most of the early morning drive home. The less arguing she had to deal with the better for them all. She would not sleep until she got home, and even then it was doubtful. Ever since finding out about Jonathan's affair less than twenty-four hours earlier, she felt like a robot going through pre-programmed movements. On the inside, the pain was so intense she had to force herself to breath but on the outside she was Mommy. She needed to return to the familiar to reduce the energy required to function. Of her children, only Jon seemed to notice his mother's fragile state. While they walked in downtown Disney, he revealed his anger with his father for leaving them. She wondered what her son would think if he knew the extent of his father's desertion. Eventually her children would have to learn about their sister, when they were old enough to understand.

It took only a few hours after Jonathan left for Lori to realize that continuing the vacation would be impossible. While eating lunch in the hotel restaurant, she watched the entrance, hoping he would join them. Unlocking the door to the hotel room, she hoped he would be on the other side. She checked her phone several times to see if she had missed his call even though she had set the ring tone to the highest level. By six o'clock, it was apparent that he had made his choice. She informed her children that they would be going home a day early. To her surprise, they showed little emotion about the change.

Despite the lack of sleep, she felt wide awake. The sky was dark enough to see the canopy of stars and the new moon. She looked at the sky thankful that God provided clear driving conditions. Jon climbed in the front passenger's seat after getting his little brother settled on the rear seat with a pillow and blanket. Traffic on the toll road was light and the car was quiet. Within a few minutes of driving, her children were sound asleep in answer to her prayers. Lori's cell phone sat in the cup holder but she did not want to call her friend, Shelia, too early. She reflected on their conversation eight hours earlier.

Shelia answered with a scratchy voice. "Hey. How's the vacation going?"

Lori cleared her throat. "Not quite as planned. That's why I'm calling. We're coming home tomorrow."

Shelia sat up on the sofa and looked at the clock. She had dozed off waiting for a television show. "Don't tell me, one of the kids got sick."

"Right now, I'm the one that's sick."

"Well make sure Jonathan and the kid's take good care of you."

Lori took a deep breath to stop the threatening tsunami of emotions. "It's just me and the kids. Jonathan left already."

Shelia noticed the trembling in Lori's voice. "When did he leave and where did he need to go that was important enough to interrupt your vacation?"

Lori relived the events while recounting them for Shelia.

Adrenaline was surging through her body by the time Lori finished. Shelia paced around the room like a caged lion ready to attack. "Has he lost his mind? What kind of man leaves his family while they're on vacation?"

"It sounds so stupid given everything else, but what hurts most was I got a weekend in Savannah and she got Hawaii. How could he do this to us?"

"I hate to say this because you're my friend, but he's a self-centered man incapable of putting the needs of anyone else above his own. I still can't believe that he would leave you and the kids."

Lori wondered if she was responsible for his leaving too. "I was so upset that I asked him to go, but he didn't put up much of a fight." Lori wished he had.

"Lori, I'm flying down there."

"Don't do that. The van's already loaded. If we get out on time, we'll be home before you could get here."

"Are you sure?"

Lori fell back on the bed and looked at the ceiling. "Yes, I'm sure...well, as sure as I can be about anything. Yesterday, I was sure Jonathan loved us. I do know that I'm not alone and God's grace will get me through. This just hurts so much. His other daughter looks too much like him!"

Shelia closed her eyes, praying for her friend. "Lori, you're a strong woman and you're right, God will definitely carry you through this."

"Anyway, I just wanted someone to know my plans."

"Promise to call me from the road," Shelia said.

"I promise. I'll talk to you tomorrow...pray for us."

"Nothing could stop me. I love you."

"Ditto...The Bible says that love covers a multitude of sin. I hope that's true. Anyway, I'd better check on the kids. I'll see you soon." Lori hung up the phone, wondering what Jonathan was doing.

Driving on the dark road with only the sounds of her sleeping children for company, Lori still wondered what Jonathan was doing. Trying to keep her thoughts of him separate from thoughts of Jessica proved difficult without the distraction of her children. The image of Jonathan and Jessica on the beach flooded her mind. Her foot pressed the accelerator harder as the van speed down the highway. The speedometer was past eighty-five miles per hour, as she darted around the slower traffic. Just as she was about to pass a tractor trailer, it swerved into her lane. Lori instinctively jerked the steering wheel. Her reaction sent the van onto the shoulder of the road. Lori felt two of the wheels leave the ground. She steered in the opposite direction fully aware that her youngest son was sleeping in the rear seat without his seatbelt. As she fought to regain control of the van, she tried to remember if any of her children had their seatbelts on. Clutching the steering wheel, a desperate plea to God left her lips.

***

Jonathan paced the terminal waiting to board the flight to Atlanta. After leaving Jessica's, he checked into a motel near the airport. He wanted to call Lori but it was too late, so he watched television until he finally drifted into a restless sleep. When he finally got the courage to call Lori after breakfast, the call went to voice mail. He didn't blame her for not wanting to talk to him. He deserved to be punished for his actions but the uncertainty of the punishment had his nerves on edge. The possibility that Lori would ask him to move out weighed heaviest on his heart but even that was a price he was willing to pay for her eventual forgiveness.

He longed for the distraction of work to channel the energy generated by his increasing anxiety. Since he had already left Lori two messages, he felt calling again would be counter productive. The fact that she had not returned his calls had him frantic. Regardless of how intense their argument, Lori always answered his calls. Regaining Lori's trust and respect was paramount to the survival of their marriage. Jonathan was certain that the exposure of his affair would enable them to make a new start, like Lori had prayed for on the beach.

When his phone rang, he checked the caller identification quickly. He did not recognize the phone number or even the area code. Disappointed that it was not Lori, he was about to let the call go to voice mail, but needing something to do, he answered.

"Hello."

"Is this Jonathan Grey?"

"Yes, it is."

"Are you related to Lori Grey?"

The female voice was subdued. Fear gripped Jonathan causing him to freeze mid-stride. "Yes, she's my wife. Why?"

"I'm calling from Orlando Regional hospital. Your wife was in an automobile accident."

His mouth went dry. "Is she okay? What about our children?"

"They were with your wife. How soon can you get here?"

He rushed to his boarding gate. The plane to Atlanta was pre-boarding. "I'm not sure. I'll need to check on flights to Orlando."

The woman looked at her notes from the rental car agent. The contract was signed by Jonathan Grey. "You're not in Orlando?"

"No, I'm in Chicago. Can I speak to my wife, please?" When there was no immediate response, he feared they had lost the connection.

"Mr. Grey, you need to get here as soon as possible. Please call the hospital, at this number, as soon as you know your plans." She rattled off the number quickly.

"Wait…I need to get something to write with." Jonathan searched his pant pockets for a pen. When he found one, he sat in the closest chair and looked for a blank area on his boarding pass. "Okay, what's the number again?"

The woman repeated the phone number slowly. "Just give them your name. They'll be expecting your call."

Jonathan saw the line at the gate counter. "Please tell my wife and children that I'll be there as soon as I can."

"Good bye, Mr. Grey."

Jonathan raced to the gate agent, by-passing the angry stares of the others waiting in the line. He frantically explained the situation to the agent, who directed him to the main ticket counter. Guilt and his heartbeat increased with every step as he zigzagged through the terminal. In desperation, he pleaded with God.

***

A pair of yellow finches took turns splashing in their neighbor's bird bath. Sharon closed her eyes and absorbed the sounds all around her. Occasionally a breeze rustled the leaves, providing background noise for the assortment of birds perched in their trees. After reading an article on developing the senses, she started doing hearing exercises the next day. When she heard the screen door open, she took a deep breath before opening her eyes.

Dale stood before her holding two glasses of cold water and smiled. "I see you're still trying to train your ears. Getting any better?" He handed her a glass before sitting in the adjacent chair.

It was a hot day, but under the umbrella it was bearable. They had been in the house all morning. Dale worked upstairs, fine-tuning the outline for his sermon. Sharon labored in the basement sorting through boxes of toys and outgrown clothing. Cleaning the basement had moved to the top of her list. Her children were given the opportunity to identify what they still wanted before she made donations. When Dale came to check on their progress, their children shot up the stairs before Sharon could protest.

Once outside, Sharon realized that she needed a break from the clutter too. "You think it's crazy, but I'm starting to hear sounds I never noticed before, like a squirrel running along the fence." Sharon watched the condensation drip from the glass. "So are you ready for Sunday?"

"Not yet. This sermon tackles a very difficult topic, but it's the most important to understand. Now, when I hear the song *Amazing Grace*, I understand why my grandmother loved to sing it. To think that God chose to save me despite what I've done is truly amazing. Unfortunately, most people don't see it that way." Dale sat his glass on the table. "This popular minister was teaching that God chose Jacob over Esau because God foreknew that Jacob would have a heart for God. If that were true, Jacob would have something to boast about. But the Bible is clear—no man can boast. God chooses us and it's not based on anything we do. I finally had to switch the radio station."

Sharon watched a rabbit dash across their yard. "I doubt if the minister was purposefully trying to mislead people. Maybe you just misunderstood what he said. God could have known Jacob's future."

"God did know, but that's not why he chose Jacob."

Dale seemed convinced that he had found something unique in the Bible, but she wasn't so sure. "It's hard for people to relinquish the illusion of control."

"There's no room for pride in God's church. Pride caused Satan's demise."

Sharon overheard church member grumblings about her husband's opinions. She suspected Dale had too. "How much flack do you think you'll get for this sermon?"

"Jesus said to make disciples. I'm going to be obedient and leave the consequences to Him. It's a shame that there are so many voices confusing people. The Bible's so clear to those who will take the time to read it."

Sharon took a long, slow drink. "It's not that clear, and I do take the time to read it."

"I'm beginning to wonder if the nudge we get from God is to join the flock and not to be the shepherd. The blind leading the blind is why Christianity's in the shape it's in today. I just want to teach God's Word to whoever wants to learn it; unfortunately, the business of religion keeps getting in the way." Dale paused. "Sharon, I truly believe time's running out."

Sharon noticed the heaviness of Dale's words. "For what?"

"God's people to do what He told us to do."

Sharon looked at Dale. "Do you really believe that?"

Dale's eyes glazed over. "I had another dream last night."

Sharon wished that Dale would not take his dreams so seriously. She was getting tired of trying to convince him otherwise.

"People have been waiting for thousands of years for Jesus to return, so I wouldn't put too much credence in your dreams. Remember the day our children said they saw Jesus and it was just the name on a billboard?" She shook her head remembering her reaction. "Some days, I can't wait to see Jesus. This world's such a mess. But somehow the thought of standing before God and finding out that I didn't do what I was supposed to scares me."

Dale nudged Sharon's arm. "Then you'd better get busy."

***

Jonathan arrived at the Orlando airport without his luggage which was on its way to Atlanta. He took a taxi to the hospital anxious to see Lori and his children. He called Lori's cell phone again in route to the hospital. The call like all the others went directly to voice mail. Not being able to talk to her had him on the brink of hysteria. Her injuries had to be preventing her from talking. He worried that if Lori was unable to talk, she could not care for their children either. When the taxi pulled in front of the hospital, Jonathan gave the driver a fifty dollar bill and left without waiting for change. His breathing was erratic by the time he reached the information desk with his insurance card in hand, prepared for any paperwork. Two elderly volunteers were talking at the reception desk. One of them greeted Dale warmly. When he said his name, the smile disappeared. Jonathan waited while she picked up the phone and dialed a number quickly. It was obvious that he was expected.

The volunteer hung up the phone. "Someone's on their way down. "

"Can you just tell me where I can find my family?"

"We can't help you, but someone will be right with you."

After five minutes of anxious waiting, his breathing returned to normal and he managed to convince himself that he was overreacting. A middle-aged woman in a blue pantsuit walked towards him. She did not look like a doctor or nurse, which was what Jonathan expected. "Where are my wife and kids?"

"Mr. Grey, I'm Wanda Moore. Will you follow me?" She gestured towards the main corridor and walked a step ahead of him.

The woman was several inches shorter. He noticed that she seemed nervous. Being in sales, he was used to making small talk to build rapport. "I have my insurance card, but I need to see them before doing any paperwork." He was confused when they stopped outside a small conference room. Wanda opened the door, walked inside and waited for Jonathan to follow. The small room had a table and several chairs neatly arranged. A phone and large clock were mounted on the wall and a box of generic tissue sat on the table.

She closed the door before speaking again. "Mr. Grey, why don't you have a seat?"

The woman's rudeness irritated him. "I'm not sitting anywhere until I see my wife and children."

Although she was trained for cases like this, it was hard to judge how people would react. "Mr. Grey, the accident was quite serious." Her eyes indicated the severity of the situation. "Can I get the names and ages of your children please?"

He wondered why they did not already have the information. "Jonathan Jr. is the oldest. He goes by Jon, with no 'h'. He'll be thirteen next month. He's looking forward to being a teenager." Jonathan's smile was not returned. "Brianna's eleven, Ashley's nine, and Jason, our youngest, is five."

The woman looked at the paper on the clipboard in her hand and wrote quickly. Jonathan waited while the woman recorded the information, trying to read what was written. "What happened?"

"I can only tell you what I know. The state troopers can provide you with more detailed information. They're sending someone right over." She took a breath before continuing. "Your wife and two of your children," she paused and looked at the paper again. "...Jon and Brianna were pronounced dead at the scene."

Jonathan's legs buckled beneath him as the air was sucked from his lungs. He grabbed the edge of the table to keep from falling to the floor. He tried to speak. His mouth opened but silence followed. Only when he gasped for air did he realize that he had stopped breathing. He looked at the woman pleading with her to take back the words.

The pain she saw was intense but she had to continue. "The two other children were flown to our hospital. Ashley died shortly after she arrived. The youngest, Jason, has been moved to the pediatric intensive care unit."

"God, no...There must be a mistake." Jonathan could no longer delay the inevitable. He fell to his knees and looked up at the woman. "My wife and children are still at the hotel."

"Mr. Grey, I wish this was a mistake."

The room spun as Jonathan clutched his head. His body convulsed with sobs and he gasped for air between painful moans.

The woman watched carefully for signs that Jonathan would need medical attention. She waited for the initial shock to run its course. "Mr. Grey, a doctor's waiting to talk to you about your son. I'll call and tell them that you need some time."

Trying to focus through the tears, Jonathan lifted his hand just as the woman picked up the phone on the wall. "...Jason needs me...take me to my son."

"Of course." The woman helped Jonathan to his feet. His body moved sluggishly. "Is there anyone you can call, in town?" She handed him several tissues from the box.

Jonathan wiped the tears from his face. "Just take me to my son, please...."

The woman led Jonathan down a maze of hallways to a bank of elevators. While they waited, Jonathan tried to remember Lori's parents' phone number. When the elevator door opened on the eighth floor, he could barely remember his own name. He followed her down several halls to a set of doors that opened automatically as they approached. They stopped at the nurse's station where Wanda introduced Jonathan before turning to address him again. "Mr. Grey. I'll send up the highway patrol when they arrive. Please let us know what we can do to help you. The entire hospital staff extends our deepest condolences."

Jonathan quickly provided the information the nurse needed and then followed him into a room directly across the hall. When Jonathan saw his son, his heart palpitated. His son's head was bandaged and the small amount of exposed flesh was covered with cuts and scraps. Of all his children, Jason looked most like Lori. A machine beside the bed seemed to be forcing air into his son's lungs through a tube in his throat.

The nurse moved a piece of equipment so Jonathan could get closer to his son. "I'll let the doctor know you're here."

Jonathan approached the bed slowly. He touched Jason's face but got no response. "Son, daddy's here." Tears flowed down his face. Lori was the one who cared for their children when they were sick. He did not know what to say or do. Looking at his son's tiny body, he hoped the absence of casts was a good sign. "You're going to be okay." Jonathan gently shook his arm. "Can you wake up for daddy?"

No response.

"That's okay. You've had a rough day." Jonathan adjusted the sheet covering his son wondering if he knew about his mother. "You've got to get well, so we can go home…."

The irony of the situation was unbearable. He had never really bonded with Jason. Now, he was the only one left.

Jonathan looked upward. "What kind of God are you to do this? Why did you take the innocent and leave the guilty? Jessica's the one who should be punished. If you won't do anything about her, I will." Jonathan looked at Jason. "Don't take my son too…please," he whispered.

The doctor stopped at the nurse's station to get the clipboard with the forms. The nurse directed the doctor's attention to the two highway patrolmen who had agreed to wait down the hall until after the doctor talked with Jonathan. The doctor acknowledged their presence before walking into the room.

"Mr. Grey. I'm Dr. Turner. I'm so sorry for what you're going through."

"How's my son?"

"I wish the news was better. Your son was ejected from the van. From what I understand it took a while for the first responders to even find him."

"But he's going to be okay?"

"Mr. Grey, your son suffered severe brain trauma and never regained consciousness. Technically, your son's dead. We left him on life support until you came in the hope that his organs might be used to benefit others."

"What are you talking about? My son's not dead. He's just sleeping." Jonathan turned to his son. "Isn't that right, Jason? Wake up for dad, right now. Show this doctor that he doesn't know what he's talking about."

"Mr. Grey, how I wish to be wrong but all the tests are conclusive. There's no brain activity."

"So now you want to kill my son so you can sell his organs?"

"Mr. Grey, we're not killing your son. He's already dead. "

"The dead don't have a heart beat."

"Your son has a heart beat because all of these machines are keeping his bodily functions going. In cases like this, a team of doctor's must concur before we can even consider organ donation. Even if you don't consent to donating his organs, our recommendation would still be to terminate life support."

"As long as there's hope, you're not turning off those machines."

"Mr. Grey, believe me. There's no hope for your son, in this life."

"Miracles happen every day."

"Believe me, if there were any chance for a recovery, we would not be having this discussion. Miracles do happen every day. There are several people waiting to see if this is the day they receive one, in the form of an organ transplant."

Jonathan watched his son, looking for any sign of life.

"Jonathan…for some hope comes at a tremendous cost to others."

Something about the way the doctor said his name let Jonathan know that he understood. He turned to the doctor. For a second, it was as if he were looking into Lori's eyes.

The doctor continued. "The accident has shaken up everyone who's been involved. I can't imagine what you're going through right now. At times like this, it's hard to see how any good can come from the tragedy. Jason can't use his organs anymore, but others can. The decision's entirely up to you. We'll respect whatever you decide." Dr. Turner clutched the forms and waited.

Jonathan knew he had been a bad father when Lori was around. He could not imagine what type of father he would be without her. There was little doubt that Jason would be better off with Lori, wherever that was. Jonathan looked at his son wondering if he was aware of what was about to happen. "Okay." Jonathan reached for the papers.

"You need to sign by the 'X'."

Jonathan scrawled his signature and handed the clipboard back to the doctor. "What happens next?"

"We turn off the machines…Would you like a little more time alone with your son?"

Jonathan nodded.

"I'll be at the nurse's station. Come get me when you're ready."

"Will it hurt him?"

"No, it won't."

"I hope you're right," Jonathan whispered. He picked up his son's small hand. As he caressed his son's fingers, he noticed for the first time that Jason bit his nails. He wondered what else he would not get the chance to discover about his children. "Jason, if I could switch places with you I would…I wasn't much of a father. You'll be happier with your mommy…Remember how she always talked about heaven." Jonathan touched his son's face. "Don't be afraid...Will you do something for me? Tell Mommy that I really did love her and that I'm so sorry for all the pain I caused...And tell your brother and sisters that I loved them too." Jonathan wanted to hold his son but was afraid to pick him up. "God's giving me what I deserve...I may not see any of you again..." Jonathan's voice trailed off as his lungs felt constricted. He raised his son's hand to his lips and kissed it gently. "Good-bye, son. Daddy loves you."

While the doctor waited at the nurses' station, the organ harvesting team waited in surgery. The matched recipients had been notified. The doctor prayed that the transition would be quick. On the brink of both mental and physical collapse, Jonathan emerged from the room. His face was wet with a mixture of tears and perspiration. "Do you need to sit down for a minute or can I get you something to drink?"

Jonathan shook his head. "Let's do this quickly before I change my mind."

He clutched his son's hand until the doctor pronounced the time of death and his body was wheeled away. Looking at his watch, he planned to remember forever the time that his son died. He ran his hand through his hair and looked at the doctor, struggling with what to do next.

The doctor spared him from having to ask the question. "The bodies of your wife and children will be held at our morgue until arrangements can be made. I understand that you live in Atlanta?"

"Yes. This was our vacation." Jonathan paused. "Do you need anything else from me?"

"We don't, but two officers from the highway patrol are waiting to speak with you."

Jonathan looked down the hallway but did not see them. He needed Lori's cell phone to call her parents "Where's my wife's purse?"

"If it was brought in with your wife, it's probably in our safe. After you're finished talking with the highway patrol, security can help you claim your family's personal belongings. If you'll excuse me, they're waiting for me in surgery. If you need anything at all, please don't hesitate to ask?"

"Where's the closest men's restroom?"

"It's down the hall and to the left, across from the waiting area." The doctor walked in the opposite direction.

Jonathan entered the restroom trying to formulate an acceptable explanation for leaving his family. Once Lori's parents recovered from the shock, it would be their first question. He needed time to get his story straight; time that he did not have.

The highway patrolmen greeted him, when he walked out the restroom "Are you Jonathan Grey?"

"Yes…"

"May we talk with you briefly about the accident?"

He was not ready to say anything that would be officially recorded. "Actually, I need to get my wife's belongings and call our families. Can this wait?"

"This won't take long. We may be able to help you."

Jonathan disliked how the men were looking at him. "Okay. Can we sit down?"

They led Jonathan into the waiting area which was empty.

Jonathan looked at the clock on the wall surprised that it was only 6:30pm. "How did the accident happen?"

"That's what we're trying to determine. The first emergency call came in before sunrise. Do you know why your wife was on the road so early?"

"No…"

"Mr. Grey, where were you this morning?"

"In Chicago. Why?"

"The rental contract had your signature. Were your wife and children vacationing alone?"

"No, I was with them until yesterday, when I had to fly to Chicago for business. My wife didn't want to cut our children's vacation short. They were supposed to drive home tomorrow."

"When was the last time you spoke with your wife?"

"Yesterday afternoon, before I left."

"Did she seem upset?"

Jonathan paused choosing his words carefully. "She wasn't very happy that my business interrupted our vacation."

"Did you speak with her when you got to Chicago?"

"No, I wanted to give her some time. Like I said, she wasn't very happy about me leaving."

"Mr. Grey, does your family usually use seat belts?"

"Always, Lori was adamant about that. Why?"

"Your wife was the only one wearing a seat belt."

"That's impossible…"

"Mr. Grey, how was your wife's mental condition when you left."

"I told you, she was upset."

"Mr. Grey, I know this is difficult but we have to ask. Was your wife upset enough to commit suicide?"

"Are you crazy? Lori would be the last person to do something like that. You need to be questioning the other driver."

"Mr. Grey, there were no other cars involved in the crash, and your wife was driving at a high rate of speed."

Jonathan covered his mouth. Had he driven Lori to take her life and the life of her children?

CHAPTER 6

WHEN THE NEWS STORY SCROLLED ACROSS THE BOTTOM OF Jessica's Internet home page Friday afternoon, it was barely a blip on her mental radar. In the rapidly changing world of ratings driven news, tragic accidents were daily occurrences. The more heart wrenching the story, the more coverage it received. Despite the fact that Jessica had the day off work, there was no time to waste reading anything that might dampen her spirits. The day was planned for her and Jonathan to negotiate their future. Instead the time was used to unpack and get ready for the following week. Her inbox was full of emails that needed purging. After finishing her email, she planned to visit some realtor websites to gauge the Chicago market for larger homes. As much as she loved living in the heart of Chicago, she was willing to consider suburban life. The possibility of having five children during the summer meant that they would need at least a four bedroom house. Simone would never have to share her room but Jonathan's other children would.

Jessica blocked out the possibility of Jonathan not returning with suitcases in hand. The book on the power of positive thinking she read encouraged visualizing the future the way she wanted it to be. Her ever evolving vision included a stately home on several acres with a swimming pool and professionally maintained grounds. With their combined salaries, Jessica hoped her own horse was finally within her grasp. Jessica also envisioned the reception awaiting Jonathan in Atlanta. No person in their right mind would take an adulterous spouse back immediately. Her ex-husband had only given her a couple of hours to get out of his house. A smile spread across her face as she sensed victory. He would crawl back to her before the week ended then they could plan their future.

Friday evening, while Jessica ran bath water for her daughter, she thought of another benefit of moving to the suburbs. A move would get Simone away from her friend's family. They lived on the same street which initially seemed good. Simone and the little girl had been playmates since the family moved in two years ago. It was convenient to have someplace for Simone to go that did not require much effort. But after the bedtime conversation with Simone, Jessica had a candid conversation with her friend's mother banning any more religious activities. The family still invited Simone on other outings. The latest was to a water park. Since Jessica already had a Saturday hair appointment scheduled, she gave in to Simone's pleading.

Jessica was helping Simone out of the tub when the phone rang just after eight o'clock. She knew it was Jonathan before looking at the display. Her cell phone was kept close in anticipation. His timing was perfect. Simone could put on her pajamas and watch a short video while they talked. Hoping he was already in Chicago, Jessica answered ready to savor the moment that her dream became a reality. Minutes later when the call abruptly ended, she could not stop shaking. Although she had hoped for years that something like this would happen, she had given up on the scenario. If the accident had happened under any other conditions, Jessica would have been dancing in the streets. Now that Jonathan blamed her, celebrating was the last thing on her mind. She and Simone needed protection. It took three shots of tequila to calm her nerves enough to go check on Simone and get her into bed. Afterwards, Jessica stayed up all night searching for news to confirm his accusations. Details of the accident came in slowly. The only information that could be confirmed was that a mother and four children from Atlanta were killed in an early morning accident outside of Orlando but the names of those killed had not been released.

Early Saturday morning, when Jessica dropped Simone at her friend's house for the weekend, her physical appearance supported the lie that a close friend had died while they were in Florida and she needed to go to the funeral. As soon as Jessica returned home, she checked the locks on every window and door. Every horrible incident of revenge on beautiful women came to mind: the woman on the talk show that was set on fire by her estranged husband and the model whose face was slashed from forehead to chin. Jessica had no intention of letting Jonathan anywhere near her until he could calm down. Would Jonathan kill her daughter and leave her disfigured out of revenge? When the entire story came to light, would anyone blame him for his actions? The possibilities were too horrendous for Jessica to dwell on very long. Her plan had taken into account everything except this.

Pacing from room to room, her lavishly decorated sanctuary felt more like a cage. Computer printouts were sprawled across the glass dining room table, next to the almost empty bottle of vodka and unopened carton of orange juice. Every accident detail on the Internet had been located, analyzed and printed. One story hinted that the wreck may have been intentional. This perspective caused Jessica the most concern. Jonathan would be completely justified in any retaliatory action. No jury would convict him. His return to Chicago was suddenly the last thing she wanted. Her only hope was that he would wait until after the funeral to confront her. The delay would allow time to prepare. According to the last news update, the funeral arrangements were still pending.

Only three people knew about Jessica's carefully orchestrated confrontation and one of them was now dead. For the first time in her life, Jessica was concerned her fate was beyond her control. Fully aware that if Jonathan succeeded with his threat someone needed to know the facts, Jessica struggled with the decision of who to trust. Her mother had been an unknowing accomplice which made her the logical choice. Given her mother's history with married men, Jessica knew her mother would be less judgmental than her only other option, but Kendra was the one she needed immediate help from.

Every time Jessica picked up the phone to call Kendra, fear that her revelation would strike the fatal blow to their friendship halted the action. By late afternoon, she decided to face the inevitable. She was willing to fight Jonathan unto death but Simone had to be spared. Kendra had to know. Simone might need her very soon. Shortly after Simone was born, Jessica made a will. At the time, Kendra agreed to be Simone's legal guardian in the unlikely event of Jessica's death. Jessica looked at her will while waiting for Kendra to answer, hoping she would honor the commitment now that the unlikely was highly probable.

When Kendra saw the name on the caller ID, she picked up the phone excited to get an update on their trip. "Hey! How was Disney World?"

Jessica forced energy into her voice hoping to mask any tremors. "It was okay. How are you doing?"

"I'm doing much better, physically and emotionally. The doctor wants me to stay in bed for the next six weeks. Then they'll do another ultrasound. Right now, I'm just so thankful that there's been no more bleeding!"

The bed rest requirement made Jessica wonder if Kendra would be physically capable of caring for Simone. "That's good… about the bleeding." She paused needing time to revive her courage. "How are Eric and the boys handling you being in bed all the time?"

"They're doing fine. Ruby stays with us during the week. On the weekend, Eric gets to take over."

"That's good. You deserve a break…"

"So what's wrong…I can hear it in your voice," Kendra said.

Despite several hours of procrastinating, Jessica struggled to find suitable words. "I don't know how to tell you…"

Kendra picked up the remote and turned off the television. "Is Simone okay?"

"She's fine…She's staying with a friend for the weekend."

"Then what is it?" Kendra waited.

"I'm afraid to tell you, especially given your situation."

"Don't worry about me, what's up with you? Just please tell me it doesn't have anything to do with you know who, unless it's over."

Kendra's tone unnerved Jessica even more. Her emotions surged at the reality of losing the one constant in her life. Tears flowed down her cheek as she whispered her confession. "I really messed up this time and need your help."

"That depends on what you need…"

"Are you still willing to take Simone, if something happens to me?

"Of course…Jessica, are you sick? Is it cancer?"

"I wish it were that simple." Jessica regretted the words as soon as they left her mouth. "I'm sorry. I didn't mean to trivialize cancer. I meant to say that I could handle being sick." Jessica took a swig of the vodka for courage. "First, let me say that you were right…you're always right…but I was just too stubborn to listen. This time I wish I had."

Kendra prayed that Jessica was only drinking water. "I don't care about being right. What's going on…You're scaring me."

"Jonathan wants to kill me…and I think he might succeed."

"Will you stop joking? The man's many things, but I doubt murderer is one of them."

Jessica remembered the deranged look in Jonathan's eyes when her actions were only a threat. How he planned to murder her was the only uncertainty. "Kendra, I did something that I probably shouldn't have and now Jonathan blames me for what happened."

Kendra rolled onto her side. Hearing his name caused anger to pulsate through her. "Jessica, please tell me you didn't call his wife?"

"Worse, I went to see her…"

Momentarily forgetting her physical restrictions, Kendra sat up in the bed. "You did what?" she yelled.

Jessica's stomach burned from the alcohol, stress and lack of food. "I went to see her…while they were on vacation…in Orlando." She remembered the expression on Lori's face after seeing the pictures and could no longer stand. She lowered herself to the floor, careful not to spill her drink.

"Jessica, no…please tell me you didn't do that."

"…It gets worse."

Kendra closed her eyes and rubbed her temples. "How could it possibly get worse?"

"His wife and children are dead. They were killed yesterday in an accident driving back to Atlanta."

Kendra bolted from the bed in disbelief.

The silence continued until Jessica couldn't take it any longer. "Are you still there?"

Kendra resisted the urge to hang up the phone. "Yes…"

"Go ahead and say it…You told me to leave him alone."

Movement in her womb reminded Kendra of her first obligation. She returned to the bed and adjusted the pillows behind her back before continuing. "Why wasn't he in the car with them?"

Jessica downed the contents of the glass before continuing. "…because he was in Chicago."

"He *left* his family in Orlando to go to Chicago with *you*?"

"Well, he really didn't have a choice. I gave his wife a ticket for him and she made sure he was on the plane. Everything was going according to the plan, until now. He called me last night. His exact words were 'I'm going to make sure you get what you deserve.' Kendra, I'm really scared."

"You should be! What were you thinking? You don't need to answer that…It's what you're always thinking about…*you*…no one else matters. Now, five people are dead thanks to you. You wanted Jonathan and now you've got him."

The harshness of Kendra's words stung but Jessica knew that Kendra was right. If she and Jonathan could survive this, their relationship might still have a chance. "I never thought about it that way."

"Jessica, I tried and failed... I'm done...I've got my own family to think about. You need to get on your knees and beg God for forgiveness right now. He's the only one that can help you."

"I don't need another lecture. I need to know that Simone will be taken care of."

"Simone will always be welcomed in our home."

The tension in her shoulders relaxed knowing she could still count on Kendra. "I'm really sorry..."

"Sorry about what? Besides, you're telling the wrong person."

"Do you think God could forgive me for this?"

"Why? Does the reality of burning in hell finally get your attention? Maybe you should have considered that a little earlier. But for the record, yes, God is able to forgive you."

"Will He?" Jessica asked suddenly needing to know.

"That's between you and God. I've got to go."

The thought of losing both her daughter and her only friend triggered a fresh flow of tears. "Kendra, if I don't talk to you again, thanks for being a friend. Besides the birth of Simone, getting you for a roommate was the best thing that ever happened to me."

"Jessica, take care of yourself."

Jessica slowly lowered the phone from her ear feeling very alone. There was only one thing left to do.

***

Saturday evening, Sharon sat at the breakfast counter, with the phone in speaker mode, drinking a glass of iced tea while Kendra spewed the unfathomable details of her best friend's effort to steal another woman's husband. Her concern for Kendra's health far outweighed any sympathy for Jessica. When Kendra finally reached the point of asking for advice, Sharon verbalized what she had been thinking since their weekend trip.

"Kendra, maybe it's time you let Jessica handle her own problems. She seems pretty determined to do things her way. If you get in her boat, you'll just sink with her."

"Eric said the same thing, in slightly different words. I'm just so conflicted. It's hard to turn my back on Jessica after all we've been through together. Do you think he'll really try to kill her?"

"The man's not thinking clearly, assuming he ever was. He just lost his entire family. His first priority will be burying his family. After the shock wears off and he has time to calm down, he'll realize he has just as much to lose as Jessica, if their affair comes to light. Remember, he's equally responsible for what she did."

"What if he isn't capable of thinking rationally? Remember, he had no problems getting involved with a married woman and then carried on the adulterous affair for years."

In Sharon's opinion, Jessica and Jonathan were getting just what they deserved but she could not say that to Kendra. "Even if he goes after Jessica, what can you possibly do about it? Are you willing to risk your own children's lives to stand guard? Jessica has taken enough lives. Don't add two more to her tally."

"But I can't just lie here and do nothing…she's my friend."

"Yes, you can. You should seriously consider the type of friends that you want. God picks our families, but he leaves it to us to pick our friends. It seems like you and Jessica have taken totally different paths in life. You said she didn't want anything to do with God."

"But she's like a sister to me. I've got to do everything I can. God put us together for a reason. I'm sure of that. She's not ready to die!"

Sharon thought about the witches in the Wizard of Oz and visualized a house falling on Jessica. "There's nothing you can do to save her. That's totally up to God." Sharon seriously doubted that Jessica was one of God's chosen, but for Kendra's sake she wanted to offer a sliver of hope. "Have you considered that your 'help' might interfere with God's plan for Jessica? Some people have to hit rock bottom before God can get their attention. At this point, the best thing you can do for Jessica is pray."

***

Sunday morning, Jonathan tried in vain to mentally prepare for the onslaught of grieving family and friends. He had spent most of Saturday in Orlando arranging for the bodies and luggage to be flown home and collecting the various reports for the insurance companies. Their decision to decline insurance through the rental car agency meant that he would have to file the claim with his own insurance. Saturday night, he was on the last flight to Atlanta. During the flight, he looked at the accident report with photos of the crash site and wondered what his wife's dying moments were like. From the report, he learned that Lori had remained conscious long enough to tell rescuers that there were four children. Beyond that, the report raised more questions than it provided answers. Walking into the empty house late that night was tortuous. Everywhere he looked was a painful reminder of all he lost. He turned off the entry light preferring the darkness. Unable to go upstairs, he sat in the family room for hours before finally going upstairs to shower and change clothes.

With the sun up, natural light filled the house. He walked from room to room trying to feel their presence. The internal rage was momentarily being controlled. He could not destroy what Lori had lovingly created. Nothing was out of place. For years, Lori had insisted that they leave the house clean when they went on vacation. He suddenly wondered if she knew what could happen. When the doorbell rang, he opened the door without hesitation.

A microphone was thrust towards him by a young man Jonathan recognized from the news. "Mr. Grey, can we ask you a few questions about the accident?

An older man stood directly behind him with a video camera. The shift from watching the news to being the news was terrifying. "What are you doing here?"

"Our affiliate station contacted us. What can you tell us about the accident?"

Jonathan pushed the microphone away and took a step back. "I'd rather not talk about this now."

"Have any arrangements been made?"

"NO..."

"Why weren't you with your family?"

The rage Jonathan struggled to control was unleashed on the reporter. The shove sent him flying backwards into the cameraman "Leave me alone!" Jonathan yelled as he slammed the door.

He pressed against the closed door, barricading it. His breathing accelerated as he wondered how he could face their families knowing that he was responsible. Even if he survived the day, the resulting media frenzy would surely usher in his demise. His manager would want to know what work had required him to leave his family on vacation. Once his affair was revealed, there would be no escaping the consequences. The absence of a gun or lethal medicine in the house limited his options. He was standing in the kitchen with a butcher knife in his hand debating the alternatives of a direct stab to the heart or slitting his wrists, when he heard a knock on the front door followed by the sound of a key being inserted into the lock. Only one person had a key to their house. He dropped the knife on the counter and raced to meet her in the entry way, uncertain of whether he would make her leave or beg her to stay.

Shelia walked past him, not giving him a chance to do either. She carried a tray with two cups of coffee and a bag that emitted the smell of bacon. "I thought you might need some breakfast."

Jonathan followed her. "I wasn't expecting you until after church." She looked like she had not slept for days.

Shelia looked at the knife and was thankful she had followed her instincts. "I wouldn't have been able to concentrate on the service. Besides, I didn't think you needed to be alone."

Jonathan quickly put the knife back in the wood block holder. "You didn't need to come over."

"Looks like I did." Shelia handed him a cup of coffee. "It's black. I wasn't sure how you liked it."

"Black's fine."

Shelia nodded in the direction of the knife. "That would only make the situation worse."

Jonathan sat in his usual seat at the table, unable to look at her. "If you only knew...you'd grab the knife and do it for me."

Shelia sat at the other end of the table. "I do...Lori called me Thursday night and told me what happened."

Jonathan felt both guilt and relief. "How did she sound?"

"She was really upset."

"Was she upset enough to kill herself and our children?"

Shelia pondered the question she had wrestled with in the initial moments of grief. "Lori loved her children and, as much as it pains me to admit it, she loved you too much to do such a thing. This was definitely an unfortunate accident."

"Then how do you explain the kids not having on their seatbelts? You know how she was about seatbelts."

"Knowing Lori, she probably felt guilty about getting them up so early and wanted them to be comfortable. I'm sure that as soon as they woke up, the seatbelts would have been on. I just wish I had insisted harder on flying down to drive back with her. Maybe if I had, this wouldn't have happened."

Jonathan sighed. "I should have never left her."

"That's an understatement of epic proportion, but it's too late to change that decision or anything in the past. Right now, we need to focus our energy on the funeral arrangements. Promise me you won't do anything foolish until after your wife and children are laid to rest."

"Why are you doing this? Especially, since you know the truth."

"Lori was closer to me than my sister. Despite what I'm feeling towards you right now, I know that Lori would want me to help you. But don't be mistaken; I'm doing this for her, not you."

He appreciated her candor. "Did you see the reporter? Once the truth's out, how will I face anyone?"

"Jonathan, that's the crux of your problems. You only think about yourself. Did you even know how hard these last few years were for Lori? You were always gone, leaving her to take care of everything at home. Do you know that she constantly felt guilty for not contributing more to the family finances? She thought that maybe if she worked, you wouldn't have to work so hard?" Shelia reached for the bag and took out a breakfast sandwich. "The irony is that you weren't working that hard after all."

"I don't need to feel any worse."

"Oh yes you do because obviously you're still only thinking about yourself." Shelia removed the wrapping and inspected the sandwich before putting it back on the table. "Lori had an interview for a job next week. She intended to tell you, if she got an offer." Shelia shook her head in disgust. "She really thought a job would fix all your problems."

"How did I let things go so wrong?"

"Maybe it's time for you to make things right. It's the least that Lori deserves."

Jonathan knew there was nothing he could do to make things right. Lori was gone. His children were gone. But justice would be served. Jessica would get what she deserved then maybe Lori could rest peacefully. "Yes, it is."

"How did Lori's parents take the news?"

"Stick around and you can see for yourself." Jonathan looked at the clock. "They should be here in a few minutes. I wish they weren't coming."

Shelia stood up. "Maybe I should make a pot of coffee. It's going to be a long day."

***

Sunday afternoon, Kendra watched Eric from the window in the family room. The chaise lounger purchased so she could recline on the deck while he grilled sat empty. She lasted barely thirty minutes in the afternoon heat before retreating to the sofa and air conditioning. A bellow of smoke escaped the grill when he lifted the lid. The matching chef hat and apron purchased on a whim at an end of summer sale was intended to be a gag gift, but to her amazement Eric loved it and so did their sons. He wore the hat with pride from the moment he started the grill until the last piece of meat was removed. After church, her father came bearing gifts for his grandsons. He dashed past the window holding Danny while being chased by Joshua with his new water gun. It was difficult to tell who was having more fun.

When Eric brought in the first batch of meat, the smell left a trail that Kendra could not resist. She followed him into the kitchen.

He gave her a disapproving look. "What are you doing up?"

"I thought you might need a taster."

"I've already tasted it, but thanks for the offer," he said with a teasing smile.

"Look mister, if you don't give me a sample, I'll have to get it myself."

He opened a drawer and retrieved a knife and fork. "This is so good that I don't think you can handle just a sample. Not to be bragging, but this is the best I've grilled."

"You always say that."

He sliced a piece off a boneless chicken breast and waved it teasingly in front of Kendra. "And I'm always right."

Kendra grabbed the fork and bit into the chicken savoring every chew. "As much as I hate to admit it, this is really good. What did you do differently?"

Eric covered the meat and put the pan in the oven. "Great cooks never reveal their secrets. Now go lay down. We should be ready to eat in about thirty minutes."

"I'm so tired of lying down.' Kendra sat in a chair. "Thanks for grilling. I know you're just trying to keep my mind off Jessica."

"Actually, I'm cooking enough meat for several meals, but if grilling kills two birds with one stone all the better." He sat next to her reeking of mesquite smoke. "Are you able to keep your mind off Jessica?"

"What do you think?"

"Go lie down. You only have three more weeks of total bed rest. Once the twins get here, you'll be begging to put your feet up."

"Putting your feet up is one thing, staying in bed twenty-three hours a day is another. I finished all the books on my list, television's sucking my brain dry and there's a limit to how long I can stare at the computer screen."

Eric stood up and grabbed his tongs. "Maybe you can take up a hobby like knitting or needlepoint."

Kendra looked at him like he'd lost his mind.

"OK...but there has to be something you can do to help the time pass faster. I'd better turn the meat before I mess up my record of perfection."

The phone rang.

Kendra stood up. "You go back to your grill. I'll see whose calling." The cordless phone was on the floor where she had left it. Waiting for some conformation from God on what to do about Jessica, Kendra was relieved the caller ID was an unknown number. "Hello."

"Hey, is this Kendra?"

The whiney voice was unmistakable. "Hello Stephanie."

"How are you doing?"

Kendra rolled her eyes. "I'm fine...what do you want?" She clamped her mouth shut before adding *besides my husband.*

"I saw Eric and the boys at church this morning."

"Eric said it was a very good sermon. Hopefully, you took notes."

"Well, I just wanted to check on you and see if you or Eric needed anything."

"No, I think we're well taken care of. By the way, thank you for the cookies."

"Oh, Eric told you about them."

"Why wouldn't he?"

"I'm just pleasantly surprised. I don't want to cause any trouble between the two of you."

"Rest assured, that won't happen," Kendra said.

"I'm glad you feel that way because Eric will always hold a special place in my heart. I really hope we can all be friends. In times of trouble, it's nice to have friends you can count on...for whatever he needs."

Her words erased all Kendra's doubt, setting off a blaring alarm. "Stephanie, I don't know if you're just that stupid or if you think that I am. I can't imagine any woman on earth wanting her husband to be friends with someone he's been intimate with. Consider yourself warned—stay away from my husband. If you're a Christian, you'll respect my wishes. If you're not a Christian, consider this...God fights my battles and you're no match for Him. Have a nice day." Kendra hung up the phone without giving her a chance to respond.

Lying on the couch, Kendra thought about Stephanie's statement about friends in times of trouble and Eric's comment about something to keep her busy. It was the confirmation she was waiting for. Despite everything, Jessica was her friend and they needed each other. Before she had a chance to change her mind or be talked out of it by Eric, Kendra called Jessica. When Jessica did not answer her home phone, she tried her cell phone. When the cell phone went to voice mail, Kendra began to worry. She dialed Jessica's home phone number again. While her greeting played, Kendra imagined the worse. After the beep, she struggled to speak. "Jess, it's me…Call me as soon as you get this message."

The ringing phone penetrated Jessica's deep sleep. She rolled over slowly and tried to make out the numbers on the clock. Her vision was blurred and her head felt like it was splitting open. When the fog in her brain cleared slightly, she picked up the phone and pressed the callback button. The faint ringing of the phone was painfully amplified.

Kendra answered immediately. "Hello."

"Hey…"

"Are you okay?"

"Yeah…I was asleep when you called," Jessica said.

"Are you just now getting up?"

Jessica put her arm over her head hoping to dull the pain. "Yeah…what time is it."

"It's almost two."

Jessica tried to sit up but fell back on the bed. "…I'm supposed to pick up Simone at three."

"Have you been drinking?"

The empty bottle on the night stand reminded Jessica that she needed to stop by the store to restock. "What do you think?"

"I think that drinking is not going to help any."

"Well it certainly didn't hurt. I wasn't about to lay awake all night, waiting for Jonathan to bust down the door."

"Are you planning to get drunk every night?"

"I'm taking things one day at a time, for whatever time I have left."

"Would you stop sounding so morbid?"

"How should I sound? One person I love wants to kill me and the other has turned her back on me."

"Jessica, I haven't turned my back on you."

"You sure have a funny way of showing it."

"Look, I didn't call to argue."

Jessica sat on the edge of the bed. "Then why did you call?"

"To see if you and Simone want to come spend some time here."

"How long?"

"How much vacation do you have?"

"Girl, my vacation days are gone but I was thinking about using some of my sick days, since I have over three weeks."

"Let's plan for a week. If you need to stay longer, you can."

"Are you sure? I don't want to cause you any trouble."

"Yes, I'm sure. Go get your daughter and promise me that you won't drink around her."

"I can only promise to try...Kendra, thanks. You doing this means more than you'll ever know."

"Hey, we've been sisters for a long time. I'd never be able to live with myself, if I didn't help you. Call me with your flight information." Kendra hung up the phone hoping the invitation was not a big mistake and that Eric would understand.

***

By Wednesday afternoon, it seemed as if the entire city was mourning the loss of Lori and her children. The grief stricken driver of the tractor trailer came forth, confessing his role in the tragic accident and igniting a firestorm of stories on deaths caused by road debris. Although school was out for the summer, the flags at the children's school were lowered to half-mast and grief counselors were available for both the children and staff. The heart wrenching funeral procession with five hearses drew the attention of even those who had not seen the news coverage. Mid morning traffic came to a halt. The chief of police escorted the procession which was covered by both local and national news. The outpouring of support from so many strangers only intensified Jonathan's guilt.

After the funeral, the traffic congestion moved to their neighborhood. Parked cars lined both sides of the street leaving a single lane for traffic. Many of their neighbors offered their driveways for parking as family and friends flocked to the house to comfort each other. Traffic inside the house was equally congested. Most of the people were still in a state of shock and moved as if in a thick fog. Comfort foods covered every inch of countertop in the kitchen and the dining room table. People crowded every room, eating, crying and reminiscing. The children, many of whom were dealing with the reality of death for the first time, made the absence of his children more prominent. Lori's sister made a video of Lori and the kids capturing happy memories for the service. The last image on the video was the family picture taken in front of Disney's Magic Kingdom. The video played continuously in the family room.

Wandering from room to room, Jonathan struggled to maintain his composure. Although no one had said it to his face, Jonathan knew that both families blamed him for the accident. Conversations abruptly stopped when he walked in the room. He was actually relieved that they only accused him of putting work before family. When they learned the truth, he feared it might lead to retaliation from Lori's family. His mother thought it a blessing that God chose to spare his life.

Jonathan questioned how long the charade could last. Leading the family procession out of the church, he noticed two pews of co-workers. At the cemetery, his manager offered his condolences and told him to take as much time off as he needed. To Jonathan's relief, his manager did not have time to inquire further about the nature of the work emergency. Shaking his hand, Jonathan knew that he would never see his manager again. The sound of his children's voices coming from the family room exceeded his ability to endure. With his car trapped in the garage, the backyard was his only means of escape. Although the yard was filled with memories too, he hoped they would be silent. No one noticed him slip outside.

After saying goodbye to the people she knew, Shelia looked for Jonathan. She found him sitting on the ground with his elbows resting on his knees beside the tree. Stopping a few feet from him, she gently touched a branch. "Do you remember when Lori planted this?"

"How could I forget?" Jonathan shook his head remembering the day he lugged the tree around the yard while Lori and Shelia tried to decide the perfect location. Almost six years had past and the tree had grown several feet, yet the memory was still vivid. It was before Lori got pregnant, again, with Jason. "I was ready to make one of you dig the hole. She made such a big deal about this stupid tree."

Shelia looked towards the kitchen window. "It wasn't just a tree. She wanted to surround herself with reminders of the promises of God. The vine wallpaper in the kitchen, the green paint in the family room and the rock fountain in the entry way all had very special meaning for her. But this tree...it was the most important. She wanted it where she could see it everyday."

"Why?"

"In Isaiah 61, God said his people would be called oaks of righteousness."

Jonathan thought about the Pocahontas video that his daughter made him watch with her. The roots of the old tree came to life and snapped at the unwanted intruders. He looked at the tree, certain that given the ability it would chase him away. "Lori was a special woman."

Shelia wiped a tear, knowing her friend's spirit was very much alive but missing her physical presence. "Yes, she is."

"Why she married someone like me, I'll never know."

"She loved you."

The words inflicted another painful cut to his nearly mutilated heart. "One minute, I hurt so badly I can barely breathe. The next minute, I'm so filled with rage that I want to destroy everything around me. But the guilt is the worst feeling of all. How will I ever live with the guilt?"

She put her purse on the ground. "I don't think anyone could."

Jonathan grabbed a fistful of grass. "I know that I'm getting what I deserve, but what about all the other people who loved Lori so much."

Shelia moved into the shade of the tree. "She will definitely be missed. You don't find many people like Lori anymore."

"Then why did God have to take her? She had on her seatbelt."

"God is merciful."

"To who? Have you seen her parents? This just might kill them. Her mother had to be tranquilized to get through the service."

"If Lori had lived and any of the children had died, she would never have been able to forgive herself. She could always forgive others but never herself. God taking her with the children was truly an act of mercy. Knowing Lori, that was probably her last prayer."

Jonathan tried to imagine Lori in the house grieving the loss of even one of their children and consumed with guilt. "You're right. It's probably better this way, for them."

She plucked a leaf from the tree. "Lori loved God more than life itself and God works all things for the good of those who love him."

Jonathan could not see any good in Lori and his children dying and he was getting tired of people talking about God and His will. "Thanks again for everything you did. It was a fitting program."

"It was a nice service." Shelia picked up her purse and carefully put the leaf in it. "Well, I'm going to head out."

Jonathan stood up. "I'll walk you to your car."

"So what are you going to do now?" She asked as they walked slowly across the yard.

"I don't know." Jonathan looked at all the parked cars. "Are you going to be able to get out of here?"

"I parked up the street, so it shouldn't be a problem." She stopped at the end of their driveway and looked him in the eye. "Promise me, you won't do anything rash."

"At this point, I can't promise anything."

She reached for his hand. "Jonathan, Lori was a very good judge of character. Maybe it's time for you to discover what she found in you."

"I think it's too late for that."

"It's never too late," she said.

He pulled his hand away and put it in his pocket. "Just one more thing before you leave. Do you know Lori's email password?"

"No, why?

He could not reveal the real reason. "I want to send an email to everyone in her address book, just in case they don't know."

"No, I don't...but try Romans 8:31. It was her favorite verse."

Shelia left him standing in his driveway. He watched her until she reached her car. She did not look back.

***

The table was set for two with their rarely used china. Sharon was relishing the brief vacation from parenting. Her children were spending the week with their aunt in Memphis. While waiting for Dale to come home, Sharon sat in the family room and watched the evening news for coverage of the funeral. After Kendra called announcing Jessica's visit, Sharon was even more curious to see the man who caused so much pain. The garage door opening squashed the urge to call Jessica to tell her exactly what she thought of her latest actions. Dale walked into the house slower than usual. Each day, he came home looking more dejected.

Sharon walked to the kitchen and hugged him hoping to transfer a little of her dwindling energy. "It looks like you had a rough day at the office?" When he pulled away, she went to the refrigerator and took out the salad.

He dropped his bag on the floor and sat at the center island. "I never realized a minister's work was so political. This makes my old job look like a cake-walk. Aren't Christians supposed to be different from the world?"

Sharon hoped that Dale was being nudged in the right direction. She carried the salad to the table, dreading another long discussion about his job. "What happened now?"

"An emergency deacon board meeting and I wasn't invited."

"How did you find out?"

Dale clenched his hands together. "How do I find out everything at that church?"

Sharon wondered who he wanted to punch this time. "Doris...I guess it helps to have the administrative assistant on your side."

"Something's brewing and it can't be good. Nothing good ever happens in the dark."

"Well, you knew some people weren't happy about your sermons." Sharon wondered if the decision would be made for them.

"I know. Somehow I hoped that since church attendance and giving are up, the board would come around. Deacon Jones has a tighter grip on them than I imagined. It seems things won't ever change. If you don't like the message, get rid of the messenger. It could not be worse timing for Jones to stir up trouble. People are growing mentally and spiritually. They're starting to ask the right questions, which is always a good sign."

Sharon looked at the television. "And they will continue to grow."

"Not if they aren't being fed." Dale looked at the television to see what held her attention. "I thought the news depressed you."

"I'm waiting for the story on the funeral." Sharon returned her attention to Dale, thankful for an opening to change the subject. "Do you think the real story will ever come out?"

"If he carries out his threat against Jessica, it definitely will. Did you call the kids today?"

"Not yet. We can call after dinner." She kept an eye on the television while putting the food on the table. "I did talk with Kendra. Jessica arrived last night, drunk as possible. I wish Kendra would leave Jessica alone before she drags her down too."

Dale stood up and walked to the kitchen sink. "Kendra's doing what she thinks is right," Dale said, washing his hands.

Sharon sat a dish down harder than necessary. "Is it *right* to bring trouble into your own house? That's exactly what Jessica is – trouble with a capital 'T'. What if that man comes after her there? With all the information on the Internet, he could get turn-by-turn directions to Kendra's house. Although I hope he does find Jessica, just not in Texas. Then Jessica could stop hurting others and he could spend the rest of his life behind bars, thinking about the lives he destroyed with his lust. Do you know that this is the third marriage Jessica has destroyed? They say the third time is a charm. I hope they both pay dearly for what they've done."

"I think he already has, but don't forget what the Bible says about grace?" Dale moved out of his wife's path. "Do you need help with anything?"

"No…Those two don't deserve grace?"

"Who does?"

"You know what I mean."

"No, I don't. God decides who receives His grace, not us. In God's sight, we're all sinners."

"But there has to be a difference. All sin is not the same."

"Yes, it is. The consequences may be different." Dale paused. "Unfortunately, none of us are immune to the consequences of sin."

Sharon poured water into their glasses, knowing that if it was up to her, there would be no way either Jessica or Jonathan would escape the burning fires of hell.

***

At Jonathan's insistence, the last group of mourners left the house as the sun rapidly descended. What he needed to do had to be done quickly and without anyone hovering around. Alone in the house, he was drawn to the room where Lori spent most of her waking hours. Looking out the window above the kitchen sink, he noticed her oak tree was central to the view. He swiftly closed the wooden slats and turned his back to the window, hoping to silence Shelia's words about the tree. He leaned against the counter and was confronted by the wallpaper. Leaf covered vines grew upward blending into the grape cluster border.

Closing his eyes, Jonathan imagined his family still with him. He heard his children in the adjacent family room arguing over who should control the television. Lori was at the sink, staring out the window while she washed the dinner dishes. Then he realized that he would be either in his study working or out of town. The new emotion of regret was added to his growing list. He filled a glass with water from the tap and left the kitchen. In the family room, he tried to ignore the bookshelves filled with family pictures that flanked both sides of the stacked stone fireplace. The memories of Jason constantly jumping off the fireplace when he was two, causing Lori to insist he install pipe insulation around the edge, produced a remorseful smile. Everywhere he looked triggered memories, some happy and others sad.

He escaped to the room with the fewest memories of his family. In the safety of his study, he turned on the desktop computer. The last gift Lori had given him sat beside the monitor. It was an eight inch ceramic cross with a metal support frame. He stared at the words on its front, 'One Day at a Time.' While waiting for the computer to startup, he picked up the cross to read the words on the back. The cross was returned to the desk, behind the monitor. Finally, two login icons appeared on the screen. Resisting the urge to check his email first and get diverted from the task at hand, he clicked on his wife's butterfly icon. The password box popped up. He tried every variation of Romans 8:31. When the options were exhausted, he remembered her comment about keeping a password list.

While searching their bedroom an hour later, he found her journal in a dresser drawer. He wondered if Lori was hiding it from him, the children or both. Three-quarters of the pages were filled with his wife's handwriting, yet he never remembered seeing her with the book. An inscription from Shelia was scrawled across the first page—'Merry Christmas to a wonderful woman and friend!' The year under the signature immediately registered. Jessica had called that Christmas night to inform him that he was definitely the father of her unborn child. His anger was unleashed on his pregnant wife. A small slip of paper served as a bookmark. On it was the information that he was looking for. He carried the journal and paper downstairs to the office. The password worked on the first try.

Opening up Lori's email seemed like an invasion of her privacy. The curser hovered over the inbox button while he debated whether to see if his wife had some secrets of her own. The possibility of her watching his every move prompted him to resist the temptation. His only desire was to locate the email that contained the scanned pictures of him and Jessica. If she were watching, he hoped she would get some comfort in him doing what she had only threatened. The perfect punishment for both he and Jessica would begin with exposing their affair. There was no doubt in his mind that they would both be fired. His resignation letter would be attached. After cutting off her source of income, he would ensure that she was never able to destroy another man's life again before taking his own. When he opened the draft folder, it was empty. Wondering if Lori had sent the email before she left the hotel, he quickly opened the sent mail folder. The last sent email went to Shelia the day before they left for vacation. His wife had been bluffing and he could not tell. Picking up the journal, he began to read his wife's view of their life.

**

As soon as Sharon announced her plans, Dale retreated to his office. After a full-day of painting the deck handrails, she needed a warm bath to soothe her aching muscles. An inflated bath pillow and novel waited on the bathroom counter. The lavender tinted bathwater was almost at the air jets. The only thing missing sent her on a quick sprint downstairs. She was in the kitchen pouring fresh-squeezed lemonade into an ice-filled tumbler when the phone rang. The name on the caller ID caused immediate pleasure. There was so much to report since they last spoke and good conversation was better than a book. "Hello stranger!"

Karly sat in her studio surrounded by her artwork. A blank canvas was on the easel in front of her. "It hasn't been that long."

Sharon walked quickly up the stairs, carefully carrying the lemonade. "Long enough. You won't believe what's going on now?"

Karly swiveled on her stool. "Hopefully it's something good."

"Guess what Jessica had the nerve to do?"

"Whatever it is, I'm sure it's not good. I'll pass on hearing her latest shenanigans for now. If you have a minute, I need to discuss something with you. Are the kids around?"

Sharon turned off the water and started undressing. "Nope, this is the week they spend with their aunt. It's just Dale and me. He's working, as usual, so I was just about to get in the bathtub to soak. You have my complete attention."

"Sharon, I've been diagnosed with cancer."

Sharon stopped undressing and sat on the edge of the tub. "What…where…"

"Breast."

"Are they sure?"

"Very. They did a biopsy last week. Two highly recommended doctors confirmed the diagnosis."

"Karly, I'm so sorry."

"Me too."

The phone was silent. Sharon tried to imagine Karly's emotional state and sought the perfect words of encouragement. "It's just so unfair," Sharon said.

"No one ever said life would be fair."

"No, I'm serious. Jessica's wrecking havoc in the lives of others and you get cancer!"

"I wouldn't wish cancer on anyone, even Jessica."

Her surging emotions forced Sharon to start pacing. "That's because you don't know what she's done now! You know that mother and her children who were killed in the accident last week?"

"Yes, it was so sad. Did Jessica know them?"

"Unfortunately, yes. It was Jonathan's wife and children! Apparently, Jessica thought it would be a great idea to tell his wife about their affair while they were on vacation in Orlando. I'll spare you the rest of the details. But if anyone deserves cancer, it's that girl."

"Too bad the decision isn't ours."

Sharon huffed in frustration. "How I wish it was, just this time…Why do the good suffer while the bad seem to prosper."

"That sounds like a very earthly perspective. What's gotten into you?"

Sharon sighed. "I don't know. I guess it's just too much bad news this week. First it was Jessica and Kendra; then Dale came home stressed about some mess at the church and now you."

"Well, don't worry about me. Everything's going to be okay…"

"I'm the one who's supposed to be telling you that. Are you going to have a mastectomy?"

"No, they just removed the tumor."

"Well, that's a good start. What's next, chemo or radiation?"

"Neither."

"Great! That must mean that they caught it early. You're really lucky."

"Actually, I'm not. It's the worst kind of cancer. My odds don't look good, even with aggressive treatment. So I've decided to let the disease run its course."

"Karly…*no*…you can't just give up."

"I'm not giving up, but I want to go out on my own terms. I feel good now. If the experts had their way, I'd be breast-less and lying in a hospital bed quarantined from my children. I have better things to do with the life I have remaining."

Sharon looked at the water in the tub. "How does Ruben feel about this?"

Karly picked at her cuticles. "He thinks I'm crazy."

Sharon wondered if he was right. "What does he think you should do?"

"Fight the disease with everything possible."

"Maybe you should listen to him."

"Sharon, we can't fight God. If this is His will, nothing I do will change it. We all have to die of something."

Sharon felt like the whole world was going mad. "Maybe it's God's will for you to use this battle to witness to others."

"Ever since I found out the type of cancer I have, I've done nothing but think about my options. I want to ask you something and I want you to answer me truthfully. What does the Bible say about the length of our lives?

The Psalm 139 verse which Sharon used so often as evidence for God's divine plan for a person's life took on a different meaning. "It says that all the days ordained for us were written in God's book before one of them came to be."

"And I honestly believe that. I can't add to my days or take away from them, but maybe I can control the quality of them. I'm not committing suicide or acting carelessly. For me, it just came down to who I want to trust."

Sharon looked at the puddle of water forming at the base of the untouched lemonade. "But don't forget that Hezekiah added fifteen years to his life by praying."

"I know, but nothing good came from those extra years. And who said that I'm not praying for God's healing. I hope that you'll pray for me too. But maybe, it's God's will for me to witness to others through my death. Thanks to Momma, I'm not afraid of dying." Karly looked at the blank canvas and saw the image waiting to be captured.

"What about Ruben and the kids? Have you thought about the impact of your decision on them?"

"If my days left on earth are limited, I'd much rather spend them living every minute to the fullest with those I love than lying in a hospital bed fighting the inevitable and causing my family and friends even more pain. The thought of intentionally poisoning my body in the false hope of prolonging my life, especially when I feel so healthy, just doesn't make sense."

"Is there anything that I can say to get you to change your mind?"

"Ruben's already said it."

"How much time do you have?"

"Only God knows that."

"You know what I mean. What are the doctors saying?"

"...Without treatment, six months to a year."

"Oh…"

"Don't sound so glum. They always give you the worst case scenario. Despite what you and Ruben may think, I'm not giving up. Sammy's proof that with God, all things are possible. Miracles happen every day. "

Sharon tried to remember the last time she did a breast self-exam. It had been months. "Is there anything that I can do to help?"

"The best thing you can do is pray for us unceasingly."

"You know that Dale and I will do that. I'll even get my Bible study group to pray for you too. How are the kids taking the news?"

"We haven't told them anything yet."

"Do you think that's wise?"

"They're children. Losing your mother's hard enough. Making them worry about it before they have to is unnecessary and cruel. When the time comes to tell them, we will."

"Oh Karly, why is life so difficult?"

"It's all a matter of how you look at it. Compared to most, I've had it pretty easy. The time that I might suffer here is so insignificant compared to eternity. God's so good and His plan is perfect."

"How can you be so calm?"

"I have a friend who can provide everything I need. Paul was so right about God's power in our weakness. For the first time in my life, I understand what Jesus meant by His peace. It truly does transcend all understanding. I can't explain it, but I just know that everything's going to be okay. Like it says on our currency, 'In God I trust.' What a wonderful privilege."

A knot formed in Sharon's stomach. "It sounds like you're in good hands."

"We both are. I'd better let you take your bath. Tell Dale I said hello."

"I will. Are you sure there's nothing I can do?"

"There is one thing. You can tell Dale about the cancer, but I'd really appreciate it if you don't mention it around the kids. Shawn and Bridgette keep in touch on the Internet and it's hard for kids to keep secrets."

"No problem."

"We're considering a visit to St. Louis this summer. Will you guys be home in August?"

Sharon was thankful for a ray of hope in their conversation. "You just tell me when you're coming and we'll be here. Don't even think about staying in a hotel."

"It will be fun to get the families together again."

"Yes, it will be," Sharon said.

"Well, enjoy your bath."

"I'll try. Call if you need to talk." Sharon hung up the phone irritated by her feelings. Karly was supposed to be the spiritually immature one, yet it seemed as if their roles had reversed. Sharon peeled off her clothes and lowered herself into the lukewarm water. Facing cancer, Karly was willing to place her trust completely in God. Sharon closed her eyes knowing what she needed to do. If Karly could do it, so could she.

CHAPTER 7

FRIDAY MORNING THE ATMOSPHERE WAS CHARGED WITH ENERGY. The clouds followed Dale as he drove east on the interstate towards the church. The seasonal 'sunshine slowdown' caused traffic congestion as some drivers struggled to see past the sun's glare, allowing Dale time to reflect on the irony of the situation. Before him was the glorious sun displaying its splendor, yet his rearview mirror displayed a wall of dark gray clouds. Thankful that he was headed in the right direction, Dale shifted his attention from the weather to his morning schedule. The first item on his agenda was getting Doris' feedback on the sermon so he could finish it before spending the afternoon visiting two hospitalized church members. Doris Brown was the only church administrative assistant. She reminded him of a perfectly toasted marshmallow. Her hard exterior hid a soft, sweet core. A lifetime member of the church, she was approaching sixty but looked much younger despite her silver hair. Dale learned quickly that despite her short statute, she was a powerful force and the perfect test audience. He left her a draft of his sermon with instructions for her to pick it apart.

Dale opened the door to the church offices ready for a lively discussion. "So what do you think of this one?"

"I never knew there was a debate about whose sins Jesus died for, much less the implications. Being a Christian's taking on a whole new dimension. I hate to put a damper on things but someone was in your office last night."

"Are you sure?"

"Unless you came back after I left, I'm sure." Doris put a hand on her hip. "And there's only one other person, besides you and me, with a key to the building."

"Maybe there was another meeting?"

"Nice try, but I doubt if it was held in your office. Pastor, you'd better watch yourself. Deacon Jones was a little too happy when I saw him Wednesday. He's up to something."

"Doris, I leave the watching to God. Whatever's going on, I'm sure we'll find out soon enough. In the meantime, grab your coffee and let's find the holes that need filling in."

Dale and Doris were both flipping through their Bibles comparing verse translations when they heard the squeal of the exterior door opening followed by the over powering voice of Deacon Jones. Dale and Doris instantly looked at each other. Doris rose first shifting her weight carefully.

Dale noticed her grimace. "Are you okay?"

She pointed to the window. "Old bones don't lie. This storm's going to be a big one."

Dale followed Doris out of his office. Deacon Jones and another gentleman were in the senior pastor's office which had been vacant since his death. Doris had tried repeatedly to get Dale to move his things into the office, but he insisted his office served him well. Doris sat at her desk and motioned with her head for Dale to investigate.

He jokingly jabbed the air like a champion boxer warming up, causing Doris to chuckle. He quickly dropped his arms before walking into the office. The conversation between the men ceased.

Dale mustered a welcoming smile. "Good morning, Deacon Jones. What brings you to the church on a Friday morning?"

The other man, who Dale guessed to be closer to twenty than thirty, maintained a forced smile and waited for an introduction.

"Dale, I'd like for you to meet Damon Manis, our new senior pastor."

While Dale's mind tried to process the words that followed the name, an awkward silence filled the office. Damon stepped forward and extended his hand. "Dale, I'm looking forward to serving with you."

Dale accepted the moist hand under the taunting glare of Deacon Jones. Dale quickly withdrew his hand and slid it into his pocket to prevent any real punches. "You were in church Sunday, sitting in the last pew. You left so abruptly that I didn't get a chance to greet you."

Damon cleared his throat and looked at Deacon Jones.

"Damon came to check out our congregation before accepting our offer. Evidently, he liked what he saw because he's graciously accepted."

Dale tried to gauge the spirit of the young man standing before him. He did not want the association with Deacon Jones to cloud his judgment "Damon, where did you go to seminary?"

"I was 'called' as a boy and have been preaching ever since."

The muscles in Dale's stomach tightened. "So you haven't attended seminary." Dale rocked onto the balls of his feet. "What did you get your degree in?"

"The Holy Ghost is my teacher. My father and grandfather, who are both ministers, agreed that I didn't need to go to a university to learn the Word, especially since experience is the best teacher. And I have a lot of experience."

"Apparently," Dale said with a sarcastic smirk.

"Jesus didn't go to college and he's our example," Damon fired back.

Deacon Jones walked to the window. "Good point, my boy. And just like Jesus, you've been groomed from the womb for this position."

"Deacon Jones knows my father," Damon announced.

Dale leaned against the door frame and watched Jones. "I'm sure he does."

Damon looked at Deacon Jones before continuing. "I understand this is your first year in actual ministry."

"Yes, it is," Dale replied.

"Well, I'm sure as my associate pastor you'll learn quickly. I look forward to teaching you everything I know about leading a congregation effectively."

Dale needed to get away before he said something he would regret. "Well, I'm sure you two have a lot to discuss. If you'll excuse me, I need to finish working on Sunday's sermon."

Deacon Jones smiled broadly. "That won't be necessary. This change is effective immediately. Damon will be preaching Sunday. Next week, you'll be informed of your new role should you choose to remain with us."

"Then I guess there's no need for me to hang around today," Dale said.

"Since we're not paying you, I could care less what you do. It's a good thing you didn't move your things into this office." Deacon Jones turned his back to Dale, dismissing him from their presence. "Damon, as soon as you pick out the furniture you want, we'll get it ordered. Now, let's discuss what else you might need."

Dale walked directly to his office ignoring Doris' pained expression. She had overheard the conversation so there was nothing further for him to add. He was rapidly turning the pages of his Bible when Doris rushed in and closed the door behind her.

"Pastor, I know you're not going to let that boy take over this church?"

Dale turned his attention to Doris. "What can I do about it?"

"You can fight it. This whole church, well most of it anyway, will support you."

Dale sighed. "Doris, enough churches have been destroyed by power struggles. That's why there are dying churches on every corner."

"Pastor, that boy is not prepared to lead a Sunday school class, much less an entire congregation. And if he's anything like his father, we're in real trouble."

Although Dale agreed with Doris' assessment, he opted to respond biblically. "Doris, what did Jesus tell us about judging?"

"I'm not judging. I'm just calling it like I see it!"

"Evidently the deacon board doesn't share our beliefs."

"Those deacons are just afraid of you know who. They need some women on that board, 'cause clearly those men don't have good sense or backbones. It's enough to make me quit this job and move my membership."

"And what would that accomplish?" Dale asked.

"I don't know. I can't remember being this mad! Short of going in there and giving that devil a piece of my mind, I don't know what else to do."

"The problem is that we're looking at the situation through human eyes. I have to admit, when I heard the words 'senior pastor', I was livid. But it's God's church, not mine, and who He puts in charge is His prerogative. Although I suspect Damon is just a pawn in Jones' devious plan to get rid of me, he wouldn't be here unless it aligns with God's will." Dale picked up his Bible. "In Ephesians 4.4 Paul says 'As a prisoner for the Lord, then, I urge you to live a life worthy of the calling you have received. Be completely humble and gentle; be patient, bearing with one another in love. Make every effort to keep the unity of the Spirit through the bond of peace. There is one body and one Spirit- just as you were called to one hope when you were called-one Lord, one faith, one baptism; one God and Father of all, who is over all and through all and in all.'" Dale closed his Bible and put it into his briefcase.

Doris shifted her weight. "What's that got to do with that boy in there?"

"Doris, please stop calling him a boy. He's the man who's in charge of this church now."

"We both know that he won't be in charge of nothing. Deacon Jones will make sure of that." Doris watched Dale pack his bag in disbelief. "Are you leaving?"

"Right now, I'm not feeling humble, gentle, patient, or peaceful, so I'm going home. Next week, I'll find out *my new* role and take it from there." Dale grabbed his briefcase, walked to Doris and gave her a hug. "I'll see you Sunday. We'll be in the front row if you'd like to sit with us."

"Thanks, but I'd better sit in the back. Listening to him might make me sick." Doris sadly watched him walk out the door.

The storm clouds hovering over the church released their load the moment Dale slammed the car door shut. Frustrated that his emotions were getting the best of him, he started the ignition and jerked the gear shift into drive. He felt compelled to leave the parking lot before succumbing to the temptation. Impulsive actions had caused too many problems in his past. In his present state of mind, discerning God's Will would be impossible. The fact that the deacon was still standing convinced Dale that the Holy Spirit had intervened. His mind believed the words he told Doris about it being God's decision, but the man in him wanted to help God.

Straining to see the road through the blowing sheets of rain, Dale wondered if the physical world was indeed a weak representation of the spiritual. He turned on the radio hoping to learn the storm's severity. After scanning several stations in frustration, Dale turned off the radio. The noise only made the situation worse. Five minutes later, the storm provided the information he needed as his car was pelted with marble-sized hail. He looked for a place to pull over on the highway. The few underpasses capable of providing shelter were already jammed with cars. The flashing hazard lights along the shoulder of the road served as his guide as he pushed on. Forty-five minutes later, he pulled into his garage. He did not even inspect the car for damage before rushing into the house to share the news with Sharon.

The latest challenge facing them made Sharon rethink the decision not to refill her hypertension prescription. She took her last pill a few hours earlier but doubted that it would last long enough to compensate for her frazzled nerves. Dale was concerned about his ministry but Sharon was concerned about the impact of the church's action on her health.

***

Friday morning, Jonathan waited impatiently for Shelia to arrive. When he called asking her to meet him at the house, the reluctance in her voice was apparent. The call was difficult to make but she was the only one he could trust. After reading Lori's journal, tears streamed down his face for hours. Thoughts of revenge and suicide mixed with his wife's words. The voice he heard that night seemed so real that his ears still tingled. Convinced of what he needed to do, he spent the following day making plans. First, he emailed his manager explaining his affair with Jessica and the events leading to his family's demise. The attached letter of resignation was a futile exercise. As he sent the email, his only regret was that he would not be present when Jessica was escorted out of her plush office where his infidelity had begun. Next, he had his cell phone number changed and the house phone disconnected. The remainder of the day alternated between working in the blistering sun and putting his affairs in order.

Fifteen minutes past the meeting time, he heard a car in the driveway. The garage door was raised and the laundry room door unlocked. Shelia was accustomed to walking into the house without knocking. Her pounding on the door seemed unnatural. He realized that she might be expecting to find his body.

"It's open," he called.

Shelia opened the door and seemed to hesitate before walking in. "Sorry, I'm a little late."

Jonathan walked towards her but stopped abruptly. Since the accident, he was programmed to hug fellow mourners. Certain that being in the same room with the person responsible for her best friend's death had to be difficult enough, he maintained his distance. "That's okay. Thanks for coming."

She noticed the wrinkled clothes which hung loose on his body. It was obvious he had lost a great deal of weight in a very short time. "How are you doing?"

"As well as can be expected, given the circumstances."

"I called before I left, but no one answered."

"The phones are disconnected."

She looked around the room. "So…what do you need?"

He wrestled with where to hold their short conversation. He walked to the kitchen table, pulled out a chair and waited for her to sit before joining her. "I won't keep you long. I'm leaving town…The neighbors have agreed to keep an eye on things, but I didn't want to leave them a key. Actually, you're the only person in the world I trust being in the house now. I hope you don't mind that I gave them your phone number, just in case something happens."

"Not at all." Shelia watched Jonathan closely. "How long will you be gone?"

"At least a month…"

She hung her purse on the back of the chair. "At least? Meaning it could be longer?"

He ignored the questions. "The mail has been stopped and the utilities have been setup for electronic payments. Would you be willing to come by a few times to make sure everything's okay on the inside?"

"What about your job?"

"I'm no longer employed."

She looked frustrated by his lack of information. "Where are you going?"

He knew what she was thinking. "Not Chicago."

"You'll need to do better than that. How can I reach you?"

Jonathan handed her the paper that was in his hand. "This is my new cell phone number."

"Have you told your family?"

He looked away. "I don't have a family anymore."

"Your parents are going to be worried about you."

"I told them that I'm leaving." Jonathan paused. "I also told them everything else. I think they're glad I'm leaving. If I'm not around, they won't have to deal with their failure of a son."

"You can't run away from your problems," she said.

"I know that."

"Then why are you leaving?"

"The main reason is because Jessica will probably show up on my door step, if she can't contact me any other way, especially since she'll be unemployed very soon. And in my present state of mind, it's probably better that I don't have any contact with her. I've hurt my parents enough. They don't need an ugly murder scandal."

"You'll get no argument from me on that. Do you really think she would come to your home...scratch that. Why did you ever get involved with someone like her? Forget, I asked that too. So what's the other reason?"

"I found Lori's journal...By the way, you were close on her password. It was Romans 8:28. Kind of ironic, don't you think?" Jonathan shook his head. "It was like she knew this was going to happen. Anyway, between two entries was a letter to me. She said that if I were reading her journal, something must have happened to her. She tried to assure me that I could be a great father. I guess she couldn't fathom that the kids would be with her and not me." His voice cracked. He closed his eyes and put a hand over his mouth.

Shelia noticed cuts and scratches on his hand, while she waited for him to continue.

"Anyway, Lori asked me to do something and I can't do it here. I've tried but there are just too many distractions, too many temptations, too many memories..."

"What happened to your hand?"

159

Jonathan inspected his hands as if seeing them for the first time. "Lori had been after me for weeks to spread pine needles in the beds. I finally had time to do it yesterday."

"Why didn't you wear gloves? Those cuts could get infected."

"If I'm lucky…"

Shelia sighed. "I know that Lori would not ask you to leave town."

Jonathan thought about the voice he heard so clearly. "In a way, I guess she did."

Shelia looked baffled. "So, when are you leaving?"

"As soon as we walk out the door…everything I need is already in the car. "

Shelia looked at Jonathan. "How far away will you be?"

"Far enough, I hope…"

Shelia stood up. "Is checking on the house all you need me to do?"

"The plants could really use some water and care. They miss Lori too."

"Okay…You have my number and I have yours. Don't worry about things here. Just do whatever it is that you need to do."

"I will." Jonathan stood up and looked around the room. "Well, I've kept you long enough." When Shelia stood up he hugged her tightly hoping to convey the gratitude he felt. When she hugged back, he felt the love that was intended for Lori. They walked out of the house without saying another word.

***

The car was packed lightly but Jonathan's mind was overflowing. He tried to concentrate on the road but kept mentally drifting. One minute he was driving so slow that cars flew pass him. His over correction resulted in a speed significantly over the limit. He wondered if that was what happened to Lori. Was her mind so overloaded that she was unable to pay attention? He set the cruise control and looked for things of interest along the way. The memory of his son Jon reading every billboard on car trips led Jonathan to give it a try. He soon wished he had not. The billboard advertising 'The Biltmore Estate' took him back to the first time he and Lori had stumbled upon the grand manor. During the fall of their first year of marriage, some friends told them about the beautiful autumn colors along the Blue Ridge Parkway. The next Saturday morning, Lori packed the car and told him they were going on a picnic. He remembered her mischievous smile as she dragged him to the car promising an adventure. Everything about their weekend was perfect: the weather, the surroundings and their love. While he stood on the balcony taking a picture of Lori, her hair blew gently in the wind and her face seemed to glow with happiness. At that moment, all he wanted to do was hold her in his arms and never let her go. He thought the day could not get any better but it did. Jonathan learned that afternoon on the balcony of the Biltmore Estate that he was going to be a father. Lori was pregnant with Jon. The picture he took of Lori on the balcony was the one he held the night he heard the voice.

Over the years, Lori talked about them getting a cabin in the mountains but as the family grew, it seemed like an impossible dream. As Jonathan drove north, he thought several times about abandoning his plan despite having already paid for the cabin. The website boasted of being able to enjoy trout fishing, tubing down the river, hiking in the National Forest, all without getting in a car. He just wanted the isolation. Afraid that the memories would be too painful near the Biltmore, he settled on a cabin in northern Georgia at the based of the Blue Ridge Mountains. The cabin was remote but had enough modern amenities to pacify his childhood fears of the outdoors. His one and only camping experience ended traumatically at the age of eleven when a bat flew out of his tent at summer scout camp. Climbing the mountainous roads, he remembered Jon's many pleas to go camping. He tried to remember the last time his son had asked him. Pulling into the grocery store the website recommended, an additional regret was added to the already overflowing list. The final twenty minutes of the drive, Jonathan did not see another car or cabin.

It took several attempts to open the door which had a keypad lock. After unloading the car, he walked onto the back deck. Two rocking chairs with a table in the center waited to be used. A weathered checkerboard hung on the wall above the table. He heard Brianna's voice begging him to play just one more game. At the edge of the deck was a long, raised wooden walkway leading to the river. He envisioned his children racing along the path while Lori hollered for them to slow down. Like a strong magnet, the sound of the river drew him to the walkway, which creaked beneath his weight. With each step, the sound of the river grew louder and his pain sharper. At the end of the walkway was a clearing to the river bank. An oversized hammock was strung between two trees on one side. He closed his eyes and saw Lori lying in the hammock smiling at him while he manned the grill. His children's laughter filled the air as they splashed in the river. When he opened his eyes, the hammock was empty and the only laughter he heard came from the birds.

He walked to the river and scanned the banks. Completely alone, he searched his mind for a reason to exist. Bending down, he picked up a handful of the small rocks that lined the river bank. He remembered his excitement the day his father taught him how to skip rocks. They counted the skips in unison and cheered each time they reached a higher number. Rolling the rocks in his hands, he realized that he would never be able to continue the family tradition. After inspecting the rocks, he selected the flattest one and hurled it towards the center of the river. When the rock skipped four times, darkness filled his soul. In a rapid succession, he threw a rock into the river for each of his children. There was a brief pause after four before throwing a fifth rock for Simone. The river current erased the ripples before they had a chance to form just as he had done to his children's lives. It did not take long for him to realize that he deserved the fires of hell. With nothing left to live for and no one who cared, he was ready to face his punishment. An eternity of suffering seemed appropriate as he stopped at the water's edge, wondering where his body would wash up. One deep breath would end his pain in this life. His focus fixed on the center of the river as he took his first step into the water. The clear cold water quickly filled his shoes. With the next step, his shoes were completely submerged.

"HEY!"

Jonathan turned quickly and saw a man walking towards him.

"You probably should put on some waders. The water's cold this time of year."

Jonathan faced a pivotal decision. He could dart into the river, hoping the stranger would not intervene, or get out of the water. The man looked like the type who would try to save him. Not wanting to put someone else's life in jeopardy, Jonathan walked out of the water in sloshing shoes.

The man approaching him had a scraggily mustache and long brown hair that was pulled into a ponytail. They met in the center of the clearing.

"There's a pair of waders in the cabin, if you didn't bring any," the intruder said, with a relaxed, friendly smile.

Jonathan shoved his hands into his pocket. "Who are you?"

"I'm Sam, the property manager for the owners. Just checking to see if you had arrived and making sure everything was okay."

Jonathan looked towards the cabin. "Everything's just fine."

Sam inspected the hammock and grill. "This is a great location. Usually the owners use it this time of year but something came up at the last minute. I don't know all the details but it must have been major. You're lucky to get it on such short notice. Everything up here usually books years in advance." Sam motioned with his hands. "You can see why. This is truly God's country."

Jonathan walked towards the cabin hoping that Sam would follow him.

Sam was in no hurry. "Are you here by yourself?"

Jonathan walked faster, ready to get rid of Sam and his wet tennis shoes. "Yes."

"We usually get couples and families. You know the cabin can sleep six. There's a futon in the loft."

For a brief second Jonathan contemplated telling Sam the entire story. "It's just me."

Sam recognized all the signs and was glad he decided to check the cabin before doing his other errands. "Sometimes solitude's just what we need in this crazy world. That's why I came up here two years ago. Now you couldn't pay me to leave."

Jonathan walked to the front of the cabin. "Is there anything you need from me?"

"Nope…" Sam waited for the usual questions. When none came, he walked to his jeep. "Well, I'll get out of your hair. If you need anything, my phone number's on the kitchen counter. Hope you enjoy your stay."

Jonathan watched Sam drive down the road before returning to the cabin deck. He paused at the walkway tempted to finish what he had started. Instead he walked to a rocking chair, sat down and removed his wet shoes and socks. Ten minutes later he was asleep.

***

The following Saturday, Kendra sat in the kitchen peeling peaches to make her mother's famous peach cobbler. As soon as she confirmed when Jessica and Simone were coming, she started planning the family gathering. When Kendra looked out the window, Simone and her niece were huddled together giggling. Although the circumstances surrounding their meeting were less than ideal, the girls, who were the same age, instantly bonded. The last doctor's appointment confirmed two securely attached placentas and rapidly growing babies but physical activity beyond going to the bathroom and taking a shower were still restricted. This was the first exercise her muscles were getting. She was surprised how quickly her strength had diminished. Eric carried the blanched peaches to the table. At her current rate, the cobbler would not be ready before midnight. In the increasingly beloved kitchen, she wondered if her mother designed every detail knowing that one day her daughter would be the beneficiary of her last project. Thoughts of her mother were interrupted by movement in her womb. Kendra smiled at the reassurance from her mother's legacy growing inside her. "Okay, Kat…"

Jessica sashayed into the kitchen wearing a halter top and low cut Capri pants. "Please tell me you're not talking to yourself."

Kendra noticed the top edge of a tattoo as Jessica passed but suppressed the urge to ask about the new body art certain to raise a few eyebrows. Eric and Caleb would overlook it because they knew Jessica, but her sister-in-law would not be as understanding. Despite the bonding of their daughters, Kendra had serious doubts about their mothers, especially since Jessica's propensity for married men was well known. Neither Jessica's outfit nor the beer she retrieved from the refrigerator would elevate her sister-in-law's opinion of Jessica.

Kendra picked up another peach. "For your information, I was talking to Katherine. She just turned a flip."

Jessica effortlessly twisted the top off the beer bottle. "Are you sure you want to name your unborn daughter after your mother? Your daughter may need her own identity. And what makes you think it's not the boy doing the flipping?"

Kendra smiled remembering the image. "You should have seen her on the last ultrasound. She looked like she was running on a treadmill. For the record, Katherine's name was decided before she was even conceived. Besides, you named your daughter after me."

"I rest my case." Jessica leaned against the counter and took a swig of her beer.

"Well it's too late for either of us to change our minds. Will you help with these peaches, so I can get the cobbler in the oven before we eat dinner?"

"No, but I'll watch you," Jessica said.

"Some friend you are." Kendra picked up a large peach that almost shot from her hands. "I thought you were going to cut down on the drinking."

"I am. It's just a beer."

"It's still alcohol. You're setting a bad example for the children."

Jessica tipped the bottle up to her lips and drained its contents. "Happy?" She ceremoniously put the bottle in the trashcan.

"I'd be happier if you'd stop drinking all together."

"Well, that's not likely to happen anytime soon."

Kendra pointed to the extra paring knife on the table. "Have you heard from him again?"

"No…and my neighbor said that he hasn't been around." Jessica washed her hands in the kitchen sink before sitting down at the table and grabbing a peach. "I'm worried about going back so soon…that damn manager of mine. You'd think he could handle things for a couple of weeks."

"You know I'll be praying for you."

Jessica carefully peeled the skin off the peach with manicured nails. "My mother thinks I should get a gun. The more I think about it, the better it sounds. I'd get one here, if I could get on the airplane with it."

"A gun? Girl, don't do that."

"Look, you handle things your way and I'll handle them mine."

"Handling things your way is what got you in this mess."

"Look, do you want some help with these peaches or not?"

Kendra decided it was best to stay on neutral ground. "How's your mother doing?"

"You know her…She's staying at my place for the 4th of July weekend. It's the Taste of Chicago and she likes to be in walking distance of all the action."

"She's probably concerned about you, too."

"Don't make me laugh! You know what she said when I told her about this situation with Jonathan?" Jessica lifted her noise in the air. 'You made your bed, now take it like a woman.'" Jessica slumped back into the chair. "...so much for concern." The peach slipped out of her hands and hit her cleavage before landing in her lap. "Look what I get for trying to be helpful...Now, I need to change clothes."

Kendra chuckled. "Shucks...this time could you put on something more suitable for a family gathering. I don't want my brother getting into trouble with his wife."

Rinsing her hands, Jessica looked over her shoulder. "Maybe I can borrow some of your clothes, since you'll never get back in them."

CHAPTER 8

JESSICA SCHEDULED THE APPOINTMENT TO HAVE HER NEW security system installed during her truncated time in Dallas but waited until Monday morning to inform her manager that she would be a few hours late for work. Pressed for an exact time, Jessica barely masked her irritation. Walking into her office, her irritation was quickly replaced by fear. Two uniformed guards were waiting with her manager, who was holding a manila file folder. She suspected that he was sitting in her chair until he heard her coming. Jessica walked past the guards and sat her purse and briefcase on the desk fully aware that all eyes were on her. The expression on her manager's face was easy to recognize. She had seen it often but not from people like him. After an awkward greeting, he suggested they go into a conference room under the guise of privacy.

Before she could sit down behind the closed door, he placed a copy of Jonathan's email on the table and asked if the information was correct. The blood drained from her face as she read. Finding suitable words to respond was impossible. All she managed was a nod of confirmation, to which her manager responded by opening the folder and handing Jessica her signed employment agreement. A short paragraph, stating that immoral or unethical conduct were grounds for immediate termination without severance, was highlighted. Her manager held the door open and she followed him to her office in stunned silence. The fact that she was given ten minutes to pack her personal belongings under the close supervision of her ex-manager and security seemed ridiculous to her. People had affairs everyday yet she was being treated like a criminal. The public humiliation of being escorted from the building by the guards only fueled her anger. The reaction of the few individuals she passed in the hall confirmed that details of her firing had been leaked, adding to her humiliation.

Jessica sat in her car for thirty minutes, hyperventilating from anger. When her breathing approached normal, she devised her plan for revenge. The trip to the gun shop moved to the top of the priority list. After a quick background check, expedited by blatant flirting with the shop owner, a thirty-five millimeter handgun was placed in her hand. The fact that she did not know how to use the gun kept her from returning to her office to kill her manager then driving to Atlanta to finish the job. The lingering hope that Jonathan would forgive and marry her once he got over his grief vaporized the moment she read the email. He belonged with Lori and his children.

The firing range had few customers the morning of the fourth of July. After her first shooting lesson, Jessica waited anxiously for Jonathan to show up so she could claim self-defense when she killed him. She was anxious to complete her last lesson while her mother was willing to watch Simone. With no prospects for another job, Jessica could not justify the cost of summer camps. Despite Chicago's size, the details of her firing spread like a wild fire within the network of hiring managers. In the past, men would jump at the chance to work with her. Despite her best efforts, she could not even get passed the company gate keepers. The swift arrival of the rejection letters left her few options. Although she loved the city, she came to terms with the fact that relocation might be necessary.

As soon as she unlocked the gun's safety, Jessica relished the power and vented her frustration with the people who had contributed to her present situation. The instructor commented several times on her accuracy. Jessica chose not to share her inspiration. At first she thought he was flirting when he said someone with her looks and marksmanship would make a great F.B.I. agent. Although he was not her type, she decided to talk with him for a while. When he learned she was unemployed, he gave her the name and phone number of a friend who was high up in the Bureau and even offered to call him the next day for her.

Walking to her car, Jessica was more excited than she had been in years. Before she left Dallas, Kendra reminded her that when one door closed another always opens. Her adrenaline peaked as her imagination raced towards the proverbial door cracking open. Not only was she ready for Jonathan but an exciting new career loomed before her. If she was good enough for the Federal Bureau of Investigation, she decided to also check out the Central Intelligence Agency and the Secret Service. The prospect of traveling around the world at the government's expense while being constantly surrounded by fearless men trained to take charge had her anxious to get home. Scenes from 'Mission Impossible' and 'James Bond' movies filled her mind. She regretted promising her mother that she would go to the Navy Pier. Surfing the Internet for details on agencies that needed women like her would be a much better use of her time. Jessica thought about Kendra and wondered what she would think about the career change. Knowing that her mother did not like to be kept waiting, she was reaching in her purse for her cell phone, when she heard the shot.

***

By early afternoon, the church picnic was coming to life. Dale joined Sharon under a large Ash tree. After two hours of nursing the grilles and breathing smoke, he understood why few volunteered for the task. Taking on tough jobs that others did not want had been foundational to his former career success. Gospel music blasted from speakers, as church members mingled within their rigidly formed alliances. As Dale suspected, the selection and hiring of the new senior pastor divided the congregation. Despite the division weighing heavily in his favor, he knew that a house divided could not stand. Anxious to restore unity and get everyone's focus back on God, he hoped food and fellowship would be the perfect solution. Since the fourth of July fell on a Wednesday, he casually suggested moving the annual church picnic up a month to combine celebrating the freedom in Christ with the country's freedom from unjust rule. Damon ran with the idea.

Watching him work the crowd, Dale realized a big part of him wanted public credit for the change.

Sharon clutched a half-empty bottle of water. Their children had disappeared as soon as they arrived. Sharon scanned the grounds looking for them. When she spotted Damon, she diverted her eyes. "I don't know how you can watch him taking credit for all your work."

Dale wondered if his thoughts were that obvious to others.

"It's just not right. He's nothing but Jones' little puppet. If it weren't for your Bible study, this church would be losing members left and right. Did you notice how many people left before he even preached last Sunday?"

Dale retrieved a bottle of water from their ice chest. "Yes, and so did Damon. It took several minutes to regain his composure." He removed the cap and took a long swig before continuing, trying to wash away the deeply rooted feelings. "Hopefully, I can put an end to that kind of behavior. We need to be patient until he finds his footing."

"And what if he never does?"

"Let's try to be optimistic about the situation."

"It's hard to be optimistic listening to his gibberish. After last Sunday's sermon, if you could call it that, I wonder if he even knows what the gospel is."

"The same could have been said about me a few years ago."

Sharon pursed her lips. "But you weren't trying to teach others and he's so full of himself. Do you know that I actually started counting how many times he said 'I'? I gave up after thirty, and he'd barely spoken ten minutes."

He was tempted to remind his wife about Jesus' parable of the speck and the log, but he was not immune. After the initial shock of his demotion had subsided, Dale re-read all of Jesus' parables searching for divine wisdom. "Once he finds God's bearings, he'll be just fine." Dale hoped he was right.

"Let me guess. You're going to be the one to point him in the right direction."

Dale looked at Sharon's eyes and was concerned. "Are you feeling okay?"

"I'm just not as young as I used to be. The heat gets to me quicker."

Dale noticed that she avoided looking at him. He feared his situation was impacting his wife's health. "How's your blood pressure?"

"Will you stop worrying about me? You have enough on your plate…It's ironic that the two things that drove you crazy at your old employer followed you into ministry—people taking credit for other people's work and incompetent leadership."

"Since it followed me, maybe I'm the source of the problem."

Sharon rubbed her neck. "You're definitely not the problem."

"I don't know. I've always wanted the credit for my work and openly questioned the competence of others. Both reek of pride."

Sharon grabbed his hand and held it tightly. "You're not the same man I married."

Dale raised her hand to his lips and kissed it. "Is that a bad thing?"

Sharon spotted Damon coming in their direction and released Dale's hand. "Speaking of bad things, here comes one now."

Damon stopped a few feet from them. "Good afternoon."

Sharon forced a cordial smile. "Dale, I'm going to check on our children."

"Don't leave on my account," Damon said.

She left without replying and walked toward the church building. Dale looked at him expectantly.

"I didn't mean to interrupt your conversation."

"You didn't." Dale rubbed his chin. "Have a seat."

Damon looked at the chair vacated by Sharon. He sat in a different one, in case she returned. "It looks like a good turn out."

"This is the first one I've attended. Doris could probably give you a better gauge on the success. You should ask her."

Damon shook his head quickly. "I don't think so. It's no secret how she feels about me."

"Don't take it personally. The circumstances surrounding your hiring ruffled her feathers."

"I didn't have much to do with that." Damon clasped his hands, propping his elbows on his knees.

"Doris has a heart of gold and a spirit to match. Give her time to adjust. It's only been a few weeks." Dale watched Sharon enter the building. Something other than him losing his leadership position was bothering her. "A great lesson to learn before you get married is tread with care around women when emotions are involved."

"My mother taught me that lesson early, which may be why I'm not married yet."

"You're still young. Take your time."

"Tell that to my father. According to him, I should have been married a long time ago. He believes that a respectable pastor needs a respectable wife." Damon paused. "Maybe, he's right. You and Sharon are held in high regard by the congregation."

"The apostle Paul says that it's better for a man to remain single, unless he lacks self-control. Unfortunately, in today's culture even marriage doesn't seem to help." Dale propped an elbow on the arm rest. "How old are you anyway?"

"I'll be twenty-five next month." Damon wiped a bead of sweat from his forehead. "I thought you already knew everything about me."

"I prefer to get my information from the source. It tends to be more accurate." Dale noticed Damon's obvious discomfort. "You should've worn shorts. It's much too warm for long pants."

"At my age, I have to be very careful to maintain a professional image in public."

Dale smiled at his candor. "Image will only take you so far." He opened the ice chest beside his chair and handed Damon a bottle of water.

"Thanks…You're nothing like Deacon Jones described to my father and me."

Dale raised an eyebrow, curious to hear the deacon's public assessment of him. "Really…how did he describe me?"

Damon tilted the water bottle to his lips and took a sip before answering. "You're better off not knowing." He looked Dale directly in the eyes. "Why haven't you left the church yet? I think that's what Deacon Jones was counting on and probably the only reason he hired me."

"Do you want me to leave?"

"Not really. If you did, most of the congregation would probably follow you."

Dale looked at the diverse group of people around him. Some were third-generation members and others still referred to themselves as visitors but they all belonged to the same God. "That's why I'm still here. Splitting the flock is not God's will. It makes it too easy for the wolves." Dale noticed him watching others.

When a group looked in their direction, Damon instantly smiled. "This is a complicated situation. The congregation is obviously biased against me and prefers your style of preaching."

The way he turned on and off his smile annoyed Dale almost as much as his statement. "Damon, what this congregation needs is teaching, not preaching regardless of the style…There's a definite difference." Dale turned in his chair. "The aim of preaching is to elicit an emotional response. Teaching, which provides knowledge or insight, aims to permanently change behavior. We're to preach the gospel of Jesus Christ to the lost and we're to teach those who respond how to be disciples of the one true God. Look closely at Jesus' final instructions to his disciples. It's not complicated. We, you and I," Dale dramatically pointed to Damon and himself to add emphasis, "are to make disciples of Jesus Christ and teach them how to obey God's commandments."

"Do you have the Bible memorized?"

"Even if I did, which for the record I don't, don't be impressed by someone's ability to quote scripture." Dale wondered if Damon had missed the point he was trying to make. "Satan and his demons know the Bible, word for word, and recognize Jesus' authority without hesitation." Dale paused wondering how far to take the conversation. "Have you started the book I gave you?"

"No, I mentioned it to my father. He said it was a waste of my time."

"Damon, you're the leader of this church, not your father. It's time you start making your own decisions. A very wise man sent me the book with a note encouraging me to read it. Trust me. The book is not a waste of your time."

Damon spotted his father's car pull into the parking lot. "I need to go greet my father. He's excited about the prospects of a collaborative outreach with this church." He stood and held up the bottle. "Thanks, for the water."

"You're welcome," Dale said.

Damon took a few steps then turned back to Dale. "I'll start the book tonight."

Doris passed Damon as she rushed towards Dale. "You need to check on Sharon. I think she might need to go to the hospital!"

***

By Friday morning, Kendra was a bundle of nerves. The numerous messages left for Jessica, both on her cell phone and at her house, were not returned. Suspecting the worse, Kendra watched every newscast and searched all the Chicago media websites. If Jonathan had managed to take revenge, Kendra was certain that it would receive heavy press coverage. There were several murders but none of the victims fit Jessica's description. Before leaving for work, Eric tried to reassure Kendra to no avail. Ruby made some tea and encouraged Kendra to do the one thing capable of making a positive difference. Kendra was on her knees pleading with

God to protect her friend when the phone beside her rang. An audible sigh of relief escaped when she saw Jessica's home phone number on the display.

"Girl, don't you ever scare me like this again."

"Kendra," the voice sounded tired but familiar. "This is Liz. I just listened to your messages and decided to call."

"Is Jessica okay?"

"There's been an accident. I've been at the hospital for the last two days and just came in to take a shower and change."

"What happened?"

"Jessica was at the firing range Wednesday morning. Simone and I were waiting for her to go to the Navy Pier."

"Firing range! What was she doing there?"

"The usual…learning how to shoot her new gun."

Kendra imagined Jonathan lurking around a corner waiting for his opportunity to strike. "Was Jonathan involved?"

"No, no. She hasn't heard from him, even though she tried to contact him after she got fired from her job."

"Wait. She was fired?"

"Yes, the day after she came from visiting you. I thought she told you."

"No, she didn't." Kendra felt betrayed after all her efforts to help. "Will you please tell me what happened to Jessica?"

"Evidently, some kid wasn't paying attention to what he was doing in the parking lot. The stray bullet hit her." Liz paused to take a drag of her cigarette. It was the first cigarette that she had smoked in her daughter's home. "He wasn't even aware that anyone was hurt…thankfully someone saw Jessie fall…"

Kendra waited, still on her knees. "Liz, what's the number at the hospital? I want to call to talk with her."

"You can't."

"What do you mean I can't?"

Liz looked around for something to put the ashes in. She walked to the coffee table and dumped the candy out of the crystal dish. "Kendra, she's in a coma."

Kendra dropped from her knees and sat on the floor. "She's going to be okay though?"

"I hope so...but right now she's in critical condition with swelling in the brain. They didn't expect her to make it through the first night."

"Oh God, no..."

"If she pulls through, there may be permanent damage." Liz shook her head in despair before filling her lung with more smoke and exhaling. "It's so bad that I don't know if I want her to live or die."

"*Liz*, you want her to live! She has to live. As long as she's alive, there's hope for her."

"You don't know my baby like I do...She wouldn't want to live like that."

Kendra pictured Liz waving her cigarette with manicured nails. "Are you thinking about Jessica or yourself?"

"Both, I guess. The burden will be mine. Frankly, I have no desire to be wiping drool or changing diapers. If you haven't figured it out yet, I'm not the nursing type, not to mention trying to raise another child."

Kendra's heart instantly yearned for Simone, knowing that she must be taking her mother's accident hard. During the visit, Kendra joked with Eric that Simone seemed more like the mother. "Where's Simone?"

"She's at one of her friend's house. She's such a smart child. Do you know that she had memorized the girl's phone number? Anyway, the hospital was no place for a child. When I called her friend's mother and explained the situation, the mother picked Simone up at the hospital Wednesday night. I guess I should call and check on her?"

"You guess?" Kendra wanted to jump through the phone to slap some sense into the woman who was probably responsible for most of Jessica's problems. Knowing what she needed to do, Kendra hoped that God would give her the strength and protection to do it. Jessica and Simone needed someone who cared to get them through the situation. First she would get Jessica out of the hospital and then they would make long-range plans for the move to Dallas until Jessica was back on her feet. All she needed was time and support. "Liz. I'll be there as soon as I can."

"Jessie told me that you're pregnant with twins and on bed rest."

"Don't worry about me; just take care of your daughter until I get there. What's your cell phone number so I can reach you?"

Liz gave Kendra both her cell phone number and the phone number for the intensive care nurses' station. Fifteen minutes later, she was packing her suitcase with one hand and talking with an airline reservation agent, trying to get on a flight, most of which were already overbooked because of the fourth of July travel into Chicago. She decided not to tell Eric her plans until after they were set. Unfortunately, Ruby did not agree with Kendra's strategy. After trying in vain to change her mind about going to Chicago and certain that Kendra was putting herself and the babies at risk, Ruby called Eric at work.

When Kendra heard the garage door opening, she braced herself for a battle. She had been struggling with how to tell him over the phone. Logic told her to wait until she was in Chicago, certain that it would be easier to beg forgiveness than to get permission. Convincing Eric that the situation required immediate action was going to be difficult, especially since it involved Jessica. Her suitcase was packed on the bed when Eric walked into the bedroom. "Let me guess. Ruby called you."

"You should've been the one to call. What are you thinking?"

Kendra rubbed her stomach hoping to calm the twins who must have sensed her anxiety. "Eric, I know you won't understand but I've got to go."

"You're right, I don't understand how you can intentionally put your life and the life of our children at risk for a woman who could care less about anybody but herself."

His blunt honesty hurt. "I'm not putting my life in jeopardy."

"If a placenta separates while you're on the plane, you are."

"The babies and I will be fine. Jessica's in the hospital on the verge of death and that pitiful excuse for a mother is totally incapable of handling things. Do you know that Simone has been at a friend's house for two days and she has not even called to check on her?"

"If it's that serious, I'm sure her mother has been busy."

"And that's not the worst of it. She had the nerve to tell me that she's not sure whether she wants Jessica to live or die. What kind of mother would say something like that?"

"Kendra, I know how much you care about Jessica but flying to Chicago will not help the situation. Jessica would not want you to do this and you know it."

"But if I'm not there, her mother will probably let her die."

"Kendra, that's her mother's decision, not yours. Now unless you have a signed document giving you authority to make the decision, there's nothing you can do."

Kendra lowered her head. "But Eric, she's not ready…"

"Baby, you've got to let it go. You can't save Jessica. God's the only one who can and he really doesn't need your help."

"Please Eric, just let me go. If I don't go and she dies, I'll regret it for the rest of my life." Her eyes conveyed her conviction.

"You probably can't even get a flight into Chicago this weekend?"

"Yes, I can. It's in first class but I don't care about the cost."

Eric closed his eyes. A decision had to be made quickly. "When does the flight leave?"

"Four-thirty."

Eric sighed, knowing what he had to do. "If you can get me a seat on the flight, we can both go. But there's no way I'm letting you go alone."

Kendra hugged Eric tightly. "Thank you."

"But we have to come home on Sunday." Eric stood up. "I'll go see if Ruby can stay with the boys or if I need to call your dad."

As soon as Eric left the room, Kendra grabbed the phone to call the airline. The fact that there was another seat available increased Kendra's hope. Before they left for the airport, she called Sharon to tell her about the accident and asked her to pray for Jessica, their safe travel and protection of her boys while they were gone.

***

Sharon regretted misleading both Dale and her doctor, but she had no choice. Technically, it was not her fault. Dale's insistence on taking her directly to the emergency room from the picnic and subsequent overnight hospital stay forced her back onto medication. Admitting that she purposefully stopped taking it would have created more stress. It was easier to let everyone believe that her elevated blood pressure was solely due to stress. Given the circumstances, she hoped that God would understand her faltering faith especially since she intended to discontinue the medicine again once things settled down. Having to deal with Dale's situation was enough turmoil. Being dragged into Kendra's self-inflicted drama was overloading her system.

Dale was in a meeting when she attempted to relay the information. Doris promised to deliver the urgent message. When Dale called home, he was relieved that his family was alright but too preoccupied for the Kendra update. An hour long conversation with Karly helped Sharon vent her frustrations but generated some serious theological questions. After searching her Bible in vain for the answers, she was more impatient for Dale to come home. Opening the pantry to get a snack launched the overwhelming task of organizing it. The center island was covered with the pantry's contents when Dale finally walked through the door.

He set his briefcase on a chair before giving Sharon a kiss. "It must be really bad to have you cleaning. Where are the kids?"

"Shawn's at the movies with a friend. He believes that I'm making him do too much work. He's not convinced that the original purpose of the summer break was to allow children to help their parents with farm work." Keeping her children productive was proving to be no small task. She was delivering plastic bags for their outgrown clothes when Kendra called. "I don't care what he thinks, I'm not about to let him be lazy all summer. Next year, he's going to summer school." Sharon tossed some outdated cereal into the trash. "Paige's in her room. I can't believe we still had Halloween candy."

Dale searched the counter for the peanuts. "Now that you have my undivided attention, why are you so angry about Jessica being in an accident? Shouldn't you be concerned?" After retrieving the jar of peanuts, he pulled out a chair and sat down.

"I'm concerned, but I'm also mad. Kendra's putting her babies at risk in a last ditch effort to save Jessica."

Dale poured some peanuts into his hand. "Is that what she told you?"

"She didn't have too. Why else would she be going to Chicago in her condition?"

"Maybe she needs to see her friend, who's more like a sister, one more time?"

Sharon tossed another box of cereal in the trash. "Well if you ask me, that's a friendship that should have ended a long time ago."

"It seems that Kendra's showing a great deal of compassion, which is sympathy combined with action. That's what Jesus had for people like Jessica."

"I'm compassionate."

"To those you think deserve it."

The blunt reprimand stung. "Is that how I appear to you?"

"Sorry, I didn't mean to take my frustration out on you. We all need to be more compassionate."

"That's okay. Hearing the truth hurts sometimes." Sharon paused. "Do you think people in comas can hear and understand?"

"I'm more concerned with the hearing of conscious people. But to answer your question, I don't know."

"What about deathbed conversions?"

"What about them?"

"Can people like Jessica when facing death, get a final chance?"

"We all face death every day and get multiple chances."

"You know what I mean, Dale. Are there any examples in the Bible of death bed conversions?"

"There's the criminal who was crucified with Jesus. He believed and Jesus said that he would be with Him in paradise. That's the only one that readily comes to mind."

Sharon wondered how she could have forgotten about the criminal on the cross. "Yeah, but he was still conscious. What about those who are unconscious?"

"There are lots of books written by people who've had near-death experiences. Maybe you should consult with the experts."

Sharon resumed inspecting items before returning them to the pantry. "Being shot seems like just punishment for Jessica's actions. Getting a last minute reprieve from hell seems so unfair, after what she did to that woman and her children."

"To me, it seems merciful...like grace."

Sharon expelled the air from her lungs in frustration. "Okay, okay...God still has some major work to do in me."

"He has 'work to do' in us all. You struggle with the sin of judgment, but I struggle with the sin of pride. Of the two sins, pride's much more dangerous. It always present before a fall. I think that's why God brought Damon to the church. Maybe I was getting too prideful."

"That's not true."

"I've been trying so hard to hear what God's trying to tell me and what He wants me to do."

"And?"

Dale rubbed his head. "I'm still waiting for His answer or maybe that is His answer."

Sharon looked at Dale, wondering if she had missed something. "What's His answer?"

"Wait…"

***

Kendra's brief trip to Chicago increased her concern for both Jessica and her daughter. Two weeks after the accident, the prolonged vigil from Texas was taking its toll. She called the hospital every morning, praying for a miracle but settling for sustained hope. Attempting to be the dutiful mother, Liz brought Simone for daily visits. Everyone who worked in the unit was charmed by the little girl with a big heart who often brought treats for the people taking care of her mother. The doctor's inquiry about Jessica's final wishes prompted Liz's search for a will.

Kendra was spreading peanut butter on a bagel when the phone rang. Jessica's name on the caller ID caused a knot in her stomach that competed for space with the twins. Reluctantly, she picked up the phone. "Hey Liz. How's Jessica?"

"It's time," she said.

The knot traveled from her stomach to her throat barely allowing enough air to breathe. "No…"

"I found her will this morning. Evidently, Jonathan's threats caused her to put all her important documents in one place. Too bad, I didn't look for it sooner. Just as I suspected, she doesn't want to be kept alive by machines. Did you know that she wanted you to be Simone's legal guardian?"

The absence of a pause between the statements that released Liz from any obligations to either her daughter or granddaughter did not go unnoticed, neither did it surprise Kendra. She watched the peanut butter melting on the toasted bagel. Jessica had convinced her that peanut butter was a healthier alternative to cream cheese the first week they roomed together. "Yes."

"Are you still willing to be her guardian?"

"Of course I am, unless you don't agree." Kendra held her breathe afraid that the potential insurance money might tempt Liz to fight for custody."

"Oh no... Raising Jessica was enough for me. Simone needs someone young with maternal instincts. Jessica knew what she was doing picking you. Anyway, I wanted to talk with you about how we should handle things."

"What do you mean handle things?"

"I'm leaning towards turning off the machines tomorrow. The doctor believes that given her condition, she should expire quickly."

"Liz, are you crazy?"

"I understand how you feel, but we need to consider what's best for Simone."

Kendra thought about how hard it was for her to say goodbye to her mother at the age of twenty. Despite the years, the pain and longing still existed. Kendra wanted Simone to have more time with her mother. "Liz, we need to think before doing anything rash. Losing a mother is hard on a child."

Liz smashed the cigarette butt in the candy dish. "Is it better for Simone to watch her mother lie in a hospital bed being kept alive by machines?"

"For a child who loves her mother, it is." Kendra wondered if she were thinking about Simone or herself.

"No child should have to watch her mother waste away. And that's exactly what's going to happen. Before long, the visits that Simone looks forward to are going to become a painful obligation. Delaying the inevitable will only cause this baby more suffering and go against Jessica's clearly stated desire."

One hand cradled the phone against her ear and the other covered her mouth. 'God, what do you want us to do? Will turning off the machines result in more suffering for Jessica?' Since leaving Chicago, Kendra constantly wondered why Jessica didn't immediately die.

Liz took Kendra's lack of response as agreement. "Simone's birthday is next month. It would be nice if she was settled with you by then. Maybe she'll meet enough friends for a small party. Jessica didn't specify whether she wanted to be cremated, but I'm leaning that way. No sense putting a lot of good money in the ground. Besides there's not much family and except for you, I don't recall Jessica having any real friends."

Kendra pondered which scenario was more disturbing—Jessica's body being consumed by fire or Simone being denied a source of solace. Being able to sit beside her mother's grave, knowing she would be resurrected made Kendra's grief tolerable. Even bed rest did not prevent Kendra from visiting her mother's grave on Mother's Day. "Liz, I don't think we should be planning Jessica's funeral before she's even dead. Regardless of what the doctors think, God can still perform a miracle."

"He'd better act fast."

Kendra fought hard to control her emotions and her tongue since Liz controlled the ultimate decision. "Can I call you back? I need to check on the boys."

"Before you go, Simone keeps asking about her father and whether he knows about the accident. I've tried his cell phone and the home number I found on the Internet. Both are no longer in service. Do you think I should send him a letter? "

"*No*...don't do that!" Kendra's heart raced imaging what Jonathan might do if he knew. "Simone's going through enough already. Why subject her to his revenge."

"I can't imagine that he'd do anything to hurt her. After all, Simone's the only child he has left. When his thinking clears, he might actually want her. After your babies arrive, you'll have your hands full. Maybe you should contact him before Simone gets too settled with you. The child doesn't need to be uprooted twice."

"Simone will not be some consolation prize for that man. Jessica wanted her with me, when the time comes," Kendra said through clinched teeth. Realizing that anger might drive Liz to take action sooner, she softened her voice. "Liz, Jessica may need just a little more time. God can do the impossible."

"If that's true, when the machines are turned off, she won't die."

"How can you be so glib?"

"I'm being a realist. Keeping her hooked up to those machines is only benefiting the hospital, which reminds me. That lawyer called again last night about a lawsuit. We definitely have a case, but I'm not sure if you want to use him or not. Anybody this desperate for business can't be any good. I was discussing the situation with a friend of mine. He recommends that the lawsuit be filed by Simone after Jessica's death so the settlement won't be subject to estate taxes. As Simone's guardian, I'll let you handle all that since I don't care about that money."

"How noble of you..."

"Kendra, this is not easy for me either. I haven't even begun to figure out what to do with this townhouse or all her stuff. What I do know is that I can't afford to pay the mortgage on this place. It was just her luck to get fired before the accident. Her life insurance was through her job."

"Maybe her policy's still active."

"Nope, I already checked. You're given thirty days before your medical coverage stops, but her company paid life insurance was terminated with her employment."

***

Jonathan scheduled his return to Atlanta to minimize the risk of encountering his neighbors. The garage door opened slowly, which usually indicated a power failure. He parked next to the van, comforted knowing another family would be blessed through his tragedy. The charity was picking it up the next morning. Peering into the passenger seat of the van, he was thankful that Lori had not cleaned it out. As soon as he opened the door to the laundry room, he saw the house through his wife's eyes. The wall plaque caught his attention – 'As for me and my house, we will serve the Lord'. Going into the family room, his eyes soaked up the sage green paint covering the walls, triggering a memory of the day Lori transformed the room.

It had been another stressful business trip. Lugging his suitcase through the garage, all he wanted to do was sit down and relax. As soon as he opened the door, the smell of paint overwhelmed him. All the furniture was pushed to the center of the room.

Lori stood on the ladder clutching a fist full of blue masking tape. "You're home early. I wanted this to be a surprise."

Jonathan looked at the walls which were ivory when he left town. "It's definitely a surprise."

Lori looked around the room with a sense of accomplishment. She had painted, almost continually, for two days in order to finish the room before he came home. "Well, what do you think?" Lori beamed with excitement.

"It looks like pea soup. I liked the ivory better."

The smile disappeared from her face, as she slowly descended the ladder. "Well, you're stuck with this until *you* change it."

"Maybe next time you could ask my opinion before making radical changes."

"This is not a radical change and if you were ever home, I would."

The remainder of the evening, they barely spoke to each other. He wished he could take back all the hurt he caused. The color of the walls no longer looked like pea soup. After being immersed in the color for almost a month, he appreciated the effect that Lori was grasping. Green was a perfect backdrop for the stacked stone fireplace. The words flowed effortlessly out of his mouth. "The Lord is my Shepherd, I shall not be in want. He makes me lie down in green pastures. If only I had known…"

The shades in the family room were down, but the mini blinds in the breakfast area were partially opened. He wondered when Shelia had been there last. Judging from the condition of the plants, he suspected she came at least weekly. He felt guilty for not informing her of his return, but he had his reasons. Continuing into the kitchen, he sat the bag containing his dinner on the center island and ran his hand across the brown granite counter top.

"Everyone who hears these words of mine and puts them into practice is like a wise man who built his house on the rock." Jonathan collapsed onto the barstool. Every highlighted verse in his wife's Bible took visual form. "God, how will I ever clean up all this rubble and rebuild." He pushed the sandwich bag away and pulled his cell phone from his pocket.

Jonathan's number was stored in Shelia's phone. When his name flashed on the display, she accepted the call quickly. "Hello."

"Hey."

"Where are you?"

"At the house."

Shelia looked at her watch. "Are you okay?"

He suspected the question was a conditioned response, but it still warmed his heart. "I'm fine. It's still hard being in the house without Lori and the kids."

"It's going to take time."

"An eternity will not be long enough." he hesitated. "I'll just be here for a day or two, to take care of some paperwork at the bank and transfer the title for the van. Having it sit in our garage when there's a family that needs it makes no sense. It's being picked up tomorrow."

"Do you need me to keep checking on the house?"

"If you don't mind. But you don't need to do it that often. I'm taking the plants with me."

"Sounds like you've found something permanent?"

"I'm buying a cabin about two hours north of here." Jonathan thought about the cabin and its previous owner. After their first meeting, Sam, the property manager, came early the next morning under the pretense of dropping off fishing bait. They had more in common than either of them would have ever suspected. When Sam's wife and infant son died tragically in a house fire, he sought refuge at the cabin. He saw the same hopelessness in Jonathan's eyes the day they met. Unable to extend his stay in the rented cabin, Jonathan asked Sam about other options. He suggested a cabin in the area about to go on the market. When Jonathan first saw the cabin, he wanted to leave without going inside. It needed a lot of work, but Sam was insistent. When he found out that Sam was the seller, his decision was made. "I finally have a reason to use all those tools Lori kept buying me."

"I wasn't sure how to tell you something. You just solved my dilemma."

"What is it?"

"Lori asked me to keep your Father's day gift. It was too big for her to hide."

Father's day, the Sunday he spent wishing for death, had subconsciously been erased from his mental calendar. "What is it?"

"I put it in the back of the van. You can call me later, if necessary."

Jonathan hung up the phone and walked quickly to the garage. His mouth gapped open with the lift gate. The exact portable workbench he was thinking about buying on the drive down, sat waiting to be used. He wondered why Lori had chosen that particular gift. Until deciding to buy the cabin, he had absolutely no need for one. Jonathan walked back into the house trying to make sense of the impossible. "Lori, how did you know? Was God truly speaking to you?" He looked out the kitchen window. The leaves of her tree fluttered in a breeze.

A few seconds later, he walked towards the oak tree with a deck chair in one hand and Lori's Bible in the other. Sitting beside the tree, he opened her Bible to the bookmarked page and began reading the words from Isaiah 61 aloud. "The Spirit of the Sovereign Lord is on me, because the Lord has anointed me to preach good news to the poor. He has sent me to bind up the brokenhearted, to proclaim freedom for the captives and release from darkness the prisoners, to proclaim the year of the Lord's favor and the day of vengeance of our God, to comfort all who mourn, and provide for those who grieve in Zion—to bestow on them a crown of beauty instead of ashes, the oil of gladness instead of mourning, and a garment of praise instead of a spirit of despair. They will be called oaks of righteousness, a planting of the Lord for the display of his splendor."

The highlighted verses had three asterisks in the margin. He wondered if the markings were for her benefit or his. "Oh Lori, your name's so fitting. You definitely were devoted to God. Why didn't I listen to you or treat you better? I'm so sorry, please forgive me...can he really change me." Jonathan bowed his head. "Lord, please, help me..."

CHAPTER 9

DALE INHALED DEEPLY THE FRESH MORNING AIR WHILE HE SAT on the weathered wooden bench and waited. He suggested moving the impromptu meeting to the church's memorial garden which served as neutral territory. Being outside also helped him feel closer to God, something he needed desperately. Two large crows perched on a sturdy branch of the towering maple tree and surveyed their surroundings. Realizing that he envied the birds' ability to see from above caused him to smile despite the tension of the situation. He tried to elevate his view but it still looked daunting. Damon usually arrived at the church after nine. When he came into Dale's office at seven-thirty and asked if they could meet, Dale knew it had to be important.

Damon, who sat at the other end of the bench, cleared his throat. "No one walked out before the sermon this Sunday. What did you say to them?"

"I'm just doing my job." Dale's instincts were triggering a fight response. His eyes followed a squirrel as it ran across the patchy spread of grass and scampered up the trunk of the tree. Searching for calming distractions was futile.

"This isn't just a job for you."

Dale forced himself to look at Damon. "Serving God is a privilege."

"Is that why you're not getting paid?"

"God provided for my family's financial needs a few years ago." Dale decided it was time to take charge of the conversation. "Why are you here so early?"

Damon rubbed his eyes. "Actually, I wasn't able to sleep after finishing that book."

Dale smiled broadly. "It was hard for me to stop reading once I got started." His concern increased when the smile was unreciprocated. "Theologians can be rigid with their writing style. It probably was too theological in some places. Since you didn't attend a seminary, I'd be happy to clarify any of the points for you."

Dale's condescending words intensified Damon's conviction that immediate action was necessary. "Is this what you're teaching in your Bible study?"

"Yes, but at the most basic level. Before you came, I was trying to teach it from the pulpit. The more interactive format actually works better." Damon's silence prompted Dale to take a different approach. "To be perfectly honest, some parts of the book only raised more questions for me. I suspect you might have a few also."

"No, I don't…It's my responsibility to control what's being taught in this church and I definitely don't support what you're teaching."

Dale felt like a thorn in his heart penetrated deeper. "There lies the problem."

"I don't think so. As I see it, you have the problem with me being the senior pastor."

"As much as I hate to admit it, you're right. I do have a problem with you leading this congregation." Saying the words that drove him to his knees each night in despair felt liberating. "But my problem is not with you personally; it's so much bigger. There are too many churches claiming to be Christian where sound Christian doctrine's not even believed, much less taught. We're entering a period worse than the Dark Ages. No wonder so many Christians believe that maybe Jesus did get married. If you asked self-proclaimed Christians to name five of the Ten Commandments, over half won't be able to. I'd wager that you can't even write down all Ten Commandments, in the correct order. Yet Jesus said until heaven and earth pass away, not one letter of the law would be eliminated. Do you know what the basic doctrine of Christianity is?" Dale waited for a response.

Damon bit his lower lip while he contemplated whether to answer the question. "For God so loved the world that he gave his one and only Son, that whoever believes in him shall not perish but have eternal life. See, I'm not as dumb as you think."

"At the risk of using a cliché, that's just the tip of the proverbial iceberg. There's so much beneath the surface. The first question that should come to mind is 'Who are the people who will believe?' The cornerstone of the Christian faith is this: We are saved by grace, through faith in Jesus Christ. The book I gave you merely explains the major aspects of this saving grace using concrete biblical proof. So, what part do you not agree with?"

Damon was too tired for a theological debate but he was not about to yield his authority. "I agree that man's sinful by nature. But I have a real problem with the notion of unconditional election. How can God randomly choose some people to go to heaven and let others go to hell? We have to choose him, not the other way around. Isn't that why he gave us free will?"

"That's exactly the point. In our sinful state, a person's incapable of choosing God. That's why God has to intervene. Hence the rebirth that Jesus told Nicodemus was absolutely necessary to see the kingdom of God."

"But clearly we have a role in our salvation."

"Yes, we do. Believers are to be thankful and praise God continuously for His mercy. Then we need to be obedient to God's will."

"But how can you be thankful for something you didn't ask for or apparently don't even have a choice about. Isn't that what they called 'irresistible grace' implies? If God chooses a person for salvation, they can't resist him."

"If Bill Gates, the founder of Microsoft, wanted to give you a million dollars, would you resist his offer?"

"Of course not."

"Why?"

"Do you know what I could do with a million dollars?"

"Do you know what you can do with God's Spirit and His favor? Jesus said that his disciples would be able to do what he did and so much more. Jesus fed thousands with next to nothing, healed diseases, calmed storms, and even raised the dead. Isn't that worth more than a million dollars?"

"Well, yes. But my father says those Old Testament miracles don't happen anymore."

"I beg to differ with your father. Miracles happen every minute of every day. How do you explain wildfires, tornadoes and hurricanes leveling hundreds of homes yet houses in the center of the destruction are untouched. And what about people who are healed and even their doctors can't medically explain why?" Dale rubbed his head in frustration. "The new trend in Christian churches is to preach the gospel of prosperity, but Jesus never promised us prosperity. He promised us power, his power. Ignorance of God is a breeding ground for the devil's deception. Read the book of Judges, if you want to know what happens when a generation who neither knows the Lord or His works takes control. That's exactly what we have now."

Dale stood up and paced in front of Damon. He wanted to yell at the top of his lungs but he doubted even that would make Damon understand. "God, help me," he uttered before sitting on the bench again. "Damon, Jesus warned repeatedly against end time deceptions. Well, there are two big deceptions that most Christians have fallen for. The devil set the bait and they've fallen for it—hook, line and sinker. The first is that people somehow have absolute control of their eternal destiny. The second relates to the events leading to Jesus' return."

"After reading that book, I can see how you might believe that God controls your destiny, but the Rapture's well documented and universally taught in the Christian community. How can you possibly believe anything different?"

"That's a very good question. If you are serious about doing God's work, I strongly suggest that you pray earnestly to God for wisdom and understanding and then read the Bible as a continuous book. Jesus said his people will have tribulation and when He returns, the whole world will know it."

Damon took a deep breath. "Because I don't agree with what you're teaching, we're suspending your Bible study until an acceptable curriculum has been submitted and approved by me and the deacon board."

Dale clinched his jaws together so hard that it hurt.

Damon continued. "You understand that this was a difficult decision for me, but you've left me no choice. Some of the people would hate to lose you, but a divided church cannot survive. " Damon stood and left Dale sitting on the bench.

When Dale was finally able to move, he stood up and started walking. The sun was descending in the sky when he returned to his car and drove home.

***

Kendra received the call from Liz a few minutes after Jessica died, which unleashed a tsunami of grief. Caleb and Ruby helped Kendra endure the rest of the week. When Caleb arrived to drive Kendra and Eric to the airport for the flight to Chicago for the funeral, Ruby's prolonged hug provided the strength needed to maintain Kendra's fragile momentum. Unlike on their last flight to Chicago, Eric seemed preoccupied and unsupportive.

The nauseating smell of stale cigarette smoke greeted them as soon as they walked into Jessica's condominium. Kendra instantly regretted the decision not to stay at a hotel as Eric suggested. He cleared his throat to emphasize the obvious.

Picking up on their disapproval, Liz sauntered to the breakfast bar and snuffed out the burning cigarette. "How was the flight?"

Kendra looked around the great room spewed with floral arrangements, newspapers, clothes and toys. Jessica liked nice things and believed in taking care of them. Clearly, the trait was not inherited from her mother.

"Excuse the mess. Jessica stopped the cleaning service before the accident to cut costs. Unfortunately, I never was much of a housekeeper and trying to stay ahead of all this…"

Simone walked cautiously down the hallway and smiled broadly when she saw Kendra and Eric. Kendra opened her arms wide and walked quickly to meet her. "How are you doing?"

"I'm fine." She looked around the room. "Where are Danny and Joshua?"

"We left them at home, but they're so excited about seeing you soon." Kendra knew her words stoked the fire burning hotly within Eric.

Simone's smile disappeared. "Auntie Kendra, I don't want to move."

"I know baby." Kendra took Simone by the hand and led her to the sofa.

Eric hesitated by the door with their luggage, unsure if they were going to stay.

"Eric let me show you where to put your luggage. I moved my things into Jessica's bedroom. I figured you two would be more comfortable in the guest room." Eric followed Liz down the hallway, leaving Kendra and Simone alone.

"Auntie Kendra, why can't I stay here?"

"Your mommy wanted me to take care of you and our home's in Dallas."

"Can't Daddy come and stay with me?"

Kendra looked into the eyes of a child searching for words to explain a situation that was too difficult for even an adult to understand. "That's just not possible."

"If he comes tomorrow, we could ask him."

"I don't think your father will be at the service tomorrow." Kendra hoped she was right.

Simone looked at Kendra. "Why not?"

"No one has been able to reach your father."

"Daddy told me that he had to go on a trip and that he would not be able to see me for a long time."

"When did he tell you that?"

"He flew home with us from Florida."

"Have you talked to him since then?"

"No, but Mommy tried to call him a lot of times. He must be really busy."

"I'm sure he is."

Liz and Eric returned to the room. From the expression on Liz's face, Kendra knew that they must have discussed his reservations about Simone coming to Dallas. Kendra looked disapprovingly at him but he avoided her gaze, pretending to be more interested in seeing the view from the balcony. Although Kendra knew that Jessica was not responsible for the accident, it was still difficult not to resent the predicament she left. Within a few minutes, finalizing the plans for the funeral took precedence over the ramifications of her death.

***

Sharon tired of the battle between her brain which needed stimulation and her heart which did not. When Karly returned to the car with two bottles of water, an audible sigh of relief preceded the door closing. Having to smell coffee in her state of mind would be torture. They stopped to fuel the rental car before getting on the highway to Chicago. Jessica's afternoon funeral required an early start. Sharon wondered why she bothered getting in bed as she reclined her seat. With Karly's family arriving later than planned, her household was abuzz with activity to well after midnight. Karly's offer to drive the first half of their journey met no resistance, despite her being Sharon's guest.

Karly placed the water bottles in the cup holders. "Put that seat back up. I came for a visit."

Sharon reluctantly complied. "I'm so glad you were able to change your plans. I really didn't want to make this trip alone."

199

She looked in the snack bag for something to keep her awake, hesitant to reveal the reasons. "Regardless of the circumstances, I'm thrilled to get away from home, especially with you. It's been a rough couple of weeks."

Karly set the cruise control. "I could tell something was wrong. What's going on?"

"That's a million dollar question. I wish I could put my finger on a specific answer. Do you know the last time I wrote in my journal was over two years ago? Ironically, it coincided with Dale's stint in counseling. And I'm ashamed to tell you I haven't picked up a Bible outside of church in months. Bible study used to bring me so much peace. The last time I attempted to study, all I did was look for verses that rebutted something Dale said. You have no idea how hard it is to live with a person who's obsessed with the Bible. But you have enough to worry about without me dumping on you. How are you feeling anyway?"

Karly pondered the question. "Truthfully, I've never felt better. Too bad it took cancer to get me to appreciate life and take better care of my body. And get this...Ruben and I went to a wellness health fair. His personal mission's to find a cure for me, but that's a whole other story. Anyway, there was a vendor selling flaxseed products. Within a minute of the sales pitch, Ruben was convinced. I agreed to try it, just to end his pestering. Talk about a blessing in disguise. My mood varied with my cycle. Not any more. Apparently, flaxseed affects hormones. You should try it."

"What does your doctor think about that?"

"I haven't discussed it with him. After making my treatment decision, I told him that I'd be back when I felt sick. A person has to do what's best for them."

"I hear you," Sharon said.

"So, how's your blood pressure doing?"

Sharon adjusted the seat for more leg room. "The last time I checked, it wasn't doing too well." She decided not to add it was so high, she was better off not knowing. "That's probably part of my problem. It's hard to be loving and patient with others when you don't feel well."

"I thought your medicine was working."

"It was…until I stopped taking it."

Karly looked at Sharon in disbelief. "Why in the world would you do something like that? Blood pressure's nothing to play with."

"Neither is cancer…"

"Is that what you think I'm doing…playing with cancer?" Karly asked.

Karly's tone caused Sharon to rethink her choice of words. "No…You know I didn't mean it like that. You're doing what you think is best…Trusting God and not man. I decided to do the same thing."

"Sharon, our situations are completely different!"

"I don't see the difference."

"For starters, look at you. You were feeling great a month ago and now you obviously don't. You're also putting yourself at risk for a major stroke. Is that what you want?"

"No…but…"

"There are no 'buts' about this. I made my decision because the course of treatment they recommended could have expedited my death, not to mention greatly impacting the quality of my remaining time. I felt healthy and I made lifestyle changes to support my decision." Karly looked at the road ahead of her. "I'm not testing God, like you."

"I'm not testing God!"

"Yes, you are! It's like you're saying 'God, I really don't believe that you healed me before, now can you do it without medication."

Sharon crossed her arms and looked out the window wondering if what Karly said was true. A faint orange light was on the horizon. "Of all people, I thought you'd understand."

"I hate to disappoint you, but I really, really don't. Actually, I feel responsible for you doing this. I completely regret telling you about the cancer and my decision."

"It's not your fault. I made this decision and I'm sticking with it. As for regretting telling me, friends don't keep secrets!"

Karly grabbed her bottle of water and unscrewed the cap. "Being my friend doesn't mean you have to do what I do. Kendra and Jessica's friendship was proof of that. Even if my decision's wrong, and for the record, I don't think it is; two wrongs never make a right. There's a difference between being foolish and having convictions." She took a sip then put the bottle in the cup holder. "What's not taking your medicine proving?"

"That I have faith in God to heal me."

"Do you honestly believe that everybody who needs medication just lacks faith?"

"Maybe…"

"I'd pull this car over and slap you, if I thought you really believed that. Have you considered that maybe God was healing you through medication or maybe your condition's for your ultimate good?"

"When Jesus heals someone, he doesn't need medication and his healings are instantaneous. That's what I want."

"Sometimes what we want and God's Will are not the same. Before I made my decision, I searched the scriptures. There's not a single incident where Jesus made the person sicker to heal them. That's the basis for my decision. Now what's the basis for yours?"

Sharon let out a deep sigh. "I don't know…what am I supposed to do?"

"I recommend getting back on your medication until you can safely stop."

"But won't that be admitting that I lack faith?"

"If you want to get off the medications, work with God. Did you even check with him before you stopped taking your medicine?" Karly jerked her head towards Sharon. "Does Dale know?"

Sharon dropped her head ashamed that the thought of confirming with God or anyone else never entered her mind. "Okay, maybe I acted a little rash."

"A little... I'm just thankful you're not the one lying in a casket. As soon as we get to the hotel, you're calling your pharmacy and getting your prescription sent to the nearest drugstore. That should handle the problem until you can talk with your doctor. Now, do you need any other advice?"

"Yeah...What do you do with a depressed husband and rebellious teenager?"

Karly looked at the clock on the dash. "I'm not sure, but we have twenty-four hours to find out. If it makes you feel any better, I've got the matching pair."

***

Fighting the summer crowd at St. Louis' most popular attraction was the last thing Dale felt like doing. He agreed to Ruben's suggestion of taking their children to the zoo because he did not have a better alternative. As soon as they entered the Living World building, their two oldest children asked if they could explore the zoo on their own. They both complained about going to the zoo during breakfast. Eating at a restaurant made that battle easier to win. After confirming it with Ruben, Dale gave his son an exact meeting time and a twenty dollar bill then followed the rest of their group to the Darwinian exhibit.

Looking at the wave of people entering, he nudged Ruben. "Since this is the only way in and out, do you mind if we don't go in with them?"

His daughter looked back. "Dad, there's no need for you to go in. You've seen it before. I'll keep a close eye on Sammy."

Ruben shrugged his broad shoulders. "It seems our children don't want to be seen with us."

"Don't take it too personally." Dale saw a bench being vacated and rushed to claim it. When Ruben sat next to him, they seemed content watching the crowds.

Ruben checked his watch. "They should be getting into Chicago soon. I asked Karly to call when they get to the hotel."

"Stop worrying. They'll be just fine."

Ruben ran his hand over his short waves of hair. "It's hard to take anything for granted anymore...Is my worrying that obvious?"

"Yes. You've been hovering over Karly since you walked in the door."

"Man, how do I deal with the possibility of losing her, especially when it seems like she's not even trying to fight it?"

"Karly looks good. Maybe you're not losing her. I read a story about a man who was given two years to live. Fifteen years later, he's still baffling the doctors."

"I hope you're right." Ruben peered into the exhibit. When he saw his daughter securely holding her brother's hand, he relaxed. "Don't take this wrong, but you don't seem like the minister type."

"Believe me, I'm not offended. Ministry work makes corporate-America seem like child's play. I can't admit this to Sharon, but I'm beginning to wonder if I've made another mistake."

"Serving God's never a mistake," Ruben said.

"I'm not talking about serving God. It seems I've misunderstood what he said to me. Clearly, I'm not ready to lead his people otherwise I wouldn't keep failing. Counseling was a bust, teaching was abruptly haltered, and now I'm fired as a minister. Before heading down this road, my career choices were focused and successful. Now, it's one dead end after another."

"If God's doing the talking, he'll make sure you get the message straight. Like you just told me, stop worrying. It's probably not as bad as you think."

Dale rubbed his hands together before clasping them firmly. "There's one positive in all of this. The original Bible study group wants to continue our study outside of the church. We were going to start today, but with Sharon out of town, I decided to wait until next Saturday."

"I would have loved to sit in on that. Maybe later, you can give me the abbreviated version."

"The book's a better teacher. Remind me to give you a copy."

"It sounds like the humble beginning of a new church."

Ruben's observation confirmed Dale's fear. "We don't need any new churches, especially in St. Louis. There are at least fifteen Christian churches within a ten minute drive of my house, several I jog past daily." He pondered which ones were true places of worship. The words 'In the place which I have chosen' came to mind. 'Where is that, Lord?' He hoped the question in his mind had not actually come out of his mouth. His attention returned to Ruben. "Besides, I have no intention of leading people away from the church."

"Dale, I think you've got it all wrong. You're not leading anyone from that church. It looks like God's bringing them to you."

"He's not leading them to me...of that I'm certain. After two years of studying the Bible on my own, I've got more questions than answers. Jesus said the Holy Spirit would guide us into all truth, but he also said that he is the truth." Dale leaned back on the bench.

"Man, I wish I could help, but you're way beyond me. But when you find the answers, will you let me know." Ruben stood when he saw their children walk out of the exhibit laughing.

***

The funeral home's chapel was dark and cold, a stark contrast to the bright, warm Chicago day. Somber mahogany walls provided the background for the floral arrangements which flanked both sides of the white marble casket with golden trim. A spray of red and white carnations rested on the closed casket. Kendra and Liz had argued about the floral colors. Liz wanted pink and yellow because they were her favorite colors. Kendra wanted red and white because they represented God's cleansing, but told Liz they were Jessica's favorite colors which seemed to pacify her. An easel beside the casket held a poster-sized picture of Jessica. The funeral director recommended the closed casket. Although Kendra thought Simone could handle seeing her mother's lifeless body, she yielded reluctantly to the more experienced voice. Even after the decision to have a closed casket, Liz still labored over selecting the perfect outfit to bury her daughter in. The fact that Liz cared more about her daughter's external appearance even in death only saddened Kendra more.

Waiting for the service to begin, Kendra reflected on the differences between her mother's funeral and Jessica's. The struggle had been to keep her mother's service from being too long. So many people wanted to take part; there had been three different eulogies. Kendra doubted Jessica's service would take thirty minutes. She opened the crumpled program in her hand. Opposite the elegantly written but short obituary was the shorter order of the service. Since Jessica refused to attend church, the person presiding over the service was provided by the funeral home. Following the opening prayers, two scripture readings were listed. Eric was reading the Old Testament scripture. The mother of Simone's friend offered to read the New Testament scripture. While mourners trickled in, music from a CD played softly in the background. For her mother's service, the choir sang several of her mother's favorite hymns.

Despite the colorful array of flowers, Kendra looked around the room disappointed by the number of mourners. She had personally sent the funeral announcement to the local papers and Jessica's company, yet fewer than twenty people waited for the service to start. Given the ages of most of them, she suspected that they were friends of Liz. The family of Simone's friend sat across the aisle. When they introduced themselves to Kendra, the bond of unity was obvious. Kendra's gaze constantly shifted from Simone, who was sitting between her and Liz, to the door at the rear of the chapel. The possibility of Jonathan storming into the service in a fit of rage had been a constant concern. When she spotted Jay, Jessica's ex-husband, enter and sit in the last pew, she nudged Eric. Jay and Jessica's divorce had been long and nasty. She hoped his intentions for being there were honorable.

Kendra tried to convince Liz to have the service at a church but Liz was adamant; saying if her daughter did not attend a church in life, there was no point pretending in death. Kendra suspected the real reason had more to do with Liz's aversion to churches than her daughter's. From what Jessica confided, her mother had been chased out of several congregations. When Kendra saw Sharon and Karly walk through the door, she wanted to greet them but it was too late. The somber man presiding over the service was at the podium.

Kendra's pulse raced as she waited to deliver the words that were supposed to be a reflection of and tribute to the life being honored. The prayer and Bible readings went too quickly, just like Jessica's life. Walking slowly to the podium with trembling hands, Kendra prayed for strength. Simone's face was the first one she focused on causing her to realize that Jessica's life was not in vain. A glimmer of God's glory stared back at her.

"They say that funerals are for the living because they serve no purpose for the dead. For those who don't know me, I had the privilege of being Jessica's friend since our freshman year in college."

Karly elbowed Sharon when she shook her head in disagreement.

"Jessica came into my life like a cyclone, literally blowing into the dorm room with so much energy and intensity that I had to take a step back. Since neither of us had a biological sister, I guess we adopted each other. Like true siblings, we had very different personalities. Jessica was impulsive, energetic and optimistic. I'm the cautious, disciplined planner which is probably why I'm struggling with what to say. How do you write a eulogy for a thirty-one year old friend taken suddenly in the prime of her life?" Kendra paused as if contemplating her next words. "Jessica was responsible for me meeting my husband. I literally pried him from her grip as she was dragging him onto the dance floor."

Eric laughed at the memory.

"Jessica always loved a challenge. She often teased me about Eric, saying that I owed her. She was instrumental in my finding love and was there when I lost it. She offered her shoulder to cry on for several weeks after my mother died." Kendra paused again, overcome by the dire reality that the two most important women in her life were snatched prematurely from her. Her eyes locked on Sharon and Karly giving her strength to continue.

"Jessica would go out to get hot donuts for our late night study sessions. I don't know how she kept her figure in college. Over the years, we celebrated each other's joys and shared each others pain, until now." Kendra gripped the podium with both hands. Eric stood up, ready to usher her back to her seat. He stopped when she motioned that she was okay.

"The one thing that I loved most about Jessica was that she always knew exactly what she wanted and never let anything stand in the way of getting it." Kendra looked at the audience and noticed a few nods and smiles. "Some of you know what I'm talking about. This trait can be a blessing and a curse. Sometimes it got her in trouble because she didn't always know what was best for her. I wish that I could stand here and say with certainty that I'll see Jessica again, but I can't. Only God knows that. What I do know is that Jessica will be missed but a part of her will always live on in her beautiful daughter Kendra Simone."

She wanted to be strong for Simone but the pain of not knowing was too great. Eric was at her side before she could object. When she sat down, Simone took her hand.

"Auntie Kendra, Mommy's okay."

Kendra wished that she could be as certain. But if the possibility of her mother being in heaven brought comfort to Simone, she knew that she could not take it away. She wiped away her tears as she nodded her agreement.

***

Kendra questioned whether she was angry or relieved when Eric insisted on parking and escorting her to Sharon and Karly's hotel room. She saw him speaking with them at the cemetery and hoped he had not drafted them into his service. Nothing was officially planned after the graveside prayer. Everyone went their own way. Sharon and Karly's invitation to spend the evening at the hotel with them provided Kendra an opportunity to avoid Liz's second hand smoke and another discussion with Eric about Simone, whose last night in Chicago was being spent at her friend's house. Liz was meeting friends for dinner. Kendra suspected they would be doing more drinking than eating. Since they were only taking a few of Simone's things with them, there was little for her or Eric to do at the condo. His plans for the next three hours were of little interest. Her body and psyche needed a brief reprieve. The magnitude of her fatigue had to be concealed in his presence and their spiritual connection intensified both their anguish.

The door to the hotel room opened and Karly greeted Kendra with a strong embrace. She walked into the room, expecting Eric to follow. He remained in the hallway, making her feel like a baton being passed in a relay race. She turned and saw him hand Karly a business card before he walked away. As soon as the door closed, Kendra sat on the edge of a bed. Sharon handed her a bag with her favorite snack foods which unleashed the flood of restrained emotions. A long group hug followed. When they released each other, all were crying.

Karly retrieved a box of tissue and passed it around. "Now that we've got all those tears out, let's get you comfortable." She helped Kendra to her feet, prompting Sharon to help.

While Sharon supported Kendra, Karly folded back the bed's comforter and adjusted the pillows against the headboard. Once Kendra was on the bed with her treats and the box of tissue within reach, her shoes were removed. Knowing that the last woman to give her such care was her mother threatened more tears. Sharon stretched out on the other bed and Karly grabbed her traveling blanket and settled into the reclining chair, keeping a watchful eye on the others. She drove Sharon to the pharmacy to get her medication after leaving the cemetery and watched her swallow a pill in the car. An easy silence filled the room while they adjusted to being in each others' presence. Kendra broke the silence when she opened the bag of Cheese puffs and started crunching loudly.

Karly laughed watching Kendra lick her fingers. "How can you eat those things?"

"Ever since I've been pregnant with the twins, I can't seem to get enough of them. I know it's strange but there must be something in them that these babies like. Do you want some?"

Karly shook her head. "I don't think so. Have you read the ingredients list?"

Lightness filled Kendra which she had not felt in a long time. "Why would I do that? Some things are better left unknown. Sharon, would you like some?"

Sharon reached for the bag.

"Kendra, don't you dare pass her that bag."

Sharon propped herself against the headboard and took the bag before Kendra could pull it back. "Will you mind your own business?"

Karly rolled her eyes. "Suit yourself, but you know you shouldn't be eating those salty things, especially now."

Sharon popped some cheese puffs into her mouth before handing the bag back to Kendra. "Party poop-er."

"Sharon, what's wrong with you?"

"It's nothing...my blood pressure's just a little high."

Karly looked at Sharon, confirming their vow. Before Kendra arrived, they had agreed not to tell her about Karly's cancer diagnosis.

Kendra looked at Sharon with concern. "You need to be careful. High blood pressure's nothing to play with."

Karly nodded her agreement. "That's just what I told her. Hopefully, she'll listen to you."

Sharon rolled onto her side. "I'm listening to you both, so let's change the subject. How are the babies doing?"

"Fine, can't you tell." Kendra rubbed her tightly stretched abdomen. I don't know how much bigger I can get without popping."

"Have they moved up your due date?"

"Not officially. My doctor wants me to go full term but he hinted that it may mean bed rest again. I sure don't want bed rest again, especially since Simone will be with us."

Karly pulled the blanket up to her chest. "It's freezing in here."

Kendra chuckled. "Actually, I think it's a little warm. Sharon, you're the tie breaker." Kendra remembered the even split at the bed and breakfast and her smile disappeared.

Sharon spoke quickly. "I side with the pregnant woman." She looked playfully at Karly. "You need to put some more meat on those bones. Do you want the comforter off this bed?"

Karly dramatically turned up her nose. "I don't think so. Did you see that special on hotel bedding?"

Sharon covered her ears. "No, and please don't share the details until after we check out."

"Don't say I didn't try to warn you."

Sharon returned her attention to Kendra. "Why isn't Simone staying with Liz? Isn't she retired?"

Kendra sighed, tired of the question. "Jessica wanted her to be with me!"

Her tone surprised Karly. "But given the circumstances, wouldn't it be better to wait a little while, like after the babies are born?"

Kendra felt one of the babies move and rubbed her stomach. "You sound like Eric."

Sharon watched Kendra and smiled. "Is that what's wrong with him?"

Kendra nodded before wiping a fresh tear from her cheek.

"It can't be that bad?" Karly said, shooting a warning glance at Sharon.

"Worse. Nothing I do is right anymore. First, he was upset because I needed to come see Jessica in the hospital and he had to come with me; which, for the record, he didn't have to."

Sharon interrupted. "Look, you can't fault him for that. I didn't think you needed to be traveling in your condition either."

"Well, I did and nothing happened."

Sharon raised an eyebrow. "So your point is?"

"He makes a big deal out of everything. Now, he's pouting because Simone's coming to live with us. It's not like we have a choice. Liz's totally unfit to keep her, even for a few months. You should see Jessica's condo, and Liz keeps a cigarette in her hand. Eric had to ask her to smoke on the balcony for the benefit of the rest of us. That's probably why she's out with her friends now. Who knows when she'll come in or her condition?"

Karly and Sharon looked at each other.

Kendra sighed. "I know you're both thinking that Jessica and her mother had a lot in common, which is why I can't subject Simone to one more minute with her? Simone deserves a real family." She grabbed the bag of cheese puffs. "And I refuse to make any effort to locate that man who fathered her. I can't believe Eric would even suggest that. What was he thinking?" She took a bite off a large one and waited for confirmation of her feelings.

Karly softened her voice. "Let's see…maybe that you have enough to worry about with your own children or maybe that her father might actually want her."

Kendra pouted. "Whose side are you on anyway?"

Sharon got up and sat next the Kendra. "We're not taking anyone's side. Right now, you're responding with your emotions. Have you paused long enough to ask God what you should be doing?"

Karly cleared her throat, hearing the words that she told Sharon in the car.

Sharon glanced at Karly before continuing. "Very recently, I was guilty of the same thing but a good friend helped me see the error of my ways. It's so easy to act impulsively, but it's much wiser to ensure our actions align with God's plans. And don't be too hard on Eric. When a man's sexually deprived, it doesn't take much to push his buttons. Once the babies are born and you two get back to normal relations, he'll be just fine. How long has it been anyway?"

"I don't know…at least, two months…since I went to the hospital."

"Believe me, Eric knows exactly how long it's been," Sharon said.

Kendra's expression changed. "Are you serious?"

"Very. Most men are wired differently from women. Absence doesn't always make their hearts grow fonder, as the old saying goes."

Kendra suddenly became concerned where Eric was that very moment. "You don't think he'll be unfaithful, again?"

"Of course not! He's vulnerable but he's also smart enough to control himself," Sharon said.

Kendra thought about Stephanie waiting for her next opportunity. The first time Eric was tested, he failed.

Karly recognized the panic in Kendra's eyes and folded up her blanket. "Kendra, I'm hungry and I'm sure your babies need something other than those cheese things." She opened the room service menu and started reading their options.

Kendra listened hoping food could deflect the thoughts and images competing for attention.

CHAPTER 10

WHEN THE BLARING ALARM CLOCK FINALLY REGISTERED IN Kendra's brain before sunrise, every muscle conspired against movement. Straining against gravity, she managed to hit the silence button on the first attempt. A minute later, Kendra sat on the edge of the bed waiting for another surge of energy to stand. She listened for hints on Eric's location but the house was silent. The faint smell of his aftershave hung in the air indicating that he had already showered and dressed. She closed her eyes and prayed fervently for the strength to get Simone ready for school.

The desire to minimize the disruptions in Simone's life created turmoil in Kendra's. The day after returning from Jessica's funeral, Kendra began searching for piano teachers and dance studios. Observing a dance class initiated the current dilemma of having to get out of bed instead of sleeping longer like the doctor had suggested. During a casual conversation, a waiting mother encouraged her to consider the school her daughter attended. The product of public schools, Kendra had mixed feelings about private schools. When her father gave them the house, it was assumed that her children would attend the neighborhood schools. The need to enroll Simone in kindergarten provided an opportunity to walk the halls of her elementary school again. The vice principal warmly greeted her. After discussing the curriculum and their most recent state test scores, they toured the school. Walking down the dark familiar hallways, Kendra hoped that the presence of teachers and students would improve the atmosphere.

Under the guise of making an informed decision, Kendra browsed the private school's website before calling to schedule a tour. As she walked through their natural light filled building, the director of admissions, a matronly woman with silver hair, answered all Kendra's questions and raised some that had not even been considered. The school's willingness to make room for Simone after learning about her mother's death convinced Kendra that Simone needed at least one year in a nurturing environment, especially with the imminent arrival of the twins. Eric was harder to convince. Besides what he considered outrageous tuition, he also could not understand why they needed to drive Simone halfway across town for kindergarten when she could catch a bus outside their front door. Kendra firmly held her ground, prevailing twice when it came to Simone's needs. Fearing that Eric had been pushed to his limits, she hoped to avoid a third.

Uncertain whether it was fear of Eric coming into their bedroom and finding her unable to stand or God answering her prayer, Kendra stood with more energy than she thought was possible, waddled to the kitchen and set the table for Simone's first day of kindergarten breakfast. She remembered her mother's first day of school tradition as she pulled a microwavable pancakes and sausage breakfast from the freezer and sat it on the counter. Guilt over not being able to make the homemade version did not last long. Besides her physical constraints, Simone had to be ready to leave with Eric at the appointed time.

Kendra sat at the table trying to muster the strength needed to climb the stairs and wake Simone. Anxiety over her first day of school was quickly dismissed as Kendra reflected on the school's open house. Leaving her sons with a brooding Eric, she took Simone and watched her closely. While the other parents had to coax their children, Simone eagerly conversed with her teacher and politely introduced herself to her classmates. That day, Kendra saw hints of Jessica's personality emerging and prayed that Simone's genetic coding would not be too much like her mother's. Driving home from the open house, Kendra wanted to be more than Simone's legal guardian. She wanted to give Simone the one thing she needed most. It was what Jessica needed and what Kendra knew made all the difference in her life. Simone needed loving parents to grow into an emotionally healthy woman. Kendra's thoughts drifted to Eric's reaction to adoption. When she heard his footsteps, she stood quickly.

Eric walked into the kitchen without saying a word. He spent most of the night reviewing every design detail of a project facing legal problems. Construction had been halted. Every day of delay was increasing his company's losses. He needed to be at the office, not waiting to drive Simone to school. It was the worst possible time to be on someone else's schedule which added twenty minutes to his commute. He agreed to this temporary arrangement to avoid Kendra going into labor while driving in Dallas rush hour traffic. But he could not cut his day short to bring her home. As usual, Ruby came to her rescue and offered to pick up Simone, who was already treated like another grandchild.

Kendra tried not to be offended by his silent dismissal. Ever since they returned from the funeral, he had been sleeping more nights on the couch than in their bed. Even when he lay beside her, he felt like a stranger and their bodies never touched. Sharon's words about him being vulnerable to temptation lingered constantly in her mind. The little romance that had existed between Kendra and Eric disappeared completely with the arrival of Simone. In her present condition, Kendra knew that there was little she could do about it. When Eric sat at the table and poured a bowl of cereal, Kendra left the kitchen with their digital camera in hand to capture the first milestone in Simone's new life. The smile on Simone's face when Kendra tickled her awake pushed all worries aside. If Simone could smile after all she had been through, Kendra knew that she could too. The energy that Kendra had been awaiting arrived as she watched Simone quickly put on the outfit they had selected before going to bed.

When Kendra returned to the kitchen with Simone, Eric was waiting by the door with her backpack in his hand. Kendra checked the clock on the wall before going to the microwave to heat Simone's breakfast. They still had fifteen minutes. Preferring to let her actions communicate her intentions, all her energy was focused on Simone. Eric could stand by the door and brood all he wanted. Simone was not leaving their house without breakfast. If she could carry his children in her body for ten more weeks, he could wait ten minutes.

***

At his cabin, Jonathan's pain was still as intense as the day the accident happened despite his plea to God for help. Knowing that Lori really did have a spiritual connection to God complicated his struggling faith. If God loved Lori, how could He possibly help the man who caused her so much pain? Time passed without formally registering in his consciousness. His firstborn son's birthday halted his feeble attempts to keep track of the date. The sun was his only connection to time. Since he could not control it, he let it control him. His body worked from sunrise to sunset. Weeks of living in and working on the cabin kept him busy. Like a hamster on a wheel, he moved constantly but stayed in the same spot. When he bought the cabin, he was concerned that the sale price was too low. As the list of needed repairs grew, he wondered if the price was too high. The previous owner kept the cabin neat but no maintenance had been done in years and it was not designed for year round use. The deck was the easiest starting point. Replacing the weather damaged floor boards and handrails matched both his skill level and mental state. The repetitive, mindless work provided a temporary outlet and the repaired deck provided visible hope that the same might be possible for him.

The cabin was devoid of a television or any other connection to the outside world. The rare ventures into town were driven in silence. The only person in the area that he had a connection with was Sam, who left after handing him the key to the cabin. Physical exhaustion helped him sleep a few hours but night lasted too long. Lori's Bible stayed open on the small kitchen table, waiting for his eyes to open. The first night spent in the cabin, he started reading the first page. His fear of God increased with every word he read, yet every night he continued reading. He reached the book of Judges the day he finished the deck.

As soon as the last nail was driven into the deck, Jonathan turned his attention to the overgrown vines that reminded him of the wallpaper in their kitchen without the fruit border. The vines were healthy and thriving, creeping up the walls of the cabin. The barely visible wooden trellises sagged under the weight. Afraid that the clinging vines would cause damage, he climbed the wobbly ladder and began pulling. When he yanked a vine to free the clinging roots, a part of the trellis broke. He descended the ladder to inspect the damage. Termites disturbed by the intrusion scattered putting an end to his work.

After an exterminator suggested demolishing the cabin, he sat alone in the woods wondering if he was also beyond repair. The hope he felt beside Lori's tree in Atlanta was quickly withering, leading him to believe that he and the cabin faced the same inevitable fate. The image of Samson chained between the columns filled his thoughts. He drove back to Atlanta to dispose of the house and his unfinished business.

Minutes after walking into the house carrying a postal container filled with mail, Jonathan regretted returning. Surrounded by so many reminders of the innocent lives that he had destroyed, Jonathan suspected that the accident had less to do with God punishing him for adultery and more to do with God's mercy for Lori and his children, who deserved a better man in their lives. He tried to envision his family's life, if God would have taken him instead of them. In his mind that would have been the ideal situation. Lori would have known exactly what to do.

It took several hours to sort through the mail. There were an astonishing number of envelopes from across the country. Some of them were addressed with only his name and the city. After opening a few, he set aside all the hand addressed envelopes. The words of comfort only increased his guilt and pain. The funeral program and letter from Liz went unnoticed into the stack. Mail from the insurance companies and any recognizable bills were set aside to be taken care of later. The rest of the mail went directly into the trash, except for a flyer from a realtor which he left on the counter. Emotionally drained from being home, he stood up and started to walk out of the kitchen. Turning abruptly, he collected the stack of hand addressed mail, put them in the trash and tied the bag closed. Starting with his children's rooms, Jonathan meticulously searched for items that would preserve the memory of his family, even if it was not for him. The sun was still his only connection to time, dictating when to turn on and off lights.

Finished with his work, he sat on his bedroom floor surrounded by boxes. The box at his side contained a collection of coffee mugs. It took the longest to pack and was carried several times between the kitchen and the bedroom. From their first trip together, Lori purchased a coffee mug to capture the memory. He laughed when she told him the significance of the first mug and her future plans. The old, gray-haired couple starting everyday with happy memories of their life together no longer existed. On top of the box was the mug that Lori had purchased while they were at Epcot. He gasped when he found it in the kitchen cabinet with the others. Remembering the unpacked luggage hastily placed in his bedroom closet before the funerals, he raced upstairs to the small storage area in the guest bedroom. The badly battered, empty luggage was exactly where it was supposed to be. Knowing that Shelia was the only one who could have done it moved her to the top of his list. She would be the next person to go through the house to collect keepsakes; then family members would have a brief opportunity to do likewise.

The sound of the front door opening followed by Shelia's voice sent Jonathan downstairs without the box of mugs. She had a stack of flat boxes in her arms. The forced smile faded as her foot crossed the threshold. "Good morning"

He took the boxes from her hands. "Thanks for coming and for bringing some boxes."

Shelia closed the door and followed him through the kitchen and into the family room. "If this isn't enough, I can get more."

"This should be enough for now." He propped the boxes against the wall. "I found the Disney mug yesterday. When did you do it?"

Shelia noticed the collection of family pictures that once lined the fireplace mantel were gone. "The day after you left the first time...I thought the mug belonged with the others."

"Why didn't you say anything about it?"

"Because you didn't…it's quite a collection."

"Yeah, it is." He started to offer the mugs to Shelia but caught himself. "Until I found the mug, I had completely forgotten about the luggage. Maybe it was a self-preservation response. The stuffed drawers in the kid's rooms should have been a clue but it took finding the mug."

Shelia looked surprised. "You've gone through the kids rooms already?"

"No." Jonathan was not ready to explain his actions to Shelia. "What time is it?"

Shelia looked at her watch. "Nine-thirty."

The walls felt like they were closing in on him. "Have you had breakfast? I've been cooped up in the house for two days and could use some fresh air and food before we get started."

An awkward pause followed. "I've eaten. You go and I'll get started here?"

Jonathan needed to talk with her away from the house. "Please…"

She picked up her purse. "I'll drive. We should be able to catch the breakfast buffet at Shoney's."

Shelia sat in the booth and waited for him to return from the buffet. His plate overflowed. She sipped her water in silence while Jonathan shoved the food into his mouth, barely chewing between swallows.

He pushed his empty plate away and finally looked at Shelia. "When we get back, I want you to go through the house and get whatever you want."

The waitress came to their table and refilled his coffee. Shelia waited for her to leave before responding. "What I want can't be had."

"For Lori to be the one sitting here with you instead of me… believe me I know," he said.

She looked out the window. "Have you decided what you're going to do with everything?"

"I called our parents last night and told them family could come by tomorrow and Sunday to get any clothing or keepsakes. The word's probably spreading like a wild fire. Will you help me move Lori's things to the guest room so I can close off our bedroom? Lori was adamant about it being off limits to others, so it just doesn't seem right now."

"Are you sure you want to get rid of the house?"

"I'm only sure that Lori and the kids are not coming back, so this seems like the next logical step. I just hope there's a family out there who's willing to overlook the house's history."

"If you find a good realtor, I'm sure that won't be an issue. It's a beautiful home in a wonderful neighborhood."

Jonathan thought about the day they found the house. They were driving through new communities on a Sunday afternoon. It was the only house on the cul-de-sac street that had not sold. The builder was anxious to move the house out of his inventory and made them a great offer. Lori told Jonathan that God had built the house for her and it was waiting for them. It had everything she wanted with plenty of room for their children. At the time, they only had one but he knew Lori wanted more. When they moved their things from the apartment into the house, it still looked empty. Over the years, Lori had lovingly filled each room. "The realtor suggested not getting rid of the furniture yet so it will look like a family's still living in it."

Shelia smiled sadly. "Just for show…"

"You probably think that's how I saw my marriage and family."

"That was between you and Lori."

"I loved her…"

"You had a funny way of showing it." Shelia bit on her lip. "Sorry…"

"There's nothing to apologize for. Believe me, if I could change things I would. Marriage is so complicated."

"That's why I refuse to get married."

"You're single by choice?"

His words stomped on a sore nerve. "Why do people like you always make assumptions on a subject you know nothing about? Since the accident, I've tried to give you the benefit of the doubt, certain that Lori would never have married you otherwise." She shook her head in frustration.

"The words came out wrong. Please forgive me. It's just a well known fact that professional women have a harder time finding men who meet their standards." Jonathan did not want to admit that he was leery of her friendship with his wife. When he confronted Lori with his suspicions, she assured him that he was wrong.

"For your information, I've had several opportunities to tie the knot."

"Then why didn't you?"

"Marriage is a risk I prefer not to take. I know too many women who've been destroyed by failed marriages."

He wondered how much he contributed to the bitterness in her voice. "You make it sound like marriage is a bad thing."

"For the man it's not. Like the Bible says, God created Eve for Adam, to provide what was lacking. Adam needed Eve." Shelia paused. "Eve's relationship with Adam was her punishment for disobeying God."

Jonathan thought about the desperate measures that Jessica had taken. Surely no woman would go through all that if they did not need a man. "Women need men, too."

"Some women think they do, I just don't happen to be one of them. But we could argue about this all day. For the sake of future generations, let's assume that God knows best. But I'm so thankful that in the resurrection there will be no marriage."

The thought of Lori waiting for him was the only comfort he was clinging to. "How do you know that?"

"It's in the Bible...direct from Jesus' lips."

He wondered if Lori was in heaven rejoicing in her freedom from him. "Was marriage that bad for Lori?"

"You should know that, since you were the one who spent the most time with her...let me ask you something. When was the last time you heard Lori laugh?"

The question seemed trite until he realized that he could not come up with an immediate answer.

Satisfied that she had made her point, she reached for her purse. "That's what I'll miss most about Lori...her laughter. Unfortunately, it died long before she did...Are you ready to go?" She stood, hoping that the work would be finished quickly.

He left a twenty on the table and walked out the restaurant searching his mind for the last time he had heard Lori's laughter.

***

Although Sharon looked forward to school resuming for weeks, she suddenly dreaded spending another day alone with Dale. His drifting through each day like a sailboat with a broken mask was unnerving and forced her into uncharted territory. From the day she watched him preside over the university's student government meeting, he had never been hesitant to take action. Even being churchless failed to ignite some since of urgency. When word leaked that Dale had resumed the Bible study, the church asked him to leave the congregation. Damon's exact words, left on their home phone answering machine, were that 'Dale's divisive actions were detrimental to the entire congregation and could no longer be tolerated'. She decided it was time for her to take action, since it made little sense for them both to be home during the day. If he was content to spend his days reading his Bible and praying, he could fulfill the responsibilities of running their household too.

She struggled all morning with the best approach to share her plans. Walking up the stairs and into their office, she questioned her fear of his response. He sat on the floor with his back against the wall and his open Bible at his side. She sat in the chair at the desk, wishing he would at least study like a normal person. "Any new revelation?"

Dale watched her every move. "No."

Sharon nervously tapped a finger on the desk. "So, what are you going to do?"

"Continue what I've been doing," he said.

Her nervousness gave way to frustration. "Which is?"

"Sharon, I've told you that I'm not going to do anything until God tells me to."

"Have you considered that getting kicked out of a church is God's answer?"

Dale tilted his head as if considering the thought. "I'm pretty certain that message was not from God."

"And how do you know that?"

"The sheep know their Shepherd's voice."

"And are you the only one that the Shepherd talks too?"

"Has God given you some revelation for me?"

Irritated by the sarcasm in his voice, Sharon crossed her arms. "Even if He had, would you listen?"

"If it was clearly from God, I would."

"Dale, I don't know why you're being so stubborn. Those other churches would be glad to have you on their staff. You're a strong, spirit-filled man of God who people will gladly follow. Look at the number of people waiting to see where you go."

"Sharon, I don't want people following me. They're supposed to follow Jesus. Besides, the same problems will be waiting at the other churches."

Sharon swiveled the chair. "You don't know that for sure, but if you're going to be so cynical, why don't you just start a new church? At least that way, you can make all the decisions."

Dale propped up his legs and rested his arms on his knees. "For the first time in my life, I don't want to make all the decisions. It's not my place anyway. God decides how He wants the church run and by whom. I just want to do God's will, which is why I need to wait."

The movement of the chair stopped. In the past, Sharon had joked about how much Dale had changed. Looking at and listening to him now, she knew beyond a shadow of a doubt that the man sitting on the floor was not the same man she had married. "Dale, you can't just sit around the house all day, doing nothing."

"Since when is praying and studying God's word nothing?"

"You know what I meant. You need a job and a purpose for living."

"I have both a job and a purpose," he said.

"Then why aren't you doing them?"

"How can I get you to understand that I am? My purpose is to draw nearer to God and my work's to help others do the same. We get so caught up in the task of doing that we forget all about being. I wonder if that's why God sent Moses into the desert for forty years of solitude. Maybe, this is my desert experience."

"Moses had a job in the desert, and I sure hope you're not planning on taking forty years to find out what you think God wants you to do. Moses could've gone up on that mountain a whole lot sooner. Because he waited, others had to suffer longer in bondage."

Dale grimaced at her logic. "God's timing is not up to me. But for the record, I'm content with however long God wants to leave me here and when He says act, I will."

The chair moved backwards, propelled by Sharon's legs. "Since this seems like a solo pilgrimage, would you have a problem with me getting a job?"

"Is that what you want to do?"

"Yes, it is." Sharon had pondered that question for years. She missed being appreciated and accomplishing more than getting the laundry done, meals cooked, and the house cleaned. Their children needed one of their parents home, but it didn't matter which one. "Now that I don't have anything to do at the church and the children are in school all day, there's no reason why I can't be working, especially since you'll be home anyway."

Dale rubbed his hand over the carpet. "Part-time or full time?"

"I tried part-time. If I'm going to do whatever it takes to get the job done anyway, I might as well get full-time pay."

Dale stretched his legs. "When do you start?"

Sharon avoided his gaze.

"I've been married to you long enough to know when you're hiding something from me."

Sharon felt like a child caught in a lie. "They want me to start next week."

"Doing what?"

"Project Management...it's a contract position. The project starts construction soon. It's only an eighteen month project."

"Any travel?"

"Nope...the project's in town. It's a hospital expansion."

"Sounds like you got it all worked out."

"All except for your blessing."

"The blessings are up to God. But if this is what you want to do, it's fine with me. Our children may have a different opinion."

Sharon huffed. "Our children could care less what I do as long as their lives are not inconvenienced, which might actually be a good thing."

Dale looked at his watch. "Do you want to go out for lunch since our daytime dates are about to be a thing of the past?"

"Sure." Sharon stood up feeling relieved that their discussion had gone so well. "While you get ready, I'll call to give them my answer." Before she left the room, he picked up his Bible and began to read.

***

Jonathan and Shelia went from room to room sorting its contents. After several inquiries were met with rejection, he stopped asking if she wanted an item. The sun was setting in the sky when she left the house with a small bag containing a framed picture, a few books, and the pewter lapel pin she gave Lori. Before walking out the door, Shelia asked him not to call her again. He felt another loss and regretted not having a friend like Lori's who was loyal even in death. He hoped for Shelia's sake that friendships continued in heaven.

Walking to his bedroom, he realized his only confidant beside Lori was Jessica. Thinking about her sent a chill through his body. Since asking God for help beside the tree, he had tried to suppress any thoughts of her. It was the second time that day thoughts of her resurfaced. Earlier when he was sorting through his daughters' belongings, Shelia had asked if his other daughter could use some of the items. He fired back that she only wore designer clothes and had too many toys and books. His answer silenced Shelia but not his thoughts. He questioned the fairness of making Simone pay for her mother's actions but a relationship with his daughter would require contact with Jessica.

Jonathan looked at the package of pictures on the nightstand. Flipping through them the night before, he wished the camera had been destroyed in the accident but was thankful it had not. Pausing at one picture of just their children, his mind added Simone to the group. He opened the bottom draw of the nightstand to put the pictures out of sight. A worn gray paper bag caught his eye. He picked up the bag and held it for a long time before being able to remove its content. His hands shook as they clutched the last frame that waited years to be used. When Jon was in Kindergarten, Lori wanted a frame for his first school picture to proudly display his gapping smile. As soon as she saw the frame with spaces for each school year picture, from kindergarten to graduation, she purchased four. Jonathan loved the frame but questioned the quantity. Lori was adamant that she wanted all their children to have one and she was not going to risk finding matching ones in the future. Before two of their children were born, they existed in Lori's heart.

The school picture frames became a family tradition. When school pictures came home, pizza was ordered for dinner and the family celebrated the addition of the new picture to the frame. The last two years, Jason had cried because he could only watch. Lori let him hold his frame and assured him that he would soon get his chance. At the last celebration, Jason was excited that it was his last year of watching. Soon after, he started checking his front teeth, hoping that they would not fall out too soon. Jonathan ached knowing that Jason would never get the chance to put his pictures in the frame. The other three frames were in the box with the photo albums that had been taped shut and put in the closet. He was about to carry the unused frame to the garage to put with the things being donated when he remembered that Simone was starting Kindergarten. Knowing what he needed to do, he put the frame on top of the dresser.

Thursday afternoon while adjusting the silk tree in the foyer, one of several additions the realtor made at her expense to expedite the sale, she assured Jonathan he should have a viable offer in a few weeks. Noticing that the fake looked better than its predecessor that died soon after it arrived at the cabin, he hoped she was right. The house needed to be sold before he could do anything else. His car was loaded with the boxes he dared not leave in the house. Once the realtor's lock box went on the front door, he lost control. The notion of strangers being in his home was hard enough to fathom. Thinking about them handling his family's personal possessions was unbearable. He questioned the wisdom of taking the items to the cabin but it was his only option. He was not ready to relinquish them or the connection that they provided.

Jonathan drove away from his house with the sealed package for his daughter resting on his lap. Stopping by the post office was the last thing he needed to do before leaving the city. By the time he parked in front of the post office, he had talked himself out of sending Simone the frame, fearing that it would complicate his situation more. The package rode beside him, taunting his cowardice all the way to the cabin. He parked at the cabin but kept the engine idling. He looked at the clock and then at the package. The certain smile on Simone's face when her daddy personally delivered a birthday present was worth a brief encounter with Jessica. He had been robbed of saying a final goodbye to Lori and his other children. It would not happen again. He wanted to make sure Simone's final memory of him lasted. Knowing that if he got out of the car to unload it, he would talk himself out of going, he pulled away from the cabin before he could change his mind.

After driving twelve hours, he struggled to keep his eyes open. Frigid air from the vents aimed directly at his face helped briefly before dry eyes forced him to redirect the stream. The car swerved in the lane as he debated whether to stop or push on. Gripping the steering wheel tightly, he reduced his speed while weighing his options. The uncertainty of when Simone started school complicated the decision. If she had started school already, pushing on would allow him to see her before she left. The closer he came to holding his remaining child, the more anxious he became. Realizing that his impromptu visit would jeopardize her going to school helped him make his decision. He pulled into the next hotel on the interstate.

The night clerk was absorbed in a television show but looked up quickly when Jonathan walked in. She checked the clock to determine the correct greeting. "Good morning, sir. How can I help you?"

"I'd like a room please."

"Do you have a reservation?"

"No, is a reservation necessary?"

"It's Labor Day weekend." The clerk typed quickly on the keyboard to appear being helpful. She had already turned away several others. "I'm sorry sir, we're completely booked."

"Are you serious?"

"Yes sir."

"But I only need it for one night."

"The only rooms available are scheduled for check in today. Since it's after midnight, the system won't let me use them."

"I'll leave early."

"I'm sorry sir but we would not have enough time to clean it."

He rubbed his head in frustration. After getting out of the car, he was more alert but waiting at Jessica's condo was less appealing. "Can you check at other locations?"

"Yes sir, which direction are you heading?"

"Towards Chicago."

The clerk laughed. "Sir, I don't even have to check. There's nothing available. That's why we're full."

Tapping his fingers on the counter contemplating his options, he looked at the sofa in the lounge. "Would you mind if I crashed over there for a few hours?"

The clerk remembered her pastor's sermon about the weary traveler who could be an angel in disguise. She did not want to miss a blessing. "If you don't mind a pullout sofa, I can let you use our conference room."

"He smiled broadly. "I would really appreciate that."

"I won't charge you, but I need to see some identification and a credit card, just in case there's any damage."

He handed the clerk what she requested. "I can assure you, there will be no damage. Thank you so much."

The room was still dark when Jonathan's eyes opened. It took a few seconds to read the time on his watch. He jumped up when the numbers came into focus and regretted not asking for a wake up call. It was almost ten o'clock. He walked to the window and opened the curtains. Pulling open the first set, he understood why the room was so dark. A second set of light blocking curtains had been installed. When he pulled back the second set of curtains, bright sunlight filled the room causing his eyes to squint. He walked into the bathroom to get a glimpse of his appearance. The reflection in the mirror confirmed the need to change clothes. At the cabin, his attire was inconsequential. Seeing his only remaining child after such a long separation mandated a conscientious effort. While sliding on his sandals, he contemplated his options, which were limited to a wrinkled golf shirt with shorts or well-worn jeans. It dawned on him that when Lori was alive, his clothes were never wrinkled. He decided to stop at the front desk to get an iron.

The parking lot and the hotel surroundings looked very different in daylight. He walked to the place he had parked his car. The parking space was empty. Hoping that his mind was playing a trick on him, he searched the small parking lot several times before realizing the inevitable. His car was gone along with everything in it. The only thing he had taken into the hotel room with him was the small bag with his toiletries. Fortunate for him it also contained the cash he had gotten for the next two months at the cabin. Walking back into the hotel, Jonathan would have surrendered the money for Simone's picture frame and Lori's Bible and journal.

***

Friday afternoon, the house was quiet. Kendra spent the morning finalizing plans for Eric's birthday, which fell on Labor Day weekend. He was so edgy. She hoped the celebration would help. Sharon's comments about his vulnerability were lodged in her brain. Convinced that Kendra needed to rest, Ruby took the boys with her to pick up Simone. Before lying down, Kendra decided to check her email. Once Eric came home, getting access to the computer was impossible. She resented feeling like he spent more time with the computer than with his family. In addition to his late night sessions, he worked at the computer in the morning while waiting for Simone. Kendra lowered her body into the chair. When she moved the mouse, Eric's work mailbox filled the screen. Afraid that she might delete something, she paused briefly before closing the window. An email with the subject 'Happy Birthday' and Stephanie's name as the sender caught her eye. She opened the email and read it quickly.

'Hey, I enjoyed our meeting. We still work well together-especially behind locked doors. Attached is an early birthday gift. '

Kendra clicked on the attached file and stared in disbelief. Her hand was shaking when she closed the window and shutdown the computer. She stumbled down the hallway to her bedroom with tear-filled eyes and both hands supporting her abdomen, fearful that the babies would be convulsed from her womb. When Ruby returned with her children, the tears had stopped but the trembling had not. She listened carefully for footsteps approaching the bedroom. When she heard Ruby orchestrating snacks in the kitchen, Kendra crept out the bed and closed the bedroom door. A cold washcloth and eye drops reduced the effects of her crying but nothing could eliminate the pain of another betrayal.

At five o'clock, Ruby's quiet knock on the door rescued her from the war raging in her mind. Pretending that she had a good rest, she escorted Ruby to the front door. Since dinner was cooked and Eric would be home soon, Ruby reluctantly left to meet some friends at the movie theater. Eric called fifteen minutes after Ruby left to tell Kendra that something came up unexpectedly and he needed to work a little later. She hung up the phone without a reply, knowing exactly what came up. The picture flashed through her mind followed by the memory of Eric's previous birthday surprise. Anger and her maternal instincts kept her going. Kendra called his office at six-thirty to see when he would be home. When she heard his voice mail, she hung up without leaving a message.

Their sons were asleep by the time Eric's car pulled into the garage. Her heart was so burdened that she labored to breath. There was no energy left to confront her husband. Sitting on the bed while Simone prayed, Kendra attempted her own. Simone climbed into bed while Kendra was still waiting for the right prayer. Her spirit would not allow her to pray for vengeance against her husband. She slowly rose to her feet. "Sweet dreams." The light in Simone's eyes dimmed slightly making Kendra regret saying the words.

"That's what Mommy always told me," Simone said.

"I know." Kendra adjusted the comforter. "When we roomed together in college, she always told me that too."

Simone propped herself up on her elbows. "I really miss Mommy."

"Me too."

"Do you think Daddy will be coming back from his trip soon?"

Kendra's back ached. She needed to get off her feet. "I don't know."

"I hope so. He needs to know about Mommy."

"It's late. I'll see you in the morning." As Kendra kissed Simone goodnight, she wondered if Jessica's perspective about men was right after all.

When Kendra heard Eric coming towards their bedroom, she grabbed her gown and escaped into the bathroom. The surgery to close her womb prevented her from taking baths and she was too tired to stand for very long. The shower chair was finally going to be put to use. She hoped that by the time she finished a long shower, Eric would be snoring or in the office working.

***

Sharon quickly realized the work environment had changed significantly in six years. The pace increased exponentially and electronic communication was the preferred form. People wanted to know everything immediately. A ten minute delay was too long. Her frustration level was high getting into her car, making her more thankful for the long weekend. Prior to returning to the workforce, she took pride in being a courteous driver but today she was anxious to get home. The holiday weekend brought downtown traffic to a snail's pace. As many people were coming into downtown, as were leaving. A car blocked the intersection and made her miss the green light. She honked her horn in frustration.

Waiting for the light to change, she looked at the stack of documents on the passenger seat. It took most of the day to print them out, but she could not effectively review the information on a screen. If she worked the entire weekend, she might be ready for the final design review. The rest of the team had been together since the project's kickoff, putting her at a disadvantage. Canceling the family vacation initially weighed heavily on her, but she had no choice. Her stomach growled, reminding her that she skipped lunch. Her prospects for a satisfying dinner were slim. Although Dale willingly accepted responsibility for meals during the week, his cooking skills were limited. When she called home offering to pickup a pizza, he assured her that dinner was already planned. Finally, the traffic moved. Driving the rest of the way home, Sharon thought of meals that she could cook ahead of time.

As soon as she walked into the house, she smelled a mixture of cleanser and ginger. Her jaw dropped open when she saw her spotless kitchen. She took her bundle of papers and drawings into the den but when she saw how nice it looked, she felt guilty about leaving them there. After totting her work upstairs to the office, she looked into every room and wondered if someone was playing a joke on her. She called out for Dale and her children but did not get a response. There was no note on the counter either. She was about to panic when she saw him in the backyard using the electric edger. She hung her blazer on the back of a barstool and walked onto the deck. Dale stopped edging when he reached the stairs and saw her.

"Welcome home. How was your day?"

"This can't be the same house I left this morning?"

"Yep."

"Where are Shawn and Paige?"

Dale looked at his watch. "They're at the pool since it's the last weekend. They're supposed to be back by six. Why don't you go relax? Dinner will be served promptly at six-thirty." Dale removed his work gloves as he walked up the deck stairs. "I better check on the main entrée." He paused to kiss Sharon on the cheek before going into the house.

Sharon followed. "What's for dinner?"

"We're having lemon-ginger chicken with a pasta and vegetable melody and banana splits for dessert."

"Where did you get it?"

Dale frowned. "I cooked it."

"You mean you're reheating it."

"I mean that I cooked it from scratch using completely fresh ingredients. I don't know why you're always complaining about cooking. How was your day?"

Sharon sat at the breakfast counter feeling dejected. "Remember the snorkeling expedition in Hawaii?"

"How could I forget? It was great. The water was so clear you could see the crater's bottom and the fish swam to you. I wish we could do it again with our children."

Sharon had a slightly different recollection of the event. She jumped off the boat before finding out the water was fifty feet deep. The whole time they snorkeled, she worried about springing a leak in her vest or becoming shark food. "This week reminded me a lot of that experience."

Dale opened the oven just enough to take a peek at the chicken. "You remember when the little boy swam behind you? Dale chuckled at the memory.

"I've tried to forget!" Sharon could not understand what he found so funny. They were in the ocean in the middle of a school of fish. "I thought he was a shark."

"I never saw anyone swim so fast."

Sharon ran her fingers through her hair. "From the looks of things around here, maybe I should have returned to work a long time ago."

"Stop looking so miserable. I had help. There's a new service in town. You select meals from a monthly menu and schedule an appointment to assemble them. It was almost fun. Six complete, ready to cook meals with detailed cooking instructions are in the freezer. This really cuts down on grocery shopping too. I'll show you their website later and you can pick the meals for next week."

"First, let's see what it tastes like. So who helped with the house? I know it wasn't Shawn or Paige"

"I never said I'd do the cleaning. I called the cleaning service our neighbor uses. They're coming every other Friday. For what they charge, it's a real deal and it took them two hours to clean the entire house. I don't know why we didn't do this sooner."

Sharon sighed while inspecting the quality of the cleaning. Even the oven doors sparkled. "I didn't know it was an option. Are the kids still upset about our trip to Chicago being cancelled?"

"A little, but we're going to be vacationers in our own city. I went to the visitor's center and got some brochures. They took a quick look at them before going to the pool. After dinner, we're going to finalize our plans. I want to take a tour of the brewery. Paige's leaning towards a Mississippi River boat ride. Shawn thinks he wants to go up in the arch. He doesn't remember the time we took him, which may be a good thing."

"It's no surprise he can't remember. He was only three. Well, count me out of the plans. I've got too much work to do."

"I hope you'll make some time for a little fun with your family. All work and no play might make you a little cranky. Besides, this weekend's the official end to summer."

"Too bad you never followed your own advice when you were working for a paycheck."

Dale smiled. "I know."

***

Sunday afternoon, Jonathan walked briskly towards Jessica's building. His shirt clung to his perspiration drenched chest. Although it was warm, he suspected his pores were responding more to his adrenaline level. The decision to stop at that motel was costing more with each passing minute. The police who completed the report offered little hope for recovering his car or possessions. Since no rental cars were available in a two hundred mile radius, he lost precious time. The only break he received was a ride into Chicago with a retired couple who had stopped at the motel Friday night. He spent Saturday at an airport hotel waiting for a rental car. After losing another day, he finally decided to call Jessica. Her cell and home phone numbers had been disconnected. He debated taking a cab to her place but without being able to confirm that she was home, and given his current string of luck, he chose not to take the chance.

Sultry blues music could be heard a block away. As Jonathan approached the building, the music got louder. Knowing how Simone would respond but less certain about Jessica, he paused when he reached the landing. Changing her phone numbers raised a warning flag, but he had done the same thing. He hoped the passing of time worked to both their benefit. Walking up the stairs, he realized the music came from Jessica's unit. The doorbell was heard faintly above the music.

Liz was in the kitchen taking her signature chicken wings out of the oven. All her invited guests had arrived. Suspecting it was a neighbor complaining again about the noise, she barked directions for one person to turn down the music and someone else to take care of the neighbor.

Waiting for Jessica to open the door, Jonathan rehearsed his opening line, confident the shock factor would disarm her. The door flew opened. He stared into the bleary eyes of a gray haired man with a smile that revealed perfect teeth.

"If it's about the noise, we turned it down." The smell of bourbon accompanied the words.

The unexpected presence of another man left Jonathan momentarily speechless. He stared at the man's face for some family resemblance to Jessica. "I'm a friend of Jessica's. Is she home?"

The smile on the man's face disappeared as he stepped back and motioned for Jonathan to enter. "Wait here." He closed the door then went into the kitchen.

Jonathan's eyes followed the man but his feet stayed planted in the entry. Smoke hanging in the air caused him to take shallow breaths. He watched the man whisper into a woman's ear before absorbing the changes. The furniture was rearranged and the place was cluttered with people and junk.

The moment Liz saw the face that looked uncannily like her granddaughter, she knew who he was. Her eyes never left him as she dried her hands on a dishtowel. She walked to him with vengeance in her heart. Not only had he abandoned her daughter, he had also abandoned his own. She had waited weeks for a response to the letter she had sent informing him of Jessica's death and his responsibility to Simone. After a month, she shared Kendra's sentiments about the man standing before her. "So you're a friend of Jessica's?"

"Yes I am. Where is she…and *my* daughter?"

Liz made him wait while she processed the information. "Did you get my letter?"

"What letter and who are you?"

Liz scratched her head before covering her mouth with her hand.

Her slow responses irritated him. "Are you going to answer me?"

"I'm Liz, Jessica's mother."

"*Oh* that explains a lot. The minute I smelled the smoke and saw this place, I should have known that they weren't here." Jonathan pulled a business card from his wallet and scribbled his cell phone number on it. He handed the card to her. "Please have her call me as soon as possible?"

Liz clutched the card in her hand.

His frustration after enduring so much to see Simone was evident. "When will they be back?"

Liz crossed her arms and tilted her head to one side. "…Never."

"What do you mean never?"

"Just what I said…"

Jonathan pushed Liz aside and ran down the hallway. He opened the door to Simone's room. An expensive treadmill occupied the space of Simone's canopy bed. A wall of mirrors was opposite the hand painted mural. His lungs struggled for air, as he rushed to Jessica's bedroom. The furniture was the same but the clothes in the closet were not. Liz stood in the same spot when he returned. Every eye in the room was on them. The man who opened the door was perched on the arm of the sofa.

"Where the hell are they?"

"If you would have answered your phone or mail, you would have known."

Every nerve in Jonathan's body sent alarms to his brain. He could not let Simone be used by Jessica. "Please tell me where Jessica took Simone. I need to see my daughter."

"Funny how your *love* child suddenly moved up in the ranks," Liz spat the words at him. "Too bad you weren't more concerned about her."

"I won't cause trouble. I just need to see Simone and make sure that she's okay."

"You can't cause my daughter or yours any more trouble. They were killed in an accident." Liz opened the door wide and stepped back. "The black widow spider has nothing on you. She may kill those stupid enough to mate with her, but at least she spares her children."

Certain that the earth momentarily stopped, he froze by the open door.

"Make sure the next woman you get involved with doesn't drive or have children. Now if you don't mind, you've taken enough of my time."

Jonathan looked around the room, searching for a keepsake, anything that would keep Simone's memory alive. He laughed when he realized the futility of his desire which would only give God something else to take.

Liz sucked her teeth. "I shouldn't be surprised you find humor in this tragic situation. Please leave, before Al has to help you. The sight of you makes me sick."

Jonathan watched Al walk towards him with an alcohol induced cockiness of someone half his age. The desire to knock out a few of Al's teeth passed quickly. He was not the enemy. The guilt that used to accompany him out Jessica's door was joined by defeat. Walking back to the rental car, Jonathan knew he was no match for God. The columns crashed down upon him; but unlike Samson, there was no pleasure in the deaths of those around him.

CHAPTER 11

SUNDAY EVENING, KENDRA WATCHED THE MOVIE SHE LOVED as a child, trying to block Eric's latest birthday surprise from her mind. Her niece was having a sleepover with Simone, so Kendra delayed confronting Eric about the email. She was thankful, her sister-in-law dropped off a complete dinner with her niece. For dessert, they made ice cream sundaes. The girls were lying on floor pillows. Their empty ice cream bowls waited on the coffee table to be collected. Kendra and Eric sat at opposite ends of the sofa with their sons between them. Eric had joined them a few minutes earlier after taking care of the leftovers and dirty dishes. When his cell phone rang, she noticed how quickly he grabbed it and the changed expression when he checked the display.

"Hello," he said quietly.

Liz looked at the setting sun. "Hey. Where's Kendra?"

He looked at his wife. "We're watching a movie with the kids."

Kendra blocked out the voices from the television and listened to Eric's end of the conversation while keeping her eyes fixed on the screen.

"Can you go in another room or call me back later?"

"Wait just a moment." Eric stood and went into the kitchen.

As soon as he left the room, Kendra moved to the other end of the couch hoping to hear what Eric clearly didn't want her to.

"OK, what's wrong?" he asked.

"Jonathan showed up this afternoon to see Jessica and Simone. He didn't know that Jessica had died, even though I wrote him like we discussed."

"What was his reaction?"

"He didn't believe me at first. He just thought they weren't home. When it finally sunk into his thick skull, the man had the nerve to laugh."

Eric leaned against the kitchen counter. "So what does that mean for the future?"

"I don't know what to tell you. After meeting the man, maybe Kendra's right. He'd be a sorry excuse for a father."

"Did you tell him about us? The last thing I need is him showing up at my house causing trouble with Kendra in her current condition."

"I'm no fool. Some things are better left unknown."

Eric sighed. "I don't want Kendra dealing with this until after the babies are born. Then we can take it one day at a time."

"Before I told him about Jessica, he gave me his phone number. I thought you might want it, just in case."

"Let me get something to write with…" Eric turned around and saw Kendra standing in the doorway with the empty ice cream bowls. He tore a sheet of paper off the notepad and picked up the pen. "Can you wait a second?" he said into the phone. "Kendra, I'll be right back. You can leave those in the sink." He went into their bedroom and closed the door. "Okay. What's the number?" He wrote the number and put the paper in his wallet. "Hopefully, I won't need this but I feel better having it. I'm worried about Kendra. She can barely make it up the stairs but she refuses to stop pushing herself."

"You do what you need to do. Your family comes first. If need be, Simone can come back to Chicago and stay with me for a while. When she left, I didn't know that I'd be getting this place. Who would have thought that Jessica would have mortgage protection insurance? Before I was worried about having two mortgages, now I don't have any at all."

"Well, I'd better get back to my family."

"I'll call tomorrow to talk with Simone."

Kendra was at the kitchen sink, when Eric returned. "Who was that?"

"Just a co-worker. Come back and watch the movie. I'll wash those up later," Eric said as he returned to the family room.

The tidbits of the conversation that Kendra heard confirmed which co-worker. Closing her eyes to block the tears and the pain allowed images of Eric and Stephanie to fill the dark canvas. The ice cream in her stomach churned with increasing levels of acid. The pain of his betrayal combined with concern for her children's future. She turned on the water to justify her absence while she contemplated her options. Regardless of when she confronted Eric, he would never share her bed again. The question of whether to put him out of her house now or later was less clear. Kendra cringed, realizing that subconsciously she thought of the house as hers. A finger sliced through the stream of warm water. She cupped her hands together and let the water flow over the sides. Her hands rubbed together, as she symbolically washed her hands of the actions that he drove her to take. Her children needed their father but she did not need an adulterous husband. Kendra turned off the water knowing that she was too smart to end up like Jonathan's wife. She would not give Eric the chance to destroy her. The mental termination of her marriage met resistance from her heart triggering a painful surge of emotions. Within seconds, she realized the pain went beyond her emotions. The first contraction dropped Kendra to her knees. Immediately she knew what she should have been praying for since discovering the email. She gripped the edge of the counter as she panted her way through the pain. Her eyes locked on the simple wooden cross hanging above the kitchen door. Her mothers' words came immediately to mind 'Remember where your Savior is.' "Father, please protect my babies. It's too soon…Jesus help me!"

Eric ran to the kitchen when he heard Kendra cry out in pain. As soon as Eric saw her on the floor, he grabbed the phone to call for help.

***

Sharon sat at the kitchen table trying to concentrate on the specification for the concrete foundations. After reading the same paragraph for the third time, she decided to switch to the drawings. The lines on the drawings only reminded her of how complex life can be. When she finally heard the garage door opening, she prepared to be the bearer of bad news.

Shawn was first through the door. He went to the refrigerator and held the door open longer than Sharon thought was necessary. "Mom, I'm never going up in the St. Louis Arch again." He grabbed a can of soda before slamming the refrigerator door closed.

"What have I told you about slamming that door and I tried to warn you."

"The cars were so little. And you could actually feel the arch swaying."

Her attention was quickly diverted from her son when Dale and Paige came in the door laughing. Sharon wished she could delay the news. "Looks like you had a lot of fun."

"Looks like you didn't." Dale collapsed into the chair next to Sharon and slid off his shoes. "The kids wore me out. It felt like we were really on vacation. You should have come with us."

"Your sister called. She's waiting for you to call her back."

Dale looked at the drawings on the table. "I'll call her later. The kids want to go to the bookstore, so we came home to get you. We don't have to stay long."

Sharon struggled with the right words. Her options were limited. "Dale, you need to call her now. Your father died."

Both Shawn and Paige looked at their father.

It took a few seconds for the words to penetrate. When he looked at Sharon, he knew that he had heard correctly. "What happened?"

"They're still trying to figure that out. When the nurse stopped by this afternoon, your mother wouldn't let her it. The agency called your sister. When she got there, she found him dead in the bed. Apparently, he died in his sleep."

"Who's taking care of Momma?"

"I'm not sure. I didn't talk to your sister very long. There was a lot of commotion in the background but she's waiting for your call."

Dale took his cell phone out of his pocket and pushed a number. "You should have called me," he said to Sharon in an overly harsh tone, as he left the room.

"What could you have done about it in the arch?" She yelled after him. When she returned her attention to her children, they seemed to be in shock. "Are you guys okay?"

Paige walked over to her mother with tears in her eyes. "Is grandpa really dead?"

"Yes, honey. He is."

Sharon slid out the chair and let Paige sit on her lap. As she cradled her crying daughter in her arms, she looked at Shawn who left the kitchen without the soda. Seconds later Sharon heard his bedroom door slam closed. With all the work that she needed to do, the timing could not have been worse for a death in the family.

***

Eric struggled to shift his focus back to work after two stressful days at the hospital. With Kendra hospitalized for the remainder of the pregnancy, the ability to work from home was crucial. He first attributed his problem accessing the company server from home to routine maintenance scheduled during the holiday to minimize disruptions. When his access failed early Tuesday morning, he was concerned about a major system failure. Driving Simone to school, he hoped the problem would be fixed before he reached his office. Simone was usually talkative on the way to school which provided a reprieve from his thoughts but this morning she was quiet. He suspected silence was her way of coping with Kendra's hospitalization.

After watching Simone walk safely into the school, Eric's thoughts returned to Kendra. He sensed that she blamed him for her hospitalization, but had no idea why. Following his father-in-law's advice, he constantly made concessions. The look in her eyes when he kissed her goodbye before leaving the hospital still haunted him. For the benefit of his unborn children, he was willing to be the scapegoat temporarily.

As soon as he placed his briefcase on his desk, he called the Information Technology Help Desk. While he waited for someone to answer, he turned on his computer. Before he could enter his password, he heard the familiar voice.

"Good morning. How can I assist you?"

"Good morning, Tish. I'm glad I got you. Is the server down? I'm having a problem with my remote access."

"Nope, we're good. Let me check your account."

Eric listened to the sound of rapid typing followed by a long silence.

"Your access has been blocked," she said.

"Blocked…by whom?"

"It doesn't say. Have you talked to your manager this morning?"

"No, but I will. Thanks."

Tish knew a blocked assess meant one thing. "Sorry, I couldn't help you."

Eric hung up the phone but kept his hand on the handset a moment longer before removing it. Discounting the information he had just received, Eric entered his password and waited. The same error message displayed. The last conversation with his manager replayed in his head. Eric looked at the calendar on the wall. They had given him six weeks to salvage the project. He still had almost a month left. He was trying to muster the courage to call his manager when the phone rang. "Good morning…this is Eric."

"Eric…How's Kendra and the twins?"

The fact his manager called him was unnerving. Usually he would pop into Eric's office and stay too long. "They're stable. My computer access has been blocked. Do you know why?"

"That's what I'm trying to find out. Can you come down to the HR conference room? We need to talk about this."

Eric wondered who the 'we' referred to. "Can it be taken care of over the phone?"

"Unfortunately not…see you in a few minutes."

When Eric hung up the phone, he noticed that the picture of Kendra and the boys was missing. He opened his desk drawers and cabinets above the credenza. Everything of his was gone. He sat down in his chair concerned that it would be the last time and looked around the office. His manager was waiting outside the conference room. His expression mirrored Eric's. When Tom put his hand on Eric's shoulder and guided him to a chair, he hoped that the paperwork would not take long and the severance package would be fair. He looked at the cardboard file box on the table suspecting that it contained his things.

"Tom, before we get started, I want to apologize for the project. With a little more time, I honestly believed that we could have fixed the problems."

"I know. Unfortunately, this has nothing to do with the project."

His manager's acknowledgment angered Eric. "Then why am I being fired?"

Tom pointed to the other man in the room. "This is Andy Land, with Corporate Security and Compliance. I'll let him explain the situation."

Eric looked at the person who barely looked old enough to be an intern. Something about him generated an instant dislike.

He cleared his throat relishing the opportunity to dispose of the first person within the management ranks. "Recently, we implemented a program to randomly check employee email accounts for compliance with our code of conduct."

Eric wondered about the randomness of the checks. "What does this have to do with me?"

"We found pornography in your files, which is grounds for immediate termination. Had you reported the incident or deleted the email immediately, it would have only been a warning. However, since you chose to keep the material, this organization has no other choice."

Eric refused to let the company get rid of him on trumped up charges. Planting evidence worked within police departments, but he refused to believe his employer was sinking to that level. "The only way you found something unacceptable in my files is if you put it there."

"I can assure you that our operations are above reproach." Andy carried his laptop computer and sat it in front of Eric. "Is this your email inbox?"

Eric looked at the screen, his eyes scrolling down the page of unopened emails that he had not had a chance to check in four days. "Yes…"

Andy opened the next page. "Will you open the last email you read?"

Eric moved the curser to the last email not in bold faced type. His eyes widened when he noticed the sender.

Based on Eric's reaction, Andy knew that he had him. The remainder of the meeting would be strictly a formality. "Do you know the person who sent the email?"

"Yes, but I did not open this email."

Andy smirked at the futile denial. His aggressive series of firings aimed at reducing the use of corporate accounts for pornography was proving more effective than planned. "Our records prove otherwise. Please open the email."

Eric opened and read the email with his manager and Andy peering over his shoulder. He regretted not taking Stephanie's threat after his rebuff seriously. "Although the message could be misconstrued, there's nothing pornographic about it."

Andy sneered. "Open the attachment."

When the file opened, the blood drained from Eric's face. His manager leaned in for a closer look prompting Eric to close the file quickly. Stephanie had sunk to a new low. Eric refused to even waste the effort of trying to convince the over zealous head hunter. He turned to his manager. "Until this very moment, I didn't know that email existed."

Andy was not going to have his authority diminished. Eric's manager was there as a courtesy. He took a few steps away from the computer. "Well obviously someone did because it was opened prior to this meeting. Who has access to your email account?"

"*No one*...I'm well aware of company policy." Eric returned his attention to the computer screen. When he saw the date stamp he felt vindicated. "This email came in Friday at 12:20pm. What time do your records show it being opened?"

Andy walked to where he was sitting and picked up a sheet of paper. "Looks, like Friday at 2:50pm."

Eric turned to his manager "We were in the project meeting from eleven-thirty until four on Friday. There's no way I was checking email in that meeting."

His manager turned towards Andy. "He's right and I was sitting next to him the entire time. The only computer in the room was attached to a projector. If that picture would have popped up on a screen, I would have definitely noticed."

"Well, if you didn't open the email, who did?"

Eric thought for a second before burying his head in his hands. "My wife..." When he looked up again, pain emanated from his entire body. "I checked my email before I left the house that morning. In haste, I must have left the computer logged on." Eric knew he needed to get to the hospital. Kendra had a valid reason for blaming him. "Look, the person who should be sitting in this room is the person who sent that email. She needs some serious help and for her sake I hope she gets it."

"Unfortunately, the email was from a personal account and I don't have jurisdiction over non-employees."

"Stephanie's an employee and you can find her sitting at the receptionist's desk."

Andy rubbed his chin. "I thought she looked familiar. From the sound of the email, you two are involved."

"We were involved, six years ago…before I got married. She stopped by my office and propositioned me. When I rejected her offer, she threatened to make trouble for me. The woman's a basket case, who apparently knows no shame. For the record, I consider this email to be sexual harassment and wish to file a formal complaint. Now, if you're going to fire me can we expedite the process? My wife's lying in a hospital bed with a high risk pregnancy and apparently she thinks I'm involved with another woman."

His manager spoke quickly. "Look Andy, Eric's integrity is beyond reproach. If he says that he's not involved with the woman, I believe him. Since he clearly did not break any rules, you can't fire him. And if you did, Eric would be completely justified in suing the company."

Andy cleared his throat. "Eric, I'm sure you understand that pornography in the workplace is a problem thanks to the Internet. Apparently you were wrongly caught in our net. If it makes you feel any better, so far you are the only innocent party."

"It doesn't." Eric stood up. "Can I leave now?"

Andy simply nodded.

Eric pointed to the box. "Are those my things?"

Andy nodded again anxious to end the meeting and get the real transgressor.

Eric walked to the box and inspected the contents before picking it up. "When will my access be restored?"

Andy sat in front of his laptop computer and began typing. "Give me ten minutes."

His manager held the door open for Eric and fell in step with him. "Do you want me to call Kendra and explain the situation?"

Eric shook his head. "If only I thought it would help."

He patted Eric on the shoulder. "Take as much time as you need this morning. Give me a call when you get back."

When they reached the elevator, Eric handed him the box. "Will you put this in my office? If I go up, I might talk myself out of doing what needs to be done immediately."

"Of course…can I give you a piece of advice?"

"I sure could use some."

"Even when you haven't done anything wrong, flowers and chocolates help."

***

The special wing of the obstetrics' unit was designed for extended stay high risk pregnancies. The rooms were larger and brighter but it was not home. When Kendra learned that the woman who vacated her room had been there for eight weeks, the tears came again.

A nurse sauntered into the room carrying a stack of blankets. "They keep hospitals cold to reduce germs. Thank goodness for blanket warmers." Starting at the top, the nurse covered Kendra with several layers of heat. "Does that feel better?"

Kendra's body absorbed the warmth but it did little to thaw her heart. "Thank you so much. I was afraid my shivering could start the contractions again."

"Try to get a little rest. Those babies need all your energy."

Kendra adjusted the pillow between her knees and tried to get comfortable on her side. The medicine and the blankets addressed the physical pain and the cold but no one could remove the vise grip on her heart. Watching the drops from the I.V. bag fall into the tubing, Kendra tried to estimate how many bags of tears she had shed over Eric. Every path in her brain led to him, sabotaging her vain attempts not to think about her husband and Stephanie. She wondered if they were together in his office rejoicing in their new found freedom. The realization that Jessica was right about men only made the pain worse and added new wisdom to her friend's assessment of men.

'When it comes to women, men are never, I repeat *never* satisfied. The more you give them, the more they want. And don't let anything be off-limits. That only makes them want it more. When you can no longer satisfy them, they move on to the next lucky woman or girl. I hate to burst your little bubble but one day, you're going to realize that I'm right. That's why polygamy works so well. At least in that system, the used up women and their children are not completely dumped. Hell, some women were probably thankful to pass on their burden of trying to satisfy their husband's insatiable desires. Unfortunately, lawyers realized that divorce was a more lucrative alternative for them.'

At the time, Kendra had attributed Jessica's attitude to her choice of men. Now she wondered if Jessica was the victim after all, causing a fresh wave of tears.

Her father walked into the room carrying a vase of yellow and white cut flowers. "Hey, why all the crying?"

Kendra dried her face with the edge of a blanket. "Hi Daddy. I wasn't expecting any visitors."

After setting the flowers on the bedside table, her father kissed her on the forehead. "Are you in pain? I can get the nurse."

"There's nothing they can do."

He pulled the chair closer to the bed. "Are you sure?"

"Very…Although I'm thankful for your company, you can't spend every day here holding my hand. I could be here for weeks."

"That's what I'm praying for. The doctor said each day in your womb will prevent about a week in the intensive care unit for the babies. I want you and my new grandchildren to go home at the same time."

"Thanks for the flowers. They're beautiful."

"You're welcome. I wanted to get a balloon but none of the messages fit the situation."

"Have you talked to Ruby and the boys this morning?"

"I called them on the way here. The boys are going to keep an eye on their grandpa this afternoon while Ruby goes to the grocery store," her father said beaming.

"If you keep telling them that, they're going to really think they're in charge," Kendra said trying to find a comfortable position.

"Isn't that the ultimate goal?"

She reached for her father's hand. "I'm so sorry for all the trouble I'm causing."

He held her hand tightly knowing who his daughter wanted sitting beside her. "You're not causing any trouble. We're just encountering a little bump on the road of life. A few years from now, you'll barely remember any of this."

"I wish that were true but I won't ever forget this nightmare." She needed to confide in someone but wondered if her father would understand her feelings, since he was a man. If he sided with Eric, it would only cause more pain. Looking into his eyes, she decided to take the chance. "You might as well be the first to know. Eric and I are finished. While I'm pregnant with his children, he had the audacity to get back with Stephanie…"

Kendra's father sat on the edge of the chair. "I don't know what drugs they're giving you, but they must have you hallucinating."

"Daddy, I'm not hallucinating. Friday, I found an email from Stephanie to Eric." Kendra clinched her eyes tightly trying to erase the image from her mind. How could he do this to me, again?" Kendra began to sob.

Her father rushed to her side stroking her head with one hand and gripping her hand with his other. "Baby, I'm sure you're mistaken. Eric loves you and would never, ever get involved with someone else, especially Stephanie. What you're thinking isn't even remotely possible."

"Listen to your father!" Eric walked into the room carrying a vase of long stem roses surrounded by baby's breath.

Her father kissed his daughter on the cheek. "I'll leave you two to clear up this misunderstanding."

Kendra sniffed. "Daddy, you don't have to go."

"Yes, I do." He gave Eric a reassuring look. "She's all yours."

Kendra tried to draw her knees to her chest while Eric placed the roses beside the flowers her father brought. Her knees barely moved an inch. The impulse to tell Eric to take the roses and leave was interrupted by movement in her womb. The I.V. constricted hand rubbed her stomach in the area of the movement while Kendra waited for another confirmation that her babies were okay.

Eric walked to the side of the bed. "Can I feel it?"

Her look warned him not to touch her.

He gripped the bed rail. "Why didn't you say something about the email?"

She locked eyes with him. "Why didn't you tell me about your meeting with Stephanie?"

"I didn't mention it because you were dealing with Jessica's accident."

"So that gave you permission to let that slut back into your life?"

"Stephanie's not back in *my* life. As a matter of fact, she's probably being extricated even farther right now, thanks to her last ditch effort. She and Jessica must have come from the same mold."

She looked away. "Jessica was my friend, whose daughter we're raising. Please don't compare her to that no class, ignorant little whining twit."

"I'm sorry. I didn't mean to cause you more pain. And for your information, it wasn't even a meeting. Do you remember the day you called the office upset because Liz wanted to turn off the life support and announced Simone might be coming to live with us?"

She faced him again. "Yes."

"I was trying to ward off a migraine when you know who barges into my office. To make a long story short, she offered to be my mistress, no strings attached. For the record, you were right about her status with God. I, not so politely, rejected her offer. She threatened to claim sexual harassment but I didn't care. Given everything else going on in our life, I put the incident out of my mind."

"What about the email?"

"I hadn't seen it until this morning, when I was about to be fired over it. Thank goodness I had an airtight alibi for the time the email was opened. The company has started a new policy of monitoring email activity for pornography."

"Isn't that an invasion of privacy?"

"Not when it's on their equipment and work time. In this case, I'm glad they were monitoring it. I just wish they would have found it before you. I hope that email was not the reason for your premature labor."

"It didn't help. You might have an explanation for the email, but what about the call."

"What call?"

"Sunday evening when you got that phone call from a co-worker, you asked if someone knew about you before running to our bedroom and closing the door." He took too long to respond. She glared at him. "It's not so easy to explain away the call is it?"

257

"No, but not for the reason you think. The call was from Liz."

Her eyebrow rose signaling her disbelief. "Nice try. Liz always calls on the house phone. She doesn't even have your cell phone number."

"I gave it to her before we left Chicago. She needed to discuss something with me."

"What could she possibly have to discuss with you?" By his look, she knew it had to do with Simone. "Was she returning your call?"

Eric sat in the chair.

"Look, I'm lying in this bed because I thought you were having an affair. All of a sudden you're working longer hours. When you finally come home, you close up in the office until who knows when. Then you get the email from Stephanie and the secretive phone call. If you're not having an affair, I need to know what's going on with you and I want the truth!"

"The reason I'm working so much is because one of my projects is in big trouble and I only have six weeks to get it back on track. As for the call, Liz had a visit from Jonathan and wanted me to know. I asked her if he would be showing up at our house. Knowing how you feel about him and your condition, she didn't want to upset you. Fortunately, Liz didn't tell him where Simone was. She did say Jessica's death was a complete shock for him."

"Good, maybe now he can crawl back under the rock where he belongs." Kendra paused as she processed the new information. Slowly she reached her hand from under the blanket and extended it towards Eric. "I'm sorry for jumping to conclusions."

Eric reached for her hand and traced each finger with his own. "Don't you know me by now? Kendra, I would gladly give my life for you. How could you possibly think I could ever hurt you like that?"

"You did it before." She wondered if they would ever be able to put that period of their life behind them.

"We weren't married and you had left me, remember. Things are different now, much different."

The differences frightened Kendra most. "Eric, there will be other women like Stephanie."

Eric's eyes held Kendra's gaze. "But there's only one you," he whispered softly.

"Jessica said if a man's not getting it from you, he'll soon be getting it from someone else."

"I wouldn't put too much credence in Jessica's logic."

"But you know that's an area of weakness for you. It's been a long time since we've been together and given my current condition, it could be much longer."

"I'm willing to wait."

"But are you able to...and after having four babies, my body may never be the same again."

"Kendra, do you want me to find someone else."

"*No*...it's just...I don't want to end up like Jonathan's wife."

Eric got up, knelt by the side of the bed and clasped both his hands around hers. "Kendra, you're right. I do have strong sexual desires but my desire to always have you in my life is stronger. Not only did we become one physical flesh when we married, we've since become a part of one spiritual body. Jesus knows our weaknesses, both yours and mine. He will never allow us to be tempted beyond what we can withstand. Besides, between this job and my rapidly growing family, I won't have time for an affair."

Kendra's eyes moistened and filled with concern. "Is your job really on the line?"

"Yep." Eric looked at his watch. "...which is why I really need to get back to work, but I'll stay as long as you need me."

"You go," Kendra said patting her stomach. "Your children and I will be just fine." She tried to roll onto her back but the weight of her womb only allowed for a slight rotation. "I'm so sorry I didn't trust you."

Eric stood up and rubbed his knees. "The next time you bring me to my knees, give me a pillow."

She touched his arm. "There's not going to be a next time…I hope."

***

Built on the side of a hill, the cabin's deck overlooked a steep ravine. Jonathan sat on the deck, staring aimlessly. Occasionally, he turned his head in the direction of rustling leaves. The squirrels' activity increased with the rapidly approaching winter, but his activity level remained unchanged. The time between leaving Chicago and arriving at the cabin was a mental blur. Although the cabin was still standing, it was a symbolic mound of ashes. The rental car parked in front of the cabin needed to be returned but he was not even concerned about the mounting rental fee. A bee buzzed around his head without generating a flinch. The same clothes that he wore to Jessica's hung loosely on his body. Once at the cabin, he found no reason to change them. Daily grooming had been abandoned. The hair on his head and face grew together creating a menacing appearance.

The pleasure he thought would accompany Jessica's death never found a foothold. Instead Simone's death struck a deeper chord. It dashed all hope that his life was salvageable. Desperation had driven him to Chicago. Simone offered an opportunity to do something right, to somehow make amends for all the pain he had caused. He sifted every detail thoroughly and came to one undeniable conclusion. Only God could have orchestrated the absolute destruction of his life so swiftly. The timing of the accidents that claimed his wife, mistress and all of his children was beyond coincidence. If God's wrath was so intense in this life, he no longer had any desire to experience it in death. Despite days of trying, he could not reconcile the God he knew with Lori's God. His wife talked about a God of love and mercy. The God he knew was ruthless and vengeful. Although he came asking for help, God answered him by taking the little that he had left.

Surely a loving God would never kill so many innocent people just to punish him. His wife's letter had almost convinced him that God had the answers. He no longer had any questions.

Several weeks later, the call from Eric regarding Simone went directly to Jonathan's voice mail. His cell phone was turned off before boarding the plane from Chicago and put in his overnight bag. After finding out about Jessica and Simone's deaths, he had no reason to communicate with anyone. The bag with his phone was left in the rental car parked beside the cabin.

***

Dale sat in the living room waiting for his sister. His father's ability to shoulder the burden without complaint was astonishing. Dale felt ashamed for not knowing the extent of his mother's condition. As much as he hated to admit it, his sister was right. Their mother could not stay alone. Several extended family and church members provided care while he and his sister made funeral arrangements. For the following two days, he struggled with his father's responsibilities. When he needed his wife most, she was not available. Sharon's decision to put her job before family obligations had him livid. He felt like she was willfully refusing to do the right thing, which was uncharacteristic. The more he insisted that she was not indispensable after only a week on the job, the more adamant she became about not missing work. When his children sided with Sharon, Dale drove to his parents' house alone, leaving Sharon to arrange her travel plans. Her early morning call, before going to work, with her travel arrangements did little to improve his mood. They were flying in Friday evening with barely enough time to make the visitation. He had purposefully left the van, anticipating his family driving to his parents' house.

He heard a car door close and opened the front door as his sister walked up the sidewalk with a box in her hands. He reached for the box. "What's this?"

She walked passed him. "It should be enough food to last until Friday. There's another box in the car. Will you get it?"

Dale walked on the cracked sidewalk. Every time he came home, his comments on its condition were met with the same response. He suspected there were many other things his father did not have the chance to address. He made a mental note to call a contractor about the repair. Now that his father was gone, he would take responsibility for maintaining the house. He paused when he reached his sister's car and looked up and down the street where he raced his friends from elementary to high school. His father used to give him updates on his childhood friends when he came home. Sadness filled him. Opening the car door, he immediately noticed the clutter. The back seat was littered with books, toys and trash. He got the box of food and locked the car doors.

When he returned to the house, his sister was in the kitchen putting an assortment of food containers in the refrigerator. She motioned for him to put the box on the counter. "What did you feed Momma for lunch?"

Dale opened the box to inspect its contents. "We had the chicken salad."

"Did she eat it?"

"Every bite." Dale took a bag of cookies out of the box.

"Good. It used to be her favorite."

"After lunch, we took a short walk for exercise. I don't think she understands about dad. Finally, I started saying 'yes' when she asks if Dad's at work." He opened the plastic bag, took two cookies out and sat the bag on the counter. "How long has she been like this?"

His sister closed the bag of cookies and put it in the pantry. "Ever since the last stroke. This past month has been really bad. Daddy worked so hard to keep Momma happy. God rest his soul. He needed more help than I could give, but he was determined to care for Momma."

Dale leaned against the door frame while he ate the cookies. "I'm sure they appreciated everything you did."

His sister put several containers in the refrigerator, irritated he still had no problem watching her work. "Dale, I've done enough."

"Thanks for bringing the food, but you really didn't have to. Mrs. Brown brought over a casserole and a cake."

"I'm not talking about food. I'm done caring for our parents. It's your turn to step up to the plate." She walked into the living room carrying the empty boxes.

His sister's tone was tense. Following her, he listened to ensure his mother was still sleeping. "Are you serious?"

His sister sat the boxes on the coffee table and crossed her arms. "Why would I joke about this? Ever since you left for college, I've been the one they've depended on for everything. No, let me correct that. For as long as I can remember, I've been the one they expected to help. I thought when I got married and moved out of the house, things would change but they didn't."

After Dale's dealings with Sharon, he was in no mood to argue with his sister. "That's because you live closer and it's easier for you to help."

"Should I be penalized for not moving away? And *easy* is a relative term that's highly dependent on your perspective. "

"Don't blame me for your choices."

"Was it my choice to be born female or how about *my choice* to go to a community college because our parents depleted their savings sending you to that high priced university? You've always been selfish but I never realized what a hypocrite you are. Your new career fits you perfectly. Be careful brother, Jesus had some harsh warnings for both religious leaders and those who don't obey his commandments."

"I didn't know about money being tight. I could have helped you with tuition. But that's in the past, so let's just focus on the present. I can't uproot my family to move here, so what do you want me to do?"

"You can take Momma to live with you in St. Louis."

This scenario never even registered with Dale as a possibility. "Look, I agree that Momma can't stay in the house alone, but moving her to St. Louis is not the answer." Clearly his sister was too distraught to be thinking rationally. "Isn't change bad for someone with dementia?"

"Yes, but either way it goes, there's going to be change. Momma can no longer stay in her house, even if we could afford twenty-four hour nursing care. What's your next excuse?"

"I'm not making excuses. But have you considered the fact that all our bedrooms are upstairs. Momma's too old to be going up and down stairs. The last thing we need is for her to fall and break something."

"Then find a place for her in St. Louis that can meet her needs."

Dale glared at his sister, hoping she was only temporarily insane. "We're not putting our mother in a nursing home."

"They're called skilled care centers. I've checked. Many specialize in dementia care. I think the sooner you get Momma settled into one, the better off she'll be."

"If you've already checked, then you can find one here; that way Momma won't have to leave the city she loves and…"

"…and I'll be around to take care of her. Wrong. My husband has a job offer in Phoenix and he's taking it. It's time I put my family's needs first. Besides, you have more time to manage Momma's care from what Sharon told me. The ball's in your court, so what's it going to be?"

Dale rubbed the back of his neck, frustrated with both his sister and his wife. "We're moving a little fast. Maybe we should worry about burying Daddy first."

"Isn't there something in the Bible about letting the dead bury the dead? What an appropriate response from you. God commands us to honor our parents. In order of importance, that commandment comes before killing, stealing and adultery. Apparently, it must be pretty important from God's perspective. When I stand before Jesus on judgment day, my conscience will be clear. If you walk away from your share of the responsibility, I don't know how you can call yourself a man of God." His sister picked up her purse and the boxes. "I need to pick up my children. Call if Momma needs anything." She paused at the door. "On second thought, don't call me. It will be good practice, since you'll be the one in charge of Momma from now on." His sister walked out the house like the weight of the world had been lifted from her shoulders.

Dale watched her car drive away before closing the door. He stood in the center of the room. "God, help me to know your will."

'Trust me.'

"God, I'm trying to."

Dale walked down the hall that now seemed claustrophobic to check on his mother. The woman lying in the bed looked so frail and helpless. She was sleeping peacefully. He reflected on the admonition of a minister that he listened to regularly on the radio. 'Be obedient to God and leave the consequences to Him.' He walked back down the narrow hallway, knowing what he needed to do and hoping that Sharon would support his decision.

***

Late Wednesday night, Sharon sat in bed with her open journal in her lap. She had read every entry in the journal she started after leaving her career to focus on her family. Finally, she picked up the pen and began to write.

Wednesday, September 7th

It's been too long since I last wrote. Unfortunately it took a major event to get me to. Dale's father died on Sunday. He's at his parent's house until after the funeral on Saturday. The kids and I fly down on Friday, much to his displeasure. I haven't seen this side of Dale in a long time. I know he's stressed, but my being there any sooner won't make the situation any better. I wish I'd gotten roundtrip tickets, so we wouldn't be crammed in his car coming back home. I guess exercising my freedom is worth a few hours of discomfort.

This is my second week on the job, which is why I couldn't go with Dale. Things are too crazy right now. There's a lot to learn in a very short time. This morning was hectic. It's been a long time since I had to get the kids to school before rushing to an office. It brought back old memories. Now, after reading this journal, it seems I've gone backwards. At least they're older and not as needy. We had pizza for dinner tonight and I did not feel the least bit guilty. Thankfully, I won't have to do this for very long. If I can just make it through the week, Dale can handle the kids. Who knows what he's going to do about a job! But that's a whole different story and I don't have that much time or paper.

I'm working with a strange group of people. Apparently not many are Christians and the few which say they are don't act like it. It's going to be a challenge working with them. One guy's language is so bad I don't even want to deal with him but unfortunately I have to. Maybe in time, I'll get used to it again. Well, I'm tired, so I'd better get to sleep. I miss the time I used to have for Bible study. I took my Bible to work with me yesterday but never got a chance to even open it. I need to figure out a workable schedule now that mornings are not an option. Until next time..."

CHAPTER 12

BY THE SECOND WEEK OF OCTOBER, KENDRA HAD CARRIED THE twins past the critical thirty-second week. Being physically separated from her home and family was difficult, despite their many visits. When her request for a shower was surprisingly granted, her joy overflowed. The stream of warm water flowing on her body felt like an extravagant indulgence. Every moment of disconnection from the tubes and wires, which had been attached to her body since being admitted to the hospital, was savored. The shower lifted her spirits and offered hope that soon she would regain a larger degree of control.

Thirty minutes later, with her dried body shrouded in a fresh hospital gown, she stared into the table top mirror and sighed. Her hair was still too short for a ponytail and too long for her natural curls to appear groomed. She heard the cart rolling down the hall and quickly ran her fingers through her damp hair before securing it beneath an elastic headband.

The radiology technician pushed the cart into the room. "It looks like someone got out of bed today."

After six weeks in the hospital, the staff had become like extended family. Kendra kicked off her slippers and reclined on the bed. "They let me take a shower. It wiped me out physically, but mentally it was so worth the effort. How are you today?"

"Very well, thanks for asking." The technician positioned the cart closer to the bed. "Are you ready to see your little ones this morning?"

"Of course…If they're good, we can get this done before they come to reconnect me." Kendra put her arm behind her head hoping to keep her hair from saturating the clean pillow case "I shouldn't say this, but I'm so ready for these little ones to be born."

The technician consulted the chart. "Yesterday, we were at three. Let's see if we can do better today."

Kendra reclined the bed as much as possible without putting too much weight on her back. Her stomach was so large she could not see her legs. While Kendra positioned her body, the technician squeezed a large gob of the blue gel on the sensor head. As soon as the gel smeared on her skin, Kendra's eyes fixed on the screen ready to count. The magic number was eight twitches, which was a sign that the lungs were fully developed. The head of the ultra-sound glided across her abdomen pausing briefly.

The technician looked back and forth between the monitor and Kendra's abdomen. "It looks like they've moved around a bit."

"I felt a lot more movement last night. They must be really cramped."

"Okay. There's one. Look at that strong heart beat. Now let's see how those lungs are doing."

Kendra realized that she was holding her own breath and exhaled loudly.

"That's right mom; you have to breathe too. One, two, three, four, five…that's great. It's up from yesterday. Now, let's see how the little lady is doing." The technician moved the sensor across Kendra's stomach. Okay…"

"She's not hiding, is she?" Kendra took her eyes off the monitor and looked at the technician, who was no longer smiling. "What's wrong?"

The technician moved the sensor slowly pausing several times.

"Jennifer, what's wrong?"

The technician reached for the nurse call button and pressed it twice. Her job was to keep Kendra calm but the signal alerted the nurse's desk of a major problem. "It's probably just the baby's position, but I want the doctor to take a look."

Kendra moved her hands across her stomach hoping to feel what the sensor could not locate, two strong healthy heartbeats. The obstetrician on duty rushed into the room with the floor nurse. The radiologist positioned the sensor to the location where she picked up the first heartbeat before moving so the doctor could take over. The doctor watched the monitor for a few seconds before moving the sensor around. She paused at one spot before quickly putting the sensor on the cart and pushing it away. "Kendra, one of the babies appears to be having a problem. I picked up a heartbeat, but it's weak. We need to deliver right now."

Kendra's own heart paused. "But it's too soon."

"We can't wait." The doctor looked at Kendra's arm before turning to the nurse. "Why isn't she hooked up to an I.V.?"

"We took it out while she took a shower."

The doctor looked annoyed. "Get her hooked up, now!" The doctor left the room quickly.

The radiologist wheeled the cart out of the way and repositioned the stand with the new I.V. bag that was waiting. The nurse reached in her pocket and pulled out the I.V. needle and alcohol wipe. She started the line with little trouble and tried to give Kendra a reassuring smile before leaving the room.

The radiologist had another patient waiting but did not want to leave Kendra alone. "Don't worry. Everything's going to be alright. Do you need to call someone?"

Kendra's brain was frozen by the thought of losing her daughter. Guilt overwhelmed her. Had she caused the problem by getting out of bed to take a shower?

"Kendra, do you want me to call Eric for you?"

Hearing Eric's name loosened the grip of fear. "No, I can do it. Will you hand me my cell phone?"

***

Eric sat at his desk carefully reviewing his resume. Despite all the unpaid overtime he worked getting the project back on track, he still felt guilty for doing personal work at the office. After a brief phone conversation, the recruiter was convinced he had finally found the perfect candidate for a position that he had been working to fill for months. The recruiter was waiting anxiously to receive Eric's resume. True to form, he never responded hastily, wanting to ensure his resume was accurate and error-free. His manager tried to convince Eric not to view the removal of all supervisory responsibilities too negatively and assured him that a bright future with the company was still possible. Eric knew it would take too long to undo the damage caused by ill-placed trust in a subordinate and malicious rumors circulated by Stephanie. In the future, he would follow his gut instincts from the start. For the sake of his family, he was willing to live with the demotion short term but he had complete peace with his decision to leave the company. Wherever God wanted to send him, he would willingly go.

When his cell phone rang, he answered it quickly without checking the display, anxious for the update. Kendra called after every ultrasound.

"Hello."

"This is Jonathan Grey, returning your call."

Eric did not know whether to be happy or concerned to receive the call that he no longer expected. A week after leaving Jonathan the message, Eric assumed he had no interest in his daughter. The backup plan for Simone to return to Liz until after the babies were born barely left his mouth before Kendra was shouting to the point of hysteria. Eric withdrew the suggestion and settled in for their new normal. "I'm surprised to finally get a call from you."

"I just listened to your message. Getting the news about Jessica and Simone's deaths so soon after losing my family was quite a shock. It's taken me a while to process it all. I'm not sure if I'll ever be able to, which is why I had to disconnect from the world before I destroyed anymore lives. I checked my messages today only out of necessity."

Eric leaned back in the chair wondering why Jonathan thought Simone was dead. "Jonathan, there's been some kind of mistake. Simone's not dead."

Jonathan's legs had difficulty supporting his weight. "But Liz told me they were in an accident. I checked Simone's room…"

Eric wondered how Liz could be so cruel. "Jessica died after being accidentally shot, but Simone's very much alive and living with my family. Liz did not want the responsibility of raising her granddaughter and we could not get in contact with you."

"I don't understand…" He paced around the suddenly cramped cabin.

"Jonathan, Simone's alive."

Once he grasped the truth, adrenaline raced through his body. "I need to see her. Where is she? I'll get there as soon as I can. She needs her father…and I need her."

Eric pictured Kendra's reaction to their conversation. "We live in Dallas, but I'm afraid the situation is somewhat complicated."

"What's complicated about it? Simone's mother is dead and apparently the woman who's supposed to be her grandmother doesn't want her."

"Jessica named Kendra to be Simone's legal guardian in her will, with an addendum concerning you."

"I'm her biological father! You can't keep my daughter from me."

Eric clearly heard the desperation in Jonathan's voice. "Calm down. I'm not trying to keep your daughter from you, especially since she's waiting for you to come back from a long trip."

The fact that Simone was waiting for him had a soothing affect. "Is she okay?"

Eric breathed a sigh of relief hoping they could work together to resolve both their problems. "She's fine, besides missing her parents."

Jonathan ran his hand across is face suddenly aware of the thick beard. "Can I please come see her?"

"I hate to ask, but can you wait a little while longer. My wife's in the hospital with a high risk pregnancy. If she thought you were anywhere near Simone, she would go ballistic. I can't take that risk. If only you had called sooner. Now is just not a good time. "

"Maybe not for you, but for Simone it's way past time. We've been kept apart long enough. How much more must she suffer?"

"Look, I want you to see your daughter, but my wife has a very different view. And right now, protecting my wife and un-born children is my first concern."

"She doesn't have to know. I just need to see Simone and let her know I'm here for her."

"There's no way Simone would be able to keep this a secret. We can't ask or expect it of a five year old." Eric's phone signaled another call. "Can I call you back? That's probably my wife call-ing." Eric stopped short of adding that he needed time to figure out what to do.

"When will you call me back?"

Eric did not want the call to go to his voice mailbox. "As soon as I can."

"Today?"

"As soon as I can…" He pressed the end call button and saw the new call was from Kendra. He forced his thoughts away from Jonathan, as he answered. "Hey, I'm glad you called."

"Eric, there's a problem with Katherine." The nurse returned with a young man in scrubs. The brakes were released on the bed and she was being wheeled out the door.

"What kind of problem?"

"Her heartbeat…they're taking me to surgery now. Please get here as soon as you can. "

Eric saved the file and removed his memory stick. The recruiter would have to wait a little longer for his resume. "I'm on the way. Don't worry."

"Eric, pray and call Daddy and Ruby."

Jonathan did not care that Eric rushed him off the phone. Before he could fully comprehend what was happening, he was smiling; something he had not done in months. For several minutes after closing his phone, all he did was shake his head in disbelief. He opened the phone again and dialed the number for the only person who would understand.

***

As soon as Dale returned home from his father's funeral, he searched for the best skilled care facilities. His sister's impending move dictated the timing of their mother's relocation to St. Louis. After visiting a few of the nicer ones, it became apparent that his mother should live with him, even if it meant moving to a house that could accommodate her needs. Sharon adamantly opposed his intentions, stating she did not need another job. Their children fed off her negative emotions and complained about their lives being affected. Dale's argument that honoring your parents was a commandment of God which required obedience even when it's inconvenient had little impact. Sharon replied he could honor his parents without turning their lives upside down and reminded him it was God's direction for a man to leave his father and mother and cleave to his wife. She was visibly relieved when Dale finally signed the paperwork to reserve a room at a facility.

On a sunny October day, Dale drove to get his mother. The trip proved more difficult than he anticipated. During the drive, she kept asking about her husband. Leaving her in the strange surrounding the first day required all his physical, spiritual, and emotional strength. The floor nurse's assurance that his mother's reaction was completely normal provided little comfort. His mother needed him, not strangers, caring for her. It was his job to protect her and make sure that all her needs were met. As soon as he walked into his house, he called the contractors with the highest Better Business Bureau rating about adding a first floor bedroom suite onto their house. Three contractors were scheduled to meet with him to get estimates. He decided to wait until he had all the information before telling his family about his modified plans.

By mid October, Dale had firm bids for the bedroom addition, making his visits with his mother a little easier. He walked into the lobby hoping his mother would be in a better mood. The receptionist sitting behind the high counter greeted him with a smile saturated with encouragement. The smell was still the first thing he noticed, followed by the sights and sounds of despair and hopelessness. It felt like he was walking through a prison for the aged. Everywhere he looked the similarities could not be missed. The mental comparison fed his desire to get his mother released as soon as possible. But until her room addition was complete, there was little he could do besides having lunch with her every day and trying to reassure them both that the situation was only temporary. The contractor estimated that he could complete the house addition before Christmas, if the weather cooperated. Dale dreaded the prospect of the three month incarceration.

The main dining room was set for lunch. A few of the healthier residents were already navigating the tables and it was barely ten thirty. Dale returned their greetings knowing that a positive attitude at the end of life was a gift from God. He wished that God would spread the gift more abundantly. His mother's room was close to the nurse's station. It was the first place he always checked even though she was rarely there. Her room was empty. The gold framed collage of family photographs hanging above the bedside table drew his attention. His sister put great effort in assembling the pictures with names written largely beneath each. When he went to get his mother, it was the last thing put into the van. His sister handed it to him with tears in her eyes. Hanging the frame, Dale was concerned it would remind his mother of all she had lost. After a few visits, his fears were put to rest. His mother barely acknowledged the smiling images of her family. The collection was more daunting to Dale.

The nurse was on the phone when Dale reached the desk. He tried not to listen to the conversation which was obviously unpleasant. Daily he witnessed the great patience required to care for the patients and deal with their frustrated family members. When he made the connection between the words patience and patients he smiled despite the irony. Frustration was written all over the nurse's face but she still managed to greet Dale with a smile. "Good morning. Are you here to have lunch with your mom, again?"

Dale returned the smile in awe. "Sounds like you're having a rough morning?"

The nurse wrote on a chart then set it aside. "Unfortunately, it's nothing out of the ordinary."

"How do you do it?"

"Some days I'm better, some I'm worse."

"Where's my mother?"

"We switched her physical therapy to the morning since she complained about being too tired in the afternoon. We try to find the best schedule for each resident." She looked at her watch. "You can go watch, if you'd like. She has another fifteen minutes."

Dale noticed the way the staff consistently referred to his mother as a resident instead of a patient. "My presence will only distract her. I'll wait for her in the dining room."

"I'll have her aide bring her there."

Dale returned down the long hallway, looking into rooms as he passed. Some had personal furniture squeezed into the small confines. Most had the standard twin hospital bed and a three drawer dresser. Adjacent to the dining room, was the activity center and lounge with a large screen television. The television was on the news channel, so Dale decided to wait in there.

An elderly man, alone in the room, looked up when Dale entered. "You're new around here."

Dale sat in the wingback chair across from him. "My mother just moved here...temporarily."

The man looked inquisitively at Dale. "Then where's she going?"

"She'll be living with my family, but first our house has to be remodeled."

The man's smile radiated warmth. "Not many children are willing to do that for their parents these days...too self-absorbed."

Dale didn't respond, but the man was not deterred.

"I'm ninety-two...outlived my wife and children. When my daughter died, I decided to live here. My granddaughter's too flaky and her children were about to drive me crazy. Twenty year-olds still living at home. Grown children should not be living with their parents unless they're caring for them." The man shook his head. "God has his work cut out for him with this generation."

"You'll get no argument from me on that." Dale was taken back by his bluntness.

"Do you have children?"

Dale looked into the dining room, hoping to see his mother which would provide a polite excuse to leave. "Yes, I have a son and a daughter."

"Do you discipline them?" He did not wait for an answer. "You know that's the secret. Spare the rod and spoil the child. The rod can take many forms but there are some children that could have used a good whack across the bottom when they were small."

"My father shared that belief."

"When did he pass? ...your father?"

"Last month. That's why my mother had to move here."

"You must think I'm a noisy old coot." He observed Dale before continuing. "I don't believe in chance encounters, so no use wasting time." He chuckled. "I have an apartment in the independent living unit, but moved to this building for a little while."

Dale smiled at the man's spunkiness. "Why did you move?"

"A good friend broke his hip and needed full time care. I was here visiting so much I decided to check in to keep him company. As long as you pay the bill, you can do pretty much what you want. Unfortunately the pain medication makes him sleep a lot."

Dale walked to the gentleman who appeared starved for conversation and extended his hand. "Please excuse my rudeness. I'm Dale."

He eagerly accepted the gesture. "It's a pleasure to meet you Dale. I'm Rubin, but most people just call me Doc."

Dale smiled. "I have a good friend named Ruben."

"Is he Jewish?"

Dale chuckled as he sat down again. "No….They seem to do a good job with activities for the residents."

Doc crossed his frail legs. "I haven't had time to do many of the planned activities. I'm too busy with the unplanned ones."

"You're a breath of fresh air in this place. What keeps you so busy?

"Whatever God wants me to do." Doc rubbed his chin. "You sound like an intelligent fellow. What do you do?"

Dale tried not to be insulted by the man from a different era. He wanted to give Doc the benefit of the doubt regarding the racist undertone of his intellect statement, but still found it uncomfortable admitting that he was unemployed. His current situation would only fuel any preconceptions of the African-American male. It was the first time someone other than Sharon had inquired about his occupation since being asked to leave the church. Dale considered carefully how to respond. "You and I have a lot in common."

Doc watched Dale sensing his uneasiness. "Are you a doctor?"

Too embarrassed to tell the truth, Dale wondered if he would ever shed the sin of pride. "No, but we both work for God."

Doc smiled. "See, no chance encounters. So, what does He have you doing?"

"That's a million dollar question. I was in church leadership until recently."

"For how long?"

"Not very long. This is a second career for me, or so I thought."

"What happened to make you doubt?"

"It's a long story." Dale saw his mother being helped down the hall. "There's my mother," he said standing up. "Doc, it was a pleasure talking with you. Maybe I'll see you again."

"Why don't you and your mother join us for Bible study on Saturday mornings? We're tackling Revelations."

Dale was baffled by the statement. "Aren't you Jewish?"

Doc raised a challenging eyebrow. "And…"

"I didn't think Jewish people studied the New Testament."

Doc smiled. "Jewish people wrote the Bible, under God's direction of course. Why on earth would we not study what we helped preserve?"

The polite smile faded. Dale looked into Doc's eyes and saw a light burning brightly. "Are you a Jewish Christian?"

"If you mean a Jewish disciple of the Messiah, I most definitely am."

Dale noticed his mother's smile when she saw him. "I really have to leave. Maybe we'll get to talk another time."

"Come see me before you leave. I'm in room 501."

Dale walked away, curious about the man, but doubtful he would honor his request.

***

The hospital's maternity waiting area had been redecorated since Eric had announced the birth of his youngest to their family. Waiting for someone else to announce the birth of his children was nerve-racking. For both of his sons, he labored right beside Kendra, pushing emotionally as hard as she pushed physically. Despite substantially exceeding the speed limit and parking at the emergency room entrance, Kendra was already in surgery when he arrived at the hospital. The fact that they would not let him in the operating room increased his anxiety. The best he could do was to send a message to Kendra's doctor that he was there. Everyone that needed to be called had been, leaving him with nothing to do but pace the hallway and pray. Eric was relieved when he saw Kendra's father walking quickly down the hall.

Caleb handed Eric a bag. "I figured you probably missed lunch. How is she?"

Eric took the food doubtful that he could eat anything. "I don't know."

Caleb led Eric into the waiting room. "Is her doctor doing the surgery?"

"I don't know that either." Eric fidgeted with the sandwich bag. "I don't even know if Kendra knows that I'm here."

"Well, there's one thing we both know, Kendra's not alone."

Eric nodded. "I just want to be with her, even if it's just to hold her hand. She sounded so scared when she called. I don't know if she can bear any more loss. Hopefully, they put her to sleep. If there's bad news, I want to be with her when she hears it."

"Don't start thinking about the worst." Caleb put his arm around Eric's shoulder and walked him to a bank of chairs. "God works all things for the good of those who are called according to his purpose. We have to believe that."

Eric thought about Jonathan waiting for his call and wondered whether Simone being left motherless was for Simone, Kendra, or Jonathan's good.

***

When the aide came to escort his mother to her afternoon therapy, Dale reluctantly kissed her goodbye. The last substantial conversation with his mother prior to this visit was well before his father's death. Her lucid awareness caught him completely off guard. It took a few seconds to realize what was happening. As soon as he sat down, his mother started their conversation with an acknowledgement of his father's death. A deep sadness filled her eyes but she seemed at peace. Her hopeful question which followed was heart-rending to answer. Dale struggled to find words to minimize the pain of losing her beloved home and quickly shifted the conversation to details of her coming to live with him. When his mother expressed her delight with his plan, the matter was settled in Dale's mind. Convincing Sharon it was the right thing to do was the final obstacle. Without warning, his mother slipped back into her confused state while discussing what she wanted from her house. Despite his best efforts, the door was closed again, but he was extremely grateful for the few lucid minutes God gave them. Walking towards the entrance, he remembered Doc's invitation and allowed curiosity to trump reason.

Doc was sitting in a chair with a well worn Bible in his lap. He smiled at Dale who seemed hesitant to enter the room. "I'm glad you came."

Dale took in the full measure of the man, who was meticulously dressed in a collared shirt and navy blue buttoned sweater. Not a hair was out of place. "I only have a few minutes," Dale whispered, not wanting to disturb Doc's roommate who was snoring rather loudly.

Doc gestured for Dale to enter. "He can sleep through anything. However, being heard over his snoring may be a challenge. Have you been to the butterfly garden yet?"

"No, I haven't."

"Then let me show it to you. I went out this morning and the day looked promising."

"It's a beautiful day." Dale followed Doc through the wide doorway which a few days prior would have been unnoticed. The contractor remodeling his house had explained that two of the door frames needed to be replaced to allow for wheel chair access. Since his father's death, a radically different perspective of elderly care materialized.

Following Doc's slow and deliberate steps, Dale discovered a small haven tucked into the recesses of the facility. A wide concrete path ran the length of the long, narrow courtyard. An assortment of plants and trees softened the brick walls. Few blooms remained and several trees displayed their fall color. At the far end of the courtyard was a raised bed garden. Dale stopped beside the sun-filled gazebo in the center of the garden. "My mother will love it here. I hope the weather stays nice."

"We should have another month to enjoy it; maybe two, if your mother's not cold-natured."

Dale pointed to the raised bed. "Is that for the residents?"

"That's what I was told, but I'm here every day and haven't seen anyone even go near it." Doc walked to one of the wooden benches and waited for Dale to sit down first, subtly defining their respective roles. "How about telling me the abbreviated version of that story?"

Dale sat at the edge of the bench and rested his arms on his knees. "I doubt it can be abbreviated."

"Give it a try."

A complete stranger seemed like an unlikely confidant but Dale needed somebody to talk with, besides God. "Five years ago, I was managing a marketing division for a large corporation. God revealed himself to me through a series of unmistakable events, even providing the funds for me to attend seminary."

"Ah...you're a trained theologian."

From the tone, Dale knew he should be offended but the twinkle in Doc's eyes indicted no malice.

Doc continued. "You're probably familiar with the first time Samuel heard the Lord as a child. He ran to Eli who taught him how to respond to the Lord's call. If you ask me, too many of to-day's 'called' are flocking to the wrong teachers. Sorry…please continue. " Doc put his hand over his mouth.

"I specialized in counseling. After earning a masters degree, I joined a small practice. Let's just say counseling was definitely not for me. Studying the Bible's my passion, so when I found an opening for a teaching minister in a small congregation, I jumped at the chance. A few months later, the senior pastor had a fatal heart attack and I was asked to be the interim pastor. Unfortu-nately, the church and I were not on the same page, so to speak. They hired someone else." Dale shook his head thinking about Damon. "Here I stand…a shepherd without a flock."

"Do you want to be a shepherd?"

Dale pondered the question which he had never been asked so directly. He loved God and desired to serve him but did he really want the responsibility and headaches that came with shepherd-ing people who really did act like sheep. "That's a very good question."

"Ah my friend, asking the right question is the heart of learn-ing."

Dale sat back on the bench. "What kind of doctor were you?"

"An Ophthalmologist…practiced for almost fifty years. We sold the practice a few years back when my son decided he was ready to retire and his sons had no interest in taking over the family business." Doc smiled brightly. "God hooked me in re-tirement!"

"Really?…most people have solidified their beliefs by then and can't be easily swayed."

'True, true…which is what led me to read the Bible. I met a gentleman at a coffee shop one morning…my wife, bless her soul, got tired of me waking her up early so I'd have someone to talk to, so she kicked me out of the house. I met Bill that morning."

Doc sighed contently at the memory. "He was a brother of strong faith who's with the Lord now. Anyway, Bill tried to evangelize me over a cup of coffee. He knew more about the Torah and Prophets than I did and mind you, Jewish people are weaned on the Holy Scriptures. Unfortunately, I didn't know a thing about what he kept referring to as the New Testament. Seeing how he had me at a disadvantage, I told him we'd continue our discussion after I did a little research. Do you know what he did?"

"What?"

"He went out to his car and came back with a Bible; said he always kept a spare just in case, even gave me his phone number in case I had any questions. We arranged to meet again the next day. That was almost ten years ago and I've been reading the Bible every day since."

Dale looked at the Bible in Doc's lap. "It looks like it."

"I have a couple of others but this is still my favorite; my gift from God." He opened the Bible to the first page and held it out for Dale to inspect. "See, that's Bill's phone number. Well, it used to be his phone number." Doc closed his Bible. "I can't wait to see him again, but it seems like God has a little more work for me."

"So what does God have you doing?"

"After being an eye doctor for half a century, I get to help people truly see." Dale's blank stare elicited a chuckle. "God has such a sense of humor or maybe it's just his divine wisdom that puts joy in my soul, but back to your question. Are you familiar with the incident in the Book of Acts where Phillip was instructed to approach the chariot of the eunuch?"

"Yes, I am," Dale said.

"What was the eunuch reading?"

"The book of Isaiah."

Dale's quick response confirmed Doc's suspicions. "And what did Phillip ask him?"

"Did he understand what he was reading?" Dale did not have time to wait for the assumed follow-up questions. "...and the eunuch replied that he could not without a guide."

"That's my new line of work...being a guide to treasure seekers. An "X" really does mark the spot, but only those with eyes to see and ears to hear will be able to find it."

"What is the treasure?"

"The Truth, of course," Doc replied.

"I thought the Holy Spirit is supposed to be our guide?"

"True, true...but the Holy Spirit needs something to work with." Doc clutched the Bible on his lap. "Do you mind if I ask you a question?"

Dale wondered why he suddenly felt obligated to ask. "No."

"What is the Bible?"

"I believe it's the inspired word of God."

"Aw...but that's only half the answer."

"Then what's the other half?"

"It's the inspired Word of God that reveals the person and work of Jesus Christ from cover to cover. Every book, every chapter, every verse reveals something about Jesus Christ, just as every cell in our body reveals our unique genetic structure." Doc paused, contemplating how to proceed. "Most people don't believe that God still speaks to us. Has God spoken to you?"

Dale looked at the garden debating how to respond.

The silence confirmed Doc's suspicions. "He has...I knew it...tell me about it."

"You won't believe me. Sometimes, I even have a hard time believing it was really God."

"Try me."

"All my life I've had an awareness of God but it was never concrete. Life's frustrations sent me looking for answers. Probably because of my upbringing, I started with the Bible. The more

I read; the more questions I had. Right before going to seminary, I prayed that God would show me what to do. That night, I had a dream unlike any other. The details are sketchy but I woke up remembering two things; the light and the clearly spoken words." Dale rubbed his hands on his knees. Other than Sharon, he had not told anyone about the dream. "At the time, I took the dream as confirmation for seminary. Now, I'm not so sure. The one thing I do know. Since that day, my life has not been the same."

"Answers are appearing before you even ask the question and there's no doubt God's intervening in your life."

"How'd you know?"

"It was so much simpler when God spoke from the burning mountain. We didn't have to guess whether it was God talking to us. Now days, we're so scattered and there's so much confusion. You should read God's prophecy against the shepherds of Israel in Ezekiel's writings. It will shed new light on Jesus' statement that he is the good shepherd who knows his sheep and his sheep know him."

Dale subconsciously looked at his watch, not wanting to be late picking up his children but wanting to continue his conversation with the first person to share his passion for the Bible.

The way Dale looked at his watch alerted Doc that their initial session was about to end. "Looks like you need to go. When you're reading your Bible tonight, write down any questions which might come to mind. Next time, we'll find the answers together."

"How do you know I'll read the Bible tonight?"

Doc pointed an aged finger at him. "You knew what scroll the eunuch was reading."

Dale stood up. "Can I walk you back to your room?"

"No, I'm going to stay out here for a while. I'll see you tomorrow."

Dale walked away, certain that meeting Doc was no coincidence.

***

Jonathan occasionally glanced at his father who insisted on driving despite the late hour. Few words were shared on the way to the Atlanta airport. Everything that needed to be said had been. When his father parked in the passenger unloading lane, Jonathan opened the car door feeling like a child going to school for the first time. He was eager to start his adventure but hesitant to leave the security of home.

His father touched his arm. "Son, remember that your mother and I love you very much. We'll be praying for you and Simone."

Fear of losing his fragile composure prevented Jonathan from responding, but his father's words lingered long after the car had disappeared from sight. If he had only loved his wife and children as much as his father loved him. He walked into the terminal aware that it was futile to dwell on the past. The only thing he could change was his future. The line at the ticket counter was short. When the ticket agent noticed Jonathan's preferred flyer status, he upgraded him to first class which dredged up bitter memories. The last time he flew first class was the trip to Hawaii with Jessica. His boarding pass was in his hand before he could decline the upgrade. He rode the escalator down to the tram barely aware of his surroundings. The plane was unloading when he reached the gate. He placed his small overnight bag with his shaving kit and one change of clothes on a chair near the television and sat down. The late evening news was coming on so there was no need to check the time; still he looked at his cell phone. With the hour time difference, Eric still could call, but Jonathan was not sure if he wanted him to.

The flight attendant spotted Jonathan in the gate area while she was waiting for the crew change and noticed the absence of a wedding ring when he took his seat in first class. "Are you traveling for business?"

The attention he once craved went unnoticed. "No."

"So, are you going on a vacation?"

"No."

She smiled. "You're talkative tonight."

"I've got a lot on my mind."

"Let me know if there's anything I can do for you." The flight attendant returned to the door to greet the other passengers.

The need to see and hold Simone grew more intense with each passing minute. Jonathan's conversation with his father after learning that Simone was alive ended with a heartfelt invitation for him to come home. Since Eric could not bring his daughter to him and Simone could not fly alone at her age, the father and daughter reunion would require him to travel. Being in Atlanta was the next logical step.

Jonathan had every intention of staying at his parent's home until he talked with Eric. Being home was refreshment for his soul. Despite his deranged appearance, his parents were overjoyed to see him. After a hot shower and meal, his parents listened intently as he described the series of events which had happened to him since the funeral, reliving the painful trip to Chicago and the unexpected joy of finding out that Simone was alive. Before long, he was telling his parents all about Simone. His parents waited with him for the call, hoping they would be able to say hello to their granddaughter.

By five o'clock, Jonathan could not wait any longer. After leaving three voice messages, every hour on the hour, he called the airline and purchased a ticket on the last flight to Dallas from Atlanta. He had never met Kendra or Eric, but thanks to the Internet, he had their home address and phone number. He even called their house after leaving the second message on Eric's phone but no one answered. Jonathan wondered if Eric was purposefully avoiding his calls. That thought was the determining factor for Jonathan being on the plane. Eric could avoid his calls but he would not be able to avoid him for much longer. He had every right to see his daughter, regardless of what Jessica might have put in her will. Simone wanted to see him too.

The fact his daughter was living in Texas made him wonder if it was coincidental or part of a larger plan. Two weeks after graduating high school, the overweight bullied kid he used to be left Texas and his painful past in search of a different future. Eighteen years later, he was returning to Texas for the very same reason.

The flight attendant was reading the pre-flight safety instructions about assisting others with their air masks when Shelia's words about him always thinking about himself resonated. He looked across the aisle at a couple traveling with a small child. At the time he purchased the airline ticket, he had convinced himself that Simone needed him and he had to get to her as soon as possible. As the plane slowly pulled away from the gate, he momentarily reconsidered the wisdom of flying to Dallas before speaking with Eric again. When the crew gave instructions to turn off all electronics, Jonathan turned off his phone committed to his plan of action. Gripping the armrest as the plane sped down the runway, he feared his actions had more to do with his needs than his daughter's. The force of the plane climbing into the sky forced his head against the headrest. His thoughts drifted back to God for the first time since leaving the cabin. He was unaware his lips were moving as he asked for help.

CHAPTER 13

DALE HAD PROCRASTINATED AS LONG AS POSSIBLE. HE BRACED himself for an emotionally charged conversation with Sharon. The issue of his mother living with them was settled for her. The deposit he mailed to the contractor with the signed contract felt like a betrayal, but his decision was not made lightly. He hoped to convince Sharon that his mother living with them was no longer something he felt obligated to do. He wanted her to live with them and waiting too long would be more traumatic for his mother. If the concrete slab could be poured before the cold weather, the contractor was willing to guarantee a finish date before Christmas. The work crew would be at the house the following week. Dale hoped seven days would be enough time for his wife to mentally accept the change.

Discussing the impending change before dinner was prevented by Sharon's call announcing that she needed to work late. By the time she came home, Dale was helping Shawn with his homework. When Dale finished helping Shawn, Sharon was with Paige. Not wanting to interfere with their time together which was scarce during the week, he went into the office to read. Starting in Acts with the story of Phillip and the eunuch, Dale followed an unending thread. Sound from the television drifted upstairs causing him to check the time. It was almost ten o'clock. He closed his Bible and reviewed his questions which seemed more numerous on paper. Dale doubted whether Doc could answer any of them but decided it would not hurt to get another perspective. He said a brief prayer and then went to have the conversation.

Dale walked into the family room and saw Sharon sitting on the sofa with her feet propped on the coffee table. A stack of bulging file folders were on the sofa beside her. The television seemed to be on for background noise. She looked up briefly to acknowledge his presence then returned her attention to the document. He sat on the loveseat pretending to watch the news while trying to decide the best way to start the conversation. "Would you like some tea?"

"No, thank you," Sharon responded with an edge to her voice.

Dale ignored the blatant message to leave her alone and forged ahead. The sooner they discussed it, the better for them all. "I had lunch with my mother today?"

"How's she doing?" Sharon asked without looking up.

Dale sensed her irritation. "We had a very good conversation. She understands about Dad's death and she's looking forward to living with us."

She lowered the paper and looked at him. "You did tell her that was not possible."

Dale rubbed his hands together. He had her full attention "No, because it is possible."

"Look Dale, we settled this last month. Your mother's better off at the nursing home. Our house can't accommodate her physical needs, we can't move in this economy, and taking care of someone with dementia is a full time job. I'm working and hopefully your situation won't be permanent."

"Sharon, our house can be remodeled in a short time for what we need. Besides a first floor bedroom makes a lot of sense. If or when we do decide to move, the addition will only increase the value of the house."

Sharon lowered her feet to the floor. "You aren't seriously considering remodeling this house so your mother can live with us?"

Dale leaned forward and rested his elbows on his thighs. "I'm more than considering it. The contractor starts work in a week."

Sharon closed the file and threw it onto the coffee table. "How could you make a decision like this without consulting me first?"

"I did consult you."

"Then you know how I feel."

"Unfortunately I do, which is why I made the decision for the family." Dale saw Sharon's jaw muscles twitching. He knew it was taking great effort to maintain her self-control. "What kind of man would I be, if I didn't do everything I could to care for my mother?"

"Your mother doesn't have to live with us for you to do that. You have no idea what you're getting this family into."

"I know exactly what I'm doing. I'm obeying God's commandments. My mother deserves to be with her family right now. Our parents took care of us and now it's our turn. I would hope Shawn would do the same for you."

Sharon closed her eyes in frustration. "If I'm going to end up like her, I don't want to live that long. Besides, I wouldn't want Shawn to do this. No mother wants to be a burden to their children."

"It's a burden only if you choose to see it that way, which I don't. This could be a blessing, for us all."

"Dale, I know you're sincerely trying to do the right thing, but this isn't the right time for you to be turning our family upside down."

"I could say the same thing about your job." Dale regretted the words once they came out of his mouth. This discussion was about his mother, not his wife.

"If memory serves me correctly, I asked you before taking this job. And for the record, you can't compare my job with moving *your* mother into *our* home."

Dale hated Sharon's tone. "You're right. *my* mother doesn't have a choice, but *you* do."

"This isn't about me." Sharon rubbed her hand across her mouth in frustration. "All of your other decisions I could go along with, but this one's different. Is there anything I can say or do to keep you from doing this?"

"No."

"Fine, do what you want. You apparently will anyway." Sharon stood up. "I'm going to bed. I need to get to the job site early tomorrow."

"Tomorrow's Saturday."

"And…"

"Sharon, please try to understand."

"Oh, I understand completely. You make the decisions and I'm stuck with the consequences. Just don't expect me to like it." Sharon left the room taking part of Dale with her.

Dale clasped his hands together and bowed his head. "God, please help Sharon understand…Help me understand."

***

When Eric returned from the hospital, his dinner was waiting to be warmed. He managed to eat a little before lifting the fork became too strenuous. The events of the day left him emotionally and physically drained. He turned off the kitchen light, hoping the worst was behind him, and crept to his bedroom. Kendra and both his children were doing well when he left the hospital. His daughter's heart was not beating when delivered. Although the doctor was able to revive her, he warned that it was too soon to know of any lasting implications. Eric knew the minute he held his daughter, Katherine, she was perfectly healthy. She looked at him and he was certain she smiled. Kendra was still groggy from the surgery, but Eric sensed her relief to have finally given birth. Under Ruby's care, Eric knew that his sons and Simone were snug in their beds and would not miss his nightly kiss.

Eric quietly closed his bedroom door. The clock on the night-stand displayed three minutes after midnight. He removed the contents of his pockets and placed them on the night stand. The sight of his phone finally motivated Eric to listen to the messages from Jonathan's numerous calls purposefully sent to voice mail. After listening to the messages, each sounding more desperate, Eric regretted his original call to Jonathan about Simone. Now that Kendra had delivered, the sense of urgency was reduced. Eric lay across the bed, too tired to take off his clothes or pull back the comforter. He drifted off to sleep thinking about what would be best for Simone.

The sky was overcast and a foreboding color of gray. Morning thunderstorms were forecasted but the rain was temporarily trapped in the thick clouds. It was the type of sky that Jonathan hated most while growing up in east Texas. The downpours were so intense that umbrellas were useless. He woke early in anticipation of Eric's call. At seven o'clock, he waited in the hotel restaurant after nibbling on a light breakfast. When that waiting became unbearable, he asked the desk clerk for directions to Eric's home. It was a forty-five minute drive from his hotel. Once he found the house, he drove around the block twice before parking in front of the neighboring house and waiting.

While he summoned courage, the front door of Eric's house opened. He gripped the car door handle, ready for a face to face meeting with Eric. The gray-haired woman dressed in workout clothes who emerged from the house surprised him. He removed his hand from the door handle and watched her walk to the end of the driveway. She bent her body slowly and picked up the newspaper. When she stood up, she looked directly at his car causing his pulse to increase further. He prepared to get out of the car just as she turned quickly and walked back into the house.

Ruby immediately noticed the car parked in front of the neighbor's house. She tried to get a look at the driver without seeming to obvious. After attending the neighborhood crime watch meeting, she took note of anything which seemed out of place. Without her eyeglasses, she could not make out the license plate number. She returned to the house with the intention of getting her eyeglasses, but she was greeted at the door by

Danny's screams. He was up and wanted the world to know. Ruby rushed upstairs to get him before he woke Eric. Half-way up the stairs, the screams stopped. She walked into Danny's room, which was soon to become the twin's nursery, and found Simone at the crib entertaining Danny.

"Well, good morning. I hope our little man didn't wake you up."

Simone moved to the end of the crib. "No, I've been up for a long time. I can't wait to see the babies. Do you think they'll let me hold them?"

Ruby lowered the crib's side, placed Danny on his back and unsnapped his sleeper. "They're pretty small. It could be a few days before they're ready to be held by little hands."

Simone looked at her hands. "Nana, my hands aren't that small."

Ruby chuckled. "Will you hand me a diaper?" She shook her head thinking about having three babies in diapers. "Danny, you're going to have to start using the bathroom like your big brother, and soon."

Danny smiled contently as he looked for Simone, who quickly returned with a diaper and the container of wipes.

"Thank you. When Kendra and the babies come home, you're going to be a big help."

"Aunt Kendra said she'll let me change Katherine's diapers, since girls are easier to change. Danny still squirts Uncle Eric."

Ruby laughed. "I suspect that your Uncle Eric's going to get better changing diapers."

Simone walked to the window. "Do you think it will rain all day?"

"I certainly hope not."

"Can I wake up Josh and Uncle Eric, so we can go to the hospital early?"

Ruby picked up Danny. "You can wake up Josh, but we need to let Uncle Eric sleep a little while longer. What would you like for breakfast?"

Simone followed Ruby into the hallway. "I don't care, but can I help you make it?"

Ruby smiled. "You sure can." Ruby whispered over her shoulder. "Make sure Josh comes down the stairs quietly."

"Okay..."

Ruby descended the stairs and had almost reached the kitchen when the door bell rang. She considered putting Danny in his high chair before going to the door, but was concerned the doorbell ringing again would wake Eric. She walked to the door and peered through the sidelight. The man staring at her looked familiar. Sensing no threat, she cracked open the door.

"Good morning. Does Eric Daniels live here?"

His politeness softened Ruby's disposition. She opened the door wider. "Yes, he does."

"I know that it's early but may I speak to him please? It's very important."

"He's asleep right now. Would you like to leave a message or a phone number?"

"*Daddy...*"

Ruby turned around to see Simone running down the stairs. Her stunned movement allowed the door to open wide enough for Jonathan to slip in. Within seconds, Ruby watched Simone fly into the man's open arms.

"Daddy, daddy...I knew you would come...I just knew it."

Jonathan swept her up and hugged her tightly. "It took me a little time to find out where you were." The emotional surge caused by holding the daughter he thought also had been taken was more than he could control.

Ruby watched as tears flowed down Jonathan's cheeks as he rocked Simone back and forth. Her own heart pounded watching the reunion. The man crying before her bore little resemblance to the monster she expected based on Kendra's descriptions.

Simone pulled back from her father and looked at him. "Daddy, you're crying?"

Jonathan reluctantly lowered Simone to the floor but kept one arm around her. He wiped away his tears. "I'm just so happy to see you."

"Daddy, you've lost a lot of weight."

Jonathan looked at Ruby and extended his hand. "I'm Jonathan, Simone's father."

Ruby looked from Jonathan to Simone, who was smiling so brightly that her joy seemed to fill the room, and understood why he looked so familiar. Ruby sheepishly accepted his hand trying to push from her mind the things she knew about the man standing before her. When his gaze shifted over her head, Ruby turned to see Eric walking towards them. The expression on his face prompted Ruby to clear the space between the two men. Simone ran to Eric, grabbed his hand and eagerly pulled him towards Jonathan. "Uncle Eric, this is my Daddy….Daddy, this is Uncle Eric."

Eric stopped two feet from Jonathan and crossed his arms. Simone returned joyfully to her father's side but her smile disappeared when she recognized the look on Eric's face. An awkward silence filled the foyer. Eric looked at Ruby who understood completely.

"I'll take the boys to the kitchen. We were just about to get some breakfast."

Eric looked at Simone. "Simone, will you help Nana in the kitchen."

Simone grabbed her father's hand. Eric looked at Jonathan as if daring him to make the situation any worse. He knelt beside his daughter and turned her towards him.

Simone tilted her head to one side and looked deep into her father's eyes. "Do you know that Mommy died?"

"Yes baby, I do…" He placed his hands on her shoulders. "Will you do what your uncle asked while he and I talk? After that, we can talk."

"Will you eat breakfast with me?"

Jonathan looked hopefully over his daughter's head. Eric's expression eliminated the need for words. Jonathan focused on his daughter hoping to mask his frustration. "I've already had breakfast, but you should probably eat something." He stood up.

"I'll go eat, if you promise not to leave."

Jonathan ran his hand over Simone's head. "I won't leave without saying good-bye…I promise."

Simone walked slowly to the kitchen looking over her shoulder several times.

Eric walked into the living room and waited for Jonathan to follow. "What the hell are you doing here?"

"I came to see my daughter since it didn't seem like you were going to return my calls."

Eric cocked his head in disbelief. "I told you that my wife was in the hospital about to deliver any minute. We almost lost one of our children yesterday. So forgive me for being a little too busy to call you back. After waiting a month for you to return my call, I thought that you could wait one day."

"I'm sorry." Jonathan lowered his head.

"You should be." Eric paced back and forth. "Do you have any idea of the mess you created by showing up like this?"

Jonathan looked around the room taking in every detail. Pictures lined the fireplace mantel. "What did you expect me to do after finding out that Simone was alive?"

Eric made no effort of mask his emotions. "You've destroyed your family. Are you trying to destroy mine too?" When Eric saw the stricken expression on Jonathan's face, he regretted his choice of words. Despite what Jonathan had done in the past, he had clearly suffered because of it. "I'm sorry. What you've been through cannot be compared to Kendra's reaction when she finds out that I called you or that you came to our home."

Jonathan rubbed his hand across his forehead. "I truly didn't mean to cause you any trouble. I just needed to see Simone and let her know that I hadn't abandoned her. Surely, your wife can understand that."

Eric tried to reconcile Kendra's feeling towards Jonathan with the man standing in the room with him. "Do you have any idea how my wife feels about you?"

"No, I don't. I've never even met your wife."

"For the last five years, Kendra's mission in life was to get Jessica to end her relationship with you and see the light. My wife feels that she failed on both counts and she holds you totally responsible. Because she failed with Jessica, she's even more adamant about protecting Simone."

"Clearly, I've made a lot of mistakes with consequences that will haunt me forever. If I could change the past, I would but I can't. The future is the only hope that I have and I want my daughter to be a part of that future. No one can keep me from her."

"You don't know my wife."

Jonathan jammed his hands in his pants pockets. "Look, I just want to do what's best for Simone. She shouldn't be forced to pay for my sins. You're a father. Surely you can understand how I must feel. Despite what you or your wife may think of me, I do love my daughter. I'd give my life for hers, if I could." As the words left his mouth, he realized that he already had, unconsciously.

Silence filled the space between them. Eric replayed Jonathan's words while struggling to discern spiritually their validity.

Simone appeared in the doorway. "Nana sent me to ask if you want her to make some coffee." Her gaze darted between Eric and Jonathan.

Eric sensed she had chosen her allegiance. He rubbed the back of his neck, knowing Kendra would not be able to keep them apart for very long. Jonathan rocked from side to side, clearly conflicted. For the sake of both Simone and Jonathan, Eric forced a smile. "Tell Nana that we would love some coffee."

"Really?" Simone eyes brightened as she reflected his smile.

"Really…Make sure you keep your eyes on the boys while she makes it. We'll come to the kitchen when it's ready."

"Okay." Simone skipped back to the kitchen.

Visible relief filled Jonathan. "I'm really sorry about showing up like this. After losing so much, I just needed to see that Simone was alive. That it wasn't someone's cruel joke. Truly, I don't want to cause any more trouble."

Eric nodded unsure what to say to the man his wife despised.

"How are your wife and the babies doing?"

Eric welcomed neutral ground. "When I left the hospital, they were fine." Eric looked at the mantel clock knowing he needed to call Kendra.

When the phone rang, Eric hoped that nothing else was about to go wrong. He walked to the doorway. "I'll send Simone to keep you company."

"Thank you."

When Eric returned five minute later, Simone was sitting on Jonathan's lap deep in conversation.

Jonathan looked up. "Is everything okay?" he asked with genuine concern.

Eric cleared his throat. "Simone, Aunt Kendra wants me to wait until tomorrow to bring you to the hospital."

"Why?"

"She needs to rest today. She didn't get much sleep last night."

"Do you need to go to the hospital right now?" Jonathan asked.

"No, she's going to call me when she wakes up."

"Can we still go out to lunch and take Daddy?" Simone turned to her father. "Nana usually goes home on Fridays and comes back after church on Sunday but the babies changed her schedule a little. She's going to her house after breakfast."

Jonathan nodded in appreciation of the extra information. He looked at Eric still standing in the doorway. "I'd be happy to stay with Simone and your sons while you go to the hospital. It's been a while since I changed a diaper but once you learn, you never forget."

Eric had no intention of leaving his children with a stranger. "That won't be necessary, but thanks for the offer. The coffee should be ready." Eric waited for Jonathan and Simone to stand. He let Simone lead Jonathan to the kitchen as he followed thankful for the extra time.

**

It was almost noon when Sharon slid into the driver's seat. Despite the cool temperature outside, the sunshine warmed the van. She put the key in the ignition but paused before turning it. There was no reason to stay at the job site but she had no desire to go home. The slight oversight on her part launched a new battle. When she agreed to the Saturday morning walk-through, she failed to check her daughter's volleyball game schedule. Dale's pointed reminder while she dressed normally would have compelled her to cancel, but her time was the only weapon at her immediate disposal. Dale was livid, again, over her decision to forego her family obligations for what he called optional work, but she was equally livid over his decision to move his mother into their home. He needed to realize that she was not going to be around to clean up the mess he was creating. The momentary guilt over missing the game was quickly soothed by recalling it would be her first absence from one of her children's activities. Dale's record was much more blemished.

A grumbling in her stomach helped solve the dilemma of how to prolong her separation from Dale. Their early morning argument had interfered with her breakfast plans. With her work issues resolved and a slightly calmer spirit, Sharon realized that she was famished. About to start the car, she decided to call Karly first to tell her about Kendra's delivery.

Since Karly was expecting a call from her father, she put the phone in her coat pocket before joining her family outside. It took a few seconds to get their attention to call for a cease fire. "Good morning. Or is it afternoon?" Karly answered slightly out of breath.

"It's still morning. Are you busy?"

Karly kicked her snow boots against the side of the door frame before retreating into the kitchen. "No, your timing's perfect. They're all ganging up on me and I needed an excuse to come in."

"What were you doing?"

"We were supposed to be building a snow family but Ruben and Bridget started a snowball fight. It snowed six inches last night, the first snowfall of the year. They can wear themselves out while I talk to you then maybe we can finish our project. My snow momma's looking pretty good."

"Should you be out in the cold?"

Karly rolled her eyes. "We live in Minneapolis. It's always cold."

"You know what I mean."

"Girl, exercise is good for me and this is how we exercise up here. Did Kendra have those babies yet?"

"She had them yesterday and I'm happy to report that mother and babies are doing well. She called me last night and sounded completely out of it."

"Did they have to do a C-section?"

"Yes, and it was an emergency one. Evidently the ultrasound indicated a problem with the little girl. Thank God she's okay but poor Kendra. Having a C-section is bad enough without having twins and two more babies at home. She sounded upbeat last

301

night, but I'm sure that was due to the pain medication. It will be a different story when reality sets in."

"Kendra's strong. She'll be okay. I know she's glad to have this pregnancy behind her." Karly looked out the kitchen window. Her family had re-teamed. It was the girls against the boys. "What do you think she needs for the babies?"

"I'm going to send her some girly things. Poor John…he's destined for a life of hand-me downs from his big brothers."

"Is that what she named him?"

"Yep…she named them John Caleb and Katherine Elizabeth. If it weren't for Kendra missing her mother so much, Katherine may have been 'Ruth' or 'Mary'."

"I'm glad to see that she takes naming her babies seriously. There are so many examples in the Bible of children being named according to either God's instruction or His purpose. The reason I chose Samuel's name was because Hannah and I had a lot in common. If God dictated John the Baptist and Jesus' names, it must be important."

Sharon felt ashamed. "Maybe I should have put a little more thought into naming Shawn and Paige."

Karly unzipped her coat. "So what are you up to?"

"You don't want to know," Sharon said cracking open the car window. "But since you asked, I'm sitting in my car at a construction site because I don't want to go home."

Karly frowned. "Why?"

"I've never been so mad at Dale. The more I think about it, the madder I get. Do you know what he had the audacity to do?"

The last time Karly talked with Sharon, she was upset because Dale had not found a new job. Karly hoped that Sharon was not upset because he found one. "Did he find a new ministry position?"

"As a matter of fact, he did. *His mother*! He's remodeling our house so he can move her in with us. Can you believe that?"

Karly shook her head at Sharon's dramatics. "You should be thankful you married a man willing to do that. You can tell a lot about a man from the way he treats his mother and remember that God commands us to honor our parents."

"Karly, this has nothing to do with honoring his mother. The woman has Alzheimer's or dementia; I'm not even sure what it is! Do you know how much care that requires? And now that I'm working, I don't want to leave one job to come home to another. I just got Shawn and Paige from under foot. I'm not ready to have another baby. Heck, having another baby would be easier. His mother's where she belongs. She will get much better care there."

"How advanced is she?"

"Advanced enough that she can't live alone. It's only a matter of time."

"I'm sure Dale's doing what he believes is right. If I had the chance, I'd gladly do the same."

"That's easy for you to say. Your mother's dead."

Karly's eyes burned. "Sharon, sometimes you can be so… never mind."

"Well, I just wanted to tell you about Kendra."

"Thanks for the call."

"Tell Ruben and the kids that I said hello." Sharon put her phone in the cup holder and started the car. Pulling out of the parking lot, she noticed a billboard advertising luxury town homes and decided to drive past, just to see what they looked like.

***

The pain medication was wearing off but Kendra was determined to delay asking for more. The doctor assured her the medication would not harm the babies even if trace amounts leeched into her breast milk, but Kendra was taking no chances. Two glass containers sat on the bed tray waiting to be collected. The quantity of breast milk in each container was disappointing, but it was all she was able to painfully extract. The twins were too small to nurse but their doctor wanted to feed them her antibody rich breast milk.

Eric walked into the room carrying a small blooming plant to cushion the impact of the news. "How are you feeling?"

"Not too good. I can't believe women would actually choose a C-section delivery. The pain this morning was a hundred times worse."

Eric kissed Kendra. "Can't they give you something for the pain?"

"I don't want to take it, unless absolutely necessary." She touched a flower on the plant as Eric sat it on the bed tray. "This is beautiful but you didn't need to bring anything. I'll be home Monday. Last night, I wanted to get out of here as soon as possible. After this morning, I'm taking the doctor's advice to stay the full three days covered by our insurance." Kendra grasped the arm rail with one hand, pulled herself forward slightly and tried to adjust the pillow behind her back.

Her grimace caused Eric to winch. "Let me get that for you." Eric adjusted the pillow. "Is that better?"

Kendra leaned back. "Much better...Did you stop by the nursery to see our precious babies?"

"No, I wanted to see you first. How are they doing?"

"Great. A nurse wheeled me to the nursery before lunch. I wanted to walk but it will be another day before I can make it that far. When they pick up this milk, I'll ask for a wheelchair and we can go see them together. I still can't believe we have a daughter; I mean another daughter. Daddy says Katherine looks like Mom. When I get home, I want to find my mother's baby picture." She noticed Eric seemed distracted and wondered if he had trouble sleeping too. "Were the kids disappointed about having to wait to meet their new brother and sister?"

"They were more disappointed about not seeing you. Danny keeps asking for you, especially at night. I don't think he understands what's going on. In a way, he's still a baby."

A frown appeared thinking about her son. "That's what concerns me most about having the twins so soon. I feel like we short-changed him. Have you moved him into Josh's room?"

"Not yet. I might try it tonight, since I need to assemble the other crib. Or maybe I'll wait until tomorrow, when Ruby's back. She's planning to come see you tonight."

"That will be nice. Is Dad at home with the kids?"

The door was opened but Eric was not ready.

"Actually, they're at your brother's. I'll pick them up after I leave here."

"Good. I'm sure Simone likes this arrangement better. She and Natalie haven't been able to play together that often." Kendra noticed the creases in his forehead. "How's Simone doing?"

"Fine."

"You could have brought her to the hospital with you. I'm afraid that the boys won't understand me not being able to hold them and I don't want to do anything to open this incision."

"Simone was okay with the arrangements," Eric said.

Simone was spending the remainder of the afternoon with Jonathan. At lunch, Eric observed Jonathan's behavior closely. By all appearances, he was a normal, dotting father. When Jonathan asked if he could take Simone to the movies, Eric had no obvious reason to refuse. Now he was concerned whether Jonathan would run off with her.

"It's probably better for us to have some quiet time alone." Eric sat at the foot of the bed.

Kendra cringed as she moved her legs to give him more space. "We'd better take it while we can." Kendra longed for Eric to hold her but was afraid that it would be too painful. "How are you doing?"

"I'm fine," he replied.

"You don't look fine. Are you still worried about the job?"

"No, the dust seems to have settled at work."

"Then what's bothering you?"

Eric paused trying to find the best way to reveal what his wife would consider nothing short of treason. "Baby, I called Jonathan."

Kendra's pain was momentarily forgotten as every muscle in her body tightened. "You did *what*?"

"A month ago, I called Jonathan."

"Why would you do something like that? You know how I feel about him."

"I thought I was doing what was best for our family. You were in the hospital and I was struggling to take care of Simone and the boys. I needed to know if Jonathan was in a position to help care for his daughter. When he didn't answer his phone, I left him a message to call me. After two weeks without a call from him, I assumed he had no interest in his daughter."

Her stomach muscles relaxed, increasing the pain. "I told you contacting him would be a waste of time."

Eric braced himself for the backlash. "Not really. He called me yesterday. Liz led him to believe that Simone was killed with Jessica."

"Please tell me that you didn't correct him."

"I couldn't let him believe that Simone was dead."

"Yes, you could have! The last thing she needs is that man coming back into her life. You need to put an end to any plans he may have. If you don't, I will."

A knock on the door made them both look up. A young woman walked into the room. "I'm supposed to pick up…" Feeling the tension, she looked around the room quickly. "There it is." She retrieved the containers of breast milk. "I'll just take these."

While Kendra waited for the woman to leave, she tried to calm herself for the benefit of her children.

Eric watched Kendra feeling completely helpless to remedy the situation. "It's too late."

"What do you mean too late?"

"Jonathan came to our house this morning."

Kendra wanted to jump out of the bed but knew that she couldn't. Tears of frustration ran down her cheeks. "*Eric*, how could you!"

He got the box of tissue. "I was only trying to do what was best." He sat it on the bed beside Kendra but remained standing.

She yanked two tissues from the box. "For who? You?"

He walked to the window and looked out. The rain had stopped but the sky was cloudy. He turned towards Kendra and sat on the window sill. "For everyone involved."

"Eric, the man is a monster. How could you possibly want him anywhere near Simone? Did you let him in the house?"

"By the time the commotion woke me, Simone was already in his arms."

Kendra buried her face in her hands. "How am I supposed to explain to Simone what kind of man he is?"

"I don't think you should. Simone's his daughter and despite what you may think of him, they both love each other very much."

"What can that man possibly know about love?" Kendra closed her eyes. "Oh Lord, please protect her...Simone doesn't deserve this." Kendra turned her attention back to Eric. "How long did he stay?"

Eric looked at the floor. "A few hours."

"A few hours!"

"Then he went to lunch with us. He's not the monster that you think."

"Eric, have you lost your mind?" Kendra wanted to go home as soon as possible. Simone needed protection and Eric was not the person to provide it. "Is he planning on coming back to the house before I'm discharged?"

Eric sighed. "I hope so. Simone's with him now."

CHAPTER 14

ONE MONTH AFTER JONATHAN RETURNED FROM DALLAS, WITH the cabin secured for the winter, he turned his energy towards helping his parents. After staying with them for two weeks, it was time for him to move on but a destination was less clear. Even though his house had not sold, returning there was not an option. His heart yearned to be in Dallas, but his head convinced him to wait. Sitting on his parents' sofa, once shrouded in plastic, triggered a surge of memories. Before long, he began questioning every past decision. When the minister said that only a fool fails to learn from his mistakes, he was certain the advice was specifically for him. Trying to distinguish the good decisions from the bad complicated his current dilemma. Even his decision to marry his wife was volleyed back and forth. It was a good decision for him but a tragic decision for her. Thinking about Lori and her impact on his life jarred his still fragile emotions. Even in death, she never gave up on him. The letter in her journal had been a life line. His body shivered thinking about his repeated desires to die and thanked God again for showing someone like him such mercy. Twice God had stopped him. His desire for her letter made his chest heave. Despite searching the Bible, he could not find a clear answer concerning his daughter. David's affair with Bathsheba was the closest thing he could find to his situation and when he read that the child died, he was depressed for the rest of the day. He did not know what he would do if his sin were to cost Simone her life.

When his mother walked into the room, he tried to conceal the cell phone still in his hand. He had hoped that giving Simone unlimited access to him via her own phone would make their separation bearable. Instead it made it more difficult for him. His universe revolved around the calls from his daughter. But as long as Kendra refused to even talk to him about Simone, his options were limited. Eric seemed more willing to work with him, even suggesting the cell phone arrangement, but being a wedge of contention in Eric's marriage was the last thing that Jonathan wanted. Secretly he feared that Kendra would eventually succeed in turning Simone against him, especially once she was old enough to understand the nature of his transgressions. For the time being, talking to his daughter on the phone was all he could do.

His mother sat on the sofa next to him. "How would you like to escort me to the grocery store?"

"Where's Dad?"

His mother laughed. "He told me to ask you, besides your father's worse than a child in the grocery store."

"Mom, I'd love to help you but I avoid grocery stores on Saturdays. Wouldn't you rather wait until Monday?"

"They're having a big sale and I don't want to get stuck with a picked over Thanksgiving Turkey or risk them being sold out of what I need."

"You can relax, Mom. Stores won't miss an opportunity to make a sale."

"I want what I want, not some substituted inferior brand. Now make an old woman happy and get your coat. Besides, it will give you something to do while you wait for Simone's next call."

"Is it that obvious?"

"Yes. I still don't know why that baby's not living with you. Your father and I are more than willing to help out. Any judge in their right mind would see that you'd be a good father."

"I wish that were true but I'm in this predicament because I wasn't a good father or husband. I can't risk a nasty court battle, which could easily go against me, or having to tell Simone things she's too young to understand. The press would have a feeding frenzy and Simone would be the one to suffer most. Simone's in a good home with a mother and a father."

"And four other children under the age of three. How much attention can they possibly be giving that child?"

Jonathan did not want to think about that. "Simone seems just fine. She likes her school and she's making lots of friends."

"Atlanta has good schools and if she can make friends there, she can make them here. She needs to be with her real family."

Jonathan reached for his mother's hand. "As hard as it may be for us to accept, Simone may be better off where she is."

"Your father and I were talking about the old house last night. It's strange that your daughter would end up in Texas. Maybe you should go there."

"Mom, I've prayed about this...believe me. What would I do in Texas?"

"More than you're doing here. At least there, you could see her."

"If I did and something happened to her..." Jonathan could only shake his head.

"Are you still staying here for Thanksgiving?"

"The chance of Kendra inviting me to have dinner with them is slim and I'd hate for Simone to have a hotel dinner with me. Besides, it's time for me to face the family. I can't hide from them forever."

"I don't think you give your family enough credit. We've all done things in our past that we're not too proud of. Remember what the Lord said, 'Let he who is without sin cast the first stone.' I doubt anybody in this family is able to throw anything. Thanks to you, I suspect your brother and sisters have cleaned up their acts."

Jonathan smiled despite himself. "Momma, you're a mess."

His mother stood up and put her hands on her hip. "Good Lord, why didn't I think of this sooner? Why don't you see if they'll let Simone come here for Thanksgiving? It's high time she meets her grandparents, not to mention her uncles, aunts and cousins. Didn't you say her mother was an only child?"

Jonathan nodded.

"Then we're all the family she has because that other grand-mother of hers definitely doesn't count. That woman needs to be hog-tied for telling you that Simone was dead. I'll even call Kendra to ask, if you think it will help. Daddy and I will buy the airline ticket."

"I can afford the ticket, but I don't think Kendra will let her come."

"You won't know unless you ask. Now, do you want to call now or wait until we get back from the grocery store?"

Jonathan looked at his cell phone to check the time. It was almost nine. "Let's go to the store first before the crowd gets too bad."

"You mean while you work up some courage."

"Mind if we stop at the post office on the way? I need to pick up the mail from the house."

"Thanks for reminding me. I need to buy stamps for Christmas cards."

"Thanksgiving hasn't even passed and you're already thinking about Christmas."

"I've never been one to wait until the last minute. You shouldn't either."

***

Once construction began on the house, Dale's visits with his mother were severely curtailed. The contractors started early and usually crossed paths with his children as they came home from school. Sharon usually walked through the door when dinner was being placed on the table. By the time dinner was finished and their children helped or prodded to complete their homework, it was too late for a visit. The weekends were his only options. As much as Dale looked forward to seeing his mother, his family was less enthusiastic. Every time he mentioned a family visit, an argument with Sharon soon followed. He took Shawn and Paige for a visit once but they complained the entire time, almost to the point of being rude. Since his mother would be living with them soon, he decided not to force the issue.

After delivering his children safely to their destinations, Dale drove to see his mother and was looking forward to a leisurely visit. He hoped Sharon's time alone would improve her disposition which seemed to be deteriorating like the weather. The forecast called for a winter storm with up to a foot of snow. It would take more than a potential threat to keep him from doing what was right. In general, Saturdays at the nursing facility seemed more chaotic. This Saturday was considerably worse. Dale suspected the approaching Thanksgiving holiday was a major factor. Visitors filled the hallways and the staffing level was noticeably insufficient. Doc was leading his Bible study when Dale walked past the activity center and acknowledged him with a tilt of the head.

Dale's visit with his mother did not go well from the start. He wondered if his frustration was affecting his mother's mood or just the amount of activity surrounding her. She was more withdrawn and easily agitated while eating lunch. Dale prayed a more controlled environment would help her condition. When it became apparent his mother wanted him to leave, Dale tried not to be offended. Hoping that Doc would have a few minutes to talk, he was heading to his room when he spotted him in the commons area watching television.

Doc greeted him warmly before returning his eyes to the television. "Things are really heating up."

Dale looked at the television. It didn't take long for the news story to register. "I'm beginning to wonder if they'll ever have peace in the Middle East."

"Aye, one day! How's your mother doing?"

"Not a good day. If you're not too busy, can we talk for a while?"

"How's the weather outside?"

"Right now, it's just cold and gray. The snow's not supposed to start until much later, but maybe the storm will miss us. It wouldn't be the first time the forecast was wrong."

Doc stood up. "Since the weather seems to be cooperating for now, will you take me to get a cup of coffee? There's a little cafe not too far from here."

"Can you leave?"

Doc chuckled at Dale's response. "The last time I checked, this wasn't a prison or an asylum."

"I...ah..."

"Relax. I know what you meant. As long as I sign out and sign back in, it's okay."

Dale checked his watch.

"If you don't have time, we can do it another day. I just woke up this morning craving some real coffee. They give us decaffeinated coffee, thinking we don't know the difference."

Dale slipped on his jacket. "Actually, I have the time and would love a cup of coffee." He stepped aside to let Doc lead the way. "Should I pull my car up to the front door?"

"Absolutely not! The exercise will do me good."

After stopping by Doc's room to get his coat and Bible, Dale slowly led the way to his car. Few people seemed willing to venture out. Traffic was light and the cafe parking lot was almost empty. While Doc chatted with the server, Dale looked for a comfortable place to sit.

Doc nudged Dale's elbow. "These cookies look too good to pass up. Which kind do you want?"

"Oatmeal raisin," Dale said without hesitation. Doc produced a crisp twenty dollar bill before Dale could retrieve his wallet. "I intended to treat you."

Doc winked at him. "Getting me out into fresh air is enough of a treat. Besides, I need to spend my money on something."

Dale and the server looked at each other when Doc put all of the change in the tip jar. "Are you always that generous?"

"I can't take it with me. Let's get a table with real chairs. Those booths are uncomfortable."

"Do you need cream or sugar?"

"And ruin a perfectly good cup of coffee?"

Dale carried the tray to a table by the window. "How's this?" He waited for confirmation.

"Perfect, except for the lack of sunshine. Can you do anything about that?" Doc sat his Bible on the table.

"You're talking to the wrong person." Dale helped Doc take off his coat before removing his own and putting both on the empty chair.

Doc carefully pried the lid off his coffee cup and raised it to his nose. Closing his eyes, he took a deep breath and smile. "This smells so good." His eyes popped open and he took a sip. His swallow gave way to a look of intense satisfaction. "Dale, always make sure to enjoy the simple pleasures. That's what life should be about. More people need to stop and smell the coffee or roses or whatever tickles their God-given senses."

Dale raised his cup, thinking about Sharon and her listening exercises. "I'll remember that."

Doc rested his aged hands around his coffee cup. "It's been a while since our last visit. How's the house project coming?"

"It's on schedule. Mom should be home for Christmas."

"Your family celebrates Christmas?"

Dale found the question puzzling. "Don't all Christians?"

Doc pondered how to respond. "I understand why the Jewish people celebrate Hanukkah, but I have great difficulty understanding Christmas from a believer's perspective. You know, it's been proven that Jesus could not have been born in December."

"I read that somewhere, but the actual date doesn't really matter as much as the reason for the celebration."

315

"Yes, the reasons…greed and busyness masquerading as joy and peace."

"Aren't you being a little harsh? I'll admit things have gotten a little commercialized, but Christmas is the perfect opportunity to reach the lost."

"Now that's an understatement, if I've ever heard one." Doc's expression became very serious. "Have you ever wondered why the Bible's very specific on the dates that Jesus died and was resurrected, but completely silent on the actual date that Jesus was born?"

"I've never given it very much thought."

"Maybe you should," Doc said before taking another sip of coffee. "Doctor Luke, a man after my own heart, in his gospel account records Jesus saying, 'No man having put his hand to the plow and looking back is fit for the Kingdom of God.' It seems like Christmas traditions emphasize looking back, combined with an awful lot of pagan customs. Wouldn't it be more logical to focus continually on the eternal, resurrected Lord who's at the right hand of the Almighty?"

Dale shrugged his shoulders. "Are you telling me I shouldn't be celebrating Christmas?"

"I'm merely suggesting you should carefully choose what you indulge in. Remember how the book of Daniel starts?"

"Daniel and his friends asked if they could keep a certain diet while they were being trained for service, so they wouldn't defile themselves."

Doc picked up his cookie and snapped it in half. "I liken Christmas to the king's food and drink. It may look and taste good but certain individuals need to avoid it." Doc pointed to his Bible. "This is the food you need."

"Then why is the Bible so hard for people to understand?"

Doc tapped his little finger on the table as if marking each second of thought. He slid his Bible across the table to Dale. "The answer to that question is clearly stated in the Bible."

Dale stood up. "Let me get my Bible from the car."

Doc raised his hand, halting Dale's movement. "Is it the King James Version?"

"No, that's why I prefer it."

"Sit back down and read it from this one."

Dale reluctantly obeyed. "Does the translation really make much difference?"

"For some people it does. Have you ever heard the saying 'prepare your children for the road, not the road for your children'?"

Dale smiled. "The head mistress at my children's school tells parents that every year."

"Wise woman." Doc pointed to his Bible. "Some translations remove the intentional bumps in the road. Hebrew scribes believe that omitting a single letter when copying a sacred scroll could lead to catastrophic consequences. Some modern Bible translations omit entire words and phrases. The Holy Scriptures were written in the language of God by God for His people. The Bible doesn't need rewriting to make it clearer. What was my first question to you about the Bible?"

"What is the Bible?"

"Always start with that question, when instructing others. Unless a person has a healthy perspective of the Holy Scriptures, they will never comprehend the person or the work of the Messiah."

Dale frowned. Doc's words sounded like parting instructions. "Today, people are convinced you can have strong faith apart from knowing God's Word. Heck, some churches teach that the Bible's obsolete."

"Ah, but you know better, yes?"

"Yes. You can have strong faith in anyone or anything, but its three interlinking components are unchanging – knowledge, beliefs, and trust. Our time together has definitely confirmed that 'knowledge' is the most critical of the three. Our 'beliefs' are merely accepting our knowledge is true and 'trust' is acting on our beliefs."

Doc took a sip of his coffee. "Since accurate 'knowledge' of God is critical to our ability to 'trust' Him, which is what Jesus told his disciples to do, let's return to your original question – 'Why is the Bible, which is the only reliable source of knowledge about God, so hard to understand?' Turn to the sixth chapter of Isaiah."

Dale gently opened the Bible to Isaiah and silently read.

Doc waited patiently for him to look up. "Who did Isaiah see sitting on a throne?"

"The King, the Lord of Host." Dale paused. "Jesus Christ?"

Doc smiled. "The one and only…the King of kings, Lord of hosts, the Holy One of Israel. Not a baby lying in a manger! Ironically, the next chapters prophesizes Jesus' birth and instructs His disciples. If people would truly search for the answers in the right place, they can be found. So, why are God's words difficult to understand?"

"God told Isaiah to prevent 'this people' from seeing the truth until the land is utterly desolate. But who are 'this people' and what does it mean?"

"Hence, you've discovered the challenge of acquiring knowledge. One question, often leads to another. Most people give up in frustration or look to others to provide the answers for them." Doc pointed to his Bible. "Have you figured out where you fit in this story? It will explain why you heard his voice and see his works."

"I believe that I'm a child of God."

Doc placed his hand on his cheek while contemplating Dale's answer. "That's a complex answer. What's your knowledge to support that belief?"

Dale looked perplexed.

"Have you considered that you might be part of the remnant of Israel?"

"In seminary, we discussed quite extensively the natural Israel and the spiritual Israel. Christians are a part of the spiritual, believing Israel."

"Hogwash. There's no such thing as a spiritual Israel! Either you're part of Israel or you're not. Today, there's too much confusion about Israel, Jesus, Jerusalem and the New Covenant. Religious leaders talk a lot about believing and receiving, which is probably why Christmas resonates with so many. People spend much effort and money teaching children to believe in Santa and expect to receive many gifts. Train up a child in the way he should go and when he's older, he will not depart from it – Believe in Jesus and expect to receive gifts." Doc shook his head sadly. "Jesus came, as promised, but not to abolish God's covenant relationship with Israel. Go to Jeremiah 31." He waited for Dale to locate the chapter. "You need to meditate on the whole chapter but for the sake of our limited time together start with verse 31. It's easy to remember 31:31!"

Dale started reading "Behold, the days are coming, says the LORD when I will make a new covenant with the house of Israel and the house of Judah," Dale looked up. "Whoa…why didn't I notice that before?"

"Because most Christians are taught to believe the New Covenant is something new. Continue."

Dale obeyed. "…not according to the covenant that I made with their fathers in the day that I took them by the hand to lead them out of the land of Egypt, My covenant which they broke, though I was a husband to them, says the LORD. But this is the covenant that I will make with the house of Israel after those days, says the LORD: I will put My law in their minds, and write it on their hearts; and I will be their God, and they shall be My people. No more shall every man teach his neighbor, and every man his brother, says, 'Know the LORD,' for they all shall know Me, from the least of them to the greatest of them, says the LORD." He looked up.

Doc broke a piece off his cookie. "Eye opening, isn't it? His people truly do perish for a lack of knowledge. Based on scripture, the chief difference between the covenants is that the original was based on God's law, or teachings, written on a scroll and stone tablets, which required human action, and the new is based on the same information being written on individual hearts, which is all God's doing-hence grace. But the covenant was made with the same group of people – the house of Israel; the chosen descendants of Abraham and those joined to them by God. These are the ones with ears to hear God. " Doc put the piece in his mouth savoring the sweetness of the cookie and his words.

"Are you saying that everyone who 'hears' God speaking with them today is part of the remnant of the children of Israel?"

"Remember in John's account of Jesus' ministry, Jesus said his sheep hear his voice but He has others not of this fold that he must bring, who will also hear his voice. But, and this is important...Jesus said there will be only one fold and one shepherd. Is your mind spinning yet?"

Dale could only nod.

"When you get home, read Ezekiel 34. It explains Jesus' reference to being the good shepherd of Israel. Today the dilemma is that devout Jews and Christians are looking at different sides of the same coin. You have to examine both sides to see that Jesus is the Messiah prophesized to Israel and understand the significance of this identity. I suspect that was the intent of Paul's admonition to make our election and calling sure." Doc paused. "While God's grace and mercy are free to all, his covenant and promised blessings are for a very specific people."

"Why can't more people see this? More importantly, why isn't this taught in the church?"

"Jesus gave that answer to his disciples when they questioned his use of parables. When the word of God falls on good soil, it always produces fruit. I can faithfully testify to this." Doc picked up his cookie and broke off another small piece. "Dale, you need to thank God that you're hearing and seeing what so many others have not."

Dale shook his head in frustration.

Doc smiled. "As for whether you're a descendent of Israel, the best way to find out is to read the book of Deuteronomy. If you're convicted of sin and are compelled towards complete obedience, you'll have your answer."

"I'm almost afraid to know."

"My friend, a man cannot teach what he has not learned." Doc looked out the window and noticed feathery snowflakes drifting to the ground. "We'd better finish up so you can get home before the snow starts sticking to the roads."

***

Saturday afternoon, Kendra sat in the gliding rocker with Katherine at her breast. Until Kendra could walk up stairs, the babies were sharing their parent's bedroom. When Eric walked into the room, he found them both asleep. Her energy level was still not where it should be but it seemed to be improving with each passing day. Home cooked dinners were on the table every night, thanks to Ruby, church members, and her sister-in-law. Kendra's biggest challenge was maintaining her strength to keep up with the twin's feeding schedules. After a frustrating few days, Kendra was finally able to stagger their feedings but it seemed like she had a baby at her breast continually. Eric offered to help with bottle feeding but Kendra was determined to provide the best for her children and everything she read agreed that nursing babies ensured a healthy bond with their mother.

"How's our little lady?"

"I think she's done. Maybe, they'll both sleep for at least an hour. I really need to take a shower." Kendra carefully detached her breast from her daughter's mouth, hoping she would not wake up. "Will you put her in the bassinet for me?" Kendra handed the baby to Eric then lowered her pajama top. "I'm going to take a quick shower and get dressed."

Eric cradled his daughter as he gently walked her across their bedroom. "Maybe you should eat something then take a nap."

Kendra firmly grasped the arms of the rocking chair and pushed herself up. "I've got to get out of these pajamas. It's been two days and I don't want to risk making it three. How can something as simple as taking a shower and getting dressed become such a major ordeal?" She walked into the bathroom and turned on the shower.

Eric was standing over the bassinets watching the twins breathe.

Kendra quietly opened her dresser drawers to get her clothes. "Where are our other children?" she whispered.

"They're eating lunch. I just came to check on you. Do you want me to bring your lunch in here?"

Kendra paused in the bathroom doorway. "No, I'll come get it. This will be a quick shower," she said closing the door softly.

When Kendra walked into the kitchen fifteen minutes later, a turkey sandwich flanked by carrot sticks and a large glass of water were waiting on the table. She could hear her sons and Simone playing in the family room. The desire to join them was momentarily forced from Kendra's thoughts, knowing she had to eat first. Despite their small size, the babies were consuming a great deal of calories that needed replenishing. The door to the garage opening quickly startled Kendra. She relaxed when she saw Eric with a new trash bag.

"Do you feel better?"

"Much. Sounds like the kids are having fun." Kendra opened the sandwich to inspect the contents. She removed a layer of the turkey and placed it on the plate then took a bite.

Eric filled the bag with air before securing it in the trash can. "You need to eat all that meat. Remember what the doctor said about getting enough protein." He sat at the table with her. "I can't believe Thanksgiving's next week."

Kendra dramatically returned the discarded turkey to the sandwich while Eric watched approvingly. "Satisfied?"

Eric took a carrot stick from her plate. "Thank you."

"We have a lot to be thankful for this year."

"Yes, we do. Are you sure you're up to having both the families here for dinner?"

Kendra chewed slowly before swallowing. "No, but I definitely don't want to take the twins anywhere, especially with them feeding every few hours. Besides it will be nice to have everyone together again." Kendra looked around the kitchen, trying to remember where she put the list of who was doing what. She spotted it on the refrigerator door and sighed with relief. "I'm just glad we have the option and aren't forced to travel for the holidays to be with family, especially now."

Eric felt a knot form in his stomach. "Sometimes you have to be away from home to really appreciate it."

His statement made Kendra think about the times she lived in other cities. When she was at college, her mother had died. While away at graduate school, she walked in on Eric with another woman. While living in St. Louis, she was almost raped and then slandered in the media. "I've experienced enough of life outside of Dallas. I'm completely content here, which is why I don't understand you going on this interview."

Eric tried to hide his excitement about the interview. The position was a perfect match for his skills and career objectives. His phone interview and research fueled his interest in the organization. When invited to Birmingham for a final interview with the company's C.E.O, Eric almost jumped for joy. Kendra's reaction to the news caused him to seek more objective counsel from their fathers. His father's advice was to pray about it, but to know exactly what he wanted from God before he called on him. That admonition caused Eric to do some intense soul searching regarding his motivations for wanting the position and his responsibilities to his family. Caleb's assurance that his daughter would be fine regardless of the decision was added comfort. However, his casual statement that it may be good to get Kendra out of her childhood home resonated with Eric. When assessing her own mothering skills, she repeatedly referenced her mother's. "I'm going because it will help me determine the type of environment I should be looking for and what skills I need to improve. Opportunities to interview with C.E.O.'s don't come around that often."

"What kind of company schedules interviews for Thanksgiving week? Apparently, they're not very family oriented."

"Actually, they're very family oriented which is one of the reasons I want to talk with them. Apparently, they want to give the person who gets the job the opportunity to move during the winter school break, which supposedly is the best time for children to change schools." Eric omitted the fact that the organization had been trying to fill the position for six months and he was the first to make it to the final interview stage.

Kendra bit into a carrot stick. "I think you just want to get away from here for a few days."

"I'm leaving Tuesday night and coming back Wednesday. That's not much of an escape," Eric said. "We need to discuss something and you need to keep an open mind."

"Eric, can we wait to discuss the job when and if they make you an offer."

"It's about Simone."

"What about Simone?"

Eric rested his arms on the table. "Jonathan called me this morning."

Kendra pushed her plate away. Hearing his name made digesting anymore food impossible. "See what you've started by encouraging him. We should have never let Simone keep that stupid phone."

Eric knew their time was too limited to rehash old subjects. He promised Jonathan he would call him today with an answer and he intended to keep his word this time. "He wants Simone to spend Thanksgiving with his family in Atlanta."

"No."

"Kendra…"

"I said *no*."

"But why?"

"Eric, have you forgotten what that man has done?"

"Kendra, you're not his judge. Simone's his daughter, not ours. We cannot shut him out of her life. I haven't discussed this with her yet..."

"And you won't either. Jessica wanted me to raise Simone, not him."

"Raising her is one thing, cutting her off from her biological father is something totally different. And I wouldn't put too much credence in what Jessica wanted. Her motivations were somewhat less than either ethical or moral. It seems to me, she was more concerned with hurting Jonathan than helping her daughter." Eric thought about the contrite man he sat next too in church. When Jonathan brought Simone home from the movies, he had asked Eric if he could go to church with them the next day. It did not take long to see that Jonathan's request and his worship were sincere. "I wish you could have been at church with us. You'd know he's being changed."

Kendra took a deep breath. "I said no and as her legal guardian, I make the decisions regarding her well-being."

"As the head of this family, I think we need to talk to Simone and let her make the decision."

Kendra stared into Eric's eyes. "She's *too* young to know what's best for her."

"She's not too young to know that she loves her father. If you try to keep her from him, you will regret it."

"What I regret is you calling him in the first place."

"It was only a matter of time before Simone would have asked us to find him. As hard as it is for you to accept, she loves her father. And if you would take the time to talk to her, you'd know how much."

"Are you implying that I'm neglecting Simone?"

"I'm saying you have enough to do taking care of your own children. There are only so many hours to the day and right now the twins demand most of them."

Kendra lowered her voice afraid that Simone might hear them. "You never wanted Simone here. Now you can't wait to get rid of her."

"Kendra, you know that's not true. I love Simone very much and she can live with us as long as she wants, but it needs to be her decision, not ours."

"She's a child. How can she possibly know what's good for her?"

"But I'm not a child," Eric said more forcefully than he intended.

"And you think she should be raised by that man?"

"I think she needs and wants a relationship with her father. Spending Thanksgiving with him and her grandparents will go a long way towards making that a reality."

"I don't trust them."

"You don't know them. Jonathan said his mother would be happy to speak with you. He gave me his parents' phone number, even their address and I didn't ask."

There was no need to ask Simone what she wanted. Kendra knew what she would say. As much as she hated to admit it, Simone had been a much happier child and the change corresponded with Jonathan resurfacing in her life. "What if they try to keep her?"

"If Jonathan wanted to take her, he had his chance. He brought her back before and I trust he'll bring her home again. I honestly think he's trying to win your trust."

"Well, he's wasting his time. That will never happen."

"Kendra, why are you so hard-hearted when it comes to Jonathan."

"I can't believe you even have to ask that." Kendra stood up intending to find Simone but was redirected when she heard a cry on the baby monitor.

Eric looked at her. "I'll go see who's crying, if you want to have a talk with Simone."

"It's John crying. Please get him before he wakes up Kat." She looked at the clock. "It's too soon for him to eat."

Eric raised an eyebrow in astonishment "I'll get John. Then we'll come get his brothers. They should be able to distract him for a while."

Kendra waited for the crying to stop before leaving the kitchen with a barely filled stomach and a heart overflowing with grief.

***

The brochures stayed in Sharon's briefcase buried between work files for weeks. One was for the townhouse she toured and the other for a beachfront resort. It was the first time she dared taking them out of her work bag at home, knowing both would be hard to explain. As soon as Dale and their children left, she made a cup of hot herbal tea with intentions for serious Bible study. Dale's employment dilemma put the family in the awkward position of having to find a new church home. They had visited four different churches with the same results. She began to wonder if he would ever be satisfied with someone else's teachings. After their second visit, her children pushed for a family church service at home, but she was suspect of their motives. If there was a time she needed a formal Bible study, it was now. Attempting to squeeze self-study into her schedule was not working. Even when she had the time, concentrating was a challenge. When Dale called to see what time Paige needed to be picked up, Sharon relished having more time but instead of directing her attention back to the Bible, she opened her journal and began to write.

November 22,

It's hard to believe that almost two months have passed since I last wrote. Looking back at that entry, things are not getting much better. Dale moved his mother to St. Louis about a month ago. She's in a skilled nursing facility right now, an arrangement I thought was final. Unfortunately, he's now tearing up our lives to make room for her in our home. Under normal circumstances, I wouldn't be so opposed but his mother needs 24 hour care which Dale's under the delusion we can provide. My house looks like a demolition zone as they turn our formal dining room into a bedroom suite, but I'm in no hurry for them to finish. Every time I even think about having his mother living in the house, my blood pressure goes up which is why I can't even go see her. Dale's leaving me very few options. We don't talk much these days. What can I say that has not already been said? He chose his mother over his wife. I seriously doubt God wants him to do this, but I can't convince him of that. If it weren't for the kids, I know exactly what I'd do. He still hasn't found a job, other than his mother. It's probably only a matter of time before the trust fund Kendra set up reverts back to her. It was set up to allow Dale to do God's work. I don't think caring for his mother falls into that category. I started to ask Kendra about it when she called but she was already overwhelmed by her situation. The twins came early. I think they're both okay. I called Karly to tell her the twins were born. We didn't talk long, but she's doing okay, I think. With her, you never can tell. We were supposed to have our annual girls' weekend in March but that was before everything happened. Now that Jessica's dead, Kendra's raising five kids and Karly has cancer, I doubt if it will happen but who knows. Maybe escaping our realities is what we all need. What a difference a few months can make. Thanksgiving is a few days away and I have no idea what we're going to do about dinner. I was smart enough to decline hosting it this year but I don't even feel like being around family. Honestly, I'm not feeling very thankful right now. I know that's a horrible thing to say or write and very unbiblical but I'm just being truthful. It seems I've taken two steps backward emotionally and spiritually. All I want to do is run away. I wonder if this is the tribulation that Jesus warned us about.'

Sharon heard the garage door opening and quickly put the brochure for the town home back in her bag. By the time her family came into the family room, Sharon pretended to be engrossed in her study.

***

Regardless of how happy Simone sounded, Kendra was still worried. It was Simone's first holiday without her mother. Spending this critical period with so many strangers was bound to backfire. Eric's reassurances that Simone was with family failed to alleviate her anxiety. The conversation during dinner was lively. Kendra sat next to her niece who bemoaned Simone's absence before moving to the subject of the twins and when she might be old enough to baby sit. After everyone finished eating, Kendra stood to help clear the table but Eric's mother took charge and ushered her out of the dining room. When Kendra noticed Eric and her father talking, she knew the topic. She was thankful that the next feedings gave her a valid reason to escape into her bedroom and close the door.

Lulled by a full stomach and the rocking, Kendra struggled to stay awake while she nursed. Eric startled her when she felt him pry John from her arm. "Baby, you need to take a nap too."

Kendra yawned sleepily and checked the clock on the nightstand. "I wish I could but Kat will be awake soon."

"What's the family doing now?"

Eric sat on the bed. "You name it. The grandpas are keeping the kids entertained and the women have taken over the kitchen. Your brother's trying to organize a card game, but he's having a hard time."

"That's because he takes the game too seriously." Kendra rocked herself in the chair and stared at the wall.

"Are you still worrying about Simone?"

"I hope she's really okay."

"It sounded like she's having a great time. I'm glad you let her go"

Kendra rolled her eyes at him. "Did I really have a choice? It was three against one. I just wish she wasn't staying so long."

Eric looked at Kendra's face. There were lines between her brows and dark circles under her eyes. "With school out, there was no need for her to rush back."

"But this is the first Thanksgiving without her mother." Kendra remembered how hard the first Thanksgiving after her mother's death was for her. She still grieved her mother every holiday. "I know how she feels."

"Do you really?"

"I lost my mother," Kendra said with pain clearly resonating in her voice.

"But your circumstances were so different. You had much more time with your mother, who embraced deep-rooted family traditions. I'm not trying to be disrespectful, but Jessica probably didn't even make a big deal of Thanksgiving for Simone. Remember back in college, she never even went home for Thanksgiving."

Jessica's life only amplified Kendra's desire to make it better for Simone. "She wouldn't even come home with me when I invited her, claiming she preferred to use the time to study for finals. After having to deal with Liz firsthand, now I understand why." Kendra's jaws tightened. "That woman hasn't called Simone more than three times since she's been here. I expected her to call today, but maybe it's good she hasn't."

Eric leaned back on his elbows. "Being with family in Atlanta may be just what Simone needs to establish new family traditions and memories."

Kendra did not want Simone to have new traditions. She wanted her to become a part of theirs. The most important things her mother taught her were waiting to be shared with Simone. "We're her family now." Kendra was biding her time to make it official. She wondered if it was a good time to broach the subject of adopting Simone.

"She knows we're here for her, but there's nothing like grandparents. I wish you could have seen how happy his parents were to meet Simone and she took to them immediately. I'm sure she'll have many stories to tell when she gets back."

Kendra did not want to hear stories about Jonathan or his family. "I'm glad you were able to fly with her to Atlanta."

"God's good. Everything worked out perfectly." When Kendra frowned, Eric walked to her and extended his hands to help her up. "Come lie down and I'll rub your back, while we wait for the princess to wake up."

"I wish you wouldn't call her that."

"Why not? She's your daughter and you're my queen."

Kendra looked up at Eric. There was a light in his eyes, which she had not seen for a while. "You can go look at the game or play cards. I'll be okay."

Eric reached for her hands and gently pulled her from the gliding rocker. "I prefer to look at you."

Kendra leered at him. "Don't get any ideas. Even if we could, we wouldn't."

Eric laughed. "All I said was look."

Kendra leaned on Eric while they crossed the short distance to the bed, enjoying a closeness that had been missing for a very long time. He positioned the pillows for her so she could lie comfortably on her side before he sat on the bed. When his hand reached under her shirt and touched the small of her back, her body tightened slightly.

"Relax." He worked his fingers in small circular motions.

Kendra closed her eyes savoring his touch. "That feels good." Kendra thought about her mother as she opened her eyes and looked around the room that her parents had shared for almost twenty years. "Sometimes I feel like all this is a dream."

He felt her muscles relaxing. "I hope it's a good dream."

The burrows between Kendra's eyes deepened. "Thinking about the future scares me sometimes. What if I'm not a good mother or worse if I die too soon?"

He moved his hand from her back to her face and smoothed the lines. "I really hope this is just your hormones talking."

She moved his hand from her face and directed it to her back. "Maybe, but my spirit seems so restless. Maybe I'm just obsessing too much about Simone." Kendra sighed. "When she gets back, I'm sure things will get back to normal, whatever that's going to look like for us now."

Eric moved his hand to Kendra's shoulder and gently coaxed her onto her back so they could talk face to face. "Kendra, I was going to wait until tomorrow, but now may be a better time to discuss something."

The look on Eric's face worried Kendra. "Is it about Simone?"

"No, it's about the interview."

Kendra propped herself up and adjusted the pillow behind her back.

"They made me an offer and it's a very good one." The panic he saw in his wife's eyes led him to reach for her hands but she pulled them away.

"I thought you weren't that serious about this job," she said.

"Knowing that it would require us to move, I didn't want to upset you about something that was a remote possibility."

Anger filled her heart. "You lied to me."

"No, I didn't lie to you. I didn't think I would get the job."

Kendra balled her hands into fists and diverted her eyes from his.

"Kendra, an opportunity like this doesn't come very often. It's a growing company with strong leaders and social principles."

Her fingernails dug into her flesh as she fought the tears.

"They gave me everything I asked for plus some things I didn't, like a hefty signing bonus."

She forced her eyes to his face. "We don't need money or the other things they offered you."

"This is an opportunity to do the things I've dreamed of doing. It's why I became an engineer. They have a talented team that's energized and ready to change the world."

"Then why do they need you so badly?" She saw by his reaction her words hurt him.

"Because the founder and C.E.O. wants someone who reports to the same person he does," Eric paused to emphasize the importance. "Jesus."

Kendra was certain a weight had fallen on her chest. Needing to stand up, she crawled across the bed to avoid contact with Eric. Once on her feet, she grasped the bedpost and took several breathes.

Eric kept his distance. "God, help her. Please," he whispered.

When Kendra felt steady on her feet, she walked to the bassinets and looked down at her babies. "Have you accepted the offer?"

"I could never make a decision like this without discussing it with you first."

Kendra turned towards him and crossed her arms over her chest. "I don't want to move especially after just having the twins."

"Under any other circumstances, I would not even think of asking you." Eric walked to his wife and wrapped his arms around her. "Just do me a favor. Pray about it."

"What about this house?"

"We can sell it."

"Eric, it was a gift from my father. It's all I have left of my mother!"

"If this opportunity is from God, and I'm pretty convinced that it is, He will take care of all the details. But I need you to be convinced too. Will you ask God for wisdom regarding this move? And as for your mother's legacy…" Eric kissed Kendra on the cheek and then turned her to the bassinets. Her mother's namesake was looking up at them.

***

Jonathan sat in his parents' kitchen reflecting on the events of the day. His first Thanksgiving without Lori and his children was difficult. Sensing the magnitude of his loss, his entire family supported him and eagerly welcomed Simone. He tried not to think about how difficult his Thanksgiving would have been if Lori would have survived without even one of their children.

Simone hopped around the corner wearing pink satin pajamas that reminded Jonathan of her mother. "I caught you! Grandma said you were probably in the kitchen sneaking more dessert."

For the first time, he found himself comparing Simone to his other daughters who always wore cotton pajamas. He hoped that Simone would outgrow the satin ones quickly. Jonathan put down his fork and wiped the cream cheese icing from the corner of his mouth. "Have you tried her carrot cake?"

"Not yet."

He pushed out the chair next to him and slid the plate a few inches. "Get a fork and I'll share."

Simone smiled before going to a drawer and getting a fork.

"You've learned your way around Grandma's kitchen pretty fast." He watched her climb into the chair and cut a small piece. "Did you have a good time today?"

"Yes. We have a *big* family," Simone said before putting some cake in her mouth.

Jonathan liked hearing her say we. "Yes, we do. How do you like the cake?"

"Yum-my! Grandma's a good cook, not like Liz."

"Have you talked to Liz lately?"

"She doesn't call much. Before mommy died, we hardly ever talked with her. She did go to Disneyworld with us."

Jonathan had to change the subject. "Did you have fun playing with your cousins?"

"Yep, except the little one kept calling me Ashley. The others said I look like her."

The palms of Jonathan's hands began to sweat. He had asked the adults to watch what they said around Simone. It had not occurred to him the children might say something to her about their cousins.

Simone's large, inquisitive eyes pierced his. "Do I really look like her?"

Jonathan cleared his throat. "Do you know who Ashley is?"

"She's one of your other children that died in the bad accident?"

"How do you know about the accident?"

"I heard Liz talking about it to some of her friends after Mommy died."

As Jonathan reached for his daughter, he wondered what else she had overhead Liz discussing and was thankful he had several days to try to explain it.

CHAPTER 15

FRIDAY AFTERNOON, KENDRA'S EYES SHIFTED FROM THE PICTURES on the computer screen to the time. The baby monitor beside the computer confirmed the twins were sleeping contently. When Eric called alerting her to the email from the realtor, she abandoned her plans for an afternoon nap in exchange for a first look at their potential next home. Leaving her sons under Ruby's watchful eyes, Kendra willed herself to keep a positive attitude. After looking at five of the listings, her attitude had moved back to the other end of the scale. By the time she viewed the last house, she doubted Eric had taken the time to preview the houses before calling her. None of the listings even came close to their home. She leaned back in the chair, contemplating her options.

Ruby walked into the room. "Well Danny and Josh are finally napping." The look on Kendra's face revealed both disappointment and dread.

"Looking at these houses was a big waste of time. Eric wanted to schedule some appointments for next week but there's nothing in this group even worth seeing. Spring is a much better time to move. Maybe these listings will finally convince him."

"Are the houses really that bad or are you purposefully creating an obstacle? Besides, you can't get a feel for a house from pictures." Ruby pointed a knowing finger at Kendra. "God has the perfect home waiting for you."

"Maybe, but this could also be a sign that we should wait to move. I'm not moving five children into any house. We might have a commuter marriage for a few months."

Ruby chuckled. "You'll never get Eric to agree to that."

Kendra gripped the arms of the chair and pouted, knowing Ruby was right.

"Are you sure you don't want me to pick up Simone?"

Even though her doctor had cleared Kendra to drive, she had only ventured out once alone with the twins for their six-week medical checkup. Ruby had stayed home with the boys and Eric met her in the parking garage to help. This was going to be the first time Kendra took all her children anywhere by herself. She didn't want to admit it to Ruby, but she was beginning to have second thoughts about her excursion. "I'm sure. All we're doing is picking her up. We don't even have to get out of the van. The boys will enjoy the ride and it's time for me to wean myself from your services."

Ruby put a hand on her hip and tried to look offended, "So now I'm hired help."

"I didn't mean it like that. Just the sooner I get back into the swing of things the better. Especially since finding someone like you in Birmingham will be next to impossible."

"You found me didn't you? If my granddaughter wasn't about to have her first child, I'd gladly move with you for a few months. I've never lived outside of Texas and I hear the southern lifestyle is very relaxing." Ruby looked at the computer screen. "That one looks nice."

"I want a house just like this one."

"Change is good. A house with everything on the same level may be ideal."

"It looks like a dark cave on the inside. I want something new or at the least updated." Kendra stood up to stretch her aching back. "This is all happening so fast, too fast. I don't want to move out of this house or this city. This is my home. It's the only home I've known and the only home I want my children to know."

"Sometimes, we have to trust that God knows what's best for us."

"Ruby, why would God want me to leave the house I grew up in and a strong family support system to move half way across the country, where I don't know a soul?"

"What does your dad always tell you?"

Kendra did not want advice. "I know God's ways are not our ways. But be honest with me, does us moving make any sense to you?"

"Sounds like you're facing the same situation that Abraham faced, but he obeyed God and he was blessed."

"But I'm not Abraham and God has definitely not talked to me about this. I'm beginning to wonder if Eric's running from one bad situation to another."

"Kendra, Eric would never do anything to harm his family. Sounds like you need to have more faith in Eric and God. One day, you'll see God's hand in all of this."

She walked to Ruby and hugged her tightly. "I hope you're right because all I see now is heartache and confusion. This has been the second worst year of my life."

Ruby patted her back like a mother comforting a small child. "You're going to be just fine."

Kendra clung to Ruby hoping to absorb some of her strength and wondering how she would manage without her. "I still miss Mom, so much."

"I know." Ruby squeezed tighter. 'Lord, help her.'

***

Dale was tempted to abandon their plans when Paige spotted a couple walking to a car. People were losing their patience and tempers were flaring. Horns blew harshly. Based on the parking situation, it was easy to imagine conditions inside the mall. Questioning the wisdom of listening to his children, he clicked on the turn signal and thumped the steering wheel while waiting for the car to vacate the space. Shawn sat in the front seat listening to music through earphones totally oblivious to his father's mounting frustration. Sharon had rushed out of the house before the children were awake, leaving him to fill their day. He suspected Sharon's Saturday work schedule had more to do with preference than necessity.

By eleven o'clock his children had reached the point where irritating each other became the preferred pass time. After refereeing the second argument he knew a change of venue was needed. His recommendation that they eat lunch at home then go to a movie was met with groans. Paige suggested they go to the mall for lunch, but he suspected her request had little to do with food. Overhearing Sharon telling their children to finish up their Christmas list or they would be very disappointed on Christmas morning, he questioned her motivations for setting such dangerous expectations. As the Christmas marketing blitz intensified, so did his concerns about following harmful traditions devoid of biblical foundations, but trying to undo the harm to his children would require Sharon's cooperation.

As construction on the new bedroom progressed so did the distance between Dale and Sharon. The contractor upheld his end of the agreement. The room would be finished three days before Christmas but Dale wavered on his original plans. Sharon's off-hand comment about him ruining Christmas for the rest of his family resulted in a peace offering. He agreed not to move his mother into their home until after Christmas. A conversation with the home health provider changed the move date again. The aide assigned to his mother was on vacation the week between Christmas and New Year's. To minimize the amount of disruption for all the parties involved, his mother would be moving into their home on January 2nd.

Christmas carols greeted Dale and his children as soon as the automatic doors opened. Paige's eyes lit up with the Christmas lights dangling over their heads. A sea of people appeared to be moving in every direction. Some faces revealed joy but most tried to hide their frustration and anxiety. The absence of God was overwhelming as he followed his children towards the food court. The masses of people impeded their progress. Realizing his dilemma was self imposed caused his facial muscles to tighten, which his children failed to notice.

Paige looked back to make sure her father was close. Seeing the distance between them widening, she stopped to wait for him. When he was at her side, she took his hand. "When we're finished eating, can we go to the game store?"

"I thought you just wanted to come to the mall to eat."

"Daddy, since we're here, we might as well look around. Mommy wants my Christmas list."

Dale wanted to remind his daughter that Christmas should be about more than getting gifts, but everything around him communicated the opposite. Shawn was in the line to order behind seven other people. While waiting for the line to move, Dale's mind lingered on one thought. 'Father, forgive us.' Guilt for teaching his children to follow Christmas traditions overwhelmed him. He tried to remember his parent's views on the holiday. Because money was scare, less emphasis was placed on presents and more on family and Jesus. He remembered the Christmas following Sharon's heart attack. They were both so focused on God that Christmas seemed so right. Moses' warnings came to mind. Paige's gentle nudge forward returned Dale's thoughts to the present. The tables in the food court were as congested as the parking lot. His son claimed a table while Dale and Paige waited for their order.

After putting the food on the table, Dale sat beside Paige to give Shawn, who quickly removed the wrapping and bit into his sandwich with gusto, more space. When Paige paused to bless her food, Dale gave an affirming nod. Looking down at his food, he hungered for what was not on the tray. "Guys, we need to discuss something important."

Shawn looked at his father and shrugged his shoulder. "Okay."

Dale struggled with how to begin. "If we knew some of our actions displeased God, what should we do?"

"Daddy, that's easy. We should stop doing it," Paige said proudly.

"What if it's something very hard to stop?"

"Like what?" Shawn asked dipping a waffle fry into a heap of ketchup.

Dale took a deep breath and exhaled. "Like celebrating Christmas."

"You must be kidding," Shawn said before putting the fry into his mouth.

Paige reached for her drink and took a sip. "Why would celebrating Jesus' birthday upset God?"

Dale locked eyes with his son. "No, I'm not kidding." He looked at his daughter who was waiting anxiously for an answer. "I've been doing a lot of research relating to Christmas. For starters, December 25th is not Jesus' real birthday."

"Duh Dad. Everybody knows Jesus wasn't born on the day we celebrate Christmas. The early Christians picked December 25th because it was already a Roman holiday. It made it easier for them to have a day off work. I learned that in Sunday school."

Dale shook his head at his son's escalating level of disrespect, wondering if he treated all adults that way or just him. "Shawn, we talked about a respectful tone. You just crossed the line. But for the record, I'm glad to know you listened to whoever taught you that."

"I'm always listening," Shawn said with concern in his voice.

Dale questioned the quality of his son's listening skills but decided to address the most pressing issue. "I haven't found anything in the Bible to justify celebrating Christmas."

"Did you find anything that says we shouldn't?" Shawn asked challengingly but in a more respectful tone.

"As a matter of fact, I did."

His son dumped his container of fries onto the tray and began picking out the ones with too much skin. "We can't stop celebrating Christmas. It would be un-American and very un-Christian."

His daughter put her sandwich down, frown lines etched in her forehead. "Daddy, what's wrong with celebrating Christmas?"

Dale paused regretting the start of such an important conversation in the middle of enemy territory. The song 'I saw Mommy kissing Santa Claus' was drowning out their words. "Let's finish our lunch. We can discuss this later."

"Yeah, when Mom's around," Shawn said flatly.

The veins on the side of Dale's temples bulged and his jaws locked closed while he prayed for the right way to respond to his son.

Paige perceived quickly her brother was jeopardizing her time at the mall. "Daddy, can we get some cookies for Grandma while we're here? Maybe we can drop them off on the way home."

Dale appreciated Paige's actions and took them as a temporary answer to his prayer. "Sure baby. I think Grandma would love getting some cookies and seeing her favorite grandchildren."

Shawn kicked his sister's foot under the table, but she ignored him and continued eating.

When Dale and his children returned home several hours later, the smell of roasted meat filled the house. Sharon was at the kitchen sink peeling potatoes. She turned from the sink with a potato in one hand and the peeler in the other and directed her attention to her children. "Did you guys have fun with your father?"

Shawn sat at the counter. "It was okay."

Sharon looked at Dale and then back to her children. "Paige, did you bring mommy anything?"

Her daughter smiled as she held out the bag of cookies, which she was holding behind her back. "Your favorites!" she said placing the bag on the counter.

Sharon put the potato and peeler on the cutting board and rinsed her hands before inspecting the contents of the bag. "I hope you guys didn't spoil your appetites with a bunch of junk food. There's a huge roast in the oven and I'm making creamed potatoes to go with it."

Dale watched Sharon bite into a cookie. "We ate lunch early. What time did you get home?"

Sharon put the remainder of the cookie in the bag. "I haven't been home too long."

Paige pulled off her coat and hung it on the back of a chair. "We took Grandma some cookies. She has a little Christmas tree in her room with fake candy canes."

The mention of her mother-in-law caused the last bite of cookie to lodge in her throat. Sharon took a drink from her water bottle, which she kept on the kitchen counter, before returning to peeling the potatoes.

Dale noticed Sharon's changed expression as he tried to hang onto a thankful attitude. His mother was having a good day and even ate a cookie while they visited. Dale wanted to get the most from their visit but his children did not share his sentiments. They left after what Dale considered to be a short visit. Passing the activity center, Dale regretted that Doc had returned to the assisted living building after his friend with the broken hip died. They talked on the phone daily but Dale preferred being in the same room with him. They were long overdue for a face to face conversation. His planned retreat to his office to call Doc was halted by the look his son gave him.

"Mom, will you please tell Dad it's not wrong to celebrate Christmas. He wants us to stop celebrating it."

Sharon carefully placed the peeler in the kitchen sink to prevent throwing it. "I can't tell your dad anything these days but don't worry. We're celebrating Christmas. Whether he joins us is up to him." Sharon said matter-of-factly. Without pausing, she began cutting the potatoes into cubes and dropping them into the waiting pot of water.

The words took a few seconds to hit the mark. Dale stepped aside so his children had an unobstructed path. "Kids, go to your rooms so I can talk to your mother."

"Ah Dad, I want to hear this."

Dale looked at his son sternly. "Shawn, don't make me repeat myself."

Shawn, who had not seen his father so angry with someone else in a long time, stood up and grabbed his sister by the arm. "Come on, Paige."

Sharon kept her back to Dale as she continued cutting. "The kids didn't need to leave."

"Sharon, I've tried to be patient but your comment to our son was completely unnecessary, not to mention damaging to my authority."

"It may have been unnecessary, but it's definitely true. You can do whatever you want but don't expect the rest of us to agree with you." She dropped the last of the potatoes into the pot and put the cutting board in the sink before turning to face him. "What do you suddenly have against Christmas, especially since we can finally afford to get the kids what they want?"

"This has nothing to do with whether we can get the kids what they want; although, I do have a big problem with that too."

"Dale, look around you. Everybody celebrates Christmas! It's the only religious holiday that all people can celebrate peacefully."

Dale raised his hands in the air. "That should be enough proof that it's not of God. It's a pagan holiday."

"I'm not about to get into a theological argument with you about Christmas. So what's this really about?" Sharon leaned against the counter.

"It's about obedience to God's word. We've been deceived by man-made rules and doctrine into doing the very things that God commanded us not to do. There's nothing in the Bible instructing us to celebrate Jesus' birthday. If God wanted us to celebrate it, He would have given us a specific date and instructions, like He did for all His appointed feasts." After making the connection between the Old Testament and the New, he was certain

Christmas was diametrically opposed to everything he knew about God.

"Look Dale, if you don't want to celebrate Christmas any more, it's fine. But you can't keep forcing your choices on the rest of us."

"I'm not trying to force anything on you."

She tilted her head to one side. "Oh really…"

"Sharon, the room's finished. I've arranged for in-home nursing help so you won't have to do anything for my mother. What more can I do? We can't keep living like this. We argue about every little thing. You haven't let me touch you in almost three months."

Sharon dramatically raised her hands, mocking Dale's earlier gesture. "So, now we're finally getting to the real problem."

"Sharon, I need you. Is that so wrong?"

Sharon looked at the floor. "You may need me, but I'm not so sure I still need you. If it were not for our children, I'd seriously consider moving out of this house. I need time and space to think. You're not the man I married."

Dale looked at Sharon in utter disbelief. For the first time he realized their current problem was not related to his mother. "You don't honestly believe that?"

"At this point, I don't know what I believe or feel anymore. All I know is I'm tired of waiting for things to return to normal." She looked at the clock. "The roast needs to cook another hour." She grabbed her purse off the back of the door and walked out the kitchen.

Dale watched her leave wishing he could stop her, but knowing he couldn't.

***

At precisely eight-thirty Sunday evening, Kendra turned off the light in the kitchen and walked sluggishly up the stairs. Despite her reservations about the move, she tried hard not to let it impact her mothering responsibilities. Eric was tucking their sons into bed when she paused at the door to check on their progress, being careful not to let them see her. On the way to Simone's room, she smiled thinking about the fun they had putting up the Christmas tree and wondered if it was the first of their new family traditions. In addition to buying Kendra and her brother an ornament every year to mark special events, her mother kept every ornament that they made at school or church events. Kendra's brother took his box of ornaments the year he married. Kendra's ornaments were carefully placed on their tree. Simone's first ornament, marking her inclusion in their family, hung prominently next to the first ornament Kendra's mother gave her.

Simone was on her knees praying when Kendra came in. She looked up briefly before continuing her prayers. Kendra waited by the door marveling at the difference between mother and daughter. All the effort invested in trying to save Jessica seemed to have paid off with her daughter.

When Simone jumped up from her knees, Kendra sat on the edge of her bed. "Just three more school days before Christmas break."

"I know."

"Christmas was your Mommy's favorite time of year. When we shared an apartment in college, she would decorate everything including the bathroom. Did your Mommy still do that?"

"Yes. We had a closet full of Christmas decorations. Last year, we put up two Christmas trees."

Kendra smiled knowingly. Jessica was obsessed with having a perfectly decorated Christmas tree. The second tree was to keep Simone from messing up the main tree. "Would you like your own Christmas tree this year?" Kendra looked around the bedroom. "There's enough room in here for a small one and you wouldn't have to worry about the boys destroying it."

"No, that's okay." Simone thought about her father who had helped his mother put up her tree the day after Thanksgiving.

Kendra noticed a flash of sorrow in Simone's eyes. "Are you worried about our move?"

"No."

Kendra wondered if she were being truthful. "Don't worry. We'll find a new school that's just as nice."

"Aunt Kendra, can Daddy come here for Christmas?"

"I'm sure your father has other plans."

"No, he doesn't. I asked him."

Kendra suspected Jonathan put Simone up to asking. "This is not a good time for him to visit. After we get settled in our new home, you can go visit him. Maybe Uncle Eric will take you shopping next weekend to buy him a present." Kendra hoped to keep their new address from Jonathan, which was the only positive she could find for the move.

"I know just what he wants," Simone said softly. She looked at the bear that never left her bed. "Daddy sounded sad when I talked with him today."

Kendra hoped he was more than sad. "I'm sure he's okay."

"I think he misses my brothers and sisters. He said they loved Christmas time."

Kendra tried unsuccessfully to hide her shock. "Did he tell you about them?"

Simone wondered why her aunt looked like her mother did when she was angry. "At Thanksgiving, my cousin said I looked like Ashley. When I asked Daddy if I did, he showed me a picture of her and my other brothers and sister. They're in heaven now with their mother and mommy."

Kendra did not have the heart to correct her. "It's late. You need to go to sleep."

Simone rolled onto her side and propped her head on her hand just like her mother always did. "Why don't you like Daddy?"

Kendra paused. "He did some bad things that hurt a lot of people."

"He's sorry."

"Being sorry won't bring your mother back."

"Daddy didn't cause Mommy's accident. He was at the cabin when it happened. That's why he didn't come to the funeral. He didn't know about Mommy."

Kendra adjusted the blanket. "When you get a little older, maybe you'll understand."

"I think Daddy needs me."

"He needs a lot of things but you're not one of them. Your mommy wanted you to live with me."

"If I wanted to live with daddy, could I?"

"Don't you like living here?"

"You have lots of children. Daddy only has me."

Kendra kissed Simone on the forehead. "Your father will be just fine. Now close those eyes and go to sleep."

Kendra was fuming when she left Simone's room. She checked on her sons again before going downstairs to check on the twins. They were sleeping peacefully, something Kendra had not done in weeks. She followed the smell of popcorn into the den where Eric was watching television. The empty bowl and the baby monitor were on the coffee table. "I don't think we should let Simone talk to Jonathan until after we move."

"That might be difficult, not to mention cruel."

Kendra plopped on the sofa beside Eric and rested her feet on the coffee table. "I think he's trying to brainwash her into wanting to live with him."

"I doubt he's brainwashing her." Eric had talked to Jonathan several times since accepting the position. Both men, who wanted to do what was best for their children, came up with a possible solution. "Baby, we need to talk about Simone."

"There's nothing to talk about. She's staying with us."

Eric muted the volume on the television. "Just hear me out."

"Fine...but you're wasting your time."

"Kendra, when you put Simone in that private school you said it was important for her to have a nurturing environment while she adjusts to her mother's death. Despite my doubts, I have to admit you were right. She's thriving there."

"I told you."

"I really hate to move her before she finishes the year."

Kendra felt her load being lifted. Had Eric finally come to his senses? "So does that mean you're willing to stay here until the school year ends?"

"Kendra, we have to move but Simone doesn't."

"And who's she going to stay with…Ruby?"

Eric paused. "No, Jonathan. He wants to move…"

"No. Absolutely not…have you lost your mind?"

"Will you let me finish? He's willing to move here so Simone can finish the school year and we can get settled in our new home. We will still be her legal guardian."

"He just wants her money."

"He doesn't even know about the money. Even if he did, I honestly don't think it would matter."

"Do you know he had the audacity to show her pictures of his dead children? What kind of man does that? He's not fit to be a father."

Eric knew about the pictures and everything else. "The person you should be angry with is Liz. If anyone is responsible for the entire mess it's her. She's the person who raised Jessica not to respect marriage vows and was the one who cared less what her granddaughter overheard. As for whether Jonathan's fit to be a father, are you qualified to make that decision?"

"I'm honoring her mother's final wishes and that's all that matters."

"You know as well as I do that Jessica's motives were always questionable. Do you want her desire to hurt Jonathan to permanently scar Simone? Was she even sober when she wrote that document?"

Kendra refused to answer his question. Hearing Eric desecrate Jessica's memory hurt more than she could admit. Her head was pounding. She focused on the muted television, wondering if Eric was truly thinking about Simone or himself.

Realizing his wife was still grieving for Jessica, he wrapped his arms around her and held her tightly. "I'm sorry."

Kendra's body stiffened as she freed herself to stand.

Eric caught her hand, preventing her escape. "Wait."

Kendra paused but refused to look at him.

"It's time to get an unbiased expert opinion on the situation. The family counseling minister is willing to work with us to determine what's best for Simone, which is what we all ultimately want. Jonathan's flying in next week for an appointment. While he's in town, he'd like for us to get together to talk."

Kendra dropped her arms to her side and shook her head. "I can't be in the same room with that man."

"Kendra, what makes his sin any worse than ours? God forgave us and gave us another chance. You have to get past this, for your sake as well as Simone's. If you can forgive a man who almost raped you, surely you can forgive Jonathan."

"I can't."

Eric stood up quickly and locked his arms around her. "You can." He kissed her cheek and whispered in her ear. "We can do all things through Christ who strengthens us." He cupped her face in his hands and looked deeply into her eyes. "Babe, we have to trust God."

***

The efficiency apartment was warm and inviting. Dale suspected the warmth came from its current occupant in spite of the sparse, generic furnishings. It reminded him of his first apartment, a temporary shelter while preparing for a more permanent home. Waiting for Doc to join him at the small round table, sadness permeated his soul. He could not distinguish the source from the symptoms. With each visit, his mentor seemed physically weaker and he was not ready to lose the friend and teacher he so desperately needed. From the moment he opened the door, Dale sensed that Doc understood his struggle to maintain his footing.

Doc sat a steaming cup of tea in front of Dale. "Having your eyes opened is the first step. It's also the easiest. Does it feel like you're being attacked on all fronts?"

Dale welcomed the launching point for their visit. "Does it show?"

The etched lines in Doc's forehead deepened. "I've been there my friend; we all have. The closer we get to the truth, the more the enemy tries to stop us. You need to be prepared because the opposition will get worse. Just remember what the devil intends for harm, our God uses for good."

Dale watched the steam disappear a few inches above the cup, remembering the last time he had experienced such pain and confusion. The scandal with Kendra that initiated his midlife career change now seemed insignificant by comparison. "I've studied the Bible extensively for over five years. But when I read it now, it's like I'm reading it for the first time."

"What you're experiencing is completely normal. Remember, Nicodemus' frustration. And don't forget the disciples on the road to Emmaus. The resurrected Lord was walking with them and they did not know it, but the Lord was not upset. He responded by patiently explaining to them the Scriptures, beginning at Moses and all the prophets. Your current state is a blessing from God. His elect must know the complete truth. In these last days, God's people will have to choose between truth and lies, life and death. We're fortunate that God promised to be our teacher."

"But how?"

Doc pointed to Dale's Bible. "Everything people need to know is in the Bible. The Holy Spirit will guide us into all truth and warn us of things to come, so we will be prepared." He paused. "And we have each other."

Dale thought about his most recent dream, questioning whether to share it. "But how do we know if it's God speaking to us?"

"The sheep know their Shepherd's voice." Doc could tell that Dale was not convinced. "How did Abraham know it was God telling him what to do?"

Dale shrugged his shoulders. He had asked the question several times but never received a satisfactory answer. "He had great faith."

"Abraham's great faith was in God's promise, not whether it was God speaking to him. He knew it was God."

"But how did he know?"

"How do we know anything? We learn from a reliable source. Who taught Abraham?"

"God?"

"Is that an answer or a question? Turn to Genesis chapter five." Doc removed the tea bag from his cup and took a sip while he waited.

Dale read the subtitle of the chapter before skimming it quickly. "What do the descendants of Adam have to do with Abraham?"

"Did you ever wonder why God gave so much detail? The age each man was when he begot his son and the age that he died."

"Not really."

Doc walked to the bookshelf and returned with an oversized book. "My wife bought this for me. It was the last gift she gave me. The woman knew me so well." He held the book so Dale could see the title before opening it to a three page, fold-out chart. "A picture is truly better than words, which is probably why our sight is so important. I'm sure you've seen a Bible time line before but have you seen this?" Doc tapped his finger next to a framed insert. "What does this tell you?"

Dale looked at the bar graph with the subtitled 'Creation to Abraham'. His eyes traveled back and forth from the chart to Genesis chapter five. Each descendant's life was represented by a bar on the chart which corresponded to the time line. When Dale finished the chapter he looked at Doc.

"Genesis 11 has the descendents of Shem." Doc sipped on his tea while he watched.

When Dale leaned back in his chair mentally processing the information, Doc pointed at his book again. "It's much easier to grasp with a picture."

"A picture really can say a thousand words."

"This paints father Abraham's faith in a different light. He had a little help getting to know God and His power. Most people doubt the biblical accounts of man's creation and the flood. Abraham didn't because he had access to a very credible witness."

"What other important information have I overlooked?"

"Most people, especially today, like to skip over the details of the Bible. But as a man of science, I know God's most apparent in the details. The more detailed in the Bible, the more important it is."

Dale rubbed his chin. "Adam was still alive while Methuselah and his son Lamech, Noah's father, lived. That means Noah's father could have known Adam, the man who walked in the garden with God?"

"It certainly appears that way, which may explain why Noah followed God's instructions to the letter and why God was the one who closed the ark door."

Dale looked at the chart as if confirming again what the Bible recorded and the diagram clearly showed. "And Noah was still alive when Abraham was born?"

"It appears that God's call to Abraham came fairly close to the death of Noah. Can you imagine getting a first hand account of the flood from the man who built the ark? Maybe that's why Hebrew 11, the great chapter on faith, jumps from Noah's to Abraham's faith." Doc looked at the timeline. "Looking back, it makes me wonder if God's call to Abraham was just a different kind of ark to save creation, again." Doc sat up with a startled look and smiled. "After all these years, I just had another revelation. God commanded Moses to make an *Ark* to hold the Ten Commandments. God promised life to those who obeyed, so in essence they were saved by the Ark of the Covenant!"

Dale could only shake his head in astonishment.

Doc slapped his hand on the table. "Our faith is so complicated and yet so simple. I'd wager that you've used Matthew 11:28 in many of your sermons. 'Come to me, all ye that labor and are heavy laden, and I will give you rest.' These words are used to lure people to the Christian faith. Let me ask you something. Since you've started seeking the truth about God, how much resting have you done?"

Dale thought about the challenges with his career, his marriage, and his children. The only area of his life not under attack was his health. "Not much."

"That's the problem with taking Bible verses out of context. Four verses before this one, Jesus talks about the unrepentant in the Day of Judgment. The next verse, Jesus thanked our Father for hiding the truth from the wise and prudent, but revealing them to babies. Dale, you and I are babies and it's a good thing to be. We're learning the truth that sets us free and allows us to enter God's rest."

"Doc, I have to be completely honest with you. I feel like I don't know anything anymore."

"You're no different than the apostles, who spent over three years being taught by the Lord. People must understand why God sent Jesus in a human body. Moses told Israel, in Deuteronomy, Jesus would come in response to the nation's request not to hear the voice of the Almighty or see the fire again. The prophet Jeremiah reminded Israel of their savior's coming. Yet, his disciples were confused until the resurrected Jesus stood before them and explained how every scripture related to him. Many people believe Jesus lived on earth and some even believe He's the Son of God, but I wonder how many truly believe He's coming again to reign and dwell on earth among men. That's what the Bible teaches from start to finish. The coming of God's Kingdom is the true gospel and the source of our hope. Remember, God's in the detail. Closely examine the Lord's Prayer."

Dale wrapped his hands around the lukewarm mug of tea.

"Be patient," Doc said.

"Once my mother moves in with us, I'm not sure how often I'll be able to come by."

"My friend, I suspect my time with you is finished. You no longer need a human guide and you're in very good hands."

Dale felt like he was losing another father. "I wanted to get you a gift, but nothing seemed adequate."

"My gift will be seeing you on that great day of celebration. Did the information on God's appointed feast help?"

"Yes." Dale hesitated. "Some people think Jesus' return is going to happen soon. Do you?"

Doc pondered how to answer. "I suspect you already know the answer to that question."

Dale gave a confirming nod.

"That's why we have to understand and carefully obey God's requirements. We should be about our Father's business, if we want to be found faithful servants."

"There's nothing I want more than to be a faithful servant. It's just so hard to know what God wants from us."

"No it's not, once you know who you are."

"It's still hard to believe I'm part of the real Israel – one of the lost sheep God returned to the flock. Our fathers walked through the Red Sea together."

"When God says He will do something, it will come to pass. He scattered us across the face of the earth and He will gather us again; each to his own family. DNA research has proven it's scientifically possible. It's funny how science confirms what God established before the foundation of the world. The Bible truly is a lamp and the treasures hidden within have no end." Doc patted Dale's hand. "As for what God requires of us, Deuteronomy has the most marvelous summary." Doc closed his eyes. "And now, Israel, what does the Lord thy God require of thee, but to fear the Lord thy God, to walk in all his ways, and to love him, and to serve the Lord thy God with all thy heart and with all thy soul, to keep the commandments of the Lord, and his statues, which I command thee this day for thy good." Doc opened his eyes and looked at Dale. "My generation feared their parents. Did you fear yours?"

Dale's eyes widened. "Oh, yes."

"Did you fear them hurting you?"

"Only if I did what I wasn't supposed to do," Dale said remembering one particular incident.

"Did you have to guess about acceptable behavior by your parents' standards?"

Dale thought for a few minutes. "No, I learned their rules at an early age."

"And how did you learn them?"

"They put the fear of God in me." Dale shook his head at his own new revelation. "How many times have I said that? I never got it, until now. My parents taught me how to fear God, when they taught me how to fear them and why."

"Those blessed with God-fearing, loving parents learn healthy, life-preserving fear, which we're able to transfer to God as adults. This generation doesn't fear their parents or God, which explains all the self-destructive choices and rampant evil."

Dale wandered if his children had a healthy fear of their parents.

"It's getting late." Doc braced his hands on the table while he pushed his chair back. He stood up with mixed emotions.

Dale looked at the timeline again before standing also. Their eyes communicated the words neither of them could say. They embraced, both sensing it would be the last time.

Doc cleared his throat. "My friend, take care until we meet again."

***

The weekend before Christmas, Kendra's arms were locked across her chest as Eric drove into the parking lot. He offered to let her out at the door. Having no intention of being alone with Jonathan, even in a crowded restaurant, she stubbornly refused. Eric picked her favorite restaurant to make the evening more bearable. She reluctantly agreed to the dinner meeting only after talking with the church counselor. Feeling betrayed by her husband, she relented to going physically but was emotionally and spiritually resisting.

Jonathan waited at the table. All around him was a flurry of activity. Christmas music played softly in the background. When he saw Eric and Kendra being escorted to the table, he stood up immediately. Eric greeted him with a prolonged handshake. Kendra's greeting was barely audible and she refused to look at him. As soon as they sat down, a waitress appeared to take their drink order. Kendra looked at the half glass of water in front of Jonathan before ordering an iced tea and waited to see if he ordered something alcoholic. When he did not, she was disappointed. She listened passively as Eric apologized for their late arrival, which led to a discussion of the parking situation. Fearing she would be pulled into the conversation, Kendra picked up the menu and pretended to be absorbed in making a decision. Eric glanced at his wife disapprovingly. She always ordered the same entree. The waitress delivered their drinks and took their order starting with Kendra. When Jonathan ordered the same entree, she was tempted to change her order but refused to let him ruin her meal.

After the waitress collected the menus, Jonathan cleared his throat. "Kendra, I want to thank you for coming."

"Did I have a choice?" Kendra looked around for a distraction.

Eric reached under the table for Kendra's hand.

"On the way here, I was listening to a song. It seemed like the lyrics were written just for me."

Kendra rolled her eyes. He could fool Eric but he would never fool her. Jonathan was still the same self-centered snake.

"The lyrics say those who know the Lord have a story to tell. Kendra, I'd like to tell you my story, if you'll listen."

"Don't bother. I already know more than I care to."

Eric squeezed her hand. "I think we should hear him out."

Kendra withdrew her hand.

Jonathan locked eyes with Kendra. "This story is about God's mercy and grace."

Despite herself, Kendra wanted to hear what he could possibly know about God. "Fine, I'm listening."

"I was raised in the church and baptized about the age of twelve. From that point on, I considered myself a Christian. As soon as I met Lori, we became the perfect couple. The kids came quicker than my ability to handle the responsibilities. Lori's faith grew under the pressure but mine evaporated. When Lori found a new church, I went a couple of times but before long she and the kids went alone. Lori had just told me she was pregnant with our fourth child, when I took a new job and met Jessica."

Kendra looked at Eric.

"In many ways, I was just like Eve. God had provided everything I needed to be happy but still I wanted more; the one thing I knew was forbidden. Before I realized what was happening, it was too late. When Jessica told me that she was pregnant, I wanted to get rid of the evidence. Every time I look at Simone, I'm reminded of what I tried to get Jessica to do. I'm so thankful I failed."

Kendra thought about David and Bathsheba. She put her hand back in Eric's. "You didn't fail. God succeeded."

"Thankfully, He always does. Once Simone was born, I was in too deep. There were many regrets and guilt, but that was as far as I was willing to go. A few months before the accident, Lori and I went away for the weekend. At sunrise on a Sunday morning, Lori dragged me to the beach. Against my better judgment, I knelt beside her while she prayed for our marriage. As much as I tried to discount the impact of her prayer, that morning changed everything. God did what I couldn't. He ended both my affair with Jessica and my wife's pain."

The compassion Jonathan's story warranted was stifled by Kendra's suspicions of his ulterior motive. It was difficult to reconcile the person sitting across from her with the man she despised for so many years. "So now you want Simone to ease your guilty conscience?"

"I completely understand your reservations. Although I want to be involved daily in raising Simone, this meeting is about God. It took losing everything, or at least thinking I had, before I was finally ready to hear what God had been trying to tell me for years, without Him there is no hope for me or anyone else. The day that I buried my family, I found a letter that Lori had written for me, in case she died. At the end of the letter, she said for me to repent of my sins and trust in God's forgiveness. When I returned from Chicago thinking Jessica and Simone died because of me that was exactly what I did. It was the only thing left for me to do. I was so afraid. Whether I lived or died, God was the only one who could rescue me from a living hell." Jonathan's voice cracked with the realization. Seconds, which seemed like minutes, passed before he was able to continue. "Last week, I stood before the congregation at the church I avoided and confessed how my sins had hurt the ones I loved before being baptized. Instead of being greeted with condemnation, all I received were tears of joy and love." Jonathan paused again, as if considering what he was about to say. "I'd gladly go through all the suffering again to gain what I have now in our Lord, Jesus. Whatever time I have remaining is his. Our suffering is never for our benefit alone."

Kendra felt Eric squeeze her hand. On the way to the restaurant, they had discussed Jesus' commandment to love one another. She responded Jonathan was not her brother. Eric reminded her that God decides his family. The look in Jonathan's eyes erased all doubt.

Sensing the change, Jonathan's eyes traveled from Kendra to Eric and back to Kendra. "Raising Simone is not your responsibility, it's mine. I want to give her all the love God gives us, yet not my will, but His."

Waiting for their waitress to return with their meals, Kendra thought about the broken eggs from the science demonstration. She wondered if God was the egg in the hands of his children or if his children were the eggs in Jesus' hand.

CHAPTER 16

PARKED DIRECTLY IN FRONT OF THE BAGGAGE CLAIM EXIT, Kendra relished both the feel of her car and the silence. They replaced Eric's car with the mini-van and he inherited her car. Although she was glad Eric finally drove a car without holes in the floor, she missed the car, which she only drove on short errands without their children. She was fifteen minutes early but her father literally pushed her out of the house. As soon as Kendra mentioned a possible weekend trip, he insisted on coming to help Eric with his grandchildren. The weekend to help turned into a week long visit. It had only been three months since the move but for Kendra it felt like a lifetime. Her father's presence was so comforting she was hesitant about leaving. The twins were six months old and no longer seemed so fragile but when it came time to actually leave her babies, Kendra was ready to change her mind. Only the fact that Karly was already on the plane kept her from doing so. The waiting escalated her concerns both about her family and what to expect with Karly. Sharon inadvertently mentioned Karly's cancer diagnosis during one of their conversations triggering repressed memories of her mother's battle with the disease. Kendra opened the car windows and resisted the urge to sample some of the lunch that she had packed for them.

The flight attendant's gentle tap startled Karly from her slumber. She brought her seatback forward and raised the window shade. The lush greenery below was a welcome sight since the trees had yet to bud in Minneapolis. She mentally captured the view which would eventually find its way onto canvas. After living in Minneapolis for six years, she longed for more balanced seasons. For a brief moment, she wished her family were with her to enjoy the scrolling view. The last time she had been away from her family was at the bed and breakfast a year ago. When Ruben dropped her off at the airport his last words were "Have a great time and don't worry about us." It was obvious to Karly he would be the one doing all the worrying. She saw the mixture of fear and faith in his eyes. Every goodbye acquired a weightier significance since her cancer diagnosis.

When the captain announced the final approach, Karly looked at her watch. They were landing on time, which meant that Kendra would not have to wait. There were no direct flights from Minneapolis to the Destin area, but there was a direct flight to Birmingham. When she first called Kendra about riding with her to Destin, she seemed delighted. When Karly called back to confirm the details, Eric thanked her repeatedly because he did not want Kendra making the drive alone. After returning her book to her shoulder bag, Karly watched the landscape get closer. The last time she saw Kendra was at Jessica's funeral and it was such a difficult time for them.

Kendra was pleasantly surprised when Karly walked out of the airport looking healthy. Despite their brief encounters, they had forged a bond Kendra had hoped would grow stronger, but given Karly's diagnosis, she was now afraid to get too attached. Kendra jumped out of the car and rushed to greet her. "You look wonderful!"

Karly dropped her luggage and reached up to hug Kendra. "Well, thank you. So do you!"

The hug felt so good Kendra did not want it to end. Reluctantly, she pulled away. "My hair's a mess but at this point in my life, who cares." Picking up Karly's bag, she led the way to the car.

Karly waited for Kendra to put her suitcase in the back of the car and unlock the passenger door. "I see motherhood's mellowing you," Karly said with laughter.

"*Oh yes.* I'm learning to pick my battles and perfect hair is not one worth fighting. I'm just thankful it's finally long enough to get into a ponytail, especially with this southern humidity." Kendra held the passenger door open for Karly before walking around to the driver's side. After she buckled her seatbelt she looked in the rearview mirror. "Jessica would never let me live this down." Kendra sighed as she put the car into gear. "I still miss her...but thanks to Simone, I'll never be able to forget her."

Karly connected her seatbelt. "How did Simone enjoy spending her spring break with you?"

"We had a blast. I can't wait until Kat's that age."

"Don't rush it. It will be here before you know it and then you'll be longing for the diaper years."

Kendra shook her head vehemently thinking about all the diapers she had already changed. "I seriously doubt that."

Karly gave her a 'wait and see' look.

"Okay, maybe. But five is such a great age. They can tell you what they want and they're unblemished people. It broke my heart when Jonathan came to pick her up. They spent the weekend with his parents in Atlanta before going back to Dallas."

Karly turned in the seat so she could take in all the beauty of their conversation. "It seems like you've got peace about her living with him."

Kendra smiled. "I guess I do. Simone's happy, which is all that really matters. It helps that both my father and Ruby keep me well informed. Jonathan even joined our old church."

Karly watched Kendra's face as she spoke and realized what she had read was true. The face did communicate more than the words. "So he really did change?"

"More like, he's been changed. I just wish it would have happened earlier."

Karly noticed a veil of sadness descend on Kendra's face. "We have to trust God's timing. Hey, this weekend is supposed to lift us up, not bring us down."

"Sorry...," Kendra said, forcing a smile. "Are you hungry?"

"Starved. Can we stop to pick up something? I'm not picky. It just needs to be edible. They only served us peanuts on the plane."

"Count your blessings for those peanuts. There's no need to stop. I packed us a lunch. It's in the basket behind you. Since I wasn't sure what you're allowed to eat, I tried to include a little of everything."

Concern was written all over Kendra's face, raising Karly's suspicions. "I'm allowed to eat whatever I want."

Kendra propped her arm on the door. "Really?"

"Let me guess, Sharon told you about the cancer?"

Kendra bit her lips and looked straight ahead.

"Relax. It's okay, if she did."

Kendra did not want to cause any problems between the only friends she had left. "It slipped out while we were talking about this weekend. She's concerned about you." Kendra was concerned about her too. Her mother's cancer treatment left her drained. "Although looking at you, I don't see why?"

Karly stretched. She had been sitting too long. "If that was a compliment, thank you."

"Your cancer must not be as bad as my mother's."

"I don't know about that."

"Sharon said that you're refusing treatment. Do you think that's wise, especially given the ages of your children?"

"I'm not refusing treatment. I preferred a different doctor. Are you familiar with Jesus' miracle involving the woman who had been bleeding for twelve years?"

Kendra set the cruise control and took her foot off the accelerator. "That's a hard miracle to forget, at least for a woman. I complained about being pregnant for ten months. Can you imagine a twelve year period?"

"No, I can't or going from doctor to doctor subjecting my body to treatments hoping for a cure. For some people, it may be better to by-pass the doctors and go straight to the only one who can heal us anyway."

"Aren't you afraid of the cancer spreading?"

"I'm only afraid of being a scientific experiment or a revenue stream. My faith is in the Good Doctor. The Bible said that those who put their trust in Him will never be put to shame." Karly leaned against the door and sighed. "Although I wouldn't mind waiting for the Lord's return with my mother; it looks like our reunion won't be for a while."

Kendra latched onto their shared sorrow. "Your mother's dead?"

"I'd rather think of it as resting. She had a massive heart attack a few days after pointing me in the right direction. Ruben and I were able to salvage our marriage because of her; although she'd give God all the glory for it."

"That sounds like some story."

Karly disconnected her seatbelt, so she could retrieve the food. "It is. What do we have to eat while I tell you all about it?"

The miles raced pass as Karly shared her long journey to finding God's forgiveness. Kendra noticed that she told the story with the same sense of solemn joy as Jonathan. Despite the suffering, they almost seemed thankful for it. When Karly got to the part about her mother, Kendra's thoughts drifted to her mother. By the time they pulled into the condo parking lot, Kendra was less concerned about Jessica's eternal destiny and more concerned about her mother's.

***

Thirty minutes after Sharon walked into the two-bedroom condominium, she longed for a distraction from the barrage of thoughts that awaited her arrival. The check-in form was completed and returned to the breakfast bar and the unpacked suitcase was in the closet. The detailed 'things to do' list, which provided a welcomed distraction for the days leading up to the trip was finally complete. Instead of relishing the start of their weekend, she paced around the room as if it were solitary confinement. Despite the oppressive heat and humidity that had generated more perspiration on the short walk to the unit than an hour on the treadmill, she ventured onto the balcony to evaluate the premium-priced ocean view. An unexpected blast of sound overwhelmed her. Sliding the door closed behind her, she walked to the railing torn between the competing intensities of the view and the noise. Beneath the cloudless blue sky, the seemingly endless ocean sparkled like a precious green jewel reflecting the sunlight, justifying its name 'the Emerald Coast'. The resort brochure posted on her refrigerator door for months failed to adequately portray the view before her or the heavily congested road between the beach and the continuous sprawl of hotels and condominium developments. The rhythmic ocean waves breaking upon the shore blended with honking car horns, pounding jackhammers, blaring radios, idling motorcycles, screaming children and squawking seagulls.

On the horizon, distinctive fins arced out of the water. Sharon leaned against the beige railing, textured from years of careless cosmetic painting, and waited for the dolphins to reappear. Her heart pounded furiously in anticipation of the arrival of two different groups of fish. One group communicated on a common frequency and traveled in a harmonious pod towards an instinctive destination and the other group struggled with communication while fighting hostile currents intended to destroy. It would be several hours before Kendra and Karly arrived completing their group and testing the wisdom of their gathering.

A gentle breeze caused a strand of hair to escape its clip, which Sharon wore while horseback riding a year ago, causing her thoughts to shift to Jessica. Sharon hoped memories of Jessica would not be as disruptive to their weekend as her presence had been at their inaugural gathering. Driving back to the airport that weekend, Kendra and Karly had suggested the foursome make their impromptu gathering an annual event. Despite the heat, Sharon shivered remembering her thought at the time that Jessica should be excluded. A casual suggestion to make their next weekend a spiritual retreat resulted in Sharon being designated the official coordinator. The others made a convincing argument it would be good training for a minister's wife.

The first tear rolled down Sharon's cheek. As she clutched the balcony railing, the suppressed feelings reverberated throughout her entire being. Looking over the railing at the concrete pool deck below, she wondered if people really died before they hit the ground. Several deep breaths slowed the emotional assault on her body. By God's grace, she had survived one heart attack. The possibility of another heart attack so far from home or an impulsive action unnerved Sharon even more, prompting a retreat to conditioned air and her journal.

March 30th

Will waiting ever get easier? I purposefully booked my flight to get in before Karly and Kendra because I wanted time to prepare. I have no idea what I'm supposed to prepare for. Jessica's dead and Karly's dying. I'm struggling with both my marriage and parenting, so there's not much I can tell Kendra. How can I guide anyone else when I don't even know where I'm going? The problems we faced a year ago seem so trivial now. What's worse is that I'm back where I started with no idea how it happened...

***

Friday evening, a dessert tray sat in the center of the table and a pot of coffee brewed. When Sharon began clearing the dinner dishes, Kendra went into a bedroom to relieve her swollen breasts. It was the first time Sharon and Karly had a chance to talk alone. Sharon returned to her chair and pinched a corner off of a brownie.

Karly yawned. "I want another glass of wine, but that coffee smells awfully good." She picked up the empty glass and stood up. "Do you want me to pour you a cup?"

Sharon hesitated. "No, I'd better pass. My blood pressure's up again and my doctor wants me to cut back." Her eyes followed Karly into the kitchen. Since they arrived, she looked for signs of sickness to no avail. "Too bad we live so far away. It would be fun to do this more often. Do you remember Friday happy hours?"

Karly chuckled. "How could I forget? Those were some of the best free meals in town. After a long week of hard work, it was nice to relax with friends over food and drinks." Karly poured coffee into a mug. "Should I leave the pot on for Kendra?"

"I don't think she drinks it while she's nursing, but leave it on just in case…I wonder who Dale had at the house tonight. He's creating his own Friday night traditions. Can I ask you something?"

"Sure," Karly said, returning to the table with her hands wrapped around the mug of coffee and sat in the chair beside Sharon.

"What do you think about the fourth commandment regarding the Sabbath?"

Karly breathed in the aroma of the coffee, reminding Sharon of Dale. "What do you mean?"

Sharon pushed the similarity out of her mind. "Do you think the commandment regarding the Sabbath is still valid?"

"All the commandments are still valid," Karly responded. "Why do you ask?"

Sharon rested her chin on her hand. "I don't know. Lately Dale's become so legalistic, especially when it comes to the Ten Commandments. You know how he turned our lives upside down to *honor* his mother."

"And from what you've told me, all your worrying was for nothing. Dale did a very good thing."

Sharon refused to admit Dale's mother living with them was the least of her problems. A nurse came every morning to care for his mother. For the first two weeks, another came in the evening to get her ready for bed. Dale was willing to help his mother get dress but did not want to dishonor her. When Paige asked Sharon why they couldn't help grandma change into her pajamas, Sharon did not have a reason. Knowing that she was modeling the kind of care that her daughter would give her, Sharon had an abrupt change of heart. When she called home before they started dinner, Paige was excited to let her mother know she helped her grandmother all by herself. "But this is different." She thought about the last conversation she had with Dale regarding Friday evening dinners. "He's acting more Jewish than Christian," Sharon said, as if the words left a bitter taste.

Karly raised an eyebrow at the harshness of her tone. "Need I remind you Jesus is Jewish?"

"But didn't Jesus' death do away with the law and all the other Jewish rituals and traditions?"

"I'm not so sure we can consider the Ten Commandments to be obsolete traditions. Jesus taught to the contrary."

Kendra walked into the room buttoning her blouse. "What a relief! Did I miss anything?" She eyed Karly's mug. "Is there some coffee left for me?"

"Of course."

Kendra bounced into the kitchen. "Goody...I feel like a kid in a candy store...coffee, chocolate, and enough energy left to enjoy it. You guys don't know how much I needed this trip," she said while fixing her coffee just the way she loved it. She returned to her place at the table and sat with her feet propped in the chair next to her. "So what are we talking about now?"

Karly and Sharon looked at each other before Sharon spoke up. "Dale's acting strange."

Karly pushed the dessert tray in front of Kendra. "Since you just poured your dinner calories down the drain, you get first pick."

Kendra eyed the selection. "The main thing I'll miss about nursing the twins is getting to eat as much as I want. I doubled my calorie intake, trying to keep up with those two. You know how hard it is to undo a bad habit once you've mastered it." She put a brownie and a slice of cheesecake on her dessert plate before passing the tray to Sharon.

Sharon took the brownie that she had pinched off and passed the tray to Karly. "How much longer are you going to nurse?"

Kendra leaned back in her chair contemplating the question she was still struggling with. "Six months is usually my limit, but their new pediatrician wants me to nurse until they're one. The thought of nursing a child with a full set of teeth scares me."

"God knows what He was doing. Babies know when to suck and when to chew, unlike some adults," Karly said with a smile Kendra found both comforting and reassuring.

The temptation was too strong. Sharon went into the kitchen. "I saw a television special on breastfeeding. There was one woman still breastfeeding her ten year old daughter. They actually showed her nursing! That child's going to have some serious issues, if she doesn't already."

"Sounds like the mother's the one with the issues," Kendra said cutting her brownie into bite size pieces. "So what's Dale up to now?"

Karly balled up a paper napkin and threw it at Kendra. "Will you stop doing that? There are no children here to share that brownie with."

Kendra halted her fork, mid cut. "I told you, it's hard to break habits."

Sharon returned with coffee, ignoring Karly's look of disapproval. "For starters, he has started...*observing the Sabbath*."

Kendra sliced her fork into her cheesecake. "What's so strange about that?"

"I'm not talking about going to church every Sunday. He's set up his week so that all 'regular' work ceases at sunset on Friday and doesn't resume until sunset Saturday. He acts like the time is holy or something."

"Having a dedicated break sounds good to me," Kendra said.

"Will you be serious?"

"I am serious! I would love a reason not to work twenty-four hours a day, seven days a week. Although with my brood, I don't know how Eric and I could swing it. A diaper might be pretty ripe after twenty-four hours."

Karly pulled her legs up into the chair. "I don't think that's what God had in mind. Remember Jesus' teachings on the Sabbath, and he talked on that commandment almost as much as on money." Her words unleashed another wave of scriptures in her mind.

Sharon nudged Karly's arm. "Earth to Karly."

"I'm not spacing out, just remembering something. Not too long ago this country had a five-day work week. Given the biblical inclination of our government's framers, I'm certain they had the Sabbath in mind. Little by little, we've allowed our belief system to be eroded...so much for our motto—In God we trust.

"Do you remember the 'blue laws'?" Sharon asked, attempting to divert the subject from discussing God's requirements, which Dale brought up at every opportunity.

Kendra paused before putting another forkful of dessert into her mouth. "They were getting rid of the blue law in Texas when I was little. My mother complied, but my dad would drive until he found an open store. Mom always teased he was paying double for the opportunity to sin."

"There's always a high price for sin," Karly said.

"I'm just thankful we don't have to kill any more animals for sacrifices." Sharon thought about Dale's latest request. "Can you believe that Dale actually wants us to start celebrating Passover? What kind of sense does that make?"

Karly hit her hands on the table in front of her. "Oh my goodness...I don't know why, but my brain is connecting the dots all the time now. It just made another one. The just shall live by HIS faith."

Sharon and Kendra looked at each other before looking at Karly who appeared to be in her own world.

Karly's feet dropped to the floor and a smile filled her face. "The just shall live by HIS faith!"

Sharon wondered if the cancer had traveled to Karly's brain. "Okay, the just shall live by faith. We all know that, but it doesn't explain Dale's behavior."

"No, no. Not 'by faith'. It's by *his faith*! Habakkuk 2:4. I stumbled upon it last night. God has blessed us with a wonderful opportunity." Karly jumped up from the table and almost ran into the bedroom she was sharing with Sharon. "Get your Bibles ladies, because I know you brought them," she yelled from the bedroom.

Sharon rolled her eyes and groaned as she stood up.

Kendra walked to her bag on the floor beside the sofa. "What's with the attitude? You and Dale were the one's who got me reading the Bible."

"Correction. Dale gets the credit for that," Sharon said as she passed Karly to get her Bible, which she left on the nightstand under her journal. When she returned, Karly was already sitting at the table with Kendra, who looked at Karly with eager anticipation. Sharon felt dejected having her position of leadership usurped.

Karly pushed her coffee out of the way. "My mother told me something before she died. I was so wrapped up in my own problems with Ruben that I dismissed what she was trying to tell me," Tears of joy trickled down the sides of her nose. "Sharon, Dale's not being legalistic. He's living by HIS faith. And Kendra, as shocking as it may be to hear, Jessica had the strongest faith of us all. It was just based on the wrong knowledge and focused on the wrong person. Turn to Psalms 118:8; it's the exact middle of the Bible. Trust me. I counted how many chapters were before and after." She noticed Sharon's expression. "You don't judge me and I won't judge you."

Sharon looked amused. "I find it hard to believe you would actually take the time to count chapters of the Bible."

"There are 594 chapters on either side of it. Multiply 594 times two and you get 1188. That's how I remember its exact location in the Bible – 118:8. Interestingly, Psalm 117 is the shortest chapter in the Bible and 119 is the longest. The Bible is truly a very deep well. Look what the exact middle of the Bible says…It is better to trust in the Lord than to put confidence in man. How many times did Jesus comment on or question someone's personal level of faith."

Kendra opened her highlighter and underlined the verse. Sharon held her finger in place and examined the end of her Bible to see if it looked like the middle.

Karly nudged her. "My mother said the problem with behaviors today is people don't know what they believe or why. Yet everything we do is based on our beliefs. Ladies, we proclaim to be Christians, which originally meant disciples of Jesus. To direct my own study, I came up with ten questions every disciple of His should be able to answer with substantial scriptural proof. At the end of this weekend, we're going to at least know the voids in our knowledge. James said if we lacked wisdom, we should pray to the Father who will supply us abundantly." Karly extended her hands to Kendra and Sharon. After they joined hands, she bowed her head. "Heavenly Father, God of all creation…"

CHAPTER 17

FRIDAY MORNING, SHARON SAT AT THE DESK IN THE FAMILY room staring at her laptop screen. She paged back and forth between her work email and the medical website. It was a new one but the information was the same. Since returning from the weekend trip with Karly and Kendra, researching the topic that could be the root cause of her problems consumed her limited time at home. Dale's mother shifted in her reclining chair. Sharon looked over her shoulder hoping that her mother-in-law would not wake up. She fell asleep watching the classic movie channel. Sharon left the television on per Dale's instructions. The regular care giver had cancelled abruptly due to illness. The disappointment on Dale's face when he hung up the phone generated emotions in Sharon that had been dormant for months. Dale needed to go to Doc's funeral and gratefully accepted her offer to work from home until he returned. He left soon after his mother finished her breakfast, promising not to stay longer than necessary.

Sharon was more concerned with what to say when he returned than the duration of his absence. Two weeks after returning from Destin, Sharon still grappled with the possibility that Dale was not the source of her discontent. The complaints against him seemed so petty when subjected to the scrutiny of her friends. Her current dilemma was how to repair the damage caused by hasty choices without having to admit her mistakes. The sound of the door opening startled her. She abruptly closed her laptop and stood.

She noticed how Dale immediately looked towards the recliner for his mother and the two bags from their favorite café. "Your mother dozed off about an hour ago," she whispered.

He sat the bags on the table. "Do you need to leave right away or can you eat lunch here? I got your chicken salad bagged separately, in case you need to leave right away. " Dale spoke in his normal voice knowing that his mother napped deeply.

Sharon peered into one of the bags. "I have time to eat here. Do you want to wake your mother?"

"No. It's better to let her wake up naturally," Dale said walking to the refrigerator. He retrieved the water pitcher then two glasses from the cabinet.

"How was Doc's service?" Sharon carefully removed the food from the bags and arranged it on the table before sitting.

"There wasn't even standing room. It was wise to arrive early. Some were turned away at the door." He filled the glasses and carried them to the table. "Several shared how knowing Doc changed their lives. I feel blessed that our paths crossed, even if it was for a short time."

Dale checked on his mother before sitting beside Sharon. "I keep thinking about my last conversation with him, after the Passover Seder. I volunteered to drive him back to his apartment just to have more time with him. It was late and we were both tired. The entire time Doc talked about the future Passover in the kingdom and our need to finish well. He never wasted a minute of our time together. When I parked in front of his apartment building, he refused to let me walk him in but he paused before getting out of the car and said 'Be strong and courageous, my friend. God never calls us to do work that he hasn't equipped us for.' I will never forget his tranquil smile as he turned to wave before entering the building."

"It's hard to believe that his granddaughter called you the next day with the news of his death."

"The sadness of my loss is trumped by joy for Doc. He's now absent from his body but present with our Lord."

Sharon nudged Dale's arm. "Do you want to bless the food?"

Dale struggled to suppress the fresh surge of grief. "Will you?"

"Heavenly Father, we thank you for this food which you have provided from your abundance through Christ, our Lord. May it be beneficial to our bodies and souls. Amen."

Dale removed the wrapper from his sandwich and opened his bag of chips. "I'm definitely going to miss him, but we'll meet again. I wonder what he's doing now."

Sharon felt ill prepared for a conversation about life after death. "Your mother was absolutely no trouble this morning."

"That was my prayer. Thanks again for changing your schedule."

"I'm glad I didn't have any meetings and was able to help." Sharon opened her salad. "Have you thought about plans for the summer? The kids get out of school in six weeks."

Dale unfolded a napkin. "Nothing's finalized yet. With you working and Mom living with us, we'll need a more structured summer. The kids have narrowed their choices for summer camps. Since a few of them are half day programs, I'm considering hiring someone to help with the driving; maybe a college student. I don't want to upset Mom's schedule, more than absolutely necessary."

"I have someone in mind for the job."

"Great. Give me their information and I'll call them this week."

"A call won't be necessary. I can handle our kid's schedule this summer."

Dale paused from putting a chip in his mouth. "You won't have the time with your schedule and commute."

"If I don't work this summer, I will."

"You don't need to do that. The kids and I will manage."

"Are you saying you don't want me around?"

"I'm saying that I don't want you pressured into doing anything because of my mother. Please do what's best for you."

"Dale, I'm not being self-sacrificing." Sharon pushed her salad away and turned to look at him. "I took this job because I thought it would solve my problems, but it only made our situation worse. Karly and Kendra helped me to understand that neither you nor your mother living with us is the problem. Even though you're definitely not the same person that I married and I don't understanding some of the things you're doing, my problem is how I'm reacting and responding. I believe the main cause for what Karly labeled as my irrational behavior is menopause."

"You're only forty-two. Isn't that too young for menopause?"

"That's what I thought too, but I've been doing a lot of research. I could be a textbook case for the early stage of menopause – night sweats, insomnia, extreme mood swings, fatigue, depression, irritability. I made a doctor's appointment to confirm it, but changing hormones levels would explain a lot of what I've been experiencing. Because I didn't have a clue what was happening, I blamed you and the changes in our life. This past year was the worst possible timing for me to enter this next stage of womanhood."

"Our adversary really knows how to time his attacks."

"That's an understatement. I had no clue that hormones controlled so much. From what I've read, my emotional and physical state could actually get worse, which is another reason why I should take a break from this job. Otherwise I'll probably get fired for saying the wrong thing at the wrong time to the wrong person. Hopefully, this summer will provide an opportunity for us to find a strategy to get through these challenges." Sharon sensed Dale's demeanor change.

"What a relief to know that we're just dealing with a temporary condition."

"I don't know how temporary. Menopause can be a long, drawn-out process. One woman said she had hot flashes for decades. Thankfully, I haven't started having those yet."

"Sharon, my constant prayer was for God to keep our family together and show me what to do."

"Aside from having relentless patience, there's not much you can do. Thankfully, God sent Karly and Kendra to your rescue.

We're starting a weekly video chat that will be part Bible-study and part group therapy. We're all going thru challenges not meant to be faced alone."

"Sounds like a good plan. I wish I could join you, but I suspect no men are allowed."

"Only one…Jesus. You, Ruben and Eric can start your own. It sounds like we'll be doing a lot of praying for the people in our lives; you can return the favor." Sharon reached for her salad. "I'd better finish eating and get to work. Knowing that my time there is limited will help tremendously."

***

Monday morning, the sun soared above the horizon as Kendra stepped onto her porch and softly closed the door. Her breasts were empty after nursing the twins and her heart overflowed with joy. A very specific prayer had been answered in an unexpected way. Eric came home Friday evening and announced that he was changing his work schedule to have more quality time during the week with his children. The man with the reputation for being the first at the office had actually committed to staying at the house until eight-thirty. Kendra had prayed with Sharon and Karly for a set time to exercise only two days before Eric's announcement. The double blessing allowed him to have breakfast and enjoy quality time with his children and Kendra could exercise and dress before her family's needs commandeered the remainder of her day.

Traversing the vibrant chalk covered path, she breathed deeply savoring the fragrant aroma which filled the air and tried not to smudge her children's artwork. She paused at the end of the sidewalk and looked in both directions pondering which way to go. She shook her head at the magnitude of the changes continually being manifested. A breeze traveled in the direction of the sun and so did she. She longed to chase the wind, but her doctor warned her that it could be a year before she reached her full stride and former endurance level. She walked along the curb content knowing that some changes might be permanent. In the past, she ran to keep disturbing thoughts in the recesses of her mind. She hoped that brisk walks could help release them.

Determined to keep her focus on God and live in the present instead of dwelling on the past, the first thought she committed to abandoning was the belief that she could, and the unconscious desire to, control events in her life and the lives of others. Prior to becoming pregnant with the twins, her life had been carefully planned and regimented. Some plans worked well while others had backfired; but she always had a strategy. The abrupt loss of control humbled her and firmly demonstrated who had the power to veto her plans. She would still set goals, but be willing to relinquish even the smallest decisions to what she hoped was spiritual guidance. The conception of the twins no longer seemed unplanned. Every incident leading up to her move to Birmingham in retrospect seemed to be carefully orchestrated. She believed her Shepherd was teaching her to recognize his prodding while leading her to a pasture of his choosing.

As Kendra increased her speed, she thanked God for his patience and provision. Her greatest fear had been that the move for Eric's career would isolate her from the people most important to her. Yet God ensured that she was more connected. Her motivated father mastered technology in order to see Kendra and his grandchildren almost daily. The most prized accommodation to close the geographical distance was the weekly video chats with Sharon and Karly. Kendra especially anticipated seeing Karly, who seemed to exude light and peace during their time together. Her matter-of-fact statement that 'she knew who she was and what God put her on earth to do' resonated with Kendra, whose assurance had been shaken to her core. She soaked up every word of Karly's experience with God. Her humble revelation that she had a dream which confirmed her work for the kingdom stunned both Kendra and Sharon to a temporary silence, yet they believed her. Kendra grinned remembering Sharon's uncharacteristically cautious probing. Karly candidly shared that the details of the dream were fuzzy but the message and source were clear – she was one of God's chosen people and her work was teaching God's truth through her art. After years of putting her favorite teachings of Jesus on canvas, Karly shifted to creating personalized works for the individuals chosen by God. The original paintings were given to the person but prints were sold to bless others according to God's Word. Walking the now familiar neighborhood, Kendra basked in the beauty of the surrounding terrain and tried to imagine the painting Karly was creating for her. Every time Kendra inquired about it, Karly admonished her to be patient.

Kendra noticed a girl's bicycle in a yard and thought about Simone. The final paperwork acknowledging Jonathan as her father and relinquishing Kendra's legal guardianship had been signed and mailed without hesitation. After years of harboring toxic feelings for Jonathan, Kendra had anticipated lingering resentment but it had yet to surface. Her attempts to save Jessica by condemning her relationship with Jonathan seemed like wasted effort. In hindsight, it appeared that Jessica's relationship with Jonathan may have been the vehicle for her eternal salvation. There was little doubt in Kendra's mind that Simone came out of the womb radically different from her mother despite possessing her DNA. Kendra was finally able to accept that Jonathan was a factor in Jessica's child being blessed with the spirit of God so early in her life.

Facing a bend in the road caused Kendra to remember the day that inaugurated the recent period of tribulation. Being unable to answer the question 'What is truth?' had opened the door to doubts about her faith in God. It was the same question that she had asked Karly several times. She always responded with Bible verses. Kendra headed home thinking about what Jesus told the Samaritan woman at the well "You worship what you do not know: we know what we worship; for salvation is of the Jews. But the hour comes and now is, when the true worshippers shall worship the Father in spirit and in truth; for the Father seeks such to worship him. God is a Spirit: and they that worship him must worship him in spirit and in truth." Next she reflected on Jesus' response to Pontus Pilate before being condemned to death. The apostle John recorded Jesus' last words to Pilate as being 'Every one that is of the truth hears my voice'. Kendra wanted to know God's truth. With her house in sight, Kendra slowed and whispered "Lord, you are the great Shepherd. Lead me and teach me your ways. I want to know you and hear you call me by name."

THE END

FROM THE AUTHOR

If you know that God exists, please act on His promptings. He led you to this book for a reason. Don't be afraid if your growing faith doesn't align with the world's view. Above all, make sure the foundation of your faith, which is knowledge, aligns with the Word of God. The following pages contain ten questions that every disciple of Jesus should be able to answer with scriptural references. My prayer thirteen years ago was for God to teach me His truth and use me for His glory. He will do the same for you. Always remember that His people are never alone!

Matthew 13:16-17

"But blessed are your eyes, for they see: and your ears, for they hear. For verily I say unto you, That many prophets and righteous men have desired to see those things which you see, and have not seen them; and to hear those things which you hear, and have not heard them."

Revelations 22:10-14

"And he said unto me, Seal not the saying of the prophecy of this book: for the time is at hand. He that is unjust, let him be unjust still: and he that is filthy, let him be filthy still; and he that is righteous, let him be righteous still: and he that is holy, let him be holy still.

And, behold, I come quickly, and my reward is with me, to give every man according as his work shall be. I am the Alpha and Omega, the beginning and the end, the first and the last.

Blessed are they that do his commandments, that they may have right to the tree of life, and may enter in through the gates into the city."

ACKNOWLEDGMENTS

This ten year endeavor would not have been possible without God's abundant patience and provision. With each novel, I am more aware of God's infinite wisdom and mercy. Specific people and situations were placed in my life for His glory and my growth. I must acknowledge my husband, Dennis, who entered my life thirty-four years ago. Thank you for the love and stability you've provide for our family. Equally important on this journey are our children, Shane and Paris. I often said that God gave you the parents you needed; the reverse is really true. God has taught me so much through being your mother. Next, I'd like to acknowledge my big sister, Dottye Rivers. You've been a constant source of support from helping me get through college to driving across the country with James to celebrate Shane's college graduation and keeping watch over Paris. Thank you. I need to thank another sister, Laurie Harris, for taking great care of our father. You're a blessing to us both. God also blessed me with a supportive extended family of aunts, cousins, nieces, nephews and in-laws.

I want to acknowledge my cherished friends who have supported my writing adventure: Veronica Shelton, Henrietta Mackey, Zanetta Harris and Kit McGrath. Thanks for your willingness to read and re-read the manuscript at its varied stages. A very special thank you goes to Cheryl McNeil who made time to help and provided insightful feedback and corrections. I want to thank Sarah Whelan for creating the book cover and website. I am grateful for Diane Goodrich, who God sent late in the editing process to provide much needed encouragement and proofreading, and her mother-in-law, Lettie Goodrich, for giving the manuscript the final approval. Thank you sorors of Delta Sigma

Theta Sorority, Inc. who have supported my writing endeavors from the beginning. I also appreciate the support of Ronald Moore and the St. Louis Gateway Chapter of the National Society of Black Engineers.

Finally, I want to acknowledge you. Thank you for reading a book that I pray will have an eternal impact.

TEN QUESTIONS
BIBLICAL KNOWLEDGE

1. What is the Bible?

   o Genesis 1:3 (Recorded words of God)
   o Genesis 2:4-5 (Record of generations of heavens and earth)
   o Exodus 24: 1-18 (Moses recording of God's words)
   o Deuteronomy 4:1-40 (Moses exhorts Israel to obedience; God's will for his people)
   o Proverbs 22:17-21 (Source of godly wisdom, knowledge and understanding)
   o Psalms 119:1-176 (Source of knowledge)
   o Isaiah 28: 9-12 (precept upon precept, line upon line)
   o Jeremiah 36:1-8 (Lord instructs Jeremiah to record and read His words)
   o Ezekiel 40: 1-4 (God instructs Ezekiel to record what he sees, hears to declare to Israel)
   o Luke 24:27,44-47 (Jesus explains source of all prophesies concerning him)
   o John 20:30-31; (John explains the purpose of his gospel)
   o John 21:25 (John explains world could not contain the books written about Jesus' works)

2. Who is Jesus Christ according to scripture?

   o Genesis 1: 1, 26-27; John 1:1-14 (God's record of creation)
   o Genesis 1:2-5 (creation of light) John 8:12
   o Genesis 11:5-9 (the Lord sees Tower of Babel, confuses languages/scatters people)

- o Genesis 12:1-8; 15:1-18; 17:1-8; 18:1-33; 22:1-18 (God's appearances to Abraham)
- o Genesis 25:19-23; 26:1-5, 24 (God's appearances to Isaac)
- o Genesis 28: 10-22; 31:11-16; 32:1-30; 35:1-15 (God's appearances to Jacob)
- o Exodus 3:2 – 4:17 (Moses at burning bush)
- o Exodus 6:1-8, 28-29; (God reveals new name to Moses back in Egypt) {John 20: 24-31}
- o Exodus 24:1-11; (Moses and elders see and eat with God of Israel)
- o Exodus 33:12-34:10 (God promised his presence and reveals his ways to Moses)
- o Number 20:2-13; (God commands Moses to get water from rock) {John 4:1-14, 7:37}
- o Deuteronomy 6:4-9, (The Lord our God is one Lord) Mark 12:28-31
- o Deuteronomy 18:15-19 (promised Prophet)
- o Joshua 5: 13 (the captain of the LORD'S host appears to Joshua)
- o Judges 6: 1-40 (Lord appears to Gideon)
- o Judges 13: 1-25 (the birth of Samson)
- o 1 Samuel 3:1-21 (The word of God appears to Samuel)
- o 1 Samuel 12:1-25; (Samuel response to people after request for king)
- o 1 Samuel 17:45-47 (David's address of Goliath)
- o 2 Samuel 22:1-52 (David's song to the Lord)
- o 1 Kings 8:22-26, 56-61 (Solomon's dedication of temple)
- o 1 Kings 9:1-9; 2 Chronicles 7:11-22 (the Lord's covenant with Solomon)
- o 1 Kings 18:20-39 (Elijah's contest)
- o 1 Kings 19:1-18 (the Lord appears to Elijah)

- o 2 Kings 19:14-19: (Hezekiah's prayer to the Lord)
- o 1 Chronicles 17: 11-15 (God's promise to David regarding his Son and His kingdom)
- o Job 38 – 41:34 (the Lord's response to Job)
- o Isaiah 6:1-5 (Isaiah sees the King)
- o Isaiah 9:6-7; Luke 1:32-33 (prophesy and fulfillment of Jesus' birth)
- o Isaiah 11:1-16 (The righteous reign of the Branch)
- o Jeremiah 2:13; (the fountain of living water)
- o Jeremiah 10:1-16 (the Lord is the true God); 23:5-6; 32:27
- o Jeremiah 32:17-41 (The Lord's identity and promises to Israel)
- o Daniel 10:1-21 (Daniel's vision by the great river)
- o Zechariah 14: 3-9; 16-19 (The day of the Lord, feet on the mount of Olives)
- o Matthew 15:17 (Jesus asks Peter who Jesus is)
- o John 14: 1-14, (Jesus discusses relationship to Father)
- o John 20:26-31 (Thomas declares who Jesus is)
- o Acts 2:22-36 (Peter's address on Pentecost)
- o 1 Corinthians 10: 1-4 (Paul statement regarding Spiritual Rock of Israel in Wilderness)
- o Rev. 1:10-20, 22:16 (John's vision on Patamos)

3. Who is Israel according to scripture/Bible?

- o Genesis 32: 24-30 (Jacob wrestles with angel; received name Israel)
- o Genesis 49: 1-28 (Jacob's prophesy to sons – events of last days)
- o Exodus 1:1-7; 3:10-15 (Israel in Egypt; Moses call to get God's people)

- o Exodus 6:5-8 (God's promises to Moses concerning children of Israel)
- o Deuteronomy 7:6-11; 14:2; 28:9-14 (A holy people unto the Lord)
- o Deuteronomy 26: 5-19 (Summary of God's relationship with Israel)
- o Deuteronomy 28: 58-66 (Israel scattered)
- o 1 Samuel 12:22 (Response to Israel's request for human king)
- o 2 Samuel 7:22-24 (David's response to God's promises)
- o 1Kings 8:51-61 (Solomon's dedication of temple; Israel God's inheritance)
- o 1Kings 11:9-13 (Israel split because of Solomon's sin)
- o 1 Chronicles 17:9,22 (God's people forever)
- o Isaiah 41:8-10 (God's chosen servant) {Isaiah 5:7}
- o Jeremiah 16:14-21; 23:1-8; 32:36-42 (those who the Lord shall gather)
- o Jeremiah 24:6-7 (Promise of the Lord, God of Israel to captives of Judah)
- o Jeremiah 31:1-40 (Message to scattered remnant of Israel; promise of New Covenant)
- o Micah 2:12-13, 5:7-8 (God's promise to the remnant in midst of people for deliverer)
- o James 1:1 (greeting to twelve tribes scattered abroad.)
- o 1 Peter 1:1-2 (Peter's greeting to scattered, elect according to God's foreknowledge)
- o Revelations 12:17 (who the dragon/Devil makes war with)

4. What is Jerusalem according to the scriptures?

- o Genesis 12:7-8; 13:3-18 (Place God appeared to Abraham)
- o Genesis 28: 10-22 (God's first appearance to Jacob first time; sets pillar of God's house)

- o Genesis 48:3-4 (Jacob explains to Joseph land that is everlasting possession)
- o Deuteronomy 12:5-12 (God's promise to put name on specific place)
- o 2 Chronicles 6:6 (Fulfillment; place that God chose to put name)
- o 2 Chronicles 7:11-16 (God's words to Solomon regarding His house in Jerusalem)
- o Isaiah 2:2-4 (Seat of Jesus kingdom) Isaiah 24:23; 25: 6-12; 27:12-13
- o Jeremiah 32: 36 – 33:16 (future prophesies for Jerusalem)
- o Zechariah 1:16; 2:10-12 (prophesy of Jesus' return)
- o Revelation 21:1-27 (John sees to bride of Jesus Christ descending from heaven)

5. What are God's law and covenants?

God's Law

- o Genesis 22:18, 26: 2-5 (Abraham's obedience to God's voice, commandments…)
- o Exodus 12:24, 47-50; Numbers 9:14 (Passover; One law for all)
- o Exodus 13: 8-10; (Lord's law in your mouth);
- o Number 15:15-41 (one law, stoning of Sabbath breaker, fringe on garment)
- o Deuteronomy 4:44 -5:22 ("the law which Moses set before the children of Israel:")
- o Deuteronomy 6: 1-9 (Moses gives great commandment)
- o Deuteronomy 28:1-68 (Moses gives blessings/ consequences; obedience to God's law)
- o Deuteronomy 29:29 ('revealed things' given enable to do law)

- Deuteronomy 30:10-14 (Moses says law in mouth and heart, so Israel can do them)
- Joshua 1:8-9 (the Lord's words to Joshua concern the book of the law)
- 2 Kings 18: 1-12 (Why Hezekiah succeeded and Samaria fell)
- 2 Kings 22:8-20; 23: 21-25 (Josiah discovers book of the law)
- Psalms 1:1-6; 119:1-176 (Benefits of the law)
- Jeremiah 16:1-13 (Lord's judgment on this people)
- Jeremiah 31:33 (Lord will put law in inward parts, and write it in their hearts)
- Jeremiah 44:10-11 (Israel's failure to obey God's law and statutes)
- John 1:17 (relationship between law and grace - Moses and Jesus Christ)
- Acts 15: 19-21 (Jerusalem council decision; those turned to God from among Gentiles)
- Hebrews 9:19-22 (Paul refers to Moses, the Law and covenant with people)
- James 1:19-27 (Admonition to be hearers and doers of word)
- 1 John 3:4 (Sin is the transgression of the law)
- Revelations 12:17 (Those whom Devil make war with)

The Covenants

- Genesis 9:8-17 (Covenant with man after flood)
- Genesis 17:1-14 (God's everlasting covenant with Abraham and his seed/and sign)
- Genesis 17:19; 26:1-5,24 (God's covenant with Isaac and his seed)
- Genesis 27:10-22 (God's covenant with Jacob and his seed)
- Exodus 19:4; 20-24:12 (Giving of the covenant to the people of Israel)

- o Deuteronomy 29: 9-25 (Moses recounts the Lord's covenant with Israel)
- o Judges 2: 1,20-22, 3:4 (God confirms covenant with Israel)
- o 1 Kings 9: 1-9 (Lord's covenant concerning the temple)
- o 2 Kings 23: 1-3 (Josiah renews covenant of people)
- o 1 Chronicles 17:9-14 (the Lord's covenant with David concerning Israel and his seed)
- o 2 Chronicles 5:10 (Solomon brings ark into the temple)
- o Psalms 105:7-11 (The Lord's wonders in Behalf of Israel)
- o Jeremiah 11 (the broken covenant)
- o Jeremiah 31:17-34 (details of the New Covenant)
- o Jeremiah 33: 17 – 26 (prophesies David's throne / seed of Abraham…) Luke 1:32-33
- o Hebrews 10: 1-10 (law, Jesus and covenant)

6. What did Jesus become man to do?

- o Genesis 22:7-14 (Abraham declares that God will provide himself a lamb)
- o Exodus 23:20-21 (God to send angel to keep Israel in the way;)
- o Psalms 22:1-31 (Work of Jesus declared)
- o Psalm 23:1-6 (The Lord is My Shepherd)
- o Jeremiah 31:10-11 (Prophesy concerning work of the LORD)
- o Jeremiah 31:31-34; Matthew26:28 (Prophesy concerning the new covenant)
- o Daniel 9:24-27 (the angel Gabriel's words to Daniel concerning the Messiah's work)
- o Matthew 9:12-13; Mark 2:17 (Jesus' words concerning his work)
- o Matthew 9:35 (the work Jesus did in all the cities and villages)

- o Matthew 15:24 (Who Jesus was sent unto)
- o Matthew 18:11; Luke 9:56 (To save man)
- o Mark 10:45 (to serve and give life for many)
- o John 3:17 (save the world)
- o John 17:1-26 (Jesus prays for disciples)
- o John 18:37 (bear witness to the truth)
- o Acts 1:3 (speaking of things pertaining to the kingdom of God)
- o Galatians 4:45 (To redeem those under the law-children of Israel)
- o Ephesians 2:17 (preach peace to far off and near)

7. What was the gospel that Jesus preached on earth?

- o Matthew 4:17 (beginning of Jesus' ministry; repent)
- o Matthew 24:14 (gospel preached as sign of end) 26:64
- o Mark 1:14-15 (Beginning of Jesus' ministry)
- o Mark 6:12 (Jesus sends out 12 to preach)
- o Luke 21:5-36 (Jesus' teaching on Signs before the end)
- o Luke 9:2, 11 (mission of twelve)
- o John 3:1-5; 5:19-47 (Jesus' teachings on himself)

8. What work did Jesus finish on the cross?

- o Daniel 9:26-27 (prophesy concerning work; confirm covenant / end to sacrifices)
- o Matthew 26:28; 27:25 (purpose of Jesus' blood being shed)
- o John 19:36 (John explains details of Jesus' death and significance)
- o Hebrews 9:1 – 10:18 (Paul explains the purpose of Jesus' death)

9. What does Jesus expect of his people?
    - Deuteronomy 4:27-31, 39-40 (Moses instruction to God's people in latter days)
    - Jeremiah 3:6-14 (the Lord pleads with Israel to return to Him and acknowledge iniquity)
    - Matt 10:5-42 (mission of twelve – lost sheep) Mark 6:12; Luke 9:2
    - Matthew 19:16-30 (Jesus questioned about requirements for eternal life)
    - Matthew 22:34-40 (Jesus questioned about the greatest commandment in the law)
    - Matthew 28:19-20 (Jesus commission to eleven apostles)

10. What is the future hope of a disciple of Jesus?
    - Job 19:23-27 (Job's statement of his faith and hope)
    - Jeremiah 3:15-23; 16:10-21; 17:7-17; 23:1-7; 29:4-14; 31:17 (Bring us to promised land)
    - Ezekiel 37:12-14 (Lord's words concerning the resurrection and final destination)
    - Ezekiel 39: 17-29 (prophesy of last days)
    - Daniel 11:32-35; 12:1-2, 10 (prophesy concerning people that know their God)
    - Matthew 8:11 (Sit down with Abraham, Isaac and Jacob in kingdom of heaven)
    - Matthew 16:27-28 (Be rewarded when Jesus returns in glory with angels)
    - Matthew 25:31-40 (Judgment of nations)
    - Matthew 26:64 (See Son sitting on right hand, coming in glory)
    - Revelation 21:1-26 (God dwelling with men and tabernacle)

Made in the USA
Charleston, SC
14 February 2017